Empower

I0638361

Publishing

Also by Louse Gore Sayer David

John Steel: The Man and the Legend

The *She Heard a Whippoorwill Cry* Series:
Green Sea Plantation
The Land Darkens
Spring's Gift of Light
The Turbulence and the Storm
The Winds Grow Gentle
The Gathering

and *Empower Publishing*

The Gathering

Book Six in the She Heard a Whippoorwill Series

By

Louise Gore Sayre-David

Empower Publishing
Winston-Salem

Empower

Publishing

Empower Publishing
PO Box 26701
Winston-Salem, NC 27114

The book is a work of fiction and is entirely the product of the author's creative imagination. No actual person, place or event is referred to in this work. The author has represented and warranted all ownership and/or legal right to publish all the materials in this book.

First Empower Publishing Books edition published January, 2021
Empower Publishing, Feather Pen, and all production design are trademarks.

For information regarding bulk purchases of this book, digital purchase and special discounts, please contact the publisher at publish.empower.now@gmail.com

Cover design by Pan Morrelli

Manufactured in the United States of America
ISBN 978-1-63066-513-5

In loving memory of my parents, Webb and Dora Gore, and siblings.
Mary Doratheta
Daniel Lucian
Joseph Thurman
Clayton Luke
Hubert Rudolph
Carrie Emma
Sally Edna
Lacy Leadonis

—Louise Gore Sayre-David

Chapter One

Barely two months later in the little mountain valley town of Lexington, Virginia, John Fillmore Lee got a sudden idea to pay a visit to the Virginia Military Institute nearby. The notion to do a write-up that would concern the freshman cadets only, came to John as he was studying a news item lying atop his desk which lauded the academy's record for first-rateness when it came to its training program, as well as praising it for the superior qualities of its present and past instructors—namely the late, "Stonewall" Jackson.

The prospect of interviewing these new, young cadets about their yearnings and aspirations, the whereabouts and distance of their home roofs and those of whom were planning to make it home for Thanksgiving and those who would be remaining behind at the institute, not only aroused John to newfound heights of interest but also fanned his energy a lot higher besides, since he ever enjoyed meeting people and making new acquaintances not to mention his excitement over writing the article for his own newspaper, "The Pacesetter."

However, even if there had been no new subject Of interest to suddenly inspire John, the mere thought Of exchanging the humdrum routine of his new office and its stuffy atmosphere for the exhilarating joy of taking a drive in the consensually bright autumn afternoon, was enough in itself alone, too, lift John's spirit a great deal. For—over the years—John Fillmore-Lee had come to love the mountain valley of Lexington and its crisp, colorful autumns, take delight in its flowery, green budded springs with speckled trout bedding aplenty in the clear rushing streams of its rocky gorges, exalt in the glory of its tile—red and purplish hued mountain sunsets, and praise the valley's people and their time - honored folklore. In short, the valley had become the bosom of what John was seeking—his consoling agent for all the past things he had lost. From the first, he had felt as being in his own element once again, embracing the valley and the ways and customs Of its people with a zeal that was little less than piety; and it appeared his trust in the course he had followed had not been ill-founded. On the lines of success and triumphing over his mental anxieties, too, John Fillmore-Lee had gone far beyond any expectations he had envisioned on that weary September day when he was trying to get his newspaper business set up.

Granted, the man who called himself, John Fillmore-Lee had not massed any fortune. Nor was he wallowing in an influx of riches. He still worked a full day every weekday—some days well into the night hours. But, even so, he had—in a manner of speaking, risen up in the world and did enjoy a great deal of contentment, too. His newspaper business was still housed in the same building where he had started upon his arrival in Lexington, though he owned the building now instead of renting it. Neither did John and his family live upstairs above the printing presses anymore. Gilford Sloan was occupying those quarters now and had been for several years. John and his family were living on a small but neat and orderly estate just beyond the outskirts of Lexington. Even though the property was small, the twenty-five-acre plat which was enclosed with a white-washed board fence was certainly not hard to look at in any season even the drab Months of winter.

Almost centrally located on the grounds, with tall chimneys at each end and white-trimmed windows spaced evenly at either side of its gleaming white colonial doorway, was a two-story, red brick house that John had built. A wide sloping, well-groomed lawn and tree-dotted meadow fields surrounded the house; and the big red barn and stables, too, that were settling out back with their white-washed fenced lots.

Having long desired to own a place that would free him from feeling as if he were forever hemmed in the rolling, uniform, twenty-five-acre site, which John had eventually built his house and other buildings on, had been his first major purchase. However, that feeling of being penned in had not been the principle element that had directed John's move to the country. Most Of all, it was his daughter's love for horses and the outside that had induced it. John had wanted a place where he could have a barn and stables for one or two saddle horses so that Beth Anne would be able to ride to her heart's content since it appeared she liked nothing better than to go horseback riding. An enthusiastic and able horseman himself—even with his lame arm, John and Beth Anne often rode together, with him taking much pride in the fact that under his own instructions and supervisions she had become a superb horsewoman—as good as any native Virginian ever was. Her talents in the saddle were superexcellent, making it seem as if she had been born with a natural gift for the sport.

Though John was now the owner of three thoroughbred hunters—one for each member of his family—plus a matched pair of carriage horses to convey the coach and also the buggy he owned, Rachelle seldom accompanied her husband and daughter on their horseback rides. She cared nothing for the sport, finding more work to it than pleasure since she had never learned to fully relax on a horse's back. Even so, never did Rachelle's failing to gain interest in the sport bring any of the hunters to start kicking the beams for want of exercise. Gilford Sloan, like both John and his daughter, loved to ride. Thus, being a frequent guest of John and Rachelle, it was not often that one of the thoroughbred hunters were left stranded in its stable without a rider. As a rule, when John and Beth Anne headed their mounts for the open countryside around Lexington to exercise their riding skills, Gilford Sloan was usually right beside them riding the hunter; who, supposedly, had been purchased for Rachelle.

Curiously, because by this date they had grown to be rather close friends, John and Gilford Sloan hardly knew any more about each other's life in the years before their meeting, than had there been no life for each of them in these years to talk about. Of course, applying to John in a literal sense this fact was unfortunately near the truth since his life before the battle of Gettysburg remained to be shrouded in a mystery of darkness —leaving little he could use for a topic to discuss had he so desired, which he did not. Though Gilford Sloan was not yet aware that John's seemingly permanent amnesia was the main reason he made no reference to this part of his life.

As far as Gilford Sloan was concerned, talking about anything that involved those years before or during the war was becoming too much of a risk in reminding himself of those things he still wanted to blank out. He seldom made mention of his late wife, his late parents, or the war. The pain of all that he had lost still cut too deep, especially that senseless tragedy which had cost him his wife and his baby.

Nevertheless, as ironic as it was, there was another main reason why the relationship between these two men was so close and, at the same time, remained as strangely remote in itself. With each thinking that he had fought on the opposite side of the other in the great conflict that almost tore the nation beyond repair forever, both men shunned from mentioning the years beyond that September day of their meeting for fear of damaging that moral strength that they had come to view the other as having in generous supply. Indeed, within minutes of their introduction, this sensing of character had come through on the part of both and had prevailed in spite of the tension between them and exchanging of high words. It had been the fundamental reason why John had made all effort to overlook Gilford Sloan's drinking problem—which had nearly ceased to be by this time—and look instead at those other finer qualities that he had been able to detect about Gilford Sloan—honor, integrity, loyalty, and above all an unwavering unfalseness. Actually, sharing an affinity which they were unaware of, both had been reaching on that September day and had eventually found what they were seeking in the other—comradeship. For John, unknowingly, Gilford Sloan represented that brotherhood alliance that he had shared with Nat so many years. And, for Gilford Sloan, John and his family represented the family that Gilford Sloan had lost and still craved. Thus, it was not hard to see why John's and Gilford Sloan's relationship had grown to true solidity and beaten the odds against it.

As a matter of fact, John's only daughter and only child, Beth Anne had also held Gilford in favorable regard from that moment of their meeting when he had bent over her small, chubby hand with such dutiful respect. Having gained her friendship immediately, it had not been long afterwards that she had replaced the "Mr." with "Uncle" when she addressed him, and Gilford Sloan could not have valued the intimacy of the ward more. She lifted the darkness in Gilford Sloan's heart, gradually warming it until he found one day that he could look through the window even in the most dismal kind of weather and feel a gladness about the day.

Her chattering nourished his somber spirit—amusing him and delighting him at the same time, filling his mind with something else besides his troubles. With her deep-blue eyes regarding him thoughtfully, she would question Gilford Sloan endlessly about this and that, as she sat perched atop a high stool beside his desk. Her father bore with the patience of her curiosity a lot, too. But, it was Gilford Sloan's easy going personality that suffered the crux of her lively interest most.

One time, her chitter-chatter became as lengthy and lively— punctuated with a lot of giggles at the way Gilford Sloan had gone about answering her questions, that it brought her father to intercede on Sloan's behalf, reminding her "Darling, you may be hindering Mr. Sloan from his work. Perhaps it'd be best if you'd run along and play with your doll for a while."

"Yes, Papa," she squealed, jumping down from the stool instantly. Still, before she had taken a step, Gilford Sloan was hastily putting in, "No, let her be, I love her chatter. It clears my mind and helps me to concentrate on what I'm doing. In fact, I've gotten used to hearing it. It's sort of like music playing to me."

"Well, in that case, darling," laughed John, "Perhaps you'd better stay and continue on to play your music for Mr. Sloan."

Beth Anne had crawled back up upon the stool. But, instead of resuming her chatter, she remained silent, shyly looking down at her hands which she had folded over the other in her lap.

John stopped and observed her silence for a moment. He regretted that he had brought attention to his daughter's talkative nature and was wondering how he should go about handling the situation, when he was suddenly relieved to see Gilford Sloan take up his pencil and poke Beth Anne under the chin as he softly drawled, "Now, what was that you were asking me? Wasn't it something about that horsefly up there, who's about to split his brains out on that windowpane?"

John was thrilled and amused, too, to see Beth Anne drop the shy look instantly and lift her head, as she clearly came back at Sloan, "But, you just told me that horsefly didn't have no brains to butt out."

Now, John saw it was Sloan who was flinching a little as he leaned back in his chair and thoughtfully began to tap his own chin with the pencil, finally drawling again, "That's right, I did say that, didn't I? Well, since he has no brains to worry about, what about his legs? He's surely going to break his legs, if we don't get busy right this minute and get up from here and catch and set him loose."

And, as John turned back to resume his work amid his daughter's laughter and excited squeals over Gilford Sloan's clumsy attempt at trying to catch the horsefly—the clattery racket blasting his ears so until it near put an end all to his own concentration, he said to himself,

"Horseflies! God, what a subject! What will it be next, I wonder?"

Well, before John's daughter was to outgrow her thirst to know the why and wherefore for a state of being, Rachelle, and Gilford Sloan were to be faced with explaining a succession of subjects to the quick-witted, inquiring Beth Anne—scads and scads Of subjects, and John was to find out that some were far more out; indeed, than horseflies!

But, now the little overly curious girl had long reached

womanhood—already in the last year of her teens, and if this fact was a little hard for John to accept at times, the fact that there was nothing mellow about her personality was harder still. Though it made his idolism Of her no less, he still wished sometimes that she had been endowed with a bit more restraint and especially in the way she went about doings things like; for instance, what she was suddenly doing now—abruptly pushing his office door wide open and then giving the door a hard kick with the heel of her boot to close it, rather than gently closing the door by hand. The bang that followed actually made the window behind John's desk rattle, to say nothing of the start it gave his nerves even though he was looking straight at her. This was not the first time this annoying habit of his daughter's had made John's nerves jump, and it slightly irritated him.

Ordinarily, any reproving look that her behavior put on his face, it was soon vanishing under that meek, mischievous way She had of suddenly stopping, when she knew she had agitated him, to cover her face with her hands and then peek at him through her fingertips. She was doing this now and as always John's nerves had rapidly begun to settle back down. Still, on an impulse, he decided to hold out this time and take her to task somewhat, anyhow. So, trying to match the banging of the door as much as he could, he sent forth a shrill cutting whistle and then said, ignoring her elfish manner this once as he dropped his head back to his desk, "If I hadn't known better, I'd surely thought war had been declared. Doors are not closed, Pet, by giving them a kick with one's heel. Doorknobs are attached for that purpose and I'll hope that you'll bear that in mind next time."

For a moment there was total silence. The calling-down for a change had been a blow. Nonetheless, John's daughter was too strong-willed to stay down for long. She let her hands fall back to her sides and went on to sweep up to her father's desk, perching herself on its edge to say, "Not Pet, Papa, please Pet sounds too much like a cow's name. You never call me that, that I don't think of Mr. Simpson's cow!"

John never failed to marvel at how quick his daughter could jump from one subject to another. He looked up, regarding her attentively. "Mr. Simpson's cow?" He questioned, thinking of their nearest neighbors, the good-natured Simpsons who not only lived by the Golden Rule on Sunday but through the weekdays as well. "I didn't know Mr. Simpson's cow's name is Pet."

"Well it is, and that's only the half of it! Did you know that that big carriage horse that Mr. Simpson just recently purchased to pull him and Mrs. Simpson around in that new buggy, goes by the name of John?"

"You don't say," laughed John, leaning back in his chair, suddenly amused. Of course, he knew the horse's name and also what had prompted Mr. Simpson to trade for him. Ever concerned for all God's creatures, Mr. Simpson had thought that his and Mrs. Simpson's rather ample build had put too much of a burden on his former buggy horse.

"You mean you don't mind that a horse who lives so close by us, goes by the name of John, too?" Beth Anne asked in a half of obvious indignation.

"Not in the least" her father replied, "since we're not likely to be flocking the same drawing room!"

"Oh, Papa" she groaned, "sometimes your jesting is simply impossible! You know what I'm getting at!"

"No, not really, but I'm making an effort," he went on to tease. "Scott Simpson wouldn't be playing a part in all this sudden concern of yours over our sharing names with the Simpson's livestock, would he?"

"Oh, Papa," she groaned again, "I give up, since it's obvious you're not! Scott has nothing to do with my not liking the name, Pet. Besides, you know perfectly well that Scott is very much involved with his studies. He has a long way to go yet before he gets his law degree."

"And, after he gets his law degree," John pried.

A crimson glow flushed her cheeks, but that was the only thing she divulged relative to answering her father's question. Suddenly, she was pretending to be very much interested in some news notices lying on the desk in front of her and asking at the same time, "Where's Uncle Sloan?"

"He's down at the lower end of town, trying to round up the facts concerning that warehouse fire last night," John said, thinking as he took in the blush on his daughter's face, 'that's one way to cut the matter short. '

While Beth Anne still pretended to be much occupied with the news notices, fingering through them, John continued to observe her—the lovely vividness of her person—her dynamic personality that, to him, came through with the intensity of chimes resounding. Yet, quite often and this was one of the times that he felt it, her

7

colorfulness brought a piercing poignancy to his heart as well—moving him to feel that at some other time—at some other place, he had looked on another like her. Still the feeling did not excite or disturb him. Neither did he start struggling to place or sort it out. The fact was, John's wrestling with what that darkened past was done on a small scale nowadays, and this was the way it had been with him for several years now. To overcome that driving urgency to regain his memory was not an easy matter to conquer, but mindful that he stood to lose too much if he failed to conquer it had caused him to struggle that much harder, and he had gradually defeated the problem. If he never unlocked the door to that darker room in his mind, no longer did he feel it was a matter of life and death with him. Those few flickers of light which he had seen and which continued to come at random—mostly in dreams, he pretty near was never disturbed any more as far as trying to place those lost years.

From time to time, he still saw flashes of that white columned mansion, with the long avenue of live oaks in his mind, and he dreamed of it. In fact, every so often, he dreamed of another mansion, not to mention a huge terraced formal garden and walking and riding in vast cotton fields. But, trying to connect what the dreams revealed with the reality of his waking hours, was something like trying to put a crossword puzzle together blindfolded.

Oh, most assuredly, he had done his damnedest, make no mistake about that. But, one day, he had learned and in a painful way at that that if there were to be any living for him with the present, he had to turn his thinking completely around—get ahold of himself, so to speak. He realized he had to let the dreams go—let them rest as they came or he was going to lose everything, his wife, his little girl, his business—everything, because for a period there he had begun to let the dream immerse him to the point that he was unable to see or think about anything else.

Instead of doing what he himself had suggested they do when he had told Rachelle about the dreams, which was to lay it aside and go on with their normal living pattern he, stupidly, had done just the opposite—let it absorb his every thought. And, if that had not been insensible enough, he had added to it by shutting Rachelle completely out—refusing to discuss one thought or share one word with her over the matter when she tried to help. Further, his beloved child, whom he loved more than life itself, also became game for his melancholy moods and self-pitying preoccupation with himself. He began to snap at her and brush her aside; that is, until that day she ran to Gilford Sloan for comforting right before his eyes. Well, he had come out of his dream world then and had not been long in doing it. Never would he forget that day. So engrossed he had been with his dreams and trying to work, too, he had hardly heard Beth Anne's cries much less realized that she had badly smashed her finger, even though she had approached him first and had tried to tell him he felt cheap to admit, until he heard Gilford Sloan drawl, "Don't you fret, little girl, I'll fix your finger up good as ever. I know all about fixing things of this sort. Yes indeed, I'm not So busy that I can't take the time to look at your finger and fix it up to boat! Yes, you bet I will!"

Well, if Beth Anne's cries had not made much of a dent upon him, Sloan's remark certainly did and something else too—Sloan's damning expression meeting him as he spun around to finally take a look at his child and dash to her aid. In fact, as he grabbed Beth Anne and bounded up the stairway with her to dress her finger, it had not been necessary to look over his shoulder to see if Gilford Sloan's scornful eye was still following his back. He had known Sloan's contempt was fixed solid on his every step.

Anyway, that incident was to mark the turning point in that depressing period of their lives. It brought him to view the situation with open eyes and, when he did, he could find little to hail. The truth was, he found himself sickened at his own behavior. He could see that he had let a few hazy, contorted visions and dreams lure him into a dream world of emptiness, which had blinded him to the worth and value of the real world around him. so, not only had he dressed his child's finger that day himself and comforted her, too, he also apologized to Rachelle. And additionally, beginning that very same day, he started making all effort to be more conscious of the present and give thanks for its blessings and live in it, rather than dwell instead in sorrowing remorse for a past world that he was unable to even place, much less see the face of one single person in it.

And now, if a sense of having looked on the very same face whom no doubt his beloved daughter had inherited her exquisite features and lively personality from, brought a pensiveness to John's heart for a moment, he merely shrugged it off in his mind and thought, so be it as he broke the silence and asked, "Were you able to find your mother's embroidery thread? I don't see any package."

Even though John and Rachelle had been blessed with only one child, neither had ever felt the existence of a missing link in the role they played as a parent. The close relationship that Beth Anne had with both John and Rachelle, and the harmony of the family unit as a whole made up for any sense of half measures that either parent could have felt on occasion. As a matter of fact, Beth Anne's waking hours came near being equally divided between her parents. Beginning with the completion of her school years, she spent the mornings with her mother while they usually engaged in lighter housework together and other general chores that goes with the makings of a household, such as embroidery and sewing. Then, when her father came home at noon to share the noonday dinner hour with his family, Beth Anne would accompany him back to his newspaper office where she helped out with various tasks till it was time for them to return home in the evening. For the most part, this had become the pattern of her day. It seldom varied, leaving out, of course, the social activities or some other goings—that solely concerned the younger set, because she was a very popular girl attending outings and "parties" quite often and also doing her share of keeping the entertainment flowing—filling the Fillmore-Lee house to full capacity with her Saturday night "parties" in rapid succession.

Now, as she let the news notes fall back upon the desk and stood up, she said, "'Wouldn't one guess, at the very last store I went to. That's why it took so long. I'd saved a lot of steps had I headed there in the first place. To make sure I didn't leave it lying around in here some place, I put it in the buggy as I passed by."

Johns smiled, "Don't you realize that drawing attention to saving steps and misplacing articles, Pet, could bring one to think that you might be on the verge of creaking with old age?"

"And, don't you think, Papa, that I don't see right through that remark," she quipped back. "What you're trying to say to me in a round about way is that if I wait around for the completion of law courses, I could don the label of being an old maid!" She sent him a wry grin. "Further, it looks as though I'm going to have to contend with being reminded of the Simpson's cow, cost what it may."

"Now, that's not showing the proper spirit, Pet. Besides, you don't really object to the name that much, do you?"

"'Would it do any good, if I did?" she laughed and added, as she turned to another desk close by and bent over it, "Papa, are these the articles you wanted me to check over?"

"Yes, but never mind about it now. I filled the space with

something else and it's already gone to press. We'll get to those some other time. How would you like to accompany your dull reporter father on a little work detail this afternoon?"

Straightening up from the desk, she scoffed, as a smile revealed ivory-perfect teeth, "You dull? Never would I use that word in relation with you. Will the work detail be conducted in town or out of it?"

Standing there, dressed in a frilly snow-white blouse and red, white, and blue plaid wool skirt with its own cummerbund cinching her small waist—her curly brown hair set off with a big white bow in back and looking like twists of candy falling around her face and into the ruffles of her blouse where a pretty cameo broach rested at her throat—her deep-blue eyes brimming to the fullest with interest, John thought his daughter made a very pretty picture.

Blessing the fact and letting his heart exult with pride over it, all at the same time, John replied, "How does the military academy strike you?"

"Rather attractive," she said, her smile growing wider.

"M-hum, I might've known," declared John, flashing a grin of his own through his gray painted beard. 'Nothing like the trimness and polish of a uniform to fan a woman's interest. " Picking up his pen, he hurriedly scribbled a note, adding, as he sprang to his feet and lifted his hat and coat from the clothes tree that Rachelle had had the sagacity to place near his desk, "Be sure to bring your shawl, dear, because it'll probably be getting late by the time we leave the academy. You'll need it against the evening chill. It's most likely we'll go on home from the academy, anyhow. I'm leaving Sloan this note so he'll know our whereabouts and what to expect, in any case." He headed on through the door to Sloan's desk in the adjoining room.

Having found that her fringed wool shawl, which was identical in material to that of her shirt, had been too much against the afternoon's sunlight when she was running the errand for her mother, Beth Anne had been carrying the shawl in her hand upon her noisy return. Now, she made a dive to retrieve the shawl and her handbag, too, from a chair sitting beside the door where she had thrown both only moments before that and then went dashing through the door herself.

The fact that she had accompanied her father to the academy on former occasions when he had sought information for other news stories, dampened Beth Anne's eagerness for this visit not one bit.

The thought of going to the military institute had always put wings on her feet, with the prospect of each visit being no less refreshing to her than had she been going there for the very first time. And, not in the least, did the case of the institution being an "all-male world" make for the unsettling of one tiny nerve in her body. The truth was, this one particular circumstance delighted Beth Anne all the more, not because; however, that she was so enamored of the male person or taken with him—though like most women she did appreciate a handsome man and his attentive eye, but for the reason she was barred from enrolling in the training school herself because of her sex. Thus, Beth Anne, merely walking through the institution's doors gave her a feeling of challenging the rule—a feeling that she was lording it over man and order alike just a fraction or two.

Still, this feeling of having the game in her own hands for a moment was a small factor compared to the other things that made Beth Anne's visits to the military academy seem so exciting. The entire aura which environed the military had never failed to intrigue and delight her. She loved the ran tan beat of the drums. Her heart swelled at the sounding of bugles reveille—taps. She was fascinated by the preciseness of marching feet, lifting and falling at the same instant. The colors, the badges, gleaming buttons and braid, flashing swords and bayonets—the whole regalia elated her and had from the moment of her first visit there with her father when they had stood and watched a body of cadets marching in a practice drill—a visit that had resulted in her father losing a half nights'sleep that night in his effort of trying to explain to her why she could not enroll in the academy, too, when she grew older!

Beth Anne recalled the incident to her mind On this afternoon as she rode through the colorful leaf-fringed streets toward the academy, remembering how hard it has been for her to resign herself to the fact that a student of the military school, she would never be. Nonetheless, the phase had passed; though, and she thought she had come through without any lasting scars, taking into account she found herself smiling at the memory even though her enthusiasm for the place was as intense as ever.

Beth Anne's smile still held as she gazed at Lexington's distant hills. She thought seldom had she seen the valley's rim banked with such a profusion of color. With the clear, shimmering sky hanging above the golds and the reds, the picturesque view reminded her of her mother's pretty blue-rimmed, flowered China plates, making it seem that in its shining brilliance the entire valley was breathing with a pulse of purity—contenting her so that she began to feel as if she were lying on the softness of a featherbed in the warmth of a glowing hearth.

She began to wish that the season would stay as it was and never change, with the intensity of her feelings bringing her to turn to her father and say, "Papa, I hope Thanksgiving is this pretty, but I bet it'll turn cold overnight and sweep every last particle of all this prettiness away."

"Well," John said, taking in his daughters own glowing prettiness, "we must remember, to everything there is a season, and a time to every purpose under the heaven" Now, why did I say that? John thought. Who else have I heard quote that same biblical verse time and again? Stop it, John Fillmore-Lee, before your thoughts trap you from the present again. Don't you see your daughter is beginning to send you a questioning look. "Maybe not overnight, Pet, but it will go, that you can count on," he continued. Still, I'd say we've been lucky this year I have seen falls that brought snow by this time. The important thing is to enjoy it while it lasts. There's the academy. I hope these drill sergeants don't have the freshman cadets so involved that I'll be forced to leave without getting my interviews."

"I hope so too, Papa, but from the looks of the grounds it appears that's what you may have to do."

Guiding the buggy to a parking place under a row of red and yellow maples that bordered the front grounds of the academy, John, shifting his gaze, replied, "I go along with you there. It looks as though the entire student body might be taking advantage of the weather today." He pulled the buggy to a stop, and jumping to the ground he threw the reins around a low-hanging branch, going on, as he sent his daughter a smile, "Well, even if we don't get our interviews, at least from all appearances you'll get the chance to enjoy a little march music and observe some of the tactical craft that's involved in making soldiers out of men." As he stepped closer to offer her his hand in alighting from the buggy, his smile erupted into a laugh. "But, I warn you now, no keeping me up till twelve o'clock tonight asking questions, that's beyond my ability to deal with competently, remember?"

"I was just thinking about that, Papa," she laughed, as she took his hand and swept to the ground. "You've discredited yourself though. The way I remember it, you were very much equal to the task." She shook her head. "What a problem I must've been at times, doubtless a regular holy terror."

"Well, I wouldn't put it that strongly," said John, as they began to walk across the grounds in the direction of where the practice drills were taking place, "'but you did have your days and nights, too, I should say." He paused his step and looked up, letting his eyes run over the milling men. "We're in luck, there's Sergeant Siders. He'll help us. Come on, we'll edge a halt to those exercises, I'll move in with my pen and notebook. He's usually pretty well up on what's happening at this place and seems to have no qualms in sharing it with the press."

It was true, Sergeant Calvin Siders was a most liberal man, although his bellowing voice and hard piercing gaze plus other marked features, kept this trait as well as other traits of his eye. His freshman students were ever in awe of his stern discipline, and his hard-looking expression helped none whatever, only adding to their misgivings. The way the sergeant's small black eyes went about sizing his students up, as he strode his portly frame back and forth among them in his endeavor of trying to create a first rate cadet, not only put most of his charges in mind of a flying bullet finding its mark, inducing them to turn their thoughts to clinched steel traps. Then, there were other things about his person for instance, always giving the appearance of being swathed in more yellow braid than the blue cloth of his uniform—with every inch seeming to blare his authority that much more, and also literally barking his orders and commands—all hindrances when it came to letting his lesser forbidding qualities shine through. However, from the first, John had been onto Sergeant Calvin Siders softness, fully aware that despite all the toughness he projected, it hardly went one fraction beneath the skin of his body.

Suddenly, John heard the Sergeant bellow out a roaring dismissal and saw him turn in his and Beth Anne's direction, giving them a most friendly wave. As the sergeant came striding on toward them, with John taking in his rare wide grin, the sudden change of the sergeant's character, reminded John of a chameleon changing its color, bringing him to wonder why it was Calvin Siders who could not bring himself to grant his students the benefit of his smile once in a while, too, because from observing the body of scattering cadets the sergeant had turned his back on, John was positive that there were few in the whole group whom Calvin Siders had not scared hell out

14

of, to say nothing of possibly frightening them away from following a military career for all time—had they been so inclined.

Granted, there were not many among the freshman cadets whom John had not pretty much sized up right, but Cadet Carson Heyward of South Carolina was not one of them even though, coincidently, he had been one among the number whom had served for John's mental reckoning and final convictions. Even as, Carr Heyward had not been frightened from seeking a military career or anything else. Nor was he scared. But, it was true, he was down in spirit. Still, Calvin Siders had had nothing to do with it. The fact was, Carr Heyward had become so wrapped up in thoughts of home that day, that he had more or less stumbled through the drilling exercise, half-hearing Calvin Siders shouts of command or anything else being said—his first spell of real homesickness absorbing his every move and thought.

Carr was not going home for Thanksgiving, like the majority of his classmates were. He was one of the few remaining at the academy. Carr had come up with the idea himself upon leaving for Lexington in early fall. Having been well aware of the great outlay of cash that his parents had already put out that year in order to make the move to the new mansion, Carr wanting to help preserve what little money would be left in their purses after all the crops were harvested and sold and most the debts paid off, had suggested that both he and his sister remain at school instead of trekking it home for Thanksgiving. He had pointed out, since Thanksgiving and Christmas fell so closely together, it would not be a great ordeal to wait those few weeks to go home, saving a lot of expenses. Jane Anne had supported her brother's suggestion and, without uttering one word of protest at that, though it was painful for her to do since it put an end to all her hopes of possibly seeing Stuart through the holiday. Luke and Eliza had also gone along with the suggestion, but mainly because they had felt to object to such sound reasoning might not be very wise of them, fearing their objection could have a lasting impact on their son. All the same, they had wondered how they were going to make it through the Thanksgiving holiday without their children's presence.

Now, Carr Heyward was wondering the same thing—wondering what he was going to do with himself through the long holiday, now that all classes and drills had been adjourned until the following week. He was finding that it was one thing to suggest something, but quite another to face it and especially when it meant sacrificing some hungering desire like going home to Green Sea for the Thanksgiving holiday.

Having strayed hardly one foot from the spot he was covering when his instructor and drill sergeant, Calvin Siders had called a halt to all drills and classes, Carr's pining for home had become so intense that he was actually smelling and seeing Pete's tempting dishes setting on the dining room table. And, adding to the thought of missing all the good food, thoughts of saddling his favorite riding mare for the traditional afternoon Thanksgiving hunt with his father and jailor trotting along beside them—in truth it was more a horseback ride than a hunt, were flagging Carr's spirit that much more.

No, Carr was suddenly reminding himself and feeling a whole lot worse because of it, even if he were at Green Sea and going on a hunt, Jailor would not be occupying his usual place because Jailor's earthly hunts were all over. He supposed all that was playing a big part in his dark mood. Not only had his mother conveyed the news of Jailor's death in a letter a few days earlier, but the sad news of Doss' death as well. Even though his mother's letters made his days, that was one he would as leave had gotten lost in the mail rather than passed on to him. With Doss and Jailor both gone, he truly thought Green Sea would never be the same. As a matter of fact, Doss holding his hand as he helped him guide his small pearl-handled knife down a piece of wood while Jailor tried to get his nose in the act, too, was the first memory of his lifetime. They both were embedded in his memory and as much a part of Green Sea as those century-old enduring live oaks that bordered the long avenue. He supposed Jane Anne had also been informed. He did not have to be told she was saddened about the news. He knew she was. His tender, gentle sister. Doss may not have taught her how to hold a knife, but he had ever been there to mend her dolls.

He wished his mother had not, all of a sudden, taken such a dislike to Stuart Drakston, because Jane Anne had fallen in love with him. He certainly saw nothing wrong with the match. Stuart admired his sister and considering all accounts, it was his thinking that she would never come by a finer husband than Stuart Drakston. Besides all Stuart's fine, honorable qualities, Stuart was also immensely rich, and he was not talking about land and holdings only, he meant thousands and thousands of cold cash lying in bank vaults—

something the Heyward family was always short on though he supposed they were considered to be rich, too, or somewhere close to it, if land and a new mansion meant anything! He knew what he would do for a start toward filling up the dragging days ahead, he would go this minute and write his sister a long letter. No doubt she was feeling as lost, if not more so, than he was.

Suddenly, it dawned on Carr that someone had been calling to him, realizing the instant he was turning that the voice trying to get his attention belonged to Calvin Siders. Looking across the parade grounds, he spied the sergeant motioning for him to come forth as he said something to a man and woman whom, it appeared, he was engaged in conversation with. Carr was puzzled as to why Calvin Siders was waving for him to join the trio, because he was well aware that his performance during drilling exercise had not warranted a pat on the back from the sergeant. More likely a good belated chewing out, he was telling himself as he began to stride forth with just a fraction of trepidation weighing on his steps.

Calvin Siders was turning a most pleasant expression toward him as he hollered out, "Heyward, I think maybe you can help my friends here. I thought I overheard you say that you'd be spending the holidays in Lexington instead of leaving for home today, is this correct?"

"That's right, sir," Carr said, seeing now that Calvin Siders companions were a very well-dressed distinguished-looking gentleman and a young woman, who had a face that was beautiful beyond description, as he slowed his steps and made all effort to keep his gaze fixed on the sergeant instead of letting it stray to the fairer features of the young woman.

"'Well, I thought I was right," Calvin Siders was saying. "'I'd like you to meet Mr. John Fillmore-Lee and his lovely daughter Miss Beth Anne. Mr. John here is owner and chief editor of the local paper, the "Pacesetter". He's preparing an editorial about the freshman class and wants to interview a number of you. I thought perhaps you could help him and maybe suggest one or two more of your classmates who'd do the same."

"Of course, Sergeant Siders, I'd be glad to help in any way I can," Carr replied, and taking his gaze off the sergeant stepped forward and offered John his hand as Calvin Siders picked up his piecemeal introduction and went on, "Good. Well, Mr. John, it appears here's your man, Cadet Carson Heyward of Green Sea Plantation, South Carolina."

Giving Carr's hand a long, gripping shake, John said, "How do you do, Cadet Heyward. I'll be much obliged for any information you'll furnish me," the mentioning of Green Sea Plantation affecting no deep emotion within him. What excitability John was feeling was being induced by his ever interest in the South and nothing more.

"It'll be my pleasure, sir," Carr replied back, "I'm honored to make your acquaintance." Then, turning, at last, to meet Beth Anne's deep-blue gaze direct, he smiled and added, as he gave his cadet cap a tip and shoved it farther back on his head, "Miss Lee, again, I feel honored."

This was one instance where there was no awareness of a uniform with Beth Anne, despite her father's remark pertaining to their luring attraction. The fact was, as Carr Heyward's shocks of coal-black curls—Carr's hair had turned black as his father's and sister's over the years, came tumbling down beneath his cap to fall on his forehead and around his face, framing his handsome features, it is doubtful Beth Anne would have noticed had he been decked out in leggings and buffalo hides. Her eyes were too busy with Carr Heyward's face, not to mention his broad shouldered tallness, which towered over that of her father's by at least two or three inches, to notice uniforms or anything else as she returned Carr's smile and took it upon herself to clarify his obvious confusion regarding her last name.

"Fillmore-Lee," she smilingly offered, knowing as surely as her name was Beth Anne that besides the pleasantries the moment was giving birth to something else, too, bringing her to wonder if Carr was also aware of it. "It's two words joined with a hyphen," she further explained.

"Fillmore-Lee," he repeated and, as he did with them continuing to exchange smiles—to Carr, the sifting maple leaves suddenly became apple blossoms falling in November because that was what the face of the girl standing before him made him think of—a delicate pink apple blossom. And, seeing this awakening in Carr's gaze, Beth Anne recognized it for what it was and pondered the state of his feelings no more, letting the moment stand as long as it would, while her father and Sergeant Calvin Siders, too, gawked at them and waited.

Luke did not open the letter that he took from the mailbox. He waited until he reached the kitchen where he joined Eliza for dinner so that they could enjoy hearing Carr's news together. During the weekdays, unless they were entertaining company, it had been Luke and Eliza's habit to shun the formal dining room ever since Carr and Jane Anne had left for school, taking their meals instead in Pete's big comfortable kitchen.

Now, taking their seats at the kitchen table, Eliza pushing her plate aside in haste, smoothed out the letters pages on the table top and began to read aloud, while Luke hang on every word and nodded his head in accordance with her occasional comments—both totally ignoring the dinner that Pete had set before them until they had first savored every tidbit of news that the letter furnished.

Dearest Parents,

Hope your normal good health is still remaining to stay with you both, and especially now that winter seems to have arrived and bringing with it its usual maladies and complaints as well. Quite a number in my class have been sore plagued by and pretty near with all the other woes that accompanies the common infirmities of cold weather.

There is no question that the weather did play a big part in the infirmity of my classmates, considering the fact that most of them were taken ill less than no time after romping like puppies, for hours, in the big snow that fell here two days after Thanksgiving. In fact, our weather changed overnight here and as did the looks of Lexington and the surrounding countryside as well. On the morning following Thanksgiving Day, the sky gradually darkened to a steel-looking grey and a cold wind started blowing at near hurricane force and, within hours, besides plunging the temperature from a balmy Indian Summer to something what the polar regions must feel like, it stripped the trees bare of all radiance—leaving most—especially the pretty stand of maples out in front of the academy, looking as naked and colorless as desert sand. But the big surprise was yet to come when the next morning everything was so laden with snow, that it looked as though the entire world had turned to one big fluffy cotton ball! However, before I leave the subject—yes, I must be honest and confess that I, too, took an active part in what I defined as being nothing but playful amusement. Well, it was more near a fight than actual play. We freshman students staged a mock battle against our upper fellow students, using snowballs for ammunition! The only thing, I decided to lay down my arms a lot sooner than some of the

19

other did—no doubt saving myself the same aches and pains they are suffering now.

I enjoyed your letter telling me about the hog-killing at Oak Grove on Thanksgiving. Though by a piece of luck I had the pleasure of meeting a most charming local family just before Thanksgiving and was hosted by them on Thanksgiving Day and did have a very pleasant time visiting with them, I still missed being home. Not only did I miss Green Sea itself, I also, more than I can adequately express, missed the company of my own family and friends, especially our afternoon hunt, Papa, even though the thought of Jailor not being there did depress me; and also, those traditional, delectable dishes, Mother, that you alone have the knack of giving the right flavor to.

Anyway, that sounded just like something that only Aunt Martha would come up with, staging a hog killing on Thanksgiving Day! Here I was having mental visions of all those traditional dishes gracing the dining room table at Green Sea, and there you two were feasting on fresh park at Oak Grove! I think had I known about that fresh backbone and rice, not to mention the sausages and all the other, it would have been goodbye Lexington, for me, whatever the cost! At any rate I don't mind revealing that I have suffered a twinge of homesickness lately but, fortunately, it has been alleviated considerably through the gaining of these friends whom I must tell you about.

Shortly, after our training instructor, Sergeant Calvin Siders had dismissed my classmates and me from all duties till after the holiday, with me still standing in my tracks wondering how I was going to fill the long hours ahead while my spirit dropped lower and lower, I heard the sergeant calling to me. It turned out that he had joined some friends of his who had arrived during our drilling exercise and whom I had not even seen, though they had been watching the sergeant put me and my fellow companions through the paces from where they stood under one of the maple trees on the grounds.

Under the sergeant's beacon and with some trepidation I might add, I hurried across the grounds toward him and, momentarily—to my easement and pleasure I was making the acquaintance of Mr. John Fillmore-Lee and his lovely daughter, Beth Anne. The sergeant went on to explain that the gentleman, who is co-owner and chief editor of a local newspaper the "Pacesetter", was there to gather information regarding an article he wished to write and feature in his paper, concerning the freshman class. The sergeant asked if I would oblige the gentleman with an interview, which, of course, I readily agreed to and before I hardly knew what was happening, not only did I find myself happily ensconced in the Fillmore-Lee buggy on the way with them to their home, but elated as well over the fact that I was going to have supper with them that night too! Mr. John, following Sergeant Siders example this is the manner I chose in which to address the editor since his surname is rather odd and unnatural sounding, is a well-thought-of, distinguished gentleman. His amiable and outgoing nature no doubt accounts for some of this esteem and, unquestionably, has aided him in his obvious success as a newspaperman, despite the fact that he is hampered a great deal in his work—so I've taken notice—by the lameness of his left arm. I have no idea what the nature of this impairment is since, so far, the subject has failed to come up even though I have spent a considerable length of time with him in conversation. However, this fact could be as a result of his seemingly staying interest in the South and its culture, once he learns one is southern born—leaving little room for other topics of interest.

Actually, aside from hearing Mr. John make mention that he and his family are former Washingtonians—having moved from Washington, D.C. to Lexington before his daughter who is an only child was of school age, I have learned nothing which I have already pointed out. I was witness to this fact when I was invited back by Mr. John to spend Thanksgiving Day with him and his family and attended a local horse show with him, his daughter Beth Anne, and his co-partner in business, a Mr. Gilford Sloan who had also been invited and who is a native Virginian, by the way! The popular regard in which he is held was clearly manifested at this event. He was hailed and greeted from all sides. The Fillmore-Lee's live on a small twenty-five-acre estate on the outskirts of Lexington. The plot is orderly and well-kept. So is their home, a moderate but attractive two-story brick, which is lovingly presided over by Mr. John's wife, Rachelle. "Miss" Rachelle is a charming and warm woman— obviously very kindhearted. She welcomed me to their home and table with no less warmth than had she known me all my life. Though one can feel the family's closeness and deep devotion for one another, "Miss" Rachelle did not accompany the rest of us to the horse show, seeming to prefer instead the domestic side of life. I gathered her fondness for the sport and, horses in general, is not as keen as her husband's and daughter's. Anyway, when we all returned from the horse show, she had dinner awaiting us—one that she had prepared herself and varying somewhat, too, from our dishes, but still very tasty, especially the roasted duckling and one unique dish that I had never seen or tasted before—Boston baked beans.

Their home site also contains a barn and stables, which houses the fine horses that the family owns, plus their other livestock. One of the three hunters that makes up the horse group is a splendid boy, who goes by the name of Thunder and who is claimed by Beth Anne. Although Mr. John's left arm is lame, both he and his daughter are superb riders. The several trophies and blue ribbons they hold attest to this. Beth Anne took part in the horse show on Thanksgiving. Needless to say, she and Thunder took the jumps with ease of a floating feather, winning another trophy to add to her collection. Mr. John was awfully proud of her. So was Sloan, I noted, whom she addresses as "Uncle Sloan."

All in all, I did have a wonderful Thanksgiving and am grateful to this family for making it so. I wish you both could meet them too, especially Beth Anne, who is the loveliest girl I have ever seen. Her eyes are as blue as the deep sea at Sandy with a gaze that sparkles as bright as its waters. As a matter of fact, Mother, her eyes remind me of yours.

I must turn in now as it is near that hour. Keep the letters coming, for as much as I do enjoy the company of these new friends of mine and take delight in the cheerful, warn atmosphere of their home, my thoughts still dwell at Green Sea aplenty—thinking of you both and all the others there, as well as Jane Anne in Charlottesville, while I continue to count the days till Christmas.

P.S. When I think about it, I find it somewhat strange that Beth Anne and my only sister, Jane Anne share the same name with their given names and are both called thus.

As she followed the lines of the letter, Eliza's frequent comments had steadily declined until they had finally ceased altogether. Now in the continuing silence with Luke noting and with some amusement at how her mouth was drawing up tighter and tighter, she neatly folded the letter's pages together and stuck them back inside the envelope.

Then quickly thrusting the letter inside her apron pocket and without even waiting for Luke to drop his head, let alone give him time to offer one word of his usual thanks for the food, she hastily drew her plate forth and started filling it from the dish of chicken and dumplings that was already barely lukewarm, hissing, "Yankees," as she furiously began to ladle the food onto her onto her plate. The word split the silence like a shot.

"What?" Luke exclaimed, seeing now that he had not sized up his wife's obvious simmering as well as he thought he did. This Beth Anne business was not all that was riling her. "Oh come, dear, the war's been over a long time. Besides, I'd say these people should hardly be branded as such, after living in Lexington, Virginia, that long.

"Once a Yankee, always a Yankee, is my concept," she retorted back. "Boston baked beans! Will you tell me what's any more Yankee than that? I'd say it's far from being a Southern dish!"

"And our son did, too, if I recall the letter correctly," Luke said deciding to forego the blessing, for this once, since Eliza was already pushing the food toward her mouth and filling his own plate as he went on. "So what are you getting so worked up about? Is it the girl? Personally, since these people appear to be a respectable and upstanding family, I'm grateful that Carr's made their acquaintance. I imagine that academy can get to be pretty boring at times."

"I won't argue the boring factor with you, Luke, because I, too, imagine he gets plenty lonesome. But I won't agree with you on the other part. I don't care how respectable Yankees are. I want no part of them!"

No longer was Luke amused. Besides having a guilty conscience over eating food that he had failed to recite a verbal thanks to his Lord for—something he had not failed to do since joining the Baptist church, he thought Eliza was not being very fair-minded, actually too biased toward the whole matter to his way of thinking.

"Listen, dear," he said lacing his words with the might of force as he looked up from his plate to stare at her, "I know you suffered a great deal because of the tragedies and hardships that hit our family during the war and afterwards, too. But, you must remember they were tragedies and hardships that were brought about by circumstances that no one person or one group of people should be held accountable for, certainly not this one family whom you say you want no part of. In truth, when we get right down to the bottom of this matter regarding Yankees and think about it, we all should see that none of us who fought in the war or participated in it to any degree, North and South alike, are totally exempt from shouldering some blame. So I hope you'll consider that aspect and be fair on the part of these new friends of Carr's."

Realizing Luke had made a valid point and no doubt was right, since to her Luke made very few mistakes if, indeed, he made any at all, Eliza carried the "Yankee" factor no further. All the same, following another long moment of silence in which Luke resumed his eating—thinking the subject was dropped, no longer was she able to hold back her sentiments in point of the girl factor, blurting out, "Well, it certainly didn't take him long to forget the looks of Grace Cooper's eyes!"

Luke almost broke up in laughter. He didn't, though, because he knew the matter was far too serious, one that could involve into an indomitable situation that just might bring a lot of unhappiness to all concerned.

So the urge to laugh was pushed way deep in Luke's throat. Then, making a halfway motion at clearing it, he told her, "That's another thing, dear. We must start realizing that our children are no longer, just that—children! They are both grown adults. We cannot nestle them to our bosoms forever. Those days are past. Certainly we can and will continue to comfort them, but we cannot limit their freedom, their wants, and their desires to the shadow of our wings only while we do this. I'll admit that the letter does sound as though Carr might be attracted to this Beth Anne. But what if he is? It may not mean anymore than what his attraction to Laura meant, which amounted to nothing but friendship in the long run. Next came Grace. Now, it appears it's this Beth Anne Fillmore—uh—"

"Lee," Eliza filled in, thinking herself that the "Lee" part of the name was the most interesting and pleasing aspect of the whole business.

"Oh, yes, Fillmore-Lee," Luke went on. "The name does sound a little odd. Anyway getting back to what I was saying. There could very well be a dozen more girls before Carr finds that one special one whom he will want to spend the rest of his life with." He reached and gave Eliza's hand a pat. "So, settle your thoughts dear, and then after dinner go ahead and answer Carr's letter, accordingly."

Eliza gave Luke a long look, but finally nodded her head at him in agreement. Just the same, she was telling herself, that is much easier, Luke, for you to say than it is going to be for me to carry through with. It was one thing to want no part of a Yankee, but to

24

pretend that it was all right with her that her son was getting Chummy with Yankees, not to mention that from all appearances he was falling in love with one, was going to be something like having to endure a mouthful of gall and wormwood.

It looked as though this problem concerning her children's courting was going to get worse before it got better, anyway, she thought, it was just yesterday that not only had her and Elizabeth Drakston's friendship—though fast it had never been to begin with—come near to the mark of a final outs over it, but she had also received another blow by learning from Elizabeth that Jane Anne and Stuart Drakston had been writing daily letters to one another ever since Jane Anne had left for the University of Virginia.

Of course, she had not forbidden her daughter to correspond with Stuart Drakston. To tell the truth, she had failed to think of it. She supposed her mind had been too busy thinking about all those miles she was putting between her daughter and Stuart Drakston, once she had her settled in college, to have much of anything else in her head, at the time. She had no idea yet what she was going to do about the letters if, indeed, there was anything she could do now since it had been going on all this time. One thing she did know. Elizabeth Drakston's support in the matter, she would never have. It had not taken her long to find that out yesterday when, much to her surprise, she had opened the front door to see a rather perturbed-looking Elizabeth standing on the threshold.

Eliza thought she would never forget how Elizabeth had looked, holding her nose so high in the air that she appeared to be sniffing some unpleasant odor, as she brusquely said, "I want to talk with you, Eliza." Just like that, without one word of greeting or anything.

"Of course," Eliza said, holding the door aside for Elizabeth to enter. Then, she closed the door and ushered Elizabeth in the living room, indicating for her to take her seat on the green brocaded sofa, then taking hers in a chair nearby where she could face her guest.

Though she hardly thought that sorrowing news had brought Elizabeth to Green Sea, if the stern set of her usual pleasant-looking features meant anything, Eliza—always thinking of her aged father every time a Drakston coach did roll up unexpectedly, still had to first make sure before another word was said, asking quickly, "Elizabeth, everyone's well? No bad news, I hope?"

"Health wise, Eliza, everyone's well thank you," Elizabeth snapped. "Regarding the circumstances of the news; however, I shall think that will depend on the outcome of our discussion!"

Eliza did not take easy to Elizabeth's remark.

"'And, I shall be thinking, Elizabeth, and soon at that, that there won't be any discussion at all, if you don't simmer down a little before you start," Eliza barked back, having no compunction about letting Elizabeth Drakston know that, guest or not, she could not jump down her throat and get by with it.

Elizabeth took heed and relented somewhat, drawing in her breath a bit. After all she had no wish to get thrown out before she succeeded in doing what she had come to do.

"Very well," she said more calmly, "I'll get to the point. I want to hear in specific detail all about those disreputable characteristics that you obviously see my son holding. I'm his mother. I think I have every right to know."

Surprised to see that the ever mild-mannered Elizabeth could indeed make a direct attack without hedging at all, Eliza was thrown somewhat but soon rallied and said, "No, despite your accusation and demand, I won't do that because I have yet to stigmatize your son in such a manner as that."

"Of course, you haven't publicly because that would discredit your own self, would it not? Still, not only your actions toward him speak differently, but you have told him in the privacy of your home that he isn't welcome to come here. You won't deny that?"

"Yes, I'll deny that, too, because it isn't following true fact. I didn't tell your son he wasn't welcome to come here. What I did tell him was, that he was not welcome if he didn't put those foolish notions concerning my daughter aside. I also told him that I thought it was improper and not very honorable of him to confess his love and desire for marriage with our daughter, without ever once approaching her father or me with his intentions."

"Had he approached you, would you have favored the match?" Elizabeth promptly fired back, eyeing Eliza intently.

Eliza hesitated, feeling cornered—cornered by something that she herself could not even grasp, let alone to define.

"I thought not," Elizabeth went on. "Everything my son said is true. He isn't welcome here and you are very much opposed to him, regardless of what you've told me."

Finally, Eliza spoke, a near pleading quality in her voice. "I want no quarrel with you or Stuart, Elizabeth. All I want is to be left in peace with my family."

"What about my family? Apparently our peace and happiness doesn't concern you in the least. Except for the day his father died, I've never seen Stuart as unhappy as he was following the night after the ball when you treated him so unfeelingly. Don't you realize when I see him this way it affects me deeply too?

"I understand that, Elizabeth, and I think that you'd understand my point of view and my deep concern regarding my daughter's well-being."

"Well-being—happiness! Eliza, you're talking nonsense and I'm not so brainless that I don't think you're aware of it! I know all the details, Stuart told me. He offered to wait a whole two years for your daughter. Besides, in point of Jane Anne's happiness, couldn't you see she was totally miserable when you packed her off to school. And not only her, but you made Stuart miserable, too."

"Well she may be miserable, but I'm positive marrying with Stuart won't remedy it. To my way of thinking she'd be more unhappy than she is now. She's too young for your son. Not only that, it's important that she gets her education. She'll adjust. So will Stuart. Just a matter of time that's all."

"I hardly see the possibility of that happening, in spite of the distance you've put between them, considering the number of letters passing back and forth. "

"Letters?" Eliza questioned.

Elizabeth regretted her remark, seeing the surprise on Eliza's face. Still, it was too late to take the words back.

"You mean you didn't know that they're writing to one another almost every day?"

"No," Eliza confessed. I haven't given that any thought, since my daughter is well aware of my views and should know I have no intention of changing them."

"I see," said Elizabeth, "and very much regret that I've revealed it, because I couldn't be more opposed to your behavior concerning this matter." Elizabeth rose to her feet. "However, before I take myself from under your roof and away from here, I want you to realize that because of your views, I would've preferred Stuart falling in love with someone else. Although I do think Jane Anne is a lovely girl and personally have nothing against her, I see nothing but a lot of pain and distress for all of us. Further, I want you to know that I also believe, after having had these several weeks to ponder the matter, that your stand against my son has more to do with Stuart's late father than Stuart himself."

Eliza had also risen and, if Elizabeth had expected the blow of her trump card to put Eliza back in her chair, her surprise was hitting that much harder, for to Elizabeth's amazement instead of the outburst of anger and provocation that She was expecting to burst forth, there was only a baffled expression covering Eliza's face as she replied,

"That's an unheeded, presumptuous remark, Elizabeth, not like you at all."

"No, I'll agree, insolence is not my style, but never have my son's good character and his future happiness been at stake before, either. Besides, the remark held truth and you know it. Still, I have no wish to go further and air details. Frank was my husband, the father of my son. I loved him and he..." Elizabeth suddenly broke Off and turned her back to Eliza, making her way toward the door. No, she told herself, she would not subject the relationship that she and Frank had shared to this kind of vulnerability, least of all to Eliza Heyward, because if Eliza Heyward did thank that Frank had not loved her, she was a bigger fool than she was thinking she was!

However, as Elizabeth was rushing on through the doorway and across the hall toward the front door, leaving Eliza wondering what to reply if anything as she scurried after her, she made a sudden stop and turned back, "Stuart doesn't know I've come here to have this talk with you in his behalf. Neither does his grandmother or Mr. Carson. In fact, Frank's mother or your father, whom I've come to love as dearly as my own father, doesn't know about any of this messy situation. Stuart wanted it that way. I'll hope you'll at least keep mine and his confidence. He doesn't want to cause them to worry. Neither do I."

Having gained Elizabeth's side, Eliza replied, "Nor I," as she reached and pulled the door aside and stood by it. "So, we will continue on as we have in the past for sake of family in spite of this, I'll too hope."

Elizabeth's mouth churned in ridicule.

"Of course," she said with a scornful little laugh." Why not let the charade continue? It's not going to present no problem for either of us, in the near future anyway, considering that it's Martha's turn to host the family Christmas gathering at Oak Grove this year!"

As she dropped her head back to her plate and busied herself with finishing dinner, Eliza was wondering again if she should tell

Luke about Elizabeth's visit. So far, she had kept it to herself. Before she could make up her mind, though, Luke was pushing his chair back from the table and saying, as he jumped up and planted a kiss on top of her head, "Don't forget to answer Carr's letter dear, this very afternoon," and was already through the doorway.

After having looked through the empty doorway for some time Eliza finally decided it might be wiser of her if she did not air her problems with Stuart Drakston and his mother right then, and especially since Luke had taken the stand he had concerning Carr and his Yankee friends.

Chapter Two

Some fifteen months later on a Sunday in late February as Eliza brought her straying attention back to the Reverend Marsh Reed who was still flailing around in the pulpit, she shifted and resettled her feet once again, telling herself that given a little more time Marsh Reed would finally outdo the late Reverend Johnson yet in long-winded endurance. And later, when she felt the reverend's strong hand grasp through the heavy cloth of her glove as he stood beside the church door pumping her hand vigorously and wishing her a most pleasant afternoon—while at the same time he was also hoping for a dinner invitation, Eliza was positive Of it and wondered where on earth these Baptist clergymen mustered their strength from. Especially in Marsh Reed's case because he was not the most robust of men to begin with. Then; however, noting that the reverend's stock and cotton shirt both looked as though it may have been July instead of February—both drenching wet—Eliza was not so sure about the minister's endurance after all.

Pulling her hand out of Marsh Reed's grasp and going on down the church steps, she told herself, fool man, doing himself in like that. Did he not see that for over one good hour he had lashed out at a congregation whom he had, either put to sleep or bored hell out of. Well, let Marsh Reed continue on without taking heed and, one of these Sundays, he was going the same way Reverend Johnson had gone. Yes, let him scream on and, for sure, he was going to shorten his days—right smack into the Promised Land if he was not more careful or, who knew, maybe right into that same hellish inferno he was forever warning his parishioners about!

It was for a fact Marsh Reed's long preaching session, which he had punctuated with screams and shouts and flailing arms in his effort to lead his congregation to the way of more righteous doings and holier thinking, had uplifted Eliza one fraction or put her on any spiritual plane. Indeed, even though the minister was unaware of it and would have been more than shocked to learn Of it, he had irritated Eliza to no end by prolonging the church service as he had, leaving her drained Of all inspiration—Godly or otherwise by the time he had finally lifted his arms upward to heaven in his last and final prayer.

Neither Eliza's mood or her health was up to its usual standard on this particular Sunday anyway, and Marsh Reed's long, stormy sermon had certainly had no calming effect on either, only aggravating her and straining her nerves that much more. For one thing, she was suffering from a wretched head cold and should not have attended church to begin with. Then, if there were one thing that needed to be seen to at Green Sea before late afternoon—or things that Eliza did not only want to do but thought should be done, there were one dozen. Now, there was no doubt about it, the prolonged church service had left her with not enough time to get to everything, even if she rushed her head off. A few things would just have to be pushed aside and it was all Marsh Reed's fault!

Late, the day before, Carr's second wire of that week had come unexpectedly. Now, despite the first wire stating the trip had been called off, Carr, his future bride to be, Beth Anne and Mr. Gilford Sloan would be arriving in Charleston on the four o' clock train that very afternoon. It seemed, at the last moment, rather than let the trip be called off altogether since Carr had already been granted a week's leave from the academy, not to mention his great disappointment at not being able to take Beth Anne to Green Sea at last to meet his parents, that John Fillmore-Lee's business co-partner had volunteered to chaperon the two young lovers to South Carolina.

The trip which had been scheduled a few days prior with Beth Anne and her parents accompanying Carr, had been canceled due to the sudden indisposed Rachelle Fillmore-Lee. Though her illness was thought to be nothing serious, Mr. John would not hear of his wife attempting the long, tedious journey. Nor would he leave her side to come without her. Thus, a decision had been reached to dispatch the honorable Gilford Sloan in John's place, since it was also unthinkable that Mr. John's daughter would journey to South Carolina with Carr Heyward alone even if she was engaged to marry him with the wedding date already set for late June.

This was something else that was nettling Eliza despite all her resolve not to cave in and weight against it. Though at this late date she did not voice it aloud anymore, it was still awfully hard for her to accept the fact that her only son had fallen in love with a "Yankee girl" and was going to marry her. A Yankee living at Green Sea! The mere thought of such a possibility existing not only still sent shock waves through Eliza, but also rendered her to mute silence every time the subject came up. She had tried, had searched time and again to

31

find adequate words for her feelings on the subject but after finding the task to be a futile and hopeless one had finally given up.

Yes, contrary to all Luke's reassurance that day that Carr was more Or less just getting a head start in his conquest to find his life's mate, Eliza had truly known when he came home at Christmas that year that his conquest had stopped in Lexington—ceased before it had hardly begun with Beth Anne Fillmore-Lee.

Constantly, it seemed, Carr had praised and lauded those Yankees, and especially this Beth Anne, till Eliza had thought she would scream. Even at the family Christmas gathering at Oak Grove that year, she had not been spared the subject of the Fillmore-Lees. Not only had Carr told everybody about his Yankee friends, but he had topped the subject off by passing Beth Anne Fillmore-Lee's photograph from hand to hand, asking each and all if they did not think the girl's eyes were identical to his mother's—as if such a possibility could actually exist, let alone expecting an answer to such an outlandish question when it hung upon a photograph that he had worn so blotchy and soiled that the girl's eyes were hardly distinctive from her other features!

Though Martha near did herself in to have everything in top-notch order at that party, and no question about it the party had been a dazzler, Eliza still could not honestly say that she had enjoyed herself. Besides having felt ill at ease—actually embarrassed over the way Carr was ranting about those Yankees, there had been the constant threat of Elizabeth Drakston's eyes on her as Stuart Drakston was making good his word by hovering as closely to Jane Anne as possible. She survived that ordeal though and much to her relief and surprise had been spared worrying about Stuart Drakston when Jane Anne had come home on Summer vacation. Stuart had gone to England with Elizabeth and spent the greater part of that summer there. She supposed it was asking too much, but she hoped they went back again this coming summer, because it looked as though she was going to have enough to contend with without worrying about Stuart Drakston, too!

Yes, regardless of Luke making light of her reaction to Carr's letter that day attaching no importance to it whatever—that letter had been the first of many, all bearing startling resemblances, that Carr had written to Green Sea until about six weeks ago when Luke had come into the kitchen at dinner time holding the unique shocker of all in his hand. In part their son had written, he had become engaged to marry Beth Anne Fillmore-Lee with the full approval of her betrothed parents. The wedding would take place in Lexington, Virginia immediately following the termination of his two-year course of military training at the academy in late Summer. Both his and Beth Anne's wish was to be married before he entered The University of Virginia in the fall, rather than wait until he completed all of his schooling. Beth Anne would continue living on with her parents while he commuted from the university to Lexington once a week. He had given the subject a great deal of thought and did not foresee his marrying, which had certainly been no spur of the moment decision because he had wanted to make Beth Anne his wife from the start, putting any additional financial burden upon them since this was the plans of living pattern they had settled on. Leastwise, he sincerely hoped this would be the case with no problems popping up, for it would indeed distress him if things were to fall otherwise. He wanted and hoped for their approval, too. Still, in a way, he felt he already had it because he knew his happiness was also their happiness.

He was cutting short his Christmas vacation to Green Sea so he could spend part of it in Lexington, since there were quite a few special events coming up there that he had been invited to attend along with the Fillmore-Lees. Then, following the holiday season when things had settled down to a less hectic and demanding state, he thought the month of February would be most congruous and convenient, the two families could finally meet and become acquainted with one another—perhaps with them first approaching his fiancée and her parents with an invitation to visit Green Sea and then the Fillmore-Lees reciprocating at a later date. Did they not think this plan would not only make for a more harmonious get-together but fall more in line with propriety besides? And, the letter had rattled on and on with more plans, more suggestions, and more hopes until Luke was sitting silently once again and taking note how Eliza's mouth had again become drawn and tight as she went through her usual motion of quietly folding the letter and slipping it inside her apron pocket.

Luke knew Eliza did this because of the number of times she would be retrieving the letter to read over and over that very same day.

In silence, Luke still sat and waited—waiting for Eliza to say, "I told you so." But Eliza surprised him. Instead of saying anything about his continual insisting that they not take Carr's courting capers too serious, she finally broke the silence by saying, "Well, whether I like it or not, it looks as though I'd better start working on my Yankee acceptance speech!" She lifted her head, surprising Luke again with the sudden look of temperance she was taking on. "Luke, it's going to be hard, welcoming Yankees to Green Sea, but for our son, I will welcome them and with an open door, you'll see." Wise enough to realize that some situations called for using wisdom and strictly nothing else, Luke merely smiled and told her, "Of course you will, dear. Knowing you, I never expected no less."

Still and all, though, despite her will to accept Carr's choice and restrain her prejudice toward all Yankees, in addition to commiserating with Rachelle Fillmore-Lee's affliction, Eliza was still finding it very difficult to hold on to her self-control. The off and on wires which her son had sent to Green Sea that week— messages that to her had begun to take on as many phases as the moon—had just about loosen Eliza's tongue to the point of sounding her frustrations in clear, distinct words. Right at this point the only thing that Eliza was taking any comfort at all from was the heartening fact of knowing that she would be entertaining the honorable Gilford Sloan, instead of those other two Yankees whom she had been expecting to entertain!

Suddenly, Eliza felt a familiar touch on her arm and was already apologizing to Caroline as she turned back, "I'm so sorry, Carolina, I didn't even see you."

"I know, dear," said Caroline, "and I'm not going to detain you for long because I can see you are anxious to get on home, but I did want to make sure if what I heard is true.

Are they on their way, after all?"

"It appears so, Carolina, on the four o'clock train this afternoon, and don't you worry about detaining me, Marsh Reed has already made helter-skelter of my plans for early afternoon, anyway.

Caroline laughed, "His sermon was rather long-spun today. At times, he sounded as though he thought we all had fallen from grace and were in dire need of a rap on the knuckles."

"Well, whether he was aware of it or not, nor do I care, that last hour, I was bored out of all patience," Eliza said, reaching inside her handbag to bring forth her handkerchief once again to catch the dribble from her nose.

"And, no wonder, Eliza, with that dreadful cold," said Caroline turning to all seriousness. didn't mean to hold you up, you'd better get onto the couch and Stay out of this air."

"I'll be alright," Eliza said, giving her nose a hard blow. "I'll wait for Luke, anyway. I thought he was right behind me, but I see the preacher's still got him covered. He'd better hurry, though, or we won't ever have time to eat our dinner before starting for Charleston. Still, trains are never on time. That's why I couldn't plan a get-together, dinner party, or anything else today, Caroline, but, somehow, I'll manage to get everybody together before they leave even this time will be limited."

"I understand, Eliza, though I do wish it were possible today. I'm so anxious to see her in person, I can hardly wait, aren't you?"

"Well. "Eliza mumbled with a sniff and broke off, with Caroline noting how conveniently she was using the time to cough several times in her handkerchief and dabbed at her nose quite a bit before going on with her response, "Yes and Carr says even if Mr. Sloan is rather quiet in nature, he still has the ability to put one at ease and cause them to feel right at home in his presence. I'm really looking forward to meeting him."

"Yes, we all are, because from what we've heard Carr say ourselves, he certainly has to be very pleasant company. But, it's still too bad that Beth Anne's parents were prevented from coming, too."

"Y-es... " Eliza mumbled again and broke off, taking another long moment to clear her nostrils, conveying her feelings so plainly to Carolina that it near brought a giggle to gurgle out loud in Caroline's throat, as she went on, "but they'll be coming later, probably at Easter when Carr gets another leave from the academy."

'Oh, that'll be wonderful! Everything will be so pretty then, with the dogwoods and so many flowers in bloom," exclaimed Caroline, just as Luke came striding up to grasp her hand and say, "Hello, dear. Where's that husband of yours? I bet off someplace to greet some little boy or girl who's decided to make their entry among us on the Sabbath."

"Precisely," laughed Caroline, "that's why he told me not to wait and come on to church without him. How are you, Luke?"

"Oh, tolerable, a little better than my girl here, I dare say," Luke said, as he shifted his hand from Caroline's to grasp hold of Eliza's.

"I agree with you," said Caroline. "I've just told her, she'd better get inside and stay there."

"'Good advice, dear," agreed Luke. should've done what Bruce did. He insisted that Martha stay home today with her cold."

"Well, I should've had sense enough myself to have stayed put, too, right where I was, considering how well I know the pleasure Marsh Reed takes in ranting and raving, once he gets started," scoffed Eliza.

Luke and Caroline exchanged a knowing smile, with Luke suppressing his as he replied, "All the more reason, sweetheart, why I'm going to insist you not accompany me to Charleston to meet that train. Carr will understand and so will the others. I don't want you to catch more cold and become bedfast."

"But, Luke, he'll expect me to be there!" Eliza cried, and was suddenly trying to muffle a loud sneeze in the folds of her handkerchief.

"Not if he were hearing you, he wouldn't, and no buts, dear, come on, I'm taking you home." Luke said, and telling Caroline to take care, he took Eliza by the arm and promptly started shepherding her toward their coach.

"And, Luke, you make her stay there, too, till she gets better," called Caroline.

"I will and say hello to Seth for us," Luke called back, with Eliza adding as she looked back Over her shoulder, "I'll let you know about the get-together, Caroline, you see I'm under his orders for now."

Caroline laughed and waved for Eliza to proceed on her way.

The train was late. The thin February sun had already dropped below the treetops with the first dusk beams of the bleak wintry evening swallowing up the distant landscapes, before Luke heard the whir of rumbling wheels and the sing-song peal of a train's whistle slicing through the air from where he sat inside the train depot. He jumped to his feet and turning up the collar of his overcoat against the whip of cold air that was reaching through the station's double doors as they were being flung aside by other waiting greeters and passengers ahead of him, he hurried along, too, now more thankful than ever that he had insisted Eliza to stay out of the cold. He gained the stations flat form just as the train came breaking in along beside it in snaps and Scrapers and was promptly witnessing the final heaving and last jerks of two long passenger coaches as their big iron wheels finally came to rest on the tracks below.

Luke shivered - not so much from the chill of the brisk weather but from the expectation of seeing his son's face most any second.

Standing in one place though and waiting for the coaches' doors to swing Open was proving to be too much for him. All of a sudden, he was edging along the flat form, peering anxiously from one lighted window to the next, searching for that first glimpse of Carr among the stirring passengers. But, even after covering the full length of the first coach, he still had not seen one person that he had recognized much less spying Carr. Now; however, that the door had finally opened and a swarm of passengers had begun to spill out of the first coach, Luke was hesitating for a second as to whether proceed on or turn back, when suddenly he heard Carr's voice shriek through the milling crowd, "Over here, Papa!"

Wondering how he had missed sighting Carr among the passengers in the first coach, Luke whirled around. But, instead of moving toward his son who came blustering forth in a gait that would near equal that of a swashbuckler's, Luke stood frozen to the same spot, his mind whirling crazily with the thought, where did Eliza come from, as he caught sight of the girl Carr pulled along with him by the hand. Then, just as quickly as he mentally rebuked himself for letting his thoughts become hurled into such a chaotic state of confusion, even if by some strange coincidence the girl did remind him so much of Eliza.

All the same, as the two young people continued making their way toward Luke where he seemed to be permanently rooted—their vibrant presence seeming to generate a bolt of electricity through the whole depot, again Luke felt there was something unnatural about the scene—something eerie. It crowded him, made him feel shivery all over once more and, this time, the weather had not one single thing to do with it.

The girl was laughing and her dynamic vividness put Luke in mind of Christmas, not long past, though not one ribbon, one bow, or one garnish or flounce of trimming about her attire did he see. Nor did she or her outfit require any Luke reasoned as he let his eyes stay fixed on her, her fire-engine red cloak, the pure-white woolen scarf thrown around her throat, and the white tam o'shanter that matched it setting at a jaunty angle atop her brown flowing curls.

Luke saw that she was taking the jostling that she was having to undergo from the crowded station in stride and sensed, right Off, that Beth Anne—Fillmore-Lee was no demure, skittish namby-pamby-more the tomboyish type. He was suddenly sure of it, for just before she and Carr reached him, she turned her head over her shoulder and yelled, as loudly as the force of her lungs would put out—Luke was positive, "This way Uncle Sloan! Where in the world are you?"

Luke never had time to look and wonder about the whereabouts of Beth Anne's "Uncle Sloan" which of whom he may be in the swarm of people before him. Letting go of Beth Anne's hand, Carr instantly had him clasped in a bear hug as he sang out, "Papa! papa!"

It made no difference how often he came home, wherever they met, whoever they met in the presence of, or how numerous their audience, Carr's affection for his father was never moderately doled out. Needless to say, Luke returned it in full measure and also never failed to marvel at the wide personality gap between his two children. Carr's voice boomed. Jane Anne's voice hardly rose above a whisper. Carr was demonstrative—open. Jane Anne was shy—timid. Carr was talkative—inquiring, wasting little time in approaching the subject. Jane Anne was sparing of words—kept her own counsel.

Luke could have gone on and on marveling at the wide, varying traits of his two children. The list was long with him knowing well every facet that was embodied in each trait. Carr surprised him none whatever when suddenly he was breaking their bear hug way short of its normal duration to ask, in a fearful voice while he let his fiancée remain waiting at his elbow to be introduced, "Papa, where's Mother? Nothing's wrong? She isn't ill?"

"No, no son," Luke hurried to reply, "nothing like that. It's just a very nasty cold. She wanted to come but I insisted she stay out of the cold air."

"Oh, great," Carr said with a sigh. "I'm really relieved it's nothing no worse. Since she's always with you when you meet me, I thought she was only lost from view until I reached you and saw she wasn't here at all. It scared me." He sighed once more before he finally turned back to Beth Anne. "Well, Papa, here she is at last, my future bride. Beth Anne, my father, the best papa that anyone ever had!"

If Luke was strained somewhat to keep another sudden chill from throwing him into a fit of trembling in front of Beth Anne, at finally being able to take in her features at close range, he was also given another start and put to task besides to hide his amusement when she piped right back letting the introduction lie where it had fallen, "Now, wait a minute, Carr. I know Mr. Heyward is everything you say he is. But, what about my own father back in Lexington? He's great, too, you know!"

Luke saw that Carr was not thrown one bit by Beth Anne's comeback; however, and decided this sort of rejoinder must be nothing new between the couple when Carr promptly flashed back, while he gave her a rather pompous bow, "As you say, Madam. Now, if you'll be so kind as to oblige me, Miss Fillmore-Lee, my father once again," indicating his presence with a much overstressed gesture.

Beth Anne laughed and again surprised Luke by leaning forward and brushing his cheek with a kiss before she told him, "Never mind us, Mr. Heyward, this goes on all the time. But, before we start again I do want to tell you how happy it makes me to finally have the pleasure of meeting you at last, and also want to thank you and Mrs. Heyward, too, for inviting Uncle Sloan and me, making all this possible for us. From what I've seen of South Carolina through the train windows, I know I'm going to love it as much as I do my native Virginia, and I must confess I'm literally counting the minutes until I'm granted my first look at Green Sea!" Her winning smile vanished fast. "My only regret is that my parents were forced to forego this trip, missing this occasion of meeting you, too."

Feeling as though some unknown force was pressing on his eyeballs, sealing his stare permanently to Beth Anne's features in spite of all he could do, Luke reached for her hands and held them in his. "You may be sure, dear, that both Mrs. Heyward and I share your remorse but have hopes, too, that they'll be able to make the trip in the near future. You must also rest assured that your pleasure at being here is indeed our pleasure, too. We're very happy to have this opportunity to welcome both you and Mr. Sloan..." Luke broke off and also forced his eyes to break their stare too and look beyond Beth Anne through the crowd as he laughed and added, "wherever he is, to our state as well as our home, Green Sea. Now, that I've had the pleasure of meeting you, too, I can see that our son is a very lucky young man to have found and won you."

By the time Luke's tongue has run the length of this introductory amenity, his mouth had begun to feel as dry as if he had actually been running in an arid wasteland, grateful to the core of his heart that Beth Anne Fillmore-Lee could not look into his mind and see his rambling thoughts like she was looking into his face and no doubt studying him as he was likewise studying her—but in a vastly different way.

Good Lord, what was this he was asking himself? He knew now

why he had thought, for a startling instant, that he had seen Eliza a few minutes before. This girl was Eliza over—the young sixteen-year-old Eliza whom he had met at Windsor! Her eyes were identical to Eliza's. No wonder Carr had said so time and again, until they all had started teasing him so unmercifully himself included. Wonder why Carr had failed to tell them that this girl actually favored his mother, too, still, on the other hand, even if the years had hardly left a mark on Eliza's face, how could he expect his son to see the resemblance as he himself saw it—vision his mother in the flower of age when she, too, had most often let her hair hang down around her face in delightful curls and waves?

Although he had tried to tell himself from the second he had spied Beth Anne's presence and been startled cold by her appearance that it was merely a coincidence and nothing else, no longer did he believe that. The likeness between her and Eliza was too close for him to continue fighting such a notion and trying to shrug it off. But, what then? Why did she favor Eliza so much, with it filling his whole being with an unrecognizable awe which he seemed to have no power over? As far as he knew—he certainly had never heard anything to the contrary—the Carson's or the Goodyear's had no relatives in either Washington, D.C. or Virginia. Nor had they ever had. Wait a minute—Virginia! Maybe no relatives in Virginia, but Eliza's brothers spent a considerable length of time there during the war years, especially Nat who did have quite a reputation for chasing girls till he lost his life there in the spring of sixty-four!

Good Lord! What about this girl's mother, if that by any chance were the case? Whatever had come over him for taking such a thought as that in his head? Such thinking not only diminished Nat's memory but dragged this girl and her family through the mud besides! He had to get ahold of himself— stop letting his thoughts run so wild and wayward.

Nevertheless, what in the name of heaven was Eliza going to think when she saw her own image standing before her in another real, live person? There was no telling what she would do, or say as for that matter! He knew what he would do. Just as quickly as he could manage it, once they reached Green Sea, he would think of some excuse to be alone with Eliza for a few minutes and suggest that they keep the subject as quietly as possible. On second thought, though, taking all that was at stake into account, perhaps it might be better if he chanced Eliza doing nothing; and also said nothing about it himself. He must remember no two people saw alike. Though he hardly saw how anybody could miss seeing the resemblance, and that went for Eliza and everybody else who was granted the opportunity to look into this girl's face. Why, as far as that went, he could even see a resemblance between her and Carr!

All the same, he would say nothing or do nothing—act as though, or try to, that there was not one thing amiss with him and see what came about—see if his eyes were playing tricks on him and if his thinking had been nothing but a mere bushel of lunacy and nonsense.

All of a sudden, Luke found his thinking had already put him in a tight spot. Even though he had done his utmost not to let his reckless thoughts absorb him entirely, he knew he had done just that when—all at once it dawned on him that Beth Anne had come to the end of her chattery little speech in response to his praising remark and was waiting for him to pick up the conversation and him with not the vaguest idea of a word she had said. Even so, he was spared from floundering too long by the sudden appearance of a man whom he thought might be his other guest ambling through the crowd toward them. Luke had heard Carr make mention of the fact that Gilford Sloan was seldom without his cigar—even attempted and sometimes did succeed in carrying on an entire conversation without once removing the cigar from the corner of his mouth. Well, there was a cigar hanging between this man's lips that, to Luke, looked like it was pretty much stationary.

Hoping he was glossing over his distracted behavior, Luke smiled and quickly looking past Beth Anne, said, "If I'm not mistaken, I think my other guest is about to join us," and as Beth Anne turned her head to look, too, he took another step forward and held out his hand. "Mr. Sloan, I presume."

Ambling to a stop, Gilford Sloan let one eye cock up at Luke from under the brim of his brown woolen derby—a habit that became fixed with him in the four years he had followed Lee's Army.

"Yep, that's me," he drawled, with his cigar still dangling from the corner Of his mouth, but then Luke noted he removed it as he let his other hand meet his and went on, "and I presume you're Mr. Heyward. Sorry about the delay, but between these two young'uns here and that conductor back there, it puts a man out to keep in step." "So, that's where you were." Beth Anne bubbled.

"Yeah," Gilford Sloan drawled again, still giving Luke a rather lengthy handshake.

He stopped me to have a few words, or maybe I should turn that back around and say we stopped one another just about the same instant. I thought I'd seen him somewhere and he thought he'd seen me somewhere and come to find out by golly, we had—Lee's Army! Fine man."

"Goes to show the world isn't as big, sometimes, as we think it is," allowed Luke, telling himself that if he were not still off his beam, he was going to have an enjoyable time visiting with Gilford Sloan—cigar included. "It's my pleasure, Mr. Sloan, to welcome you to South Carolina."

"Thank you," replied Gilford Sloan, finally breaking the long handshake. "It's my pleasure to be here, and just Sloan if you will, that's what I tell everybody."

"Very well, first name basis it is then," agreed Luke.

"Now if everybody will, let's make tracks for Green Sea. I think Charlie must've already attended to the baggage by now," indicating that he would lead the way to where the carriage was parked.

"Good old Charlie," said Carr as he reached for Beth Anne's hand and they fell in behind his father and Gilford Sloan who were walking side by side. "I bet he could make his way around this train depot with blindfolds on."

"Wouldn't be surprised, son," said Luke. "He's certainly been here often enough, over the years, to know his way around."

Carr and Luke both thought of the faithful Doss, too, but neither chose to share their thought with others.

If Luke were holding any notion that Eliza would breathe any word about the remarkable likeness that she did indeed see between herself and her son's betrothed by the time the party arrived at Green Sea, or as for that matter during the entire visit, he did not know his wife as well as he thought he did. To begin with, Eliza was far too modest about her looks to broach the subject and was that much more inclined to remain mum on the topic, if it meant comparing her features with the striking perfection of the youth, and especially in a case where the young girl was slated to become her daughter-in-law. Why, to her, talking about it—even to Luke—was unthinkable.

Nevertheless, that was the first thing that Eliza did notice no sooner than the carriage stopped at the front steps and she saw its occupants begin to file through its doors. Yes, even though it was way past dark with the air growing chillier by the minute, Eliza was standing on the lighted porch waiting when the carriage pulled to a stop. Never mind that her head cold still raged. Eliza was making good her word that she would be of favorable disposition toward her Yankee guest, despite the fact that she had loathed all Yankees for a long twenty-three years and still saw no prospect of her feelings for them in general ever undergoing a great change. She had simply relented because of her deep devotion for her son.

Regarding her two children there was no hurdle—no matter how great the burden upon herself—that Eliza would not attempt to remove if she thought her children's wellbeing and contentment depended on it. This very fact made the circumstance of Stuart Drakston all that more difficult and tormenting for her. Why she could not relent in favor of the love that he and her beloved daughter obviously held for one another, was beyond her scope of vision to see no matter how hard she tried when she did put her mind to the task, which; in truth, had come to pretty much a lasting mental chore with her.

Sometimes, seeing the unhappiness On Jane Anne's face, Eliza would resolve to go ahead and do no less by her daughter then she was doing by her son—accept Stuart Drakston as Jane Anne's choice. Then, just let Stuart come within her sight, and once again, she was hell-bent to row the galley on—so to speak—in keeping him and her daughter apart.

At any rate, seeing her own young image very near duplicated all over again in the youthful, vibrant Beth Anne as she stepped from the coach on Carr's arm did unnerve Eliza, though not as much as Luke had been shaken at the train depot. In truth, through her overwhelming Joy at sighting her handsome son at the same instant that she sighted Beth Anne and having her eyes riveted more on him than the girl on his arm, Eliza had greatly lessened the blunt of her shock. In addition, there were others to distract her attention and keep her thoughts from dwelling on this strange phenomenon—her taxing responsibility as acting hostess to two new, unfamiliar guests, as well as the dinner party which she also gave in their honor on the following night. Though unlike most celebrations and dinner parties at Green Sea, this affair was small and intimate with a short guest list.

Those who did make the list were Elijah's father, her Aunt Amy—Elizabeth graciously declined on the pretext of having a sick headache, and Eliza was spared the ordeal of what to do about Stuart since he was away at the time representing a client—Bruce, Martha,

43

Caroline and Dr. Seth, the Reverend March Reed, and surprising everyone even herself Lucy Randolph, whom Eliza coaxed till Lucy finally gave in and came.

If any of those present noticed anything out of the ordinary about Beth Anne Fillmore-Lee's looks, likewise to Luke, the oddity of the circumstances which undoubtedly each realized could lead one straight into a rather ticklish situation, must have persuaded them to keep the detection to themselves, or until they were granted a more expedient time for discussion anyway. Then, perhaps again, the presence of Lucy Randolph at Green Sea again after so many long years distracted everyone's attention so, that the close resemblance between the hostess and the girl from Lexington went undetected after all. For it was no accident that these close friends of Lucy Randolph were very happy as well as bemused over the obvious fact that Eliza had deliberately prevailed upon her to come in contemplating of pairing her and Guilford Sloan together! Even so, neither Lucy nor Guilford Sloan seemed to mind one bit that their hostess had seated them side-by-side at the dinner table. They turned to one another often appearing to have a lot in common to talk about throughout the entire meal and afterwards as well.

Yet another factor that could have induced those who may have been absent of the Carson features in Beth Anne, to keep quiet about it was their fear of Eliza's reaction to their discovery. For, saving the two Lexington guests, there was not a person present who did not realize that to suggest that Eliza had anything in common with a Yankee would be the nearest thing to telling her she and a rattlesnake had something in common! It mattered not that Carr was marrying a Yankee and, from all appearances, Eliza accepted her. They were well aware this fact had changed nothing on the part of Eliza's feelings for Yankees as a whole.

Nonetheless, despite all Eliza's aversion for Yankees—something she had come by through no want or misdeed on her part, but by the horrors of war—a repulsion ever lying there like a live wire just beneath the surface all through this making welcome of her guests and becoming acquainted with them, so far everything had gone pleasantly enough for her during this time.

Following the dinner party at Green Sea, Martha—in turn—had honored the young couple and Gilford Sloan with a dinner party at Oak Grove the next night. With the subject of horses and horse racing domination the evening's conversation, all with that affair had gone well, too. In addition, for both Luke and Eliza, there had been a number of pleasurable and interesting chats with Gilford Sloan, especially for Eliza when Gilford Sloan told her he could vaguely remembered seeing the officer who some said was heir to a vast plantation called Green Sea in South Carolina, while he was serving with Lee's Army.

Stunned, Eliza felt as though her breath was cut off. For what seemed like time everlasting, all she could do was sit and mutely stare back at Gilford Sloan, wondering if she had heard him correctly or if she had missed out on part of what he had said because she was not used to his lisping, dragging voice.

Finally, with Luke staring, too, and also appearing to be as stunned as she was and while Gilford Sloan seemed to remain no more moved than had he dropped a remark about the weather, Eliza drew a deep breath and ventured to say, "I'm sorry, Mr. Sloan, but did I understand you to say you did see my older brother during the war?"

"Well, everything certainly seems to add up that way, Mrs. Heyward," Gilford Sloan drawled with a little more zest, as he finally noticed the impact of his disclosure on Luke and Eliza's face and especially Eliza's. "But only vaguely and, unfortunately, things never changed in that respect so I never had the pleasure of meeting him personally."

Laying down his cigar on an ashtray near his elbow, Gilford Sloan reshifted his feet, settled himself further back in his chair and went on with his story, "You see, I was just a plain foot soldier in General Lee 's Army, stayed that way, too, through the whole four years of the war. Your brother being an officer, made our worlds wide apart. It was only by chance that I saw him. It happened one day just before General Lee started us on the march toward Gettysburg. I was restless, homesick would be more like the truth. Anyway, just to kill time, I set out on a walk through camp and venturing in on a group of my comrades, happened to hear something being said about someone being heir to Green Sea Plantation in South Carolina. Well, I liked the sound of the name and just being curious, I said to the soldier who I was standing next to, 'who is it here, who's got a plantation in South Carolina?' Then, he said back, 'Hell, friend, what's with you? Does anybody in this group look like they own a plantation? Wish I did though, I'd start tramping toward it this minute. I wouldn't stay away like that officer you see yonder sitting astride that horse. He's the heir to Green Sea, friend, and hasn't gone back once since he left it, or so they say. Setting a good example for the rest of us, I guess so, that's how I happened to see the officer who's turned out to be your brother, Mrs. Heyward."

"But, listen," Gilford Sloan went on, his voice having gradually become a little impassioned since he saw Luke and Eliza was savoring every word with rapt attention, "the incredible part about this whole thing is, I never remembered your brother's name, but Green Sea stuck in my memory like glue. When I learned that Carr was actually from Green Sea Plantation, I just assumed the name of the officer whom I'd seen that day was Heyward. Then, the day that Carr and I finally got around to talking about the war, soldiering and such, it all came out when Carr remarked that his two late uncles had also attended military school. I remarked back that I guess that being the case and, what with father also an officer in Lee's Army, that I didn't reckon the males in his family knew much about marching through mud on foot, and went on to add that I remembered seeing his father one day when this group of soldiers were talking about him being heir to Green Sea. Well, Carr looked at me like I was plain crazy or something. Then, the questions really started flying back and forth and that's when I learned the officer I'd seen that day was Phil Carson instead of you, Luke. Didn't Carr tell you about our talk, how dumb I've been about the whole matter? Carr said the officer I'd seen had surely had to been his late Uncle Phil Carson since the soldiers had told me he was heir to Green Sea."

"N-o-o...," allowed Eliza, her thoughts seemed to have suddenly turned more to other things than staying on the subject at hand. "Carr's never mentioned it, Mr. Sloan, or at least to me, he hasn't."

"Nor me, either," Luke put in. "But, I suppose what accounts for his failing to tell us is, it either slipped his mind Or the fact he just hasn't had the chance, since he's been wiring a few words home lately instead of writing for fear he wouldn't get a letter to us in time telling his plans to make their visit home."

"Well—like I said," Gilford Sloan continued, as he inclined a fraction forward and picked back up his cigar. "It hasn't been long back that we finally get around to having our talk together. You see, at the very best, I'd still say I'm not much of a conversationalist. Never have been. I have no trouble putting things down on paper. But talking it out, is altogether a different matter with me."

Eliza suddenly appeared to come back from wherever she had

let her thoughts take her to.

"Nonsense, Mr. Sloan," she smiled. "You're disfavoring yourself for no good reason, because Luke and I find you very enjoyable Company and certainly hope from now on you'll make it a practice to visit Green Sea often."

"Well—thank you—Mrs. Heyward," stammered Gilford Sloan, the dull glint in his eyes taking on a sudden spark, "I'll do my best to keep your kind remarks in mind and just maybe, with some luck too, I'll improve on my record for silence. I'm truly sorry about your two brothers and regret, for what little it's been worth, that I failed to mention this to Carr before I did. Of course, I don't suppose it matters much at that, taking into account that I saw your brother just before he became missing at Gettysburg It certainly shed's no light on what occurred afterwards."

"Even so, Mr. Sloan, we appreciate your telling us. You see, since my brother's fate remains to be unknown to us to this day, any tiny bit of information regarding him that we can come by, is always a great help," said Eliza, and although Gilford Sloan's insignificant disclosure did not turn all her thinking back in time, it did occupy Eliza's thoughts to the extent that those few short chitchats that she had engaged in with Beth Anne—when she could catch up with her since Carr constantly had her on the go showing her off to relatives and friends—had been nothing but mere trivial discourse. Certainly, Eliza—so far—had not procured that information that she had counted on obtaining and thought she had a right to hear from her future daughter-in-law! It was not that Eliza meant to start probing at this late date, even if family names did carry a lot of weight. She was simply curious, and on this last night before Carr and his party were to leave the next morning, it suddenly came to her at the supper table that time was fast running out.

Hence, it was with no malice, in the least, that Eliza smiled at Beth Anne across the table and said, "Beth Anne dear, your last name is so unusual. Since linking two family names is a custom that's seldom practiced in our culture, I just wondered, dear, you wouldn't by any chance be related to the Lee's of Virginia, would you?"

As swift as a shot Eliza had her answer.

"No, Mrs. Heyward, and I hope that doesn't disappoint you," Beth Anne flashed back, leaving Eliza feeling as though her hand had fried against her cheek.

Adoring his mother and sharing a close bond of harmony with

her, Carr also felt put down—actually embarrassed, with the notion swiftly settling in his head that his fiancée's snappy comebacks did not sound so amusing after all. Though Gilford Sloan and Luke, too, were taking it in quite another way. They both were suddenly attempting to hide their smiles in their water glass. Even so, if Beth Anne noticed anybody's reaction, she gave no indication of it.

As nonchalantly as though she had said nothing at all, Beth Anne went on, jumping to another topic that was far wide of the one that she had responded to so curtly, "Mrs. Heyward, this fried chicken is so crisp and tender? I'd love to get your recipe for my mother. We have fried chicken often. It's one of our favorite dishes, but our way of cooking it surely doesn't compare with this."

"I really have no recipe, dear," Eliza tersely replied, more or less feeling her way as she tried to hold her calm, "but I'll be glad to write down what few details we do follow for your mother."

Still appearing as though the name issue had never surfaced at all Beth Anne blithely kept the chatter rolling, "Oh, if you will, Mrs. Heyward, I promise you the very first thing I'll do when I get home, is have a try at it myself. I already know many of Carr's favorite dishes and hope by the time we're married, to be able to prepare a few of them, just exactly the way he's been used to having them prepared."

In the face of such a loving and bubbly spirit Carr's disconcertion had little chance of holding. Smiling at Beth Anne, he said, "I know I've picked the right girl now."

"I'll go along with that, son," Luke finally put in, "because it's always been my opinion being married to an excellent cook is one of life's good blessings." He smiled at Eliza. "Since I was fortunate enough to marry one, I feel I'm more than qualified to make such a statement."

"But we mustn't forget Pete, dear," protested Eliza. "He deserves credit, too, you know.

"True enough, love, and I don't know what we'd do without him. But I was mostly referring to all these years Pete did nothing but sit and watch, while you labored at your culinary skills," smiled Luke.

Taking in the dry smile that Eliza did manage to grow and send to her husband, Gilford Sloan saw that she was having trouble in holding with Beth Anne's snippiness over the name matter. Indeed, Gilford Sloan sensed that Eliza Heyward was not going to hold out much longer and promptly decided, for what little it be worth, to volunteer a few words of his own in hopes of helping matters.

"Well, comparing all these delicious dishes and all those others that's been set before me, since I've been here at Green Sea, with the junk I've thrown together for myself over the years, I'll sanction every word you stated, Luke, and then some," he drawled, and cutting his eye at Eliza knew she had hardly heard him, much less one word he had said.

Gilford Sloan was right. Barely one word of his remark had reached Eliza's ears. She was too busy with her mental lecture, telling herself that if she did not take issue, then and there, with Beth Anne Fillmore-Lee 's remark that, no doubt, she would be paving the way for more remarks in the future that would even be harder to hold with. After all, she and this girl would eventually be living under the same roof together. No, she did not take kindly to being put down by anybody, and especially by a Yankee at that and in her own home and at her own table to boot when there had been no sound cause for it to start with! Yes, for the sake of future harmony, she must pursue the matter further. Besides, this Yankee girl might as well have come right on out and said she could care less about the Lees of Virginia. Well, nobody was going to insult General Lee in her presence and get by with it!

Suddenly, in the dropping silence that was settling over the table, Eliza's voice rang out, clearly conveying her pique as she said, "Beth Anne, if I did offend you some few moments ago by mentioning the Lees of Virginia, I'm sorry. It's just that to us here in South Carolina, Lee is a great and admirable name. We honor it."

"Oh, think nothing of it, Mrs. Heyward," Beth Anne quickly offered, trying to cover her surprise that Eliza had reopened the subject—a subject that she thought she had killed and one which she had, unknowingly, flouted because of the unfortunate circumstance that surrounded her name, though she had been fully aware of her brusqueness to Eliza Heyward and indeed was not very pleased with herself for having succumb to such behavior. so, before she hardly knew what was happening she was spurning the question all over again and heard herself racing on, unable to stop, "Evidently, my father must honor the name a great deal, too, because of all the names he may have chosen for his last name, he still selected the name, Lee!"

Had a bomb come crashing down through the ceiling, it is doubtful the shock of it would have been more startling. Knives and forks were paused where they were being handled, as electrified faces came up from supper plates to stare at Beth Anne in heavy silence.

All the same, Beth Anne stared back, but she hardly saw them. Her thoughts were on a mill course, covering the miles to Lexington where her adored father was. For the first time in her life, the impact of his misfortune was coming home to her. Not only was she seeing the vulnerability of the tragedy and the hazards it had ever posed for both her parents, but was feeling the pain of it herself for the first time that she could remember. Why, no wonder her father had preferred they keep quiet about it, she was thinking. It was almost like having one's name on the danger list! She thought now that perhaps she had always been in defiance of the tragedy and its beatable side, though she had been unaware of it until now. She certainly could offer no other explanation for her behavior because being insolent was something new with her. She thought that was why she had snipped so contemptuous at Carr's mother's question and had also been unable to stop her tongue from rolling the facts of the matter on, despite her father's wishes that they not talk about it. In fact, she was positive of it.

Well, what was done was done. There was no turning back. She was not sure, because she had never given it any thought until this very minute, but she reckoned she would not have married Carr without telling him, anyway. She wondered if her father had given any thought to the question. If he had, so far, he had not mentioned it to her, or to Carr either she didn't believe. Apparently, noble names and bloodlines meant a lot to these people. Well, her father may not know his direct lineage, but as far as she was concerned that still had no bearing on his honorable character. To her, he was every much as aristocratic as any blue blood—yes, General Lee included! And, if Carr Or any of his family were to view it otherwise, she would still have no regrets that it was finally out in the open. No, she had nothing to hide! Nor did she have anything to hang her head over!

Suddenly, through her crowded thoughts, it dawned on Beth Anne that Carr's mother was saying something, that Eliza Heyward's croaking voice was asking her for the second time while all the rest still continued to hold their frozen expressions on her too,

"Selected? Did you say he selected to be called, Lee?"

While a pride such as she had never experienced before surged through her, seeming to lift her ten stories above the chair she was sitting in, Beth Anne looking Eliza straight in the face replied, in a steady and clear voice, "Yes, Mrs. Heyward, that's what I said. Except for the Fillmore part of my name, which happens to be my mother's maiden surname, I really have no idea what my last name is!" Her shoulders rose higher above the haughty, proud height she had brought them to. "It could very well be Lee, even if my father did choose it out of a million or one other names he could've chosen, I don't know!"

For Luke and Gilford Sloan both, no longer did they see one single thing to smile about. Now, with the subject having turned into a matter of perplexing uncertainty for one and all around the table, they both remained to sit silent and motionlessly with their paused dinnerware in their hands.

Carr, however, failing to grasp the gist of Beth Anne's remark in his anxiety was quickly telling her, while he looked as though he wanted to jump up and go rushing around the table and take her in his arms, "Darling, I'm so sorry. I didn't have any idea you were adopted, not that it makes one bit of a difference to me."

"Adopted!" Beth Anne exclaimed, her deep-blue gaze swiftly darting to Carr, looking at him as if he had suddenly lost his senses—despite the tender expression he held for her. "Whatever gave you the idea I'm adopted? I'm very much John Fillmore-Lee's daughter, I'll have you know!"

"But, darling, I thought you just said you didn't know what your last name is. So I thought—"

"Well, you thought wrong," Beth Anne told him, making it plain in the look she sent him that his effort at lightness was failing to reach her because he had greatly offended her. By even thinking she was adopted, let alone mentioning the word out loud. Carr merely stared back, too bewildered to go on. The subject had completely lost him.

Luke and Gilford Sloan had become lost, too. So had Eliza. In fact, right at that moment, not only was Eliza deeply regretting that she had ever risen the name subject at all, but for the sake of her son's comfort would have preferred the subject dying altogether and going no further. Nevertheless, despite her regrets, Eliza, in her attempt to learn what she now felt had become imperative to know, heard herself stumbling on, "But you are a Lee-Fillmore, I understand. Is that correct?"

"That's correct, Mrs. Heyward," Beth Anne replied more calmly, "and I'm sorry for startling you people like I have. I can see that family name and bloodline means a great deal to you."

Beth Anne's forthrightness and obvious sincerity threw Eliza off guard again.

"Well..." she muttered, finding it a most convenient time to let her paused dinnerware start moving again as her mind rapidly searched for some reply that would sound no less sincere and, at the same time, be fitting enough, too, to justify her prying. "I suppose, dear, it does appear that way and I'm sorry for that, but hope you'll overlook the fact because we really aren't all that biased. It's just that we cherish the general's memory so, that let one mention the word Lee, and, instantly, our feelings and our interest, too, I must admit are stirred a great deal."

"Oh, I can understand that, Mrs. Heyward," Beth Anne said, "because my father has always been pretty much the same way about General Lee! In fact, I'm sure the deep respect he's ever held for the Southern general is what prompted him to take the name Lee for his own name."

Heavens and earth! Eliza thought. The conversation was growing worse instead of better. She was right back where she started! It was true, the Heyward's did love and cherish General Lee like she said, but their devotion was still not so deep that they had ever given one thought to forsaking the Heyward name for the Lee name! Nor would they! Well, she was left no choice. She would have to probe on!

"Really?" Eliza went on to quiz, her voice a bit uneven. "But— I would think with your father being..." She stopped. No, surely there was a more delicate way to put it. Coming right out and calling her father a Yankee would not be in good taste. She was not that improper, even if the name did fit the subject! She would try another approach. "I mean... " Knowing full well what she had in mind to say was going to sound even worse, Eliza was halting again, feeling so awkward and inadequate all of a sudden that she wanted to slide under the table out of sight.

"That one would hardly expect to see such loyalty and devotion from one whom had opposed the general and his army during the war," Beth Anne finished for her, with a little amused smile cursing her pretty lips.

The manner in which the plucky Beth Anne went after a subject, was not lost on Eliza. Neither was the amused smile. The fact was, these two identical personalities were playing a game of hit and miss with one another, though they had not the least knowledge of it. At any rate, Eliza bucked up quite a bit, and putting on a half-smile of her own, came back, "Well—yes, dear, I will admit I was thinking along on that line somewhat, and if you'll forgive me for saying so, it appears to me your father served in the wrong army, considering that his esteem for our beloved general was so deep that he was willing to forsake his own name in favor of adopting the name Lee!"

By this time, though they remained to be squeamish and especially now since the subject seemed to be shifting to the Yankee versus Rebel cause, all the rest had resumed eating too. Now; however, their focus was coming up from their plates again to stare at Beth Anne in suspense—waiting for a similar retort.

But, for some few seconds, there was nothing from Beth Anne. She appeared to be puzzled, losing her smile altogether as she thoughtfully observed Eliza. At last, though, she was telling her, causing faces to freeze even more, "I'm afraid, Mrs. Heyward, through my own blundering, you've misunderstood me and have the wrong impression about my father. My father didn't forsake his name. Unfortunately, in his case, there was no name to forsake simply because he hasn't been able to recall but very little, if anything, about his true identity for a good many years now!"

Eliza's face did more than freeze at Beth Anne's statement. It paled too as she thought to herself, dear God, can such things be? What on earth had her child let himself in for? And, not only him, but what about the rest of them too? On top of everything else, now it appeared as though they all were slated to battle the burden of having a deranged man in the family! Further, what about the future grandchildren, if the couple were so blessed? No, this additional disclosure was just too much. The will to pry or hear anything else about this girl's family, was not in her anymore. Not for the present anyhow. Let Luke or someone else take up the subject, if they had a mind to, she was finished with it. She had to get away this very minute—be alone with herself so she could think!

Suddenly, Eliza was murmuring something about being so sorry to hear such sad news and asking everybody to excuse her as she started to rise from the table. She had no more than gotten half-way out of her chair though before Beth Anne was stopping to plead, "Please, Mrs. Heyward, won't you wait until I clear up this matter up. I can see you're very upset."

Having made it to her feet, Eliza hesitated, letting one hand cling to the table's edge as she acknowledged, "Yes—but there's really no need to go any further into it, I'll be all right." She let her eyes sweep around the table. "Please, everybody go ahead with your supper. I'd better check with Pete about the frozen dessert, anyway." She started to move on, but Beth Anne was stopping her again.

"No, Mrs. Heyward, it's too important to all of us to push aside. Won't you wait and let me explain."

Eliza slid back down into her chair.

Heart fluttering somewhat, Beth Anne commenced with her story, telling it exactly as her father had related it to her some years back, finishing by adding, "Had it not been for my mother's sharp eye, along with the deep concern and interest she took in her duties as a volunteer nurse, especially with the more severely ill patients who often times were more or less abandoned since hope appeared futile anyway, my father would be lying somewhere today in an unmarked grave. Father has always said that God and Mother together saved him."

Recognizing that all the miseries and tribulations of the war had not been born by Southerners alone, Eliza could not help letting her heart swell in sympathy for the Yankee ex-soldier as she murmured, "'How terrible—for all of you this must be. I'm so sorry," and as her words met with similar echoes of sympathy from Luke, Gilford Sloan, and Carr who managed to show Beth Anne his deep love for her as well by stretching his hand across the table to touch her arm, Eliza went on to inquire, "And, after all this time, he still doesn't recall anything connected with his past life before Gettysburg?"

"Only a blurry scene or two that's flashed across his mind every so often and that also comes in a dream from time to time, Mrs. Heyward, but he refuses to dwell on this or talk about it. He says the scenes are too outrageous and absurd to apply to him. The truth is, few people are aware Of my father's impairment because he prefers to keep it quiet. Mother says that he fears if people know, they might think that—he's..." For all her habit of being outspoken, Beth Anne's view faded into dead silence as she dropped her eyes back to her plate. She could not make herself go on and say one word that could be taken to mean insanity.

Even so, she heard Eliza saying, finishing for her, "Mentally deficient?"

Beth Anne lifted her eyes. "Yes, something on that order, Mrs. Heyward," she said, and turning to Gilford Sloan, added, "This is the first you've heard of my father's affliction, isn't it, Uncle Sloan?"

Without hesitating Gilford Sloan affirmed, somewhat emphatically, "Yes, dear, it is, so if there is any lack of mental strength in your father's head, that makes me forty times worse than he is because in all the fourteen years I've known him, I have yet to detect it!"

Beth Anne sent Gilford Sloan a grateful smile. She had counted on him and he came through. Although his remark had carried a bit of witticism, its message as a whole was precisely what she had secretly hoped he would bring out when she had turned to him.

All the same and unknown to Beth Anne, Gilford Sloan was experiencing a feeling of gratitude, too, grateful that she had trusted him enough to turn to him and give him the opportunity to put in his two cents worth. Though he was every bit as shaken if not more so, over Beth Anne's story as the Heyward's were, he; nevertheless, had been reading Eliza's whirling thoughts all along and had secretly hoped for an opening in the conversation, so he could express his views on the part of John Fillmore-Lee's sanity if nothing else. And; indeed, much to Gilford Sloan's pleasure he noted, his remark did seem to have made a favorable impact, especially on Eliza Heyward.

It was true, Eliza had calmed down considerably, even if it had taken hearing the true facts of the whole story related and the addition of Gilford Sloan's statement besides to achieve it. And, Gilford Sloan was not the only one noting the change in her. The others as well had her more subdued behavior in the direct line of their eye—happily regarding it, even if they did remain to be a bit uneasy as she suddenly picked up the subject again and began to state in detail her own view. Though no one had asked for it.

"Well," she said rather subtly, "I can certainly understand your father hearing people's reaction to something of that nature. With amnesia being an affliction that even a physician would have no ready explanation or answer for, I'm not so sure that he didn't make the right decision when he chose to keep it a private matter. His choice no doubt has saved him a lot of distress and worriment. Yet, there's another side to your father's problem that we shouldn't overlook and that is, his choice for silence all these years may have been a very costly silence to him because it could have very well played a big part in keeping that door to the past firmly closed where otherwise it may have opened by this time." She stopped and sighed somewhat resignedly. "Anyway, if silence is your father's preference, have no fear dear, that we'll disclose anything you've told us." Now that she was beginning to perceive what had really been at the bottom of Beth Anne's curtness when she had questioned her about her family name, Eliza was more willing to define things for what they actually were and more eager, too, to try to keep a middle course regarding all aspects of the situation.

Luke, always ready to back Eliza up and did in most things, quickly added, as they passed a meaningful look between them across the table, "Of course, it'll be a sealed book, Beth Anne dear, as far as we're concerned."

"Thank you, I'm most grateful to you both, you're very understanding," Beth Anne replied, relieved and yet suffering a twinge of apprehension, too, in wondering how her father was going to take it when she told him what she had done; therefore, prompting her to go on and add, "I promise, if what I have revealed does distress either of you in any way, once you meet my father, it'll all vanish."

Carr never gave his parents a chance to comment.

"Oh, don't let anything like that concern you, darling," he hurriedly put in. "I shall think that both Mother and Papa are sensible and reasonable enough, too, not to give way to needless worry of that nature. Besides, although I love you dearly for speaking up for your father and know he would, too, and be proud of you if he were here, I don't think there should be any pleas or amends offered on the part of Mr. John, no matter what the case, because his commendable standing requires none." Now, more than ready to close the subject before something else was said that might play havoc with the seemingly present calm, he flashed Beth Anne a loving smile and laughed, "You'd better finish that chicken leg or you'll be fast changing your mind about wanting Mother's recipe. But be careful. It must be so cold and dried-out by this time, it could very well pull your teeth out!"

Beth Anne smiled back and picked up her chicken by eying Carr with a meaningful look, too, as she bit into it.

If anyone had been anticipating that Gilford Sloan would add anything else to the subject, it was just as well that Carr had made it plain he wanted the topic dropped because it is doubtful Gilford Sloan could have managed a simple phrase right at that point. Likewise, to Eliza some few minutes earlier, his mind was too much in a whirl—his spinning thoughts chilling him through and through as they jumped here and there piecing incidents together which were telling, he was stumbling on a startling discovery John Fillmore-Lee was no Yankee, no Fillmore, no Lee or anybody else, but the late Phillipe Carson in living flesh!

It had all started while Eliza was in the process of giving her long viewpoint. Listening to her and telling himself that most of what Eliza Heyward was saying made a lot of sense, it suddenly came to Gilford Sloan that there was something very familiar about his hostess' features and like a sudden flash of lightning he knew! Why, of course! Beth Anne and her father! Eliza Heyward's eyes were identical to theirs—the same spellbinding violet-blue gaze. Why he had not detected it before, he had no idea. Then, just as suddenly again, and something else that he could not explain, his thoughts went straying clear back to the day when John had asked him to feature the editorial on General Lee and he had addressed John as "Lieutenant," and, all of a sudden, he was linking John Fillmore-Lee with the late Confederate officer from Green Sea whose name he had been unable to recall; and like a thunderbolt once more, a startling conceivability had popped in his head. John Fillmore-Lee had to be the, supposedly, late Philippe Carson, heir to Green Sea Plantation!

Feeling as though his head might explode any second as another chill went racing clear to his toes, Gilford Sloan was suddenly thinking in past tense no longer. John Fillmore-Lee was Philippe Carson! Yes, as surely as his name was Gilford Sloan, his Yankee business partner was Eliza Heyward's long missing brother! He was positive of it.

What in the name of God should he do? Steady his hand for one thing or his fork was going to go clattering back down to his plate, he told himself. Still, he had to think and think fact, get hold of himself. He'd been in tighter spots and made out all right. Surely, he could do the same this time. Do nothing for now—that's it—say nothing and do nothing, except pick up every bit of information on Philippe Carson that was possible to pick up in the little time that was left before he went back to Lexington! No doubt that was best. Luke Heyward's wife had already been jarred considerably. So had his own nerves and everybody else's. If he were to convey his thoughts, he could cause the whole bunch to go into hysterics. Yes, just keep it to himself for the time being. Another little while wouldn't hurt. After all, it had been long years since Gettysburg. Yes, regardless of John Fillmore-Lee's attire upon his arrival in Washington, from Gettysburg, he had been no Yankee. He would stake his life on it.

Still chilling, Gilford Sloan took a firmer grip on his fork, smiled at the two young lovers, who obviously were lost in each other and resumed his own eating.

Chapter Three

John Fillmore-Lee's hand stalled on the doorknob that opened into the newspaper office. Up until that moment, John's reluctance to face Gilford Sloan had escaped him altogether. Now; however, with the awareness of it washing over him, John became a bit irritated. For being skitter about something as trivial as facing someone whom he had known and worked so closely with for so many year-s was not only downright idiotic to him but very hard for him to accept besides, even if his common sense did tell him he had good cause to be disinclined over the prospect of facing Gilford Sloan when the door did swing open.

That out-of-the-way subject matter which John had discussed with his wife and daughter upon the latter s arrival home the night before from South Carolina—that is after Carr Heyward had bid his night's farewell—was one thing, but the thought of facing those beyond the family circle whom he knew were now aware of it, too, was quite another matter with him.

Despite all though and also the fact John did recognize he was overly concerned about the turn of events—more than he had ever thought possible those times he had let his problem cross his mind lately—he found he was still luxuriating in a certain degree of delight that morning. The knowledge that his daughter had refused to let Carr Heyward's mother's probing over that Lee business intimidate her—standing unflinching and spilling everything, was giving John's heart a great deal to feast on. He was proud of her. True, he had reasoned that she may have been a little too blunt as Rachelle had pointed out. But, the fact remained he still took a lot of satisfaction in knowing that she had indeed born up and not weakened under Eliza Heyward's obvious prying and wondered if he could have handled it as well, had he been in the same circumstance. He doubted it.

The instant he had set his eyes upon his daughter the night before, John had known that something was bothering her. Rachelle had also known and they both had anxiously awaited Carr Heyward's departure so they could find out what she was on pins and needles about. Though John was sure that Carr had not lingered more than thirty minutes after escorting Beth Anne home from the train depot, because the hour had been rather late besides their obvious fatigue from the long train ride, it still had seemed like hours to both him and Rachelle before he had taken his leave. Even so, it had been apparent that they had not been the only two whom had anxiously awaited Carr to buzz along, for the sound of his feet had hardly cleared the porch before Beth Anne had blurted out to them, "Papa, I'm certain you and Mother both are going to be very disappointed with me, maybe even angry, because I'm afraid I could've shown a better side of my nature to the Heyward's than what I did!" And, without pausing once, she had gone on and related the details of the whole dining room episode at Green Sea before she had stopped.

In spite of his sudden attack of nerves, John smiled, recalling the incident to his mind. Yes, he thought, as he and Rachelle had sat and listened in wide-eyed astonishment, their daughter had gone on to describe the scene so vividly, he believed almost word for word that they themselves had begun to feel as though they had been present, too, with the wrath that she had pointed out to them never surfaced, though Rachelle pointed out to her that she may have exercised a little more reserve. As for himself, he had not said much of anything, only saved him the task of telling the Heyward's himself and that he was proud of her. As a matter of fact, though he did not tell her so, he felt that he had sort of let Beth Anne down by being hesitant in telling Carr Heyward about his problem before she and Carr had gone to Green Sea.

At any rate, since it appeared his family and the Heyward family were slated for a rather close association with one another through the marriage of their children, he did feel somewhat relieved that they had been informed of his problem and gratified, too, that the disclosure had not stirred any worse commotion than it had. Apparently, once the shock waves were finally spent, the Heyward's had accepted it with good grace.

Strange though it was as far as Sloan was concerned, his emotions were mixed. Though it made him feel awfully good to know that Sloan had also stood up for him and, as much as he appreciated it, he still in all honesty could not say that he did not regret Sloan's knowing about it. It was certainly a puzzle to him why he felt that way, because in all probability it was Gilford Sloan's remark that had calmed Eliza Heyward down, no doubt the one thing that had convinced her that he was in possession of his faculties and not a raving lunatic! He didn't know for sure, but his lack of comfort over Sloan's knowledge of the matter could stem from their near daily connect with one another. Perhaps, deep-down, he feared that Sloan's eye would constantly be vigilant upon him now—scrutinizing for some sign of defectiveness. Well, one thing for certain, he had to face Gilford Sloan and he might as well quit stalling. He had work to do. He would act as natural as possible and let the subject lie like he always had unless Sloan mentioned it first.

Hoping that he would see the same unexcitable Gilford Sloan he had always known, John suddenly turned the doorknob and said, as he stepped through the door into the outer office where Gilford Sloan was already seated at his desk working, "Hi, Sloan! Welcome back. I see you're buckling down to the grind again." He moved on to Sloan's desk and stretched out his hand.

Gilford Sloan raised his head, displaying the usual cocked eye as he dropped his pencil and let his hand meet John's most eagerly, shaking it heartily as he drawled through a wide smile, "Hello, Partner, sort of good to be back." Then, in the same relaxed manner that he had ever exercised—John happily noted, Sloan leaned back into his chair and drawled on, "Yeah, thought I'd start wading through some of these notices, but we can talk about them later. How's Rachelle? I'm more anxious to hear of her."

Feeling much easier now, John propping himself on the edge of Sloan's desk said, "She's a lot better, Sloan, I'm grateful to say. Still a little weak, but able to be out of bed for several hours a day now."

"That's good news," Sloan replied. "I thought about going on out to your place last night with Carr and Beth Anne to inquire of her, but then thought better of it since it was sort of late. Thought you might've already gone to bed. When you go home for dinner, give her my regards."

"Sure thing, Sloan, and how was your journey? I trust it was pleasant enough." John grinned, "I know it must've been, if what I heard wasn't exaggerated."

"What was that?" Sloan asked, cocking his eye at John more closely.

"Oh, come now, Sloan," John laughed, "Don't play like you've never heard of that schoolteacher!"

"Who you mean, Miss Lucy Randolph?"

"Oh, so it wasn't exaggerated," John chuckled again.

"Well—whether it's been blown out of proportion or not, I couldn't say," Sloan drawled. "Before forming an opinion, I'd have to hear the telling first." Appearing now to be a little on edge—John observed—Sloan leaned forward and picking back up his pencil began to roll it back and forth in his hands as he added, "I will admit I found her awfully easy to talk to for some reason. The two times I was in her company, once at Green Sea and once at her home in Oak Grove, it seemed we never ran out of subjects to discuss with one another."

Suddenly, John very much regretted that he had made an effort to have a lighter spirit than what he actually felt by razzing Sloan.

"Oh, I was just ribbing you a bit, Sloan," he admitted, "forget it." He shrugged and sprang to his feet. "I'd better quit hindering you from your work, anyway, and get busy myself." Heading for his own office, though, he suddenly stopped and turned back. "I almost forgot, Rachelle asked me to tell you we'd be expecting you for supper tonight. She said she was having two of your favorites, ham and Boston baked beans."

"But is she well enough for all that?" Sloan asked with obvious concern. "She shouldn't be standing over a stove this soon."

"I, too, pointed that out to her, but she assured me that our daughter would be doing most of it. The truth is, I think she can hardly wait to hear all about your trip to South Carolina. Not only that, but you do realize, of course, that Rachelle has grown quite fond of you over the years and enjoys your company as much as I do. As a matter of fact, I think Rachelle looks on you as a brother she never had. Anyway, with Beth Anne and Carr planning to attend a social right after supper, we'll be alone and would like to have you come, if you will. Shall I tell her to expect you?"

"Of course," smiled Sloan. "Tell her I'm looking forward to it and thanks a lot." Suddenly, something else came to Sloan. "Listen, do you think Rachelle's up to discussing something of a very important nature? I've thought of putting it off for a few days, but since she's better and I'll have the opportunity to be alone with you both together, I guess I might as well get it over with, unless you think I could upset her or tax her strength too much."

Immediately, to John, there seemed to be something ominous about the day. Though he was completely at a loss as to why he felt that way.

"Well," he replied, "since I can't say for certain, Sloan, I don't know the nature of the subject you have in mind, but I suppose she is. Is it something I could help you with?"

"I really don't know, John, maybe you could. Still, I'm

depending more on Rachelle to help me clear things up, so perhaps I'd better wait. Besides, I think it might be best to wait until the three of us can discuss it together."

"As you wish," said John. "Tonight then?"

"Tonight," Sloan assured, his usual cool manner appearing once more as he dropped his head back over his work.

For a few brief seconds, John lingered, fastening a puzzled expression on Gilford Sloan before he turned away to his own work.

Hardly is it necessary to point out that John made little headway in his work that day? The more he thought of Gilford Sloan's purposed discussion coming up that evening with him and Rachelle, the more baffled and mystified his thoughts became. Save the one thing that Sloan was planning to discuss, John's thoughts hit on more than a dozen things that Sloan might have had on his mind before the day was over—some as farfetched as his partner possibly selling his half-interest in the Pacesetter, to marrying his school teacher friend and moving to South Carolina! And, when Rachelle learned that Sloan's visit that evening was going to be for the purpose of having a discussion with her and John that no doubt would be far adrift from Sloan's normal line of talk, plus all the news she was expecting to hear about the Heyward's besides, it became quite an ordeal for her to keep her mind on anything else, including ham, Boston baked beans, or her supper in general.

The day finally passed though and now with Beth Anne and Carr having just excused themselves from the supper table and hurried on off to join their friends at the social, Rachelle—sensing that Gilford Sloan had become somewhat tense as she guessed that he was ready to embark upon the subject matter which she and John had puzzled over all day, suggested that they all refill their coffee cups. When it came to easing tense situations, Rachelle had ever been one to think that there were not many things that could do the trick like a good cup of coffee.

"You sit still, dear, and let me oblige," said John as he quickly jumped up and dashed for the kitchen to get the coffeepot which Rachelle had left on the stove to keep the coffee warm. Filling the coffee cups, John was sliding back into his chair when Gilford Sloan suddenly surprised him by clearing his throat and saying, "John, you know as long as I've known Carr, I never knew until recently he has an uncle who remains to be among the missing casualties of Gettysburg to this day."

Sloan's statement surprised Rachelle, too, because the war was one subject that her husband and Gilford Sloan had made it a practice to shun. She wondered what he was leading up to.

John wondered the same and was also thinking at the same time that regardless of what his friends motive might be, he still saw no cause for him to open a subject which they both refrained from discussing since the day they met for fear of damaging their relationship. Not only was he surprised at Gilford Sloan, he was disappointed in him, too, and it clearly came through in his brusque response.

"Neither did we," he replied, the tone of his voice quite guff, "until our daughter mentioned it a few weeks ago."

Giving no indication that he had noticed John's displeasure with the subject topic, Sloan continued, "Well, I don't suppose we should be too surprised that he failed to mention it before he did, considering that it all happened before he was born. You may be sure, though, had he been at Gettysburg like we were, it would've made a sight of difference in his attitude."

Thinking about their own silence over the years when it came to discussing the war, John, giving Gilford Sloan a puzzled, discontented eye over the rim of his coffee cup, thought his statement sounded like a lot of stuff and nonsense and, in so many words, made an endeavor to tell him so without spelling it out.

"Don't be too sure about that," he snapped, his impatience with the subject coming through again.

Even so, Gilford Sloan, appearing undaunted to John's amazement, went on, "Before his time or not though, I'm still surprised that he's never mentioned the fact that his other uncle, the late Nat Carson rode with our mighty, brave Jeb Stuart. As a matter of fact, I learned this uncle of Carr's lost his life at Yellow Tavern in spring of sixty-four, the same battle that our great Stuart was mortally wounded in. It's a shame that both Mrs. Heyward's brothers came to such a fate. I learned a great deal about these men while I visited Green Sea, things I've never heard Carr talk about. Especially about the older brother, Philippe Carson, whose fate Mrs. Heyward says she's never fully accepted."

Observing her husband's mounting discontentment with Gilford Sloan's persistence on keeping his tongue rattling off facts about the war which John had totally lost track of because of his impairment, Rachelle—though she was every much as baffled over the behavior of their guest as John was, started to interrupt at this point in an attempt to change the subject. She was too late, though, for before she could open her mouth, John was already fiercely retorting, "Well, taking into account our daughter, Sloan, is marrying into the Heyward and Carson families, I certainly hope that what you learned about these two men would meet with applause, or could it be that you' re leading up to reveal some shocking closet news to Rachelle and me? If that's the case, come on out with it. You're well aware that I grow weary and impatient when one plays at hide and seek in conversation! "

"John dear!" Exclaimed Rachelle. "Gilford's our guest. Don't be so on edge. If it's fact that he does have some black marks to disclose to us about this family, I'm certain he's doing it and trying to be easy about it is because he has only our best interest at heart and nothing else."

Gilford Sloan had never gained the courage to tell Rachelle he detested the name Gilford, ever bearing it in silence coming from her. "'I'm sorry, dear. That goes for you, too, Sloan. I guess I am suffering from a case of nerves, been that way all day," said John.

"I'm sorry, too, John, I didn't know," Sloan said. "Maybe I should've started this at another time. Since I have, though, I might as well tell you that your hunch about me beating about the bush is right, but what I have on my mind has nothing to do with closet news. In fact, to settle that question, if it's ever risen with you, from what I saw and heard about the Carson's and Heyward's, too, it's my guess that their closets are pretty much free of hidden skeletons."

"Well, I must confess I'm somewhat relieved to hear you say that. However, I'm still in the dark as to why you seem to be inclined to go back and bring up long ago events into the conversation, which to my way of thinking, bears no fundamental importance, whatever, to the principal interest that Rachelle and I mostly have on our minds these days," John said.

"Maybe not, but for now and the near future, my plans are to talk of nothing else to you every chance I get," Sloan emphatically asserted, realizing that John himself had initiated his most opportune moment for the dropping of his bombing belief and conviction.

"For what purpose, if I may ask?" John thoughtfully questioned, finally finding himself at a nonplus with his supper quest and openly admitting it. "'What's come over you, Sloan? Suddenly, you seem more like a stranger than the Gilford Sloan I 've known and worked with all these years.

There was no interference from Rachelle this time; for, silently, she was agreeing with John, thinking to herself that Gilford Sloan was indeed not his usual self.

Sloan took a long swig of coffee. Then, setting his coffee cup down and ignoring all John's remarks except his first, he said, looking John straight in the eye, "For what purpose, you say. Well—mostly because not only do I admire, respect, and hold deep affection for you, Rachelle, and your daughter, you're all closer to me than anyone I know. But, most important of all, I'm doing it to try to help you gain your true identity, because from the instant I heard Beth Anne disclose to the Heyward's the misfortune you suffered at Gettysburg, I have every reason to believe you're Philippe Carson, heir to Green Sea Plantation! In fact, I'd stake my very life on it!"

For a fleeting moment, nothing could be heard in the shattered silence but the intake of Rachelle's breath and the movement of her hands as she—feeling as though her chair was slipping out beneath her, grasped the table's edge for support. Then, John's voice was exploding over everything, as if his nerves had truly blown, at last, he cried out, "Christ almighty, Sloan! Have you lost your senses? Apparently, you only half-heard what Beth Anne told the Heyward's. I was a private in the Union Army, lying in a Union ambulance wagon with several other mortally wounded Union soldiers from Gettysburg, whom had expired before reaching the hospital, when Rachelle spotted me and saw that I was still living! I should think that's a long way from being this Confederate officer from South Carolina whom you've recently heard about!"

Sloan waved John's protest aside, saying, "I know all about that, John, and before you say anything else, I beg you to first hear me out. I have a lot of valid points that we can't dismiss in this matter." He turned to Rachelle. "Rachelle, I'm depending on you, too. With John's help, you and I are going to help him conquer this problem of his. I deeply regret that I didn't learn about it sooner. Now, if you're up to it, I'd like for you to tell me every detail that you remember taking place the day you found John. Then, I'll fill in my part and, when I do, I'm certain you'll share my belief that John is Philippe Carson, if he doesn't."

Rachelle; however, did not respond to Sloan's remarks, or to the question of her strength regarding a long, and no doubt, taxing discussion. Still shaken, she merely murmured, "He's heard my prayers," appearing as though she were unaware of Gilford Sloan or her husband's presence, which, of course, strained John's nerves that much more and caused his supper guest to bear the brunt of his tension and frustration all over again.

"Can't you see, Sloan, that your nonsense about my being Philippe Carson has been too much for her," he burst out and jumping up, he made a dash for Rachelle's side, pleading, "Don't be upset, dear. Everything's going to be all right. Please, won't you blot it all out from your mind, I'm going to!"

Suddenly, to Gilford Sloan's profound relief though—he could have hugged her and, to her husband's surprising astonishment, Rachelle came back to them, saying in a tone of voice that John had seldom heard her use in the many years he had been married to her, "I'll do no such thing, John! Neither will you! Go back to your chair and try to simmer down for goodness sakes! As Gilford says, you've got to help us see this matter through!" She turned a radiant smile upon Gilford Sloan. "Of course, I feel up to discussing it with you, Gilford. Nothing could delight me more. The fact is, right now, I feel as though I could talk all night. I remember every detail as well, as clearly as if it all happened yesterday."

And, as John yielded to his wife's wishes and went back and took his chair, even though it was plain to see he still did not share her and Gilford Sloan's view, Rachelle commenced with her part and before the discussion was brought to a halt; indeed, she had near talked—off and on—the remainder of the night! For the discussion had hardly gotten underway that John was to perk up and take a keen interest himself when a most important factor was made clear to him.

Turning to John, at one point, in Rachelle's relative Of events, Sloan interrupted by asking John, "And, in all this time, John, never has one glimpse of anything came to you, in dreams or otherwise, that you think might be related to those years that were blocked out?"

It was obvious that John was diffident to impart anything, concerning the matter, to Gilford Sloan. But, with Rachelle's anxious eyes hanging on him, he was almost forced to come across with what little he could furnish, finally replying, "'One or two scenes, but I don't see how they could possibly be related to me, unless by some coincidence, I possibly had relatives or friends in the South that I visited fairly often."

"Great! That's something to go on," exclaimed Sloan. "'What were the scenes?"

Suddenly, John felt he was being stripped of all dignity—the urging gaze of both Rachelle and Gilford Sloan crushing his noble pride. Right at that moment, he wanted to dash through the door and become as lost to the present as he was lost to those long ago years. Realizing he was covered though, he went ahead and volunteered, "'Well—from time to time, there's a long avenue of live oaks, which at first seemed to lead to nowhere. Then later on, I felt my mind's eye was focusing on something that I knew was there at the end of the avenue, but I was unable to make it out in the darkness. Then suddenly one day, it was there—a huge mansion."

"Why, you're seeing the live oaks at Green Sea!" cried an excited Gilford Sloan.

"The devil you say?" John came back, leaning forward in his chair while Rachelle appeared to be holding her breath.

"You bet I am," whooped Sloan, "a long avenue of them that leads straight to the mansion! Mrs. Heyward told me that they were planted by the first Matthew Carson and his bride over a hundred years ago, when I remarked of this unique beauty!"

"But, the mansion, Sloan? Does it have columns on all four sides?" John hastily asked, his eyes growing brighter.

"The mansion at Green Sea?" Sloan questioned. "No, only eight tall columns in front. Why do you ask that?"

"See, you're all wet, Sloan." John sighed disheartened as he settled back again into his chair. "Not only does the mansion I see have columns in front, but it's completely surrounded with them."

Thwarted, Sloan was thoughtful for a moment. Then, he was crying in excitement. "Wait a minute! The Heyward mansion is practically new! Luke Heyward told me that after a long fifteen-year struggle, he and his wife finally completed it about two years ago! The Carson mansion, the one that his wife and her two brothers were born and grew up in, was destroyed by fire only a year or two following the war!"

"Oh, John," cried Rachelle, "I just know that burned mansion is the one you see, dear!"

Though doubt remained to stay with John, he could not bring himself to turn his mind away from what his wife was suggesting. Weighing it in silence as he stared back at her he was finally to murmur, seeming to be expressing his thoughts more to himself than to those around him, "Could it possibly be?"

"Why not, John?" Sloan thundered once more, "and when you hear the rest of what I have to tell, you won't be asking questions like that ever again, you'll be as convinced as I am!"

"But, I was in the Union Army, Sloan! Before you go any further with this conversation, will you explain that fact to me, for God's sake!" John thundered back.

"That's easy." Sloan readily told him. "A number of things could explain it. the most likely, though, is you were dressed in a Yankee uniform in order to get a closer look at the Yankees—no doubt doing reconnaissance work of some sort. I understand Philippe Carson was a first lieutenant. He could've been doing this strictly on his own. Don't forget that rank has the authority to judge situations and act accordingly without waiting for approval from higher officers, if that were the case or otherwise."

"John!" Rachelle was crying again, "never once in all these years have we thought of that possibility. You see, having fought in the war himself, Gilford has thought this all through. I'm positive now that Gilford's going to Green Sea was an act of Providence on your behalf, John." She took her eyes from John and-let them rest on Gilford Sloan. "John didn't tell you all of it. He's also dreamed of walking through vast cotton and tobacco fields."

"Cotton and tobacco fields," repeated Sloan. "Well, I can vouch for Green Sea's vast acreage. The fields are immense. But, now,   I want to pursue two other incidents that are very important in the matter. I think once I go through the details of those two happenings with John, he'll then be as convinced as we are that I'm on the right track. He was involved in both of them. One, he won't recall but the other he will."

"What incident was that," John asked, his interest promptly repressing his doubts and dampened spirit.

"The day you handed me that editorial to feature on General Lee's death. The other was an incident I was involved in, which dealt with a conversation pertaining to you, just before the general and all his army hit the road for Gettysburg," said Sloan. "So listen, here goes..."

"Wait, Sloan," John interrupted, his face rather anxious looking, "before you go any further, I'd like to know if you've discussed any of this with Beth Anne or Carr." "No, John, I haven't. In fact, except for you and Rachelle here tonight, I haven't said a word about it to anybody."

"Good," said John. "I'd prefer we all continue to keep it quiet. Besides our hopes, there's a lot at stake here." He looked at Rachelle. "Rachelle dear, since you're in on this, there's no way I can protect you if all this comes tumbling down around us, but I can spare our daughter and that I want to do, come what may. Never do I want Beth Anne to suffer any unhappiness because of it. We all must remember one important factor in this matter and that is, these people at Green Sea may not take too kindly to someone who suddenly appears on the scene claiming to be the late Philippe Carson, heir to their holdings."

"I've thought of that too, John, and I fully agree with you. Neither do I want to cause any unhappiness for anybody, especially for Beth Anne and Rachelle here." Sloan said.

For the first time that night, John's grimness seemed to lift. As a faint smile began to play at the comers of his mouth, he told Sloan, "I might've known you've covered all aspects of the matter, Sloan. That's what makes you such a good newspaper man."

"Well, I try to look at all angles," said Sloan. "I do realize Beth Anne's marriage is to take place in a few months and, for that very reason, I want to wait until I can present definite proof that you are Philippe Carson before I do or say anything publicly. But, you may be sure when I do have my work completed on the matter, Beth Anne will be writing her true name, Beth Anne Carson, on that marriage certificate! "

"You sound determined, Sloan." John said, his smile more pronounced.

"I am determined, John." Sloan replied. "Come hell or high water, I'm going to prove you're Philippe Carson, Mrs. Heyward's brother! You'll soon believe me, too, because I don't plan to let up or allow you to let up until the battle is ours!"

"Heaven be praised! I truly believe he's going to do what he says, John," laughed Rachelle, reaching to touch John's arm. Then, she rose from her chair, telling them "I'll be back shortly. I'm going to put on a fresh pot of coffee. I have a feeling we're going to need it, before we cover everything that's on our minds tonight."

Indeed, before many days had passed, John saw that Gilford Sloan was very much decided to the task he had set his mind upon. Holding hard to word—saving the hours they were on the job at the newspaper office, Sloan did not let a day pass that he did not dig, probe, and recount with John some major happening that the latter could no longer remember. In fact, Sloan became so adapt in his war battle descriptions—drawling incessantly it seemed, at times, to John about some master stroke of General Lee's, that in some instances it soon got to the place where it was quite difficult for John to separate the real from the imaginary, in that, he began to wonder if he were not seeing a measure of Sloan's storytelling in the scope of his own mind's eye, rather than visualizing the scene through those vivid narratives which Sloan could give words to so skillfully. Then, there were sessions upon sessions of other discussions where Sloan covered other aspects of the situation with John and Rachelle. Since it was Gilford Sloan's belief that the past would open to John that much sooner if he were informed of all facts—past and present—that anyone could furnish him. Sloan spent hours bringing John up to date with all the things he had learned about him, Green Sea itself and its surroundings, plus Drakston Hall, Oak Grove and also Elms.

Of course some of this information that Sloan had come by in his visit to the low country and was now making known to John, not only astonished John but was awing to him too. Rachelle was likewise. Granted, it was a fast rule with Sloan that he tell John nothing that Rachelle's ears could not also hear. She heard it all. Though Sloan was to note that both Rachelle and John appeared overly astonished to hear that John had been engaged to marry the former Caroline Wilton of Elms, who remained to be a very dear and close friend of the family, he also noticed at the same time, that their astonishment did not seem to go so far as to disturb their own relationship. To Sloan, it appeared to be as solid and secure as ever, which, in truth, it was. Of all the news that Sloan was to relate, which among other things were the deaths of Anne Carson and Nat Carson in addition to the startling resemblance between Beth Anne and Eliza Heyward and the pronounced violet-blue Carson eyes that John had also inherited, Sloan thought that John was most affected when he informed him that he still had a living father. As a matter of fact, any news that Sloan had to relate—he observed—that dealt with Matthew Carson, seemed to overwhelm John.

However, at all events, in addition to all their drilling that Sloan was putting John through—telling and questioning and discussing—Sloan was also in the process of making contact with a number of former Confederate officers of Lee's Army of Northern Virginia whom he thought might have served with John in close contact, or, in any event, might know a little something about him and the circumstances which surrounded the matter. Besides gathering this information which he thought might hold some clue in helping him to bear out his claim that John and the late Philippe Carson was one

71

and the same person, Sloan was banking on one or two of these former comrades of John's to identify him—if it came to that. First, Sloan was trying it another way and planned to ask these men to identify John as a last resort only, because he well recognized that time and the burdens brought on by John's impairment had altered his person a great deal.

The fact was, when Gilford Sloan stopped to ponder over this factuality of circumstance, he very much doubted that Eliza Heyward would recognize her own brother when John and Rachelle made their first visit to Green Sea at Easter. For as certain as Sloan was that he was dead right about John, he would have been the first to admit that with the exception of John's eyes, the man who called himself John Fillmore- Lee and the young, vital man whom he had observed in the portrait at Green Sea, indeed had little in common.

At any rate, providing Rachelle's health kept improving, she and John were slated to finally meeting the Heyward's at Easter time. Hence, before this meeting and visit took place, Gilford Sloan— continuing to believe that any one thing he told or described to John could be the key that would unlock the dark void in his mind once he did find himself in the midst of Green Sea and its surroundings with family and friends, was cramming John's head with every bit of information that he could gather that bore any correlation at all with the matter.

Gilford Sloan could hardly wait for John to go to Green Sea. His faith that some incident was going to turn the tide for John when he arrived there, could not have been more solid. He firmly believed that as surely as Easter marked the Resurrection of Christ, that the forthcoming Easter Time would be the period when the darkness in John's mind would tum to light. Even so, having picked up a word here and a word there from Rachelle, Gilford Sloan had begun to hold another belief. Even though there was no doubt in his mind that John was telling him the truth when he said he could not recall one thing that he was trying to hammer into his head, day in and day out, that still did not keep Sloan from taking on the notion that if John had tried as hard to remember as he apparently had tried to forget— that in all probability—he would have been able to recall more to his mind than an oak lined avenue and a white-columned mansion, Though he; nevertheless, could still understand, knowing John's nature. Thus, Gilford Sloan kept to his task, drilling John as laboriously as ever in the weeks that followed.

Chapter Four

The days awakened to bird song and drowsed to sleepy darkness upon a mellow land. Spring had come and, in the midst of this whisper-soft gentleness, birth was reigning everywhere. Dogwoods bloomed. Pink, green strawberries ripened in strawberry fields.

Cotton seeds swelled in silk-like soil, while, at the same time, in another mellowed field row upon row of tender, satiny tobacco plants were cradled in their infancy. Corn shoots inched along in the warmth, and, once again, the cornfields were taking on the look of a rippling sea that seemed to join the gleaming far horizon beyond.

Springtide—the essence of rebirth. The season of Easter—a period of awaking to light and natures reigning beauty. A time of renewal. The revival of faith—of hope. And, although Eliza was mindful and appreciative of all these things and the present divine entity surrounding her as she rode beside Luke to church on this bright Palm Sunday morning, the lightness of heart which she craved and knew she should have possessed just wasn't there. Even though the morning could not have been more luminous, she felt if she were to look up at the sky, there would be clouds meeting her eyes instead of a radiant blue universe, though experiencing these phantasmal encounters in the ensuing years had been a rare happening—if at all. Even so, having no wish to chance meeting one on this day, Eliza did not look up. She turned her head and looked at Luke instead and suddenly—in doing so—her depression seemed even worse because the verity of that long ago vision that she had seen on another Sunday morning was coming home to Eliza in full force—Luke, her vibrant, handsome husband, was growing old!

Yes, studying Luke's aging profile—his white temple, the deep crosses around his eye and those that ran the entire length of his jawline, plus the thickening of his neck, that long ago experience of having visioned Luke as being aged, was called to Eliza's mind. The vision had deeply distressed her. But, then, on second thought, she had taken heart that day, had to a certain degree been grateful for this gift of second right which she possessed, because she had been able to see one message that it was conveying to her then, that had made her heart sing—she and Luke were going to be together a long time because she was going to see him grow old.

But now that it dawned on her that it was happening and appeared to be happening rather fast at that—the trueness of the vision taking place before her very eyes—Eliza's heart was dealt a hard blow. And, the fact that she was to see more evidence of time and all the hard toil that Luke had been exposed to, as she let her eyes fall from his profile to rest on his strong, coarse-lined calloused hands holding onto the horse's reins, did nothing at all as far as lifting her spirit. In fact, her heart plunged that much farther.

Assuredly, despite her knowing that Luke was still a long way from becoming old and feeble, Eliza was still unable to see anything heartening in the fact that her beloved husband was not young anymore, as a matter of fact, was on the brink of his declining years, if; indeed, he was not already well into them.

Yes, Eliza was thinking, this was a fact of life taking place now instead of some supernatural experience that she was seeing in the future. This was for real—the present. This was the year 1886. Luke was growing old and she was not even a decade behind him. He was fifty-two. She was forty-four. Indeed, time had gone and where had it fallen

Was this why she was so depressed today—the knowledge of all this weighing on her? Was she wishing that time would cease to be, stop altogether? Well, she supposed she did, when it came to the matter of it turning one more jet-black hair to white in Luke's head. Curious as it was, when it came to the matter of herself again, she did not worry about the years. It appeared to be only Luke's age that concerned her. She didn't know, but maybe that vision of seeing him aged, long ago, had had something to do with it. Whatever the reason, all she did know was, that Luke's head was rapidly turning white and the years were piling up their evidence on him and she could do nothing to stop either, though her love for him was more intense than ever.

On the other hand, maybe the main reason why she was so concerned with the aging process today was due to her anxiety over her beloved father. No doubt about it, being eighty-one years of age, he was old! Even though Seth had assured her that that black out spell that her father had suffered about two weeks ago at the stables was mostly caused by overspending his strength—being foolhardily enough to take that reckless, madcap

Fancy out for a gallop and stayed too long, she still worried about him. Josh had revived her father and had had the good sense to send another stable groom to tell Aunt Amy, while he had been busy going about it. Of course, it had frightened Aunt Amy half to death, but in her calm way, she wasted not one minute in sending for Seth. Though when Seth arrived, he found her father already recovered and sipping a brandy, which Seth said was as good as any medicine he himself could have prescribed him.

All the same, Seth had warned her father to let his horseback rides be few and far between in the future, if at all, telling him that he would be wiser to let Fancy kick the stables all she wanted than for him to be taking chances on a horse's back at eighty-one years of age. And, Seth had pointed out to her that even though he could detect nothing seriously wrong with her father's heart, she still must keep in mind that he was quite up in years, his heart having been ticking for a long time. Might as well have come right out and told her not to be surprised if his heart did give out, to her way of thinking. Whit should be there seeing to Fancy's gallop's himself, rather than writing home and reminding the rest to keep his mare in tune, as he puts it. Eliza smiled to herself, Whit and his lopsided grin, so much like Nat's. Right, Lucy, I've finally acknowledged—well, mentally anyway—that Whit is the result of your and Nat's taking of the forbidden fruit! Whit's grin is proof of that! No, Lucy dear, neither you, or Nat if he were here, can ever deny that period of dalliance, no matter what! She would have to hand it to Lucy to work it out, though. Most girls would not have had the courage, the strength, or the brains to have carried through with it like Lucy had—herself included, she supposed!

At any rate, undoubtedly, her worriment over her father did have a lot to do with her depression today—why she felt as though some premonitory warning was threatening her, because aside from that as far as she knew everything else was going fairly well with her. Though she would have to be honest and admit that it had taken quite a few encouraging words from Luke, in those past weeks, to effect the change in her attitude concerning Carr's forthcoming marriage to that Yankee girl!

Yes, she thought she had finally reconciled herself to what appeared to be the inevitable. Moreover, she thought she had also quelled her anxiousness over John Fillmore-Lee's hapless misfortune and infirmity, although she had not forgotten that she was going to have to be, constantly, on her guard when carrying on a conversation with him. Naturally, the same applied to Luke too. She and Luke had discussed this problem of Mr. John's several times and now were pretty certain they had more or less prepared themselves when it came to the matter of dealing with his problem in conversation. As a matter of fact, they both were looking forward to meeting the Fillmore-Lee's whose plans were to make their first visit to Green Sea the coming week—in fact, on Good Friday; and the way she looked at it, a more promising day for a first meeting and visit, they could hardly have chosen.

She certainly hoped so—hope that their visit went off better than their daughter's first visit had. She would never forget all the commotion that Lee business had stirred! Although she had kept her word and not told one soul about how John Fillmore-Lee had come by the Lee part of his name, she; nevertheless, had made certain that everybody had been informed that there was no connected bloodline between him and the Lee's of Virginia! She especially had pressed this upon Martha, having taken no chances with her! The truth was she and Martha had passed a few "hot" retorts not long back. No, not about that Lee name business but about how much that Yankee girl favored the Carson's!

It had all started when, at one point, during their discussing of this peculiar and one in a million incidents regarding the startling resemblance between Beth Anne and herself that Martha—Martha having been the one to launch the subject no sooner than the first chance they had gotten to be alone together after Beth Anne's visit, had promptly reminded her not to forget that, at some time or other during the war years, both her brothers and her father as well had served in the near abouts of the same locality that the Fillmore-Lee's were from originally; and had also had the nerve to go on and tell her that this fact could very well shed a great deal of light upon the matter as far as explaining it, if she were to give it some thought!

Well, she had told Martha that she needed to go back to school and take a course in arithmetic because, in no way, could one make the gap between the years the Carson men had served in those places and Beth Anne's age, add up. Then, Martha had dared to come back and say that Beth Anne herself or someone else was dressing up her real age because the Carson features in her were too pronounced to deny! And, the retorts had gone on and on with both of them really letting their tempers flare aplenty. But, in the long run and as may be expected, they not only had made up but, for sake of family honor, had also made a bargain to keep their mouths shut about the matter—

finally having agreed that they were totally stumped when it came to arriving at a reasonable explanation.

Another little smile faintly curved Eliza's mouth.

Of course, in point of Martha's unvirtuous thoughts, she had stopped at letting Martha know that she was not the only one whom had harbored thoughts along that line. Both Luke and herself, when they had finally gotten around to mentioning the subject of Beth Anne's Carson features to one another, had confessed of letting their minds stray in the same direction; that is, until they had stopped to consider the age factor—a fact that could not be ignored. Thus, they too, had agreed to try to view it as being merely some odd and prodigious incident that had occurred and nothing more. Well, she didn't know about Luke, but she was having quite a bit of difficulty in bringing her mind around to fully accepting that, though she had said no more about it to Luke, and certainly not Martha! After all, who was to say that she was duty bound to let Martha in on most her thoughts and opinions, anyhow?

Eliza's rambling thoughts had long taken her eyes from her husband's hands and had, instinctively, settled her closer to his side where she continued to let them ramble on, as she let her nonchalant gaze drift at nothing in particular. Noticing her obvious depression and unusual disinterest in conversation, not even Luke's attempt at jollity and teasing her while they had proceeded on toward Church, had done much in the way of lifting her spirit or calming her mind down either. Nor had Marsh Reed's clamorous sermon, once Eliza found herself at the mercy of his hell-bent, high-geared oratory. The fact was, barely had Eliza taken her seat before she were wishing that she could escape to the outside grounds and get out from under the reverend's thundering voice altogether; and, eventually, that was where she did find herself and was feeling all the better for it, immediately. For not only were spring's balmy, inviting weather and leafing landscape a great improvement over the Church's somber, bare interior, but the small group of people who Eliza was the midst of and conversing with, were a far sight more interesting to her and soothing, too, than any one rap or bellow that Marsh Reed had pounded and barked out. Eliza had heard it all before. But, she had born with it and stayed put, because whereas she had not only half-heard the sermon out of sheer boredom, she had been well aware that Luke was not bored—gazing upon Marsh Reed as intensely as ever.

At any rate, Eliza was now outside and Martha was asking her, as the conversation turned to the Heyward's expected guests, "What day will they arrive Eliza?"

"Friday afternoon, if their plans stay on schedule." Eliza said, and turning her smile on everybody, added, "and all of you are invited to be at Green Sea no later than six o'clock Saturday evening when you'll meet them and help Luke and me entertain them at a dinner party we're giving in their honor. Sorry about the delay, but we thought since Beth Anne's mother has suffered a recent illness, it might be better to give her a little time to rest and relax from the hazards of traveling, before we besiege her with too many of our low-country customs."

Caroline laughed, "Even if you were to change your mind, Eliza, and not make us wait, I doubt she'd be too uncomfortable, because your dinner parties are always such a delight for everybody. I simply love them."

"Me too, dear," said Doctor Seth. Then, he looked at Eliza. "But, don't count one hundred percent on us being there, Eliza! Caroline hasn't felt well, lately." Suddenly, Eliza felt a weight on her heart again.

"I'm so sorry, Caroline, why didn't you let me know," she cried.

Making light of her husband's disclosure Caroline replied, "Oh, every time I sneeze, Eliza, Seth thinks I'm ill. Doctors are like that I suppose."

"No, Caroline dear," Luke put in, "it's not because Seth's a doctor. It's because he loves you and is concerned for your welfare."

"I'm trying to get her to see that she isn't as young as she used to be," said Seth, quite seriously.

Coming back in a lighter tone, Luke laughed, "'But, Seth, you're going about it the wrong way. No woman fancy's being reminded of her age. You should know that, you're being a doctor."

Trying to go along with Luke's lighter mood, Eliza laughed too, saying to him, "Well, look who's talking about age; and besides, who does want to be reminded of what our mirrors are already telling us and quite frequently at that!"

"You're right about that, Eliza," chimed Martha. "I simply hate it every time I think I see a white hair."

"Think?" Bruce questioned with a smile and then went on to inform, "Undecided on the color or not friends, I've noticed she doesn't hesitate at pulling them out!"

Observing how Martha was scowling at Bruce, Luke quipped,

"Oh, you shouldn't be all that concerned, Martha. Haven't you heard the old saying? A woman's like good bourbon, she gets better with age! So, why worry about the grey hairs."

"Luke!" Eliza exclaimed as a blush covered her face and also Caroline's. "What's come over you?" She turned to Martha. "Never mind him, Martha, he's been like this all day."

Undaunted, Martha merely made a face at Luke, and one that was not showing a blush, either. In fact, Martha wanted to match Luke's quip and could have but thought better of it, since it appeared Eliza and Caroline's modesty had already been shocked considerably. Thus, she forewent the comeback to Luke and instead inquired of Eliza, changing the subject altogether, "Eliza, did you hear from Jane Anne? Has she decided to come home for Easter? We haven't heard one word from Laura yet."

"Yes, we got a letter yesterday. I meant to tell you, but I got sidetracked with all this talk about aging. She mentioned that Laura was writing a letter home too. You should've gotten it. You'll probably get it tomorrow. Anyway, Jane Anne isn't coming home. She's decided that since final examinations will begin immediately following Easter, she should stay at school and study. Not only that, but she pointed Out that she'll be coming home for summer vacation in about three weeks, anyhow. Although I'll confess that Luke and I are greatly disappointed that she won't be with us, I'll also have to admit we think her decision is wise and sensible and we respect it. I wrote right back and told her so too!"

"It is wise of her, Eliza, and wise of you and Luke to look at it that way. I know I'd be petrified if I were facing college examinations that I hadn't prepared myself for," said Caroline.

"Well, she does take her studies seriously and, so far, it's paid off for her. Luke and I are proud of her academic record." Eliza said.

"Jane Anne is doing really well, no question about that," said Martha. "But, if I know her like I think I do, I bet she isn't near as serious about what she achieves regarding grades and degrees as she is about hurrying and getting it all behind her, so she can come home for good and marry Stuart."

Instantly Eliza's face flushed pink again, with those around her well recognizing its

"Really, Martha," she flared, "couldn't you let one conversation concerning our daughter pass without bringing Stuart Drakston's name into it? For the life of me, I can't understand why you insist on trying to match those two children up!"

"Children!" Martha snorted. "If Jane Anne at going on eighteen years of age and Stuart at already twenty-four years, are children, I'll regret to think what their appearance will be, when they do reach maturity! What's more, your accusation that I'm trying to match them up is completely fake and you know it!"

"Well in my book she's still too young for Stuart Drakston," retorted Eliza.

"Well, in mine," Martha flared back, "she's a full-grown woman, who's deeply in love with my nephew, and you'd be sensible to see it and accept it!"

Seeing that neither Bruce or Luke was going to interfere, and fearing their tempers were going to get worse before they got better, Seth decided to take it on his own to try to soothe things over before a full-fledged fight was staged, said, I remember the day Jane Anne was born as clearly as though it were this morning. I knew the instant I laid her in Luke's hands, that his heart was hooked for all time."

The doctor's intervention seemed to work.

Appearing much calmer, Eliza said, "you're right, Seth. As far as Luke's concerned, she could get away with almost anything. He could never bring himself to paddle her, even when she deserved a thrashing."

"Well," smiled Bruce, "I'm not the least surprised at that, because it's been said that men are for a fact, more partial to their daughters and women more partial to their sons." If anybody there thought that Luke was going to make light of the saying, they were in for a surprise.

Looking at Eliza and sending her a smile, he said, 'Well, dear, it appears that you and

I just might exemplify that saying, seeing that it does seem to be that way at our house."

Martha, appearing as cool and collected as though not one retort had passed her lips for months, suddenly rose to the occasion and volunteered, "I don't know about the saying regarding a son since we weren't blessed with one, but in support of your admission, Luke, I'll have to confess there must be something to it, for in point of the father, daughter relationship, you're not the only example around, if Maggie's behavior means anything. I don't believe that she and Seth Junior have ever passed a cross word that she didn't either write Bruce about it, or save every word to relate in person to him, once she made another trip home.

"And, I'll admit I am ever ready to turn her a sympathetic ear," laughed Bruce, "and also want to make it known that while I'm loaning Maggie a shoulder to cry on, my wife, at the same time, is loaning hers to our son-in-law. Whether Martha left that part out by intention or just plain forgot to tell it, I wouldn't know!"

Obviously, it was by intention. For seeming a bit self-conscious which was a rare thing with Martha, she said, "Now, Bruce, you didn't have to tell that."

Caroline smiled, "Oh, don't fret so, Martha. Bruce didn't tell us anything that we didn't already know through all those flattering remarks that Seth Junior lets fall about you."

"Yes, Martha," agreed Doctor Seth, "my son thinks highly of you, I'm certain he's never given one thought to all that nonsense that's forever being quoted about meddling mothers-in-law." The doctor pulled forth his watch. "Sorry to break this up, friends, but we 'd best be getting along. Besides having a patient, I must see to this afternoon, Caroline could overtire herself."

"See what I mean about being married to a doctor," laughed Caroline, and turning to Eliza went on to add as she squeezed her hand, "We'll be there, Eliza, you can count on it."

As the doctor and Caroline turned to leave and all the rest began to follow suit, Eliza suddenly called out to Martha, "Martha, I'll expect to see you and Bruce there, too."

Martha whirled back, hollering, "Of course! Whatever gave you the notion we wouldn't be!" And before the started Eliza could come back with a reply, Martha whirled back around and proceeded on.

Seeing that Martha's cutting retaliation was slowing her husband's feet and turning his head around to stare anxiously at those behind him, Caroline shot her hand out to grasp Seth's, saying, "Oh, come on, Seth, and don't let their short tempers get at you so. It doesn't mean a thing."

But, it did matter. That is, the source of the retorts mattered a great deal to Eliza, more than Caroline or anyone else realized.

She and Luke had been on their way home only a short while when she said, "Luke, I love Martha, but she does provoke me to no end at times. Did you hear what she said about our child wanting to marry Stuart Drakston?"

Even though he let it pass, his wife labeling their grown daughter a child did not escape Luke's notice.

"Doll, you know full well how Martha is. Whatever may pop in her head, she usually comes out with it. Pay it no mind."

"You mean—you think there's no cause for my being concerned—that there's nothing to Jane Anne's attraction for Stuart Drakston?" Eliza added, no longer feeling weighed down for the first time that day.

"No, I didn't mean that at all," replied Luke. "I said pay no mind to Martha."

"Oh, I see," murmured Eliza, her relief dying rapidly. "Then you agree with Martha to a certain extent, if not fully?" she went on and asked, her voice increasing in intensity.

"No, not fully, but partly—yes." Luke said. "I don't go along with her statement regarding Kitten's good marks in school, sounded like she might be a little anxious of our daughter's excellent academic standing. Relative to Stuart, though, I think she may have summed our daughter's feelings up about right."

"Well, if she has, I won't have it, Luke, I'll never consent for a daughter of mine to marry a Drakston!" Eliza affirmed in a voice that now sounded as if it were on the brink of flooding over with emotion.

Luke turned his head, saying, "Don't make statements like that, dear. Stop and think a little, won't you?"

Meeting Luke's gaze, her distress and a trace of annoyance with him, too, plain to be seen in her eyes as she held them steadily to his, Eliza told him, "You're not only agreeing with Martha, you're beginning to sound like her, too. I should think you wouldn't go against my wishes like this."

"Against your wishes?' Luke questioned, his dark, heavy brows coming together as his expression tensed. "You know perfectly well, sweetheart, I'd never go against you on anything, because, so far, you've always come through and exercised good judgment when a situation called for it, and I shall hope that you'll, eventually, come through and act accordingly about this matter. Those youngsters are in love with one another and we might as well accept it."

"But, how can they be after all this time? Stuart Drakston hasn't set his feet inside our house in eighteen months or more. When do they see one another? No, I won't go along with the idea of their being in love. Nor will I ever. Jane Anne's settled now in her studies. She wants to teach. That's her desire—not Stuart Drakston!"

Luke might have told Eliza that Stuart no longer came to Green Sea because of her hostility toward him, but being Luke he didn't. Instead, he merely shook his head and turned his eyes back upon the road.

However, after patiently letting a long moment of silence pass, he did tell her, "You think she has no desire for Stuart Drakston, dear, because it's what you want to think. You're closing your eyes to what happens to be a normal functional emotion which each and every single individual meet with, our daughter being no exception, and I, for one, thank God for that. It's true, they see one another very little and no doubt this very fact has increased in their love and desire for one another, rather than diminish it. When it comes to separating them, the distance between them hasn't solved one thing." "You sound so positive about this." Eliza said.

"I sound that way because it's fact and I'm doing my best to make you see it, too," Luke came back somewhat forceful. "Kitten talked to me at length about her and Stuart's love for one another and their desire to marry when she was home at Christmas time. Don't think for one moment that Stuart Drakston has given up the notion of making her his wife. He's more determined than ever. She told me so."

"Well, if that's the case, why hasn't he been able to persuade her then," Eliza suddenly exploded with a vehemence in her voice that near made Luke jump, "I can tell you why. It's like I just pointed out. She doesn't have any desire to be his wife!"

Despite his ever self-control and his all overwhelming love for Eliza, Luke's patience with her started pitching violently—which indeed happened to be a first occurrence with him where the matter applied to Eliza herself. Instead of raging back at her though, he gripped the reins in his hands that much harder, letting them be the outlet for his emotion until he thought he had conquered it.

Finally, endeavoring to get his point across to her once more, he said, "She hasn't given in and married him not because she doesn't desire to, but because of her intense devotion for us all, you, me, and Stuart. She wants us to be a family together, bound by affection and regard for one another, rather than one separated by discord and contention. You know well enough how gentle her nature is. It's just not in her to openly oppose anyone, much less you or me, no matter how much she loves him…"

"All the more reason why I can't bear to see her marry a Drakston." Eliza interrupted.

Luke's eyes left the road once again, falling on Eliza in contemplation. He was well aware that he might have used the word "revenge". But, for fear of bringing up the one subject that he himself could hardly bear to think about much less discuss with Eliza—Frank's rape of her—he recoiled at the thought of saying the word. Even so, he was almost certain that Stuart Drakston was, innocently, having to bear the brunt of his wife's hostility towards him for no other cause but those long ago loud, shabby deeds of his late father.

The mere thought of it put an unpleasant taste in Luke's mouth. He felt helpless, almost sicken—actually near loathing himself for not having the courage and self-preservation to go ahead and dig further into the matter to see if, indeed, he was not on the right track about his wife's behavior.

None the less, he turned his head back to the road and went on with what he was saying before Eliza had interrupted him, "She assured me she has no thoughts of eloping with Stuart. Above everything else, she wants to win your approval, so they can be married at Green Sea in a home wedding, like we were. She thinks if she continues her schooling and does as well in the future as she has been doing, that you will give in and give them your blessings..." Luke paused, hoping that part of what he had said had gotten to Eliza, and he would be hearing a favorable response from her for a change. But, when sometime passed and Eliza had yet to speak, he further added, his displeasure over the entire matter plainly coming through, "I suppose, come to think of it, there's more to Martha's theory about this whole mess than I ever realized."

To Luke's surprise Eliza still made no comment, and they rode on for some few minutes more before she did speak, surprising him all the more by sweeping aside the topic of their conversation as though it never existed, telling him, "I'm so sorry, Luke, for having stormed at you back there, please try to forget it. I guess my black mood today has about gotten the better of me."

Turning to look at her again and meeting with the troubled depths of her lonely violet eyes as she turned to him, Luke became more distressed.

"'I'm sorry, darling, I didn't know," he quickly said. "Don't you feel well?"

"No need for you to worry, Luke. It's only a mood, it'll pass," she replied, and edged closer to his side, with nothing concerning her problem in the matter of their daughter's love for Stuart Drakston being brought out in the open and settled upon as they rode on home sitting closely together.

Although staring at people was far from being a common trait in Luke's nature, he feared that was precisely the impression of himself that he was giving John and Rachelle Fillmore-Lee. Because the longer Luke sat opposite Beth Anne's parents in the open carriage as it rolled on toward Green Sea, the harder it became for him not to stare and stare hard. Especially in the case of the middle-age, grey-bearded man whose mind seemed to be so far separated from those of whom he was in company with, not to mention the social intercourse flying back and forth. Despite the man's seemingly remoteness; however, Luke observed, he was still managing, somehow, to contribute a fair amount of responses and replies to the conversation taking place; and very cultured, polished rejoins at that! Luke wondered how he did it. For not only did John Fillmore-Lee seem remote and apart from those around him, he also gave every appearance of wanting to be anywhere except where he was at, actually shrinking within himself. And, it was Luke's opinion that was growing worse with every additional mile that brought them closer to Green Sea.

It was obvious John-Fillmore-Lee was very much ill at ease, which made Luke wonder if it were because of what his daughter had revealed about him when she had made her first visit to Green Sea. Luke decided that in all probability that must be his trouble and, immediately, strived harder to be more open and affable so that his male guest might gain more confidence in himself.

Luke soon saw; however, that he might as well have saved himself the effort. For it was clearly manifested in John Fillmore-Lee's behavior the only element of comfort he was experiencing, was the seemingly reassuring protection that he appeared to seek and obtain from the woman who sat beside him. He seemed to want to keep himself as closely to her side as possible, as a matter of fact, making it look as if he might constantly hang upon his wife's skirts. He kept one arm linked through one of hers, gripping her hand, while his other arm stayed in an almost inert position by his side—his hand and withered arm resting on his knee.

Though she did look to be on the fragile side some-what; and, certainly, conveyed the fact that she had indeed extended her strength a little too far—obviously overtired and in need of rest and possibly a nap, Luke still thought that Rachelle Fillmore-Lee was a rather comely looking woman despite these detriments. With a flower petal softness remaining to cling to her well-proportioned features, Luke decided she must have been a very pretty woman in her youth; and also, concluded that what evidently had been a great help in making her prettiness endure—still come through and shine so—was her Open warmth which promptly came through, to others effectively easiness that seemed as gentle and soothing as soft rain drops. Certainly, this was the case as far as Rachelle Fillmore-Lee's husband was concerned. It was plain to be seen the—presence of the woman was the mainstay for which John Fillmore-Lee's state of confidence depended.

In this spring of 1886, the Heyward's had finally seen their way clear to purchase their first open-carriage, and Luke now was glad he had told Charlie to hitch the carriage horses to the new carriage that morning, rather than hitching them to the older enclosed coach which they were still using for most their travels; that is, when they did not travel by buggy. For the bright spring day had quickly turned to summer in April. And, what made it seem like a summer day all the more, every little while, faint rolls of thunder had started rumbling in the distant horizons. Luke was not too concerned about the thunder though. He was sure if there were a summer-like storm in the making, he would have his guests safely ensconced within the walls of Green Sea long before it commenced. He was more concerned about keeping his promise to Bruce to look in on the latter's favorite Jersey milk cow again that afternoon. The cow had taken ill earlier that week and, even though Luke was sure he had her on the mend, he had promised Bruce that just as quickly as he could fetch his guests to Green Sea and bid them his regrets for having to leave he would set out for Oak Grove.

The truth of the matter, having tried to reach John Fillmore-Lee and feeling that he had failed, Luke, though he did feel for the sick cow, was sort of taking a little comfort by this time—from the fact that he had something else to do for the remainder of the day besides keep the company of his strange behaving male guest.

Apart from the man's remoteness and Luke's urge to want to stare at him, there was also a pervading uncanniness connected with the meeting, which had Luke much baffled anyway; and what made it all the more baffling was the fact that he was at a complete loss to identify it—something amiss from the normal run of meeting someone for the first time. It crowded Luke, made him feel uncomfortable, and he had felt that way from the moment his hand had met John Fillmore-Lee's at the train depot. But, with being forced to mind his manners since besides the older gentleman there were others in the party from Lexington to greet and bestow his compliments upon also, his son Carr among them, Luke had pushed the feeling off and tried to forget it.

Even so, once Luke had seen that Charlie had gathered all the luggage and put it aboard the carriage and he himself and all the rest had gotten settled down in their seats—with himself, Carr, and, Beth Anne sitting on one seat and Beth Anne's parents sitting on the opposite seat facing them, not only did the same eerie feeling come rushing back to Luke with a driving force, but he also found he was hardly able to keep his eyes off John Fillmore-Lee's face.

Though Luke thought he had experienced the ultimate in astonishment the day he had met Beth Anne—having later convinced himself that the startling resemblance between her and Eliza was merely a coincidence, this meeting with her father, in other respects, was beginning to be every much as disturbing to him.

Trying to be as discreet as possible, Luke cut his eye at John Fillmore-Lee once again, his sidelong look keenly scrutinizing, and, suddenly, like a flash, the luring attraction was finally revealed—the eyes! The man's eyes were identical to Eliza's. The same externals, size and shape. The same violet-blue depths—Carson eyes!

Carson eyes? Now, was that business starting all over again? It had been puzzling enough to have Carr's fiancée emerge on the scene one day, looking in every respect almost like his own mother—give or take a few years, but to see that her father had also been endowed with this same unique Carson feature was quite a load for the mind to go about trying to make sense out of, thought Luke, feeling a quiver tingle along his spine and mystified as to why it was there.

But, by this time; however, the carriage had reached the meadow field, and, all of a sudden, Beth Anne was giving a delightful little squeal at spotting the aged Bullitt, turning Luke's attention to her as she said, "Oh look, Carr, there's your mother's stallion, looking trim as ever."

Carr laughed, "Fat as ever, darling, not trim."

"Oh, you would," Beth Anne scoffed, pretending put out with Carr as she shaded her eyes with her hand and continued to gaze on across the field, chirping instead to her father, "Papa, look. He's the big black stallion, standing near the big magnolia tree over yonder. He must be getting close to thirty years old. Mr. Heyward brought him all the way from Virginia to Carr's mother before they were married. He was Mr. Heyward's first present to her."

"You don't say!" Smiled John, appearing to be more alert—Luke observed—then he had been since stepping off the train in Charleston, going on to add, as he and Rachelle both turned to look across the meadow, "And, as far as I can tell from here, he's still a fine looking stallion, too, despite your future husband's lash against him."

"Oh, he is, Papa, and so gentle," gushed Beth Anne. "All one has to do to get him to come running straight to them, is stand by the meadow fence with an open palm and call his name."

"What special significance does the open palm express to him?" John questioned.

"Oh, I forgot that part," giggled Beth Anne. "It means sugar cubes to him, Papa. Every time he sees an open palm extended toward him, he thinks he's going to get a handful of sugar cubes."

"And, believe me, he's gotten his share, too." Carr put in. "Through a prankish accident a long time ago, in fact before I was born, he became permanently winded, near ran himself to death. Even since then Mother's babied him something awful, spoiled him rotten and Papa will vouch for that, won't you, Papa? Papa—?"

"Uh—what's that—oh—yes, son, I'll say she has," Luke finally replied, hoping his response—if not completely by what Carr had expected, was not too far off base. For John's remark about Bullitt had taken Luke far back, clear to his first meeting with Philippe Carson when the latter, had, virtually, made the same remark. It started Luke, and, instantly, brought his gaze focusing straight as an arrow upon the man who had phrased it now. There was no eye cutting with Luke this time. Further, if his spine tingled, he wasn't aware of it because as he took, in John Fillmore-Lee's appearance from head to foot, he became too numbed to feel or think of anything but the one name pounding again and again through his head—Philippe Carson! Philippe Carson!

Then, suddenly, like a river—running wild, a surge of questions came racing at Luke, awaking his senses to the occasion once more as he asked himself, could it be possible that this withdrawn, handicapped and prematurely-aged gentleman and the handsome, mirth loving Phil Carson he had known were one and the same person? Was there a possibility that this man's tragically mental elapse had robbed him of his true identity, that being no other than Phil Carson himself in the living flesh, all those years? Wait Luke, not so fast, hold your horses! This man really has no perfect likeness to the Phil

Carson you know. No, that wasn't quite true. One couldn't dismiss those Carson eyes. Further, if John Fillmore-Lee were to part with some of his beard, maybe there would be more of Phil Carson under it to see than what was presently meeting his eye. Had a badly scarred face prompted John Fillmore-Lee to wear a full beard, or did he adhere to the practice because it was fairly fashionable to do so, though he himself had refrained from growing One on the account of Eliza. She didn't go for beards. A trim mustache, yes. But no beard, said a beard reminded her of Abe Lincoln too much! At any rate, he must remember the Phil he had known had not even sported a mustache, let alone a full beard. Yet, he must also keep in mind that one's likes and dislikes did change over the years. Moreover, one's looks did too. His own included. It had been going on twenty-four years since he last saw Phil Carson. Thus, even if there were no beard, Phil's features certainly would have altered from what they had been in his early twenties. In no way, should he expect to see the same youthful, animated Phil of those days; that is, if he were indeed looking at Phil Carson, which, of course, he believed he was!

Well, there was the house. And, there was Eliza standing on the porch, too. Now was no time to try to make sense out of these questions. But he would. One way or another, he meant to get to the bottom of this baffling matter before those people took their leave of Green Sea. He'd go slow though, make certain his steps were cautious. For besides his wife to consider, there was also Matthew Carson to think about. Under no circumstances would he want to heedlessly alarm Eliza's father, especially at his advanced age. Trying to give the impression that his nerves were not only perfectly calm but his mind had been totally thought-free besides, except, of course, for listening to the yackety-yak still going on between Beth Anne and Carr about Bullitt, Luke said, "Well, here we are folks," wondering as he did if there would be any reaction from Eliza when she saw John Fillmore-Lee's face.

"'And, there's Mother!" Carr suddenly joined in and swinging the carriage door open he sailed out and made a grab for Eliza even before Charlie managed to bring the wheels to a standstill at the bottom of the steps.

Never mind that he had brought his and his future bride's prattle to an abrupt end, and had left her to sit where she was at or descend on someone else's arm, which turned out to be his father's, he was greeting his mother!

Even so, Beth Anne seemed to not be put out with Carr's impulsiveness in the least.

She was wearing a broad smile for him as he turned and made it back to her side and took the introductory proprieties upon himself, leaving Luke hard put not to show his astonishment when Eliza scarcely spared a single glimpse at John Fillmore-Lee's face as she gave him her hand.

However, noting that his wife was being most attentive to both, Beth Anne and Rachelle, welcoming each with a most warm and lovely greeting, Luke on second thought and with a bit of amusement at that, decided that it must have been John's full beard—though neat it was—that had induced his wife to short-change him a full look upon acknowledging his acquaintance!

At all events, she smilingly continued to hold both Rachelle's hands as she went on to tell her, while everybody remained standing where Charlie had deposited them, "I feel, Mrs. Fillmore-Lee, as though our meeting really isn't a first meeting at all. Now that it's finally happened, it seems like I've known you far longer than the duration of these last few minutes."

Rachelle smiled back, candidly expressing her own feelings since she sensed Eliza was indeed sincere, "I feel likewise, and I must admit it's no wonder, because not only have I had the Heyward family in my thoughts a lot these past months, I've wanted to make a visit to this lovely place from the first moment I heard the name, Green Sea. This was especially so after Beth Anne came back and shared the delights of her visit here with us. But, from this moment on, while we're here or otherwise, it's just John and Rachelle Fillmore-Lee is too long and formal and much too awkward sounding for one to have to repeat more than once."

Eliza's laugh was easy and free.

"Very well and we're Luke and Eliza," she said. "Now, let's everybody go on inside where I trust it'll be more pleasant weather-wise. It's turned out to be more like July today than a spring day in April. I have refreshments all ready and waiting in the parlor."

"Great!" Carr grinned. Sure hope it's lemonade, Mother, and that you had a hand in making it, I think I could drink a gallon!"

His son's animated levity made Luke feel good. He smiled, "I agree your mother does make good lemonade, son, but if I keep my appointment at Oak Grove to look in on Bruce's milk cow again, I fear it'll only be one glass for me, this time." He turned, calling out to Charlie, who had just finished setting the last of the baggage on the porch and was crawling back up upon the carriage, "Charlie, would you ready the newer buggy and bring it around front in a few minutes."

"As good as done, Mister Luke," Charlie called back and then chucked to the horses to move on.

"Oh, Luke, do you have to leave so soon?" Eliza cried.

"If I get there and back before suppertime, dear," said Luke. "The sooner I leave, too, the less chance I think I'll have in meeting with a storm, possibly, on my way back, for it's my guess one's going to visit us by late evening, if not before. So, it looks as though, for the time being, I must leave the whole of entertaining these good people in your and Carr's hands. I trust they'll understand and excuse my absence."

"Of course we will," said Rachelle. Carr's already made us well aware how much you're depended on in these parts for your veterinary service, and also the possibility of your being called away at any given time, too, so don't give a thought to us regardless of how often you must be elsewhere while we're here."

"I should say not," John quickly put in and then seeming as though he had suddenly caught some of Carr's lighter spirit, he flashed a smile and went on, "The fact is, after we all appease our thirst, I was going to make a suggestion that we turn the parlor over to the younger set, anyway. My wife should lie down for a while, and if nobody has any objection, I thought while she's resting, I might go for a walk, stretch my legs a bit from that long train ride."

"I know what you mean," said Luke. "The confinements of traveling can get to be pretty tiring on one's legs. Of course, feel free to walk or go anywhere you wish to. I'd love to join you and would, if l didn't have to leave for Oak Grove."

"That's all right. I'll make it a point not to get out of sight of the house. That way, I shouldn't get lost," laughed John, with all the others joining in, too.

Then, Eliza was saying to Rachelle, "Rachelle, if you'd prefer to go ahead and lie down now, I could have refreshments sent up to your room. Everything is already seen to, no inconvenience at all. Bessie will soon have the luggage inside, too." She smiled at Beth Anne. "Your room is also ready, dear, the same one you occupied before, just ahead at the top of the staircase, in case you want to freshen up a bit."

Trailing her daughter's beaming thanks to Eliza, Rachelle said, "Oh, no, I'll take refreshments with everybody else in the parlor. I'd like to visit a little while first, then I'll rest, though it's so thoughtful of you to suggest it."

"Well let's everybody move on inside," Eliza chuckled, or Luke could very well get into that storm that he thinks is on its way, even before he starts out. I declare, anymore, it seems as though he stays about as busy doctoring the animals of this neighborhood as Doctor Seth Roalf does doctoring its people."

Suddenly pausing on the last doorstep, Rachelle asked, her eyes widening in quizzical interest, "Did you say Doctor Seth Roalf? Doctor Seth Roalf who's originally from Virginia?"

Pausing her step also, Eliza replied, "Why, yes, are you acquainted with him?" Thoughts of the war which had turn families, neighbors, and friends apart flashing through her mind, Rachelle instinctively hesitated, but only briefly.

"A long time ago," she said as she went on up the steps." It was during the war when I was doing volunteer work as a nurse. Little would one expect our paths to run together again, and especially after all this time. All things considered, I suppose our world isn't as large a place as it seems to us sometimes."

Thinking about how he had come face to face with both Tom Green and Rebecca Wainwright after he had had no hopes of ever seeing either again, Luke said, "I should hope not, dear. A number of times, I've had friends whom I never expected to see any more, walk right back into my life." And, as he motioned John to proceed him through the doorway, Luke was telling himself that he was almost certain it was happening again, at that very minute.

In less than an hour, the parlor had been cleared of all its occupants, excluding, of course, the beaming couple who still sat beside one another on the sofa—directly beneath the smiling portrait of Anne Carson—sipping lemonade and continuing to munch on the various types of dainty sweet cakes, cheese canapés, and the chicken salad sandwiches that remained setting before them in their silver containers on the parlor's center table.

Luke, his unnerving thoughts still nagging his every move, was rapidly closing the distance between himself and his destination, Oak Grove.

Rachelle, having finally shed her traveling attire for the more restful comforts of her lawn dressing gown, as she and John had whispered a few excited remarks to one another about this taxing and overwhelming adventure they were experiencing before he had slipped through the door, had at last succumbed to her long-needed nap despite all her will to stay awake.

To be sure, Rachelle had begrudged her strength every minute that it was taking to reinvigorate it. Too many exciting things abounded for one moment to be relinquished to sleep. Besides wanting to stay wide awake so she could keep on trying to make sense out of all the upheaval—past and present—erupting around her, Rachelle had also wanted to keep a wakeful mind so she could savor her old friend and beau, Doctor Seth Roalf once again. Wondering what their meeting would be like, an endless stream of questions had raced through Rachelle's mind even as sleep was claiming her. Would Seth recognize her? Would she recognize him? And, what about the woman who'd be on Seth's arm the woman whom her beloved John had been engaged to? What would be John's reaction to this woman? Would he remember her? And, how would Caroline Roalf react to John? Questions and faces too, all whirling so rapidly around Rachelle that suddenly, there had not been a single distinguishable face as she, faces, questions and all sank into oblivion together.

After seeing to the comfort of her guests, Eliza had excused herself and gone on to more endless tasks that were forever awaiting her supervision and final word; for instance, had "Miss Eliza" decided on the dessert yet? Which of the two cakes would they be serving for supper that night—the caramel laced with pecans, or should they go ahead and prepare the strawberries and whipped cream for the sponge cake?

"I think not, Pete," Eliza replied, looking up from a hamper of fresh-picked strawberries setting before her to gaze through the kitchen window as a louder roar of thunder seemed to have boomed at no great distance from them. Momentarily; though, she was looking at the strawberries again and going on, "Let's have the caramel and lemon meringue pie tonight and save these for tomorrow night when Father will be dining with us. He loves strawberry shortcake. Those need to ripen a little more, anyway."

"That's what I thought too, Miss Eliza," said Pete. "Now, about this ham, here?" And, the questions or the seeking of Eliza's approval continued on until Pete had, once again, checked over each and every dish that was to be served that night with her.

The thunder continued to roar louder, too, and although the peels did penetrate John's ears, unlike Eliza and most everybody else, he totally disregarded them. Having stuck his head into the parlor to say a word or two to Beth Anne and Carr on his way out to take his walk, John had even gone so far as to shrug of Beth Anne's warning, that he had better stick close to a shelter, with a little laugh. Indeed, ironic as it was taking into account the all absorbing and heart-rending experience which was to be John 's before the day ended, as he had laughed off his daughter's warning remark he had told himself that maybe something like being caught out in a thunderstorm just might be the sort of thing he needed—that maybe the lash of a violent downpour would have some effect on all those obscured, amorphic thoughts in his head, which seemed to be holding him in a near stupor—help clear his mind a bit!

Granted, nobody was any more cognizant of John's distant and aberrant behavior that day than John himself. He knew the image he was projecting of himself was way from being anything impressive, to say the least. Even so, no matter how hard he tried to bring forth a fraction of his lighter nature, not only did he feel his endeavor, most often, fell flat; but he also found that when it came to trying to temper his disposition to something of a more desirable nature, he might as well have saved himself the effort. In truth, John was a tortured man. Moreover, as he had been on the morning he had hesitated in facing Gilford Sloan after the latter's return from South Carolina, John, to a certain degree, was irritated with himself, too. And further, having stopped in the hallway to gaze up at the handsome young man in the portrait, whom Gilford Sloan had tried to pound in John's head was no other than John's own likeness staring back at him, had only added to his torment rather than abate it. Thus, trying to dismiss the thought that his appearance might once have been the likes of all that youthful handsomeness, John had turned his back on the portrait and forcing a smile he did not feel had donned his nonchalant air. All the same, when he laughingly said to Beth Anne, "What's a little rain? Besides, the suit's about done for anyway," he knew that starting Out to take a walk under heavy roar of a thunderstorm making up was nothing less than foolhardy if not downright stupid, and especially in a case where one had no idea where one was headed to!

Nevertheless, despite another long roll of thunder booming in the rapidly darkening clouds directly overhead, to say nothing of the fact that he was feeling almost as helpless and vulnerable as he had on the day he had awakened lost and frightened in a Washington, D.C., Union Hospital, John strode on out the door and down the steps.

Now, having hit the yard, John stopped and looked about him. Then, as his gaze came to the long line oak canopied avenue, resting upon it, he knew that was the place he wanted to head to first, telling himself as his feet strode forward that Rachelle understood his actions if the others didn't. She knew he needed to be alone for a while, with only his thoughts for company. Whether it was woman's intuition or what he didn't know, but he thought it was simply miraculous how quickly Rachelle could grasp his feelings—see into the ulterior motive inducing his behavior and understood it, no matter what. As a matter of fact, had it not been for Rachelle's quick, steady hand, he thought he would have gone sailing right out the carriage, running straight for the live oaks lining the avenue when he first spied them.

Yes, the oak-lined avenue did appear to be the same one he saw in his dreams and the same one he visioned in his mind. But, the newly built mansion with its eight Doric columns and simple, sleek lines setting on the knoll at the end of the avenue in place of the tall colonnaded mansion he dreamed about and was able to recall, seemed to diminish even this little bit of realism the place held for him. Still, he wanted to walk down the avenue, sort of test his thoughts among the live oaks, he supposed. Or could it be that he merely wanted to bask in the one small thing, that from all appearances did indeed link him to a part of his life which, for long years, he had been unable to identify himself with? He reckoned that must be it—why he was willing to brave thunder, lightning, or anything else just to be able to finally touch these century-old trees and feel the realness of their presence.

Yet; in truth, did the live oaks actually impart any real meaning to him? In all honesty, he thought not; and also thought nothing would change if he were to stand and let his hand caress their gnarled, leather-like trunks for the remainder of the time he spent in South Carolina. The truth of the matter, from the instant his eyes had swept over the train depot in Charleston, his thoughts had become so warped and confused that he was sure he would have been far better off if Sloan's drumming sessions had never taken place. To be told he was Philippe Carson was one thing, but trying to bring himself to think it, let alone accept it, was quite another. Furthermore, if Eliza Heyward's behavior toward him meant anything, it was absurd for one to think he was her brother, anyhow. It was plain as day there had not been one fraction of affinity in their meeting. In fact, she had actually shrunk from him. No question about it. To a degree, so had her husband, though he would have to admit that Luke Heyward tried and did meet the traditional conventions of making him welcome until he had taken his departure.

If Rachelle had noticed Eliza Heyward's withdrawal of him, she had failed to mention it in the few minutes they were alone. He wondered why? The reason he had hesitated in broaching the matter to Rachelle was simply because it was his opinion she had had enough to fret over lately, particularly today, for him to go drawing her attention to that, too. At any rate she and Eliza Heyward had appeared to hit it off, immediately. Maybe hearing that Doctor Seth Roalf was now residing here in Carolina and had been for several years and was not only the Heyward's family doctor but the husband of the girl he himself was supposed to have been engaged to, had had more effect on Rachelle than she had been willing to reveal, absorbing her thoughts so that Eliza Heyward's coolness toward him had passed her notice altogether. Come John. Your thoughts are making it appear that you might be a little jealous of the doctor! Well, maybe he was! Because if there was any one thing he could recall to mind, it was how Doctor Seth Roalf's eyes had hang upon Rachelle during that horrible time he had lain almost helpless under the doctor's care in that Union Hospital.

Well, whatever the case was with himself regarding the doctor's long ago infatuation for Rachelle, there was one thing for certain since it appeared he and Rachelle were destined to meet the doctor again and also his wife and soon at that, his own, supposedly, long ago relationship with Caroline Wilton Roalf shouldn't make Doctor Seth Roalf uncomfortable in the least, because he could not remember one solitary thing about her nothing—absolutely nothing!

All of a sudden, John's hand was falling away from where he had it resting on the old, rugged live oak and, instinctively, sliding into his trouser pocket. Odd though it was, his mind had started going back to things he could remember, the night he discovered he loved Rachelle Fillmore and found that his love was returned, the day their beloved daughter was born, his move to Lexington, Virginia, his meeting with Gilford Sloan and their struggle to make the Pacesetter a success—all this—began to absorb his thoughts So that he was hardly aware he had turned back toward the mansion, much less the ground his feet began to cover.

Retracing his steps back up the oak-lined avenue and then down the lane that joined it leading to the stables and on alongside the other outer buildings, including the old abandoned slave cabins where he hit a wagon road that led him through the orchard and on to the fields beyond, John never once tried to place or recall again any one person or any one thing that was connected with Green Sea Plantation. It were as if he had separated himself entirely from where he walked at, seeing none of those outbuildings that he had passed, the grounds, or anything else, conscious of nothing at all save that which was real to him—Lexington and all that which was symbolic of it; its people and the lasting friends he had made there; his newspaper business; and last but not least the small, comfortable estate that he called home and shared with his beloved wife and daughter.

On and on John walked, his head down, his mind finding relief for the first time that day as it dwelled on things that required no mental guesswork of any kind—undoubtful facts that were full of true meaning. Not something that he could only see or grasp through a sense of intangibility or the telling of someone else.

Still wrapped in his newfound mental ease and revealing in its comfort, John had given not one thought to his whereabouts—even though green corn shoots were rippling all about him—until a sudden splashing of raindrops brought his head up to see, that he not only had deposited himself in a vast cornfield but had also laid himself open to one of the heaviest down-pouring clouds he had ever seen whipping rapidly across the field straight in his direction; and not one single thing in his sight to take cover under!

Suddenly becoming panicky, along with being much repelled with himself, too, for his lack Of regard as to the weather conditions because it was not missing his farsightedness that he had now surely put himself in a position that was going to make him look like a fool in the eye of the Heyward's—if he hadn't already—John whirled around, frantically looking in the other direction in hopes of seeing something that might, to some extent, protect him from becoming drenched to the skin of his body. He saw it; and even though his sighting of it had given him another start, John still, driven by one's natural instinct to shield oneself, found himself bolting in its direction—a tall massive tomb setting under the spreading branches of a huge elm tree!

Running hard across the cornfield, John soon cleared it for, surprising to him again, the tomb was not too far from where he had been walking at. Jumping the low border of boxwoods which enclosed the cemetery and separated it from the fields that surrounded it, he dashed on across the sloping embankment that lay between the boxwoods and the tomb, seeing as he reached the tomb and crouched himself down beside it against the lashing storm that had already caught up with him, that he had missed sighting the other overlarge tomb that was erected right beside the taller one. The taller tomb had hidden it from his view.

Of course, because of Gilford Sloan's disclosures, John was instantly aware of whose family burial ground he had stumbled upon and whose tombs he was taking refuge near those of the late Anne Carson and Captain Nathan Carson, his mother and only brother. Even so, the discovery stirred him little. Actually, saving the fact of being reminded that none are immortal, which did lock his heart in despair for a moment, he experienced no emotion at all. The truth was, other than being grateful for what little protection the tombs and the leafed out elm tree were providing him with, John's mind was far more occupied with the storm and its fury and what Rachelle must be thinking—knowing nothing of his whereabouts—than it was with his surroundings.

Pulling the collar of his lightweight summer suit higher up around his neck as he crouched lower against the cool, wet granite, his cheek pressing it tightly, John was sure he had never witnessed a thunderstorm that had met the volcanic violence of the one raging around him. Hardly one or two minutes had passed before the force of its furor seemed to be shaking the earth under him. In fact, with the never-ending continuous roar of booming thunder and flashing lightning cracking all about him and streaking the darker heavens above him with long trails of cracking fire, it was no wonder that John began to feel as if he were sitting on the rim of an active volcano that, any second, might open its fiery insides upon him.

Thus, as he continued to observe the storm's violent intensity, doubting not that he was caught in the very center of its eye since it seemed to be bearing down harder and from all appearances looked as though it was going to be sometime before it abated, John suddenly thought of moving on—abandoning his perilous, water-soaked shelter altogether and try making it on to the house. Observing that he was rapidly becoming dripping wet, anyhow, in spite of all his effort to prevent it, he decided that when it came to dryness, or, as for that matter, being on the safe side either, he would be none the worse for his decision. In addition, there was his mounting anxiety regarding Rachelle. He wanted to quiet those fears of hers, that he knew without a doubt she was harboring, as quickly as possible even if he did realize that he was going to look no less inelegant than a dejected, mournful-looking wet mongrel when he did reappear.

Promptly, knowing he had no way in helping matters; though and also hoping that everyone would focus their attention more on the circumstance of his predicament than his making Of it or his appearance when they did see him, John, weighing his decision no longer, started to rise. Suddenly; however, in one split second, he had felt as though he had no feet to rise on. Moreover, his thoughts were with him no longer. For an ear-deafening bolt of lightning had him reeling in a blazing, cracking inferno where for, only an instant, he was aware of nothing but a vague smell of brimstone and shattering sound of a tree splitting open! Then, he was plunging into an unfeeling, blank darkness which was void of everything.

Meanwhile, back at the house; in fact, at the same time that the beautiful elm tree overhanging Anne and Nat Carson's graves was falling in its destruction from lightning—the shock of the blast rendering John out cold—Rachelle was hastily descending the stairway. Having awakened to the rage of the thunderstorm to see that John was still gone and also seeing no sign of his returning to their room, either while she had slept, Rachelle wasted no time for dressing. Still wearing her dressing gown, she raced for the staircase, hoping to find John downstairs; but, at the same time, a deep fear within her telling her that she wouldn't.

Now, seeing Beth Anne and Carr both peering anxiously through the inset of etched glass panes on either side of the front door and John nowhere in sight, Rachelle's fear deepened, the severity of its force plainly showing in the way her hand gripped onto her dressing gown at the throat as she called to her daughter from the stairs, inquiring of her, "Beth Anne, did your father return from his walk? Is he in the parlor?"

Beth Anne turned from the door, her eyes telling of her own fright as she said, "No, Mother, I haven't seen Papa since shortly after you retired for your nap."

Covering the last step of the stairs, Rachelle deplored, despite her effort not to, "But, that's been quite sometime ago, dear. Surely, you don't suppose he's out in..." She stopped, looking anxiously from her daughter to Carr, who had also turned away from the door upon hearing her voice.

Feeling somewhat like he was offering an excuse for something he had had no hand in addition to wondering why he felt that way because had someone asked him why he certainly would have been unable to have named anyone particular thing, Carr offered, "Maybe, Miss Rachelle, he's taking cover in some of the outer buildings." Suddenly, upon Carr's words and before Rachelle could reply, the hallway was gaining others in the household, Eliza and Bessie.

Bessie, who had been Eliza's chief mainstay for years regarding the household chores and especially since the mansion's completion, was rapidly making her descent from her final chore upstairs. Looking as though she was ready to clap both hands over her ears and start running, she made it to the first floor just as Eliza came rushing in from the kitchen and upon seeing Rachelle made an apology for her absence and, then added, "Let's all go back into the parlor and sit the storm out, you too, Bessie. But first, what's this about the outer buildings, Carr?"

"It's Mr. John, Mother," said Carr. "I was saying that maybe Mr. John had taken cover in one of the outer buildings. Miss Rachelle and Beth Anne are worried about him. They think that maybe he's been overtaken by the storm!"

"You mean he hasn't returned from his walk?" Eliza asked, feeling like she could grab something and give the man a whack over the head with it, if she could only get near him wherever he was, now that she had gotten a good look at Rachelle's face.

"No, Mrs. Heyward, he hasn't," Beth Anne put in. "The storm started raging so quickly, I'm afraid Papa didn't have much of a chance to reach shelter."

Eliza could see that John Fillmore-Lee's daughter was obviously distressed, too. Endeavoring to soothe her and Rachelle's fears also, she said, "That's the way it is with these thunderstorms sometimes, dear, but I'm sure your father's all right. He's probably taking shelter outside some place as Carr suggested."

She seriously doubted that he was though and, to save herself, could spare the man little pity, telling herself that John Fillmore-Lee deserved everything he was getting!

Making an attempt to get it across that she thought it was time they all go on inside the parlor and take their seats like she had suggested, without coming right out and saying so, since it was obvious nobody could now rescue a "dry" John Fillmore-Lee to say nothing of the fact that the storm was raging too hard to try, Eliza turned to proceed in the direction of the parlor. However, she suddenly felt herself being somewhat restrained by Bessie who was timidly tugging at her arm and murmuring, "Miss Eliza—Miss Eliza."

Halting and turning to Bessie, she said, "Yes, Bessie?"

Looking absolutely miserable, because she knew Eliza's nature inside out and was well aware that the Virginia gentlemen's behavior was getting to her, Bessie shyly volunteered, "Ma'am, the Misses there, her husband is under no shelter! Just before I com' downstairs, I looked through the window at the sto'm and seen him runnin' 'cross the cornfield towa'ds the cemete'y!"

"Good heavens! Are you sure it was him, Bessie?" Eliza pressed, the intake of Rachelle's breath pricking at her conscience in no small measure!

"'Yes ma'am, it wus him," said Bessie. 'Nobody but the gentlem'n from Vi 'ginia."

Though she wanted to openly defend John's actions—his urge to want to explore Green Sea's surroundings no sooner than he had hardly entered the house—Rachelle, ever true to her husband's wishes, refrained from doing so. Instead, she merely said, as she took on a look of helplessness, "Then, John is out there in that terrible storm."

Feeling that he should do something, or at least suggest doing something since he happened to be the only male member in the group, Carr promptly put in, "Miss Rachelle, if it'll make you feel better about Mr. John, ease your mind any at all, I'll dash to the stables and hitch up our other buggy and go see if I can find him."

Again, whatever she may have replied, Rachelle was prompted from stating it for Eliza was readily exclaiming, before Carr had hardly said the last word, "Goodness gracious, Carr, not out there, now, in all that thunder and lightning! Besides, you'll get drenched to your hide!"

"I'll be all right, Mother, I'll grab a topcoat from the coat-rack in the kitchen and make a dash from there," said Carr, feeling rather manly all of a sudden for coming up with the idea, not to mention his eagerness to get on with it in view of the fact that his betrothed or her mother had yet to get around to making a protest, or, as for that matter, voicing any other remark.

Nonetheless, as Carr started to dash on off down the hallway, Beth Anne suddenly shrieked, running after him, "Wait, Carr, I'm going with you!"

With his mother looking on in disbelief, having come to a nonplus as to what to do or say and while observing, too, that Beth Anne's outburst seemed to have surprised her son little, he turned back, saying, "No, darling, not this time. The weather's too rough. As Mother pointed out to me, you'd get drenched."

"I don't care about that, Carr, I'm going with you. Come on!" Beth Anne came back in no subdued tone of voice, grabbing hold of Carr's hand.

While Eliza still looked on, unable to believe what she was seeing or hearing and wishing that Luke were there, Carr, knowing that Beth Anne meant to do what she said gently pulled her hand from his and said, "Wait here at the front door, then. I'll bring the buggy around front and pick you up in a jiffy." He dashed off again with Beth Anne's cry of, "Hurry, Carr," ringing after him. Then, she turned and ran back to the front door, pasting her face against the etched-glass panel again and looking through it anxiously.

Finally, Rachelle got around to saying something, telling Beth Anne, "Dear, if you're determined to go with Carr, run and get your blue cape with the matching shawl. I packed both in case we had unfavorable weather. Drape the shawl over your head. Maybe it'll keep your hair from becoming too disheveled," surprising Eliza somewhat by going along with her daughter in what Eliza thought was nothing but headlong behavior.

Suddenly, seeing Beth Anne as the most courageous girl she had ever laid her eyes upon. The fact was, Bessie had become so impressed with Beth Anne's willingness to brave the storm that she wanted to assist and hastily went racing back up the stairway, shrieking out excitedly, "I'll git yo' cape an'shawl, Miss Beth Anne! I jist unpack 'em an' hung'em up, know jist where they be!"

And shortly, with Rachelle doing likewise beside the door's other glass panel, Eliza was occupying the same spot that Beth Anne had occupied and now vacated. All the same, as her gaze followed the jolting buggy vanishing down the drive through the lashing storm, her thoughts could not have been any more diverse from those that had whirled in Beth Anne's head when she stood there, than had she been performing on a flying trapeze. The fact of the matter, not only had Eliza begun to feel unconfident and put out she was thoroughly disgusted, too, at the turn of events, thinking to herself that when it came to punctuating a visit with the unexpected, that she was certain nobody on earth could match the Fillmore-Lee family!

Even so, she finally turned to Rachelle and said, as kindly as she could manage, "Rachelle, we might as well go on into the parlor and sit while we wait."

Chapter Five

Sprawled face up, John lay on the rain-soaked ground. He was alive! The bolt of lightning had not hit him, but the severity of the blast had shocked him into unconsciousness. The lightning's full charge had centered on the tall elm tree, splitting it straight down the middle in half! In fact, so precisely had the tree separated into the halves, it looked as though someone might have taken a saw to it and sawed it that way a bizarre, awing sight since in its crash to the ground the two halves had remained to stay separated. One half had fallen one way while the other half had gone another, falling directly over the graves of Anne and Nat Carson.

Although John was lying right direct in the path of the half that had fallen over the graves, by some miracle again, not one of the charred limbs had hit him. Though branches and limbs were dangling above and all about him, not one single one was lying directly upon him. The tombs had saved John; in that it was apparent the seared divided trunk would have taken his life in the fall had it not landed across the tall tombs, leaving him lying unharmed beneath it. Though he and the tombs alike were nearly hidden from view in all directions by the elm's leafed out foliage.

Even though by this time the storm had abated somewhat, it still remained to be rather prevalent. Along with the thunder continuing to roar and the lightning still flashing, the rain, too, continued to fall and had, by now, soaked John's clothing through and through—rendering his body no cozy sensations to be sure. Still, for all its discomfort, the penetrating cool wetness seeping through to his body and trickling into his face from the dripping wet branches above and around him, was doing John a great deal more good than harm. For, to a certain degree, it was helping his shocked nerves to revive—stimulating them, and before long they were sending messages that his senses started rallying to and he slowly, but surely, began to rise from that dark void into which he had plunged.

However, it was a very confused consciousness that John revived to. Aside from the excruciating pain that was throbbing in his head like a knife pricking in raw flesh and his awareness of lying in a bed of water with wet, soggy clothes clinging to his body—surrounded by a dripping wet treetop—he was totally unable to grasp anything about the incredulous predicament he found himself in, the reason for his being in such a strange circumstance, his whereabouts, or anything else.

Anxiety, coupled with the burning pain in his head sent John's heart flying a mile a minute and, for just a brief little while, all he did was lie in his painful, transfixed state and stare—staring in awe at the dripping wet treetop he was buried in. But, suddenly, as a peel of thunder boomed overhead and the sound of a faint cry came to him, simultaneously, from somewhere in the distance, the literal meaning of his circumstance zoomed through his head like an exploding rocket, freezing him in terror but clearing everything and making it real—too real—for he had gone plunging headlong into all the pain and the hell and the furor of Gettysburg!

Now, seized with the cold terror—a terror so frightening that it stopped him fast from recognizing the difference between the sound of thunder and that of exploding guns, or, as for that matter, having the logic to clearly reason out anything, John, thinking that some Yankee might be peering through the tree branches at him any minute with a plunging bayonet in hand, told himself he had to move and had to be more quiet. Yes, he was thinking, by venturing too close upon the enemy, he had almost done himself in this time. Moreover, considering the noise and the power of those damn shells—one had blown a treetop off and swept him up with it, had it not—no wonder the heavens had begun to weep since he had blacked out! All the same, he had no time for thinking about the enemy's artillery now, its efficiency or otherwise. He had to get a move on and be quick about it to boat! But oh, God! How his head did ache!

Still thinking he was back at Gettysburg and wondering how he was going to dodge the Yankees as well as their artillery shells and make it back to the lines of his own artillery guns without being taken prisoner, killed outright, or maybe blown to bits, John lifted his head somewhat and let his right hand come up from his side to assist himself in rising. Suddenly though, involuntarily, he became stock-still. Neither head or hand moved another fraction. Something else absorbed his whole attention—markings the years had left on his hand—flesh that was not that of a young man and, least of all, not that of the twenty-three-year-old Philippe Carson whom he had suddenly become in his mind and remembered! Philippe Carson! He thought, and his heart began to go even faster than the pounding beat it was already racing at as the name drummed over and over in his head, snuffing out all other sound in his ears.

After what seemed like the infinity of all time to John but, actually, was only a few brief seconds and while his eyes still stayed riveted upon his right hand, he brought himself on up to a setting position. He was consumed with belief and doubt, believing what he saw one second, doubting his eyes the next. But then, as his gaze made a quiet shift from right to left and all the naked infirmity of his other hand was suddenly revealed, that little vague suspicion which had begun to creep along his mind and which he found himself harboring so delicately for fear of its fading out, was instantly made as whole and solid as the earth he sat upon. For likewise to the thunder crash that had opened the gate to all the hell of Gettysburg, the sight of his impaired hand had begun swinging open a whole bulkhead of gates, bringing both past and present washing at him with all the impact of being swept over a waterfall in wild rapids! The wonder of it near took his breath! God Almighty! He was Philippe Carson! He was! Sloan had been right all along! He was no damn Yankee! He was no one but the real Philippe Carson in living flesh, heir to the Green Sea Plantation! Why, heavens and earth! He could remember every inch of it as clearly as though it were yesterday, how it had looked when he had left for the battlefields of Virginia!

But, wait a minute! What had really happened here? Why in the name of God was he in such a place as this, thinking he was back at Gettysburg fighting the war? He supposed trying to absorb everything all at once was a little too much for his aching head. He'd have to slow down. The thunder! There it was roaring again. It was the thunder!

Yes, it was all coming back. He'd been walking in the fields, trying to recall something of those long ago years when the storm had overtaken him, and he had run to the first thing he had seen to take cover. Then, just as he had thought of trying to make it on to the house and ease Rachelle's mind, the lightning had struck.

Christ! Between the tree and the lightning bolt, he was more than lucky to be alive! God had spared his life though. Not only that, He had given him his memory back by directing his feet toward this place. He reckoned like the severe shock and injury that had blocked it all out for him at Gettysburg, it had taken a shock of a similar kind to bring it back to him!

It was all so unbelievable though. Here he was back at Green Sea and to think not one living soul had recognized him, not even Eliza! Neither had Luke, after spending all that time with him. Had he really changed all that much? Yes, he reckoned he had, if his hands were any indication of what time and misfortune could bring to one. Misfortune that, in a sense, was his own doing. Him and his reconnaissance operation, that play the spy thing that had cost him "much. What a ness he had made of it. God! Everything was coming back so clearly. Why in the hell had he not seen to it that he could have been identified in case his luck ran out? Still, who would have thought that he would have forgotten who he was, least of all himself! His uniform had not been too far away; though. It carried his initiates and rank. Wonder what had happened to it? He guessed he would never know some of the answers, because his situation had sure been far from the normal run of things—definitely out of the pale.

He must get on a move, try to get out of those tree branches and make it on to the house. He wanted to tell Rachelle what had happened—wait! There was that cry again. Why, that was Pet! That had been her cry that he had heard a moment or two ago when he had come to and thought he was back at Gettysburg Christ! No wonder his head was splitting. She was looking for him. Considerably, the suddenness of so many things happening at one time, it was a marvel his head could take it all in much less hold together under the weight of it. Gettysburg itself was a big enough load to carry, all at once, besides having a million of other things running through his mind at the same time, not to mention those other battles too—battles like Antietam; Chancellorsville; Fredericksburg; and Bull Run. They were not in order, of course, but beating at him, nevertheless, Bull Run. Now, that was the one! Well, the one that had served him and Nat their first dish of warfare, anyway—the agony and the glory all dished up together, if he could be excused for using the word "glory" in conversation with war. In truth, in his opinion, a battlefield was an entirely inapt place for the word. All the same; however, he and Nat had really celebrated that victory. Nat—

Suddenly, the man who had called himself John Fillmore-Lee for twenty some odd years and who had now been able to the onto true identity Philippe Carson, looking back came to a stop as he turned his head towards the tombs. Peering through the tree branches and seeing Nat's name engraved on the rain-swept stone, he instantly became engulfed with grief, which only moments before that he had been incapable of feeling. Immediately, despite his elation over regaining his memory back, John plummeted into black despair and, physically, went into a nosedive as well.

With his nerves all in a flurry due to his startling excitement and suffering from severe shock, too, which the two combined already had him shaking like a leaf, he became much worse, shaking all the harder as a sob contracted in his throat. Then, all at once, his stomach began to roll and only, seconds later, it was doubling him over in a violent retch. Thus, small wonder it was that John was barely able to groan one word when, suddenly, he heard his daughter clawing at the tree branches above him and sobbing hysterically as she cried, Papa! Papa! Over and over!

The storm had almost spent itself by this time. The peels of thunder and flashes of lightning had let down considerably. Only occasionally now did the thunder roar and when it did it seemed to have moved miles away. The rain had also slackened—tempered to something like a slight drizzle. But, as far as Beth Anne was concerned—regarding appearance or otherwise—it could have been pouring hard as ever for all the difference it made to her.

From the moment Carr had picked Beth Anne up at the front steps with the buggy, the weather and her concern for her appearance, too, had gone zipping to the bottom of her worries. In fact, she might as well have saved Carr the bother of going to all the trouble to fetch the buggy in the first place, for all the good it had done when it came to protecting her from the elements. Further, the weather shields that he had fastened on the sides of the buggy had been wasted effort and time too. For no sooner than she had climbed up on the seat, the weather shield on her side had been unfastened and flung behind her as she had leaned halfway outside in the lashing storm, frantically looking all about for some sign of her father. And, she had remained in this same exposed position most all the way to the cemetery. To say her precarious position had taxed Carr, is coloring it some, even if she had gripped onto the guardrail that supported the buggy's top to help prevent herself from toppling out. As they moved along Carr had tried to coax her to pull herself back inside the buggy, but no amount of coaxing on his part had worked. He had pleaded with her, teased her, even had feigned annoyance with her, but she had held firm in her attitude, giving the impression that she was not hearing a word he was saying. Nonetheless, if her heedless attitude regarding her safety, to say nothing of the fact that she was becoming sopping wet, had troubled Carr plenty, the fright and alarm that she was soon to cause him made those things seem small in comparison.

Luckily, as they were approaching the cemetery, Carr spied the felled elm tree before Beth Anne did and spontaneously slowed the buggy some in fear of what they may find. For, still having seen nothing of her father, the instant she sighted the shattered tree, to Carr's startling amazement she gave a leap from the buggy and nearly landing on her face regained her balance and started running in that direction as fast as she could, tearing through the rain, the rivulets, and the mud puddles like a demon possessed; and losing the scarf on her head in the process. It slipped when she leaped from the buggy, and, gradually, kept sliding until it finally fell off, landing in the running rivulet that she went splashing through.

Petrified, and also relieved and thankful, too, to see that she had indeed made it and was still on her two feet, all Carr could do for the moment was sit and stare. But promptly; however, his fear of what she may encounter, once she reached the fallen tree, had him yelling at the top of his voice for her to stop and go no further.

Beth Anne paid no attention to his yells though. She kept right on running, making a beeline for the spot of destruction.

Now, deeply regretting that he had given in and brought her along, Carr hurried the buggy on a little way further and then throwing the reins aside, he, too, leaped out and started running, reaching her just as she had begun to claw at the tree branches. He pulled her back, saying, with somewhat shallow breath, "No, darling, I won't let you do this!"

"But, Papa's in there, Carr," she cried. "I heard him and I know he's hurt and needs help. Let me go!"

Suddenly, Carr could have cried himself—for joy that is—when John said, quite unsteadily, "Don't cry, dear, and do as Carr says, I'm alright."

"See there! Now, you calm down and stay put, I'll help your father," Carr told her, and breaking his hold on her he turned and quickly started pulling the branches apart to where John sat—still weak and nauseated, though he had stopped retching.

"Good Lord, Mr. John, what happened!" Carr exclaimed, as he hopped over a limb and gained John's side.

"A bolt of lightning almost got me, that's what," said John, his voice a little steadier. "Give me a hand, will you."

"Of course, sir, but are you able to start moving just yet?" Carr questioned, his eyes missing nothing about the scene. "Maybe you should wait a few more minutes."

"I think I can make it," replied John, his hand grasping hold of Carr's as he began to rise on rather weak feeling legs. "A moment ago, I'd had doubts."

Of course, once again, Beth Anne had not concerned herself with Carr's wishes or, for that matter, heeded to the words of her father, either. Also having scrambled over limbs and through the branches, too, she was right there to assist in helping her father rise to his feet and get Out of the shattered treetop. She was also still sniveling.

Now seeing the pallor above her father's bearded cheeks and taking in the wretched state of his person, Beth Anne cried between snivels, "You're not all right, Papa, you look awful!"

Trying not to give in to his shaky legs and go toppling back to the ground, John, putting on a bold front forced a smile and retorted back, "Of course, I look awful, but I have good cause to look this way. I wonder about you though. You look as if you might've discovered a swimming hole along the way and decided to jump in!"

Finally, as Beth Anne's eyes quickly went traveling down the front of her lightweight cape, which she had donned for the purpose of not only protecting herself but the pretty yellow lawn dress that she was wearing as well and which now along with the cape looked like a wet dishrag, it dawned on her for the first time how she must look. Even so, there was no comment from her. Most unusual for her, the only indication that she gave that showed she was aware and also in full agreement with what her father had said, was the faint smile she managed to send back to him as she lifted her hand to brush back a look of wet hair that was plastered across her face.

All the same, having inherited some of the same lighter spirit of the pained and grieved man before him, whom he had no idea was his own blooded uncle, Carr did comment, laughing, "Mr. John, if she'll be half as devoted to me through our lifetime as she is to you, I know I'm going to be one contented man!" With Beth Anne still saying nothing, only making a face at him, as he promptly turned to all seriousness going on, "Don't try walking, sir. I'll run and fetch the buggy up here. I'll be back in a jiffy."

As Carr turned away and went spurting back through the drizzling rain to get the buggy, John, pulling forth a rather soggy handkerchief from the pocket of his coat, said, "Here, darling, before your mother sees us, let's try to pull ourselves together a little. If there's any way to help it, we wouldn't want our tears heaping more distress upon her."

With her blithe spirit on the rise once again and while one hand reached for the handkerchief and her other moved to circle her father's waist, Beth Anne came back, "Yes, Papa, and while we wait for Carr you lean on me. I may look like I've been in a swimming hole, but I still haven't been blasted to the ground and buried in a treetop by lightning like you have!"

While Bessie had remained huddled nearby she was actually crouched down in the darkest corner of the living room that she could possibly find—Eliza and Rachelle had attempted to carry on a minimal of small talk, which neither had barely heard much less had their minds on. Now, while they both made an attempt to gain a hold upon the lull that had permeated their conversation from the beginning, finally almost dissipating it into nothing at all, the sound of a buggy squeaking brought their effort at words to an abrupt stop as their heads turned from the other in the direction of the front door.

Barely audible, more like a whisper, Rachelle was the first to speak, saying, as she began to slowly rise from her chair, I do believe they're on their way back, Eliza. I So hope they've found John and that he's all right."

As anxious about her son, and for that matter to see Luke returning too, as Rachelle was for her husband, Eliza, already out of her own chair and rushing from the room before Rachelle's last word had fallen, said, "Well, let's find out," reaching the front door and flinging it aside to gaze intently at the buggy as it rounded the drive and halted.

Directly behind her and even before she herself was certain that the buggy was holding a third party, Eliza heard Rachelle's whispery voice crying again, "Oh, thank God! John is with them!"

If for no other reason than for the mere sake of Rachelle's peace of mind, Eliza was also thankful to see that their strange behaving male guest was indeed inside the buggy. Still, her earlier conclusion relative to the Fillmore-Lee's springing the unexpected, had been mild thinking compared to what jumped in her head when she saw the two drenched, bespattered people whom her son was helping alight from the buggy. Indeed, Eliza's sum total of the whole episode could not have risen more hairsplitting thoughts; that is, until her eye caught the obvious shattered state of the man who was being helped up the walk and at the same instant, heard Rachelle gasp, "John's ill," as she rushed on by her to meet the returning trio at the edge of the porch.

With Bessie hovering behind her in the doorway—Bessie's fearful expression was rapidly turning into one Of triumph now that she could see she had not stirred up a hornet's nest for nothing—Eliza tried to get a clear scrutiny of John Fillmore-Lee's face as he more or less came hobbling up the walk with Beth Anne and Carr on either side of him. She failed though because he never lifted his head once, giving every appearance of wanting to keep his face hidden. She wondered why.

Now, as the returning party began to mount the steps and just as she had begun to wonder again—along with her conscience hurting a little too—if John Fillmore-Lee had stumbled and fallen into one of Green Sea's deeper ditches, Eliza was startled cold when Carr suddenly offered, somewhat tremulously as he gained the last step, "Mr. John's had a narrow escape. Lightning struck the big elm at the cemetery and almost got him, too."

As Rachelle cried, "Merciful Lord!" and made a grab for her husband, seeming to want to be convinced of his nearness, Eliza, at the same instant and with her conscience stinging all the more, too, was crying, "What! Lightning struck at the cemetery!"

"Yes, Mother," Carr affirmed, "the pretty elm tree over grandmother and Uncle Nat's grave is gone. It'll have to be cleared away tomorrow, but we'll talk about that later. I think Mr. John needs a doctor as soon as I can get him here. Will you see to things while I go after Uncle Seth, see that a hot bath is quickly prepared for both Mr. John and Beth Anne." He whirled back around and was taking the long flight of steps backdown two at a time, with his mother's "Yes—certainly—son" falling on his back, when John's voice stopped him midway, suddenly barking out to him, "No. no doctor, Carr! I don't need Doctor Seth's attention. Forget it!"

"But, Papa," Beth Anne cried as John kept on continuing his rather wobbly gait across the porch without stopping, "you're still shaking like a leaf. Please don't stop Carr from going for Doctor Seth. He's a very good doctor, I know he'll help you!"

Coming back to his daughter, in a softer tone Eliza observed, John told her, "No, Pet, I don't need Doctor Seth, nor will I see him. But, you may need his attention, and soon, if you don't hurry and shed those wet clothes you have on."

"But. . ." Beth Anne's protest went no further.

Steadfast on John's side, her mother had suddenly interrupted, telling Beth Anne over her shoulder as she sensed that there was something more troubling her husband than his narrow escape from the bolt of lightning, "Do as your father wishes, dear. I'll see him to our room and be with you shortly."

Having observed that John Fillmore-Lee had not halted his pronounced laboring steps once for any exchange of words or otherwise since he had crawled from the buggy and, obviously, had no intention of halting them—plainly making it clear that with the exception of his wife he wanted to get out of everybody's sight as quickly as possible, Eliza readily cleared the doorway, stepping aside and also holding to her silence, too, as he and Rachelle passed her and went on inside.

The industrious Bessie had already fled the scene, without waiting for someone to suggest it, she had hurried away to start the kettles of water boiling no sooner than she had heard the word "bath."

Although hearing about the elm tree's destruction had hit Eliza hard, taking her thoughts back to long ago happenings and, at the same time, setting her mind's eye to work in trying to gather a picture of what the family burial ground was going to look like without the huge graceful tree, she still was not so wrapped up in her own interest that she was failing to sense the feelings of her son, who was still pausing in a quandary of uncertainty on the steps, and the exasperated, disheveled girl before her.

Without delaying another second, Eliza crossed over to where Beth Anne stood, saying to her as she draped an arm about the girl's shoulders, "I'm sure if the doctor were here, dear, he'd order the very thing that your father seems to be seeking himself—rest and quiet! With plenty of rest after a good hot bath and one of Pete's hot toddies, he'll soon be feeling better, I know." She then looked at her son, going on, "When Carr gets the buggy put away and changes into dryer clothing himself, he's going to be expecting you to join him in the sitting room to help drink the pot of hot chocolate that I'm going to run right this minute and make myself. In this rapidly changing weather, it should do as much for out taste buds as the lemonade did earlier today."

There is no doubt that Eliza's lifelong deep devotion for her own father had played a big part in moving her to take this step—

completely reversing her line of thinking in those last few minutes relative to Beth Anne's behavior regarding her father. In any case, Eliza's move seemed to work, not only when it came to the question of whether to fetch the doctor or not, but easing Beth Anne's anxiety and fears as well.

Though she did not do so before assuring Carr, by the warm smile she turned upon him, that she liked the idea of his mother's suggestion, Beth Anne promptly thanked Eliza and hurried on into the house. And Carr, silently praising his mother for the way she was handling the whole episode, seeming to take this taxing, tense situation and turn it into a mere nothing, shared a meaningful look with her, too, before he turned and dashed on about the business of putting the buggy away.

But, despite all this affinity and also the continuing endeavor on Eliza's part to keep at least a minimum of calm flowing, the atmosphere in the household was anything but tranquil for the remainder of that day. For one thing, it was well over two hours later before anyone—with the exception of Bessie who was preparing baths and running other errands—was to see Rachelle, including her daughter. And, when she did make her appearance, looking even more shaken and pale, too, than she had been when she had accompanied her husband to their bedroom, Eliza felt that she had finally emerged then for no other reason than her desire to have no further disturbance take place by her failing to occupy her place at the supper table. Though her husband's chair was conspicuously empty across the table from her. Certainly, Rachelle had not come downstairs because of her want for something to eat, Eliza had concluded when she noted how Rachelle was picking at the small portions of food she had helped herself to. Indeed, Eliza had not known that Rachelle would even make an appearance for supper until short moments before she had appeared. Just when Eliza had decided that she was not going to see Rachelle Fillmore-Lee another time that day and had already begun to make preparations for Rachelle's supper, as well as John's too, to be carted upstairs and sewed in their bedroom, Bessie had finally come dashing down to the kitchen with Rachelle's message, "yes'um, Miss Rachel'say she'll be comin' down but not Mister John, he still too poo'ly."

What Eliza was unaware of was the fact that her older female guest was doing remarkably well to be participating in the supper hour at all—picking at her food or otherwise, taking into account all the additional stress and anxiety that she had undergone, and was still submersed in, since she and her husband had disappeared into the privacy of their bedroom upon his return. For no sooner than the door had closed behind them, John had flung himself— his water— soaked clothes and all—down across the bed sobbing uncontrollably. And, in spite of all Rachelle's pleas for him to tell her what was troubling him, he had kept on sobbing in silence until she had threatened to take exception to his objecting to seeing a doctor, telling him unless he told her what was grieving him so that she was going to send for Seth Roalf, anyway.

Though she had known that John had received a severe blow from the lightning striking and doubtless was suffering from shock, which could account for some of his tears, that did not stop Rachelle from being convinced that besides that aspect of the situation that there was some other juncture involved that had induced the flood of weeping—grief that appeared to totally consume him.

The fact was, even if Rachelle had been aware that John was on the brink of breaking down when she had seen him and had sort of prepared herself for it, in no way was she expecting him to immediately go stumbling for the bed and collapse upon it in such a fit of weeping. His behavior had startled her, had put her already tout nerves under such a strain that on top of feeling like she was going to start wailing herself, she had found herself reeling and had been forced to catch and hold onto a side chair nearby till she could steady her balance.

At any rate, Rachelle did pull herself together and making on to the bed had sat down beside her husband's prostrated body, comforting and pleading to him to tell her what the trouble was until she had finally given up and made her threat. Even so, she still had to wait out quite a few long minutes before John was to confide in her—his continuing silence exasperating her to no end.

As a matter of fact, Rachelle had already formed the notion that her design to get John to open up by threatening to send for Seth Roalf was not going to work either, when to her astonishment, he suddenly rolled over and reaching for the hand towel that she had placed near him, he told her between sobs, as he wiped at the flowing tears and the wet locks of hair plastered on his forehead, "It's—Nat."

"Nat?" Rachelle questioned, her brow knitting in puzzlement as she wondered what he meant by bringing up the long-deceased Nat Carson's name, something he had never done before. "You mean the

Captain Carson who was supposed to have been your brother?"

"Please, dear, don't—say—supposed," John muttered, his croaking voice separating his words, "not—anymore. He was my brother!"

Though his remark had thrown Rachelle again, she tried not to let it show, coming back calmly as ever, "Well, yes, dear, or so Gilford wants us to believe. But what about this Captain Carson?"

"Understand my mourning him like this." John finished for her, now appearing to have his grief under control as he wiped at his face again and let the towel fall back down beside him, going on to tell her as he fixed his eyes upon the ceiling, "It was the bolt of lightning that did it, Rachelle. Don't you see, it opened up everything! Nat, the war, Green Sea, all of it—everything!"

Rachelle thought she was going to keel over in a dead faint. She caught one or two long breaths though and managed to hold on, faintly whispering, as her fingers dug at the counterpane for support, "Holy Father, John, what are you saying?"

He took his eyes from the ceiling and, for a long moment, let them rest on her face. Then, sensing her shock, and, at the same time, not only appearing as though he wanted to make sure she was all right but also seeming to want to assure himself of her presence, he reached for her hand and gripping it tightly drew it to his side, telling her, "I'm saying, dear, that I can finally remember who I am. I remember each and everyone who was connected with Green Sea in those long ago years. Pa, Ma, Eliza, Luke, Nat, everybody and everything as it used to be here. I can see Nat as clearly as I'm seeing you. I can remember all the great times we had together. You see, with me, Rachelle, it's as though his death has just happened. You can understand that, I know."

Tears swam in Rachelle's eyes. But, right at that moment, nothing was as important as the marvel that John had revealed. The mere thought of it refreshed her.

"Yes, Oh, yes, John, I do understand, so very much," she said, and I'm truly sorry for that part. But, to think it's just like Gilford's been trying to tell us. Why, it's like a miracle. I mean—well, it was one thing to believe that you might be Philippe Carson, but to truly know that you are, indeed, Philippe Carson, it's—it's. Feeling that anything she might say would not come within a mile of expressing how she really felt, Rachelle had broken off.

Even so, it appeared to be a different case with John.

Shifting his eyes back to the ceiling, he gave a somewhat resigned sigh and said, "Yes, I'm Philippe Carson, or should I say, what's left of him, anyway!"

His dry humor gladdened Rachelle's heart and yet it pulled at it, too." He seemed not to hear her though, saying, "You know, Rachelle, for a brief little while back there, when I came to in that treetop, I thought I was back at Gettysburg. There were no years between then and the present. In my mind, I was young, the young and vital Philippe Carson until when I started to raise myself up and suddenly saw my hands. Take my word for it, what I saw almost done me in as much as the lightning did."

Feeling that the miracle she saw and had spoken of was rapidly slipping away moving into a new light and a dim one at that, Rachelle asked, as a fraction of fear began to edge its way into her heart, "You're not regretting that you're not young, that there have been years between then and now, are you, John?"

His eyes quickly fell from the ceiling, fastening on her again.

"Regretting the years?" He questioned, thoughtfully studying her. "Of course I'm not, dear. Knowing the happiness that you and our beloved daughter have given me, how could I regret them, ever. Yet, to say that I'm not affected by what the ravages of time has left, to suddenly be able to know and see myself as I was then compared to what I am today and still feel no heaviness of heart over it, would be lying to you."

"'Well, undoubtedly, John had somethings worked out differently, you would've been saved a lot of those hard, dark years that you've waded through. Still we should take heart and not mourn the time too deeply, because you're not that old yet," comforted Rachelle.

"Well—no, I don't suppose I am. But, we must face it Rachelle, I'm still a long way from being the twenty-three-year-old Philippe Carson, too. To tell you the truth, considering the way my head is pounding right now, I think if I don't pull myself together and be doing it quick, push some of those things from my mind, I 'm going to be on my way to the loony bin; beyond mourning, worrying; or doing anything," he said and took his hand from hers and moved it to his head.

Suddenly, observing how hard his hand was pressing down on his brow , Rachelle was far less interested and concerned over the state of John's mental health, in spite of his low opinion of it, than she was with that of his physical condition.

Springing to her feet she went sailing for the water closet and bringing back a cold, wet clothe, she said, as she laid it across his forehead, "Please, John, let me send for the doctor, I'm worried about your headache.

"No, dear, no," he groaned.

Sighing, Rachelle pressed him no further about seeing the doctor. Instead, she turned to the night table beside the bed and picking up the Waterford tumbler with its brimming amber contents that Bessie had brought to the door some minutes before that and slipped through to her, she leaned back over John and handed it to him, saying, in a tone of voice that sounded far more demanding than pleading, "Here then, drink this, John. I won't stand by and let you continue on like this for another minute without doing something. It's still warm, I know it'll help you. And further, it's past time you get out of those wet clothes. The counterpane is already wet by your lying on it."

Her no-nonsense voice got through to John. "What is it you want me to drink?" he asked.

I've told you, it's a hot toddy, or it was hot when Bessie brought it. You should've drunk it then as I suggested. I'm positive it'll relax you. Here, dear, drink it while it's still warm.

"Well, I reckon I can manage it now," he said, and taking the tumbler from Rachelle 's hand he raised up and took a long sip. Then, despite the searing pain in his head and his anguish too, he went on to add, "Hum—if this is noted for settling one's nerves, pass me more. It's really good," his light expression lifting Rachelle's heart a little higher once more, as she then turned and picked up the dressing robe that had already been unpacked and laid out for him on the foot of the bed sometime earlier.

Seeing that his wife had meant no nonsense regarding the removal of his soiled, wet clothes, John set the drink back down on the table and readily submitted to her bidding.

Now, that the damp counterpane on the bed had also been removed and along with John's clothes had been taken to the bathing chamber and dumped into a soiled clothes hamper, Rachelle, sitting back down beside John where he sat on the edge of the bed sipping his drink, ventured to say, "I gather you haven't told anybody else about all this, have you John?"

"No, only you, Rachelle," he said, holding his head with one hand while he nursed his drink from the other. thought that might be best, considering that no one here had given any indication Of recognizing me. I've got to have time to think it out, plan some way to handle it. I can't spring something like that, all at once." She observed how his hand was suddenly pressing down hard on his brow again. "Christ! Rachelle! Have you given any thought to what a disclosure of this sort could lead to—to all the ruckus it could cause? I have a good notion to say nothing more about it and high-tail it out of here and back to Lexington as fast as I can get there!"

For all Rachelle's softness she could also be somewhat tough; that is, if circumstances called for it.

"You'll do nothing of the kind, John," she said. "Have you forgotten Beth Anne? She's marrying Carr Heyward in June. Besides, would you let vanity, fear, or whatever it is that has pushed this thought into your head, prompt you to bend to such cowardly behavior, not only turning your back on your own blood relatives, now that you've finally found them, but also deny your own daughter her rightful name and heritage? I think not."

John studied the floor for a moment. Then, as he drained his glass and set it back down, he said, "No, of course, I wouldn't. These lame brains of mine have already cost you and her enough as it is."

"Nonsense, John. And, I won't listen to any more such remarks of that nature, from you or anyone else. This mental handicap which you've suffered from all these years wasn't inborn. Nor was it of your own making. You know as well as I do what it all resulted from, severe injuries which were dealt you under trying circumstances and which nearly cost you your life, if I might add."

"But, I should've listened to you, Rachelle, and not given up like I did. You can't say that wasn't stupidity."

"That's past, dear," Rachelle told him, her tough side taking a fast dive. "The important thing now is you finally do know. so, let's think of it in this regard and go forward instead of backward."

"But, I can't take any more today, Rachelle," he said, turning and looking at her beseechingly. "Regarding any social amenity, discourse or otherwise, including supper, you'll have to beg my regrets. Even if I were to go ahead and force myself to make an appearance for supper, I'm certain I wouldn't be able to stomach one bite. I feel awful." John didn't have to tell Rachelle how he felt. The pallor above his iron-grey beard was self-explanatory enough.

"I know, John," she said, "and I wouldn't hear to your trying to do anything but take a good hot bath and go to bed." She stood up. "I think Bessie's drawing your bath now. I'll go see if it's about ready." She started to turn away but then turned back, asking him somewhat hesitantly, "John—you do remember—her too, don't you?"

"Her?" John asked, the vagueness of his wife's question puzzling him. "Whom do you mean, dear?"

"The girl you were once engaged to, Caroline Roalf, I believe she is now."

The haze had cleared quickly, leaving a trickle of amusement running through John, which in spite of his troubles and pain urged him into deviling Rachelle a bit.

Managing a faint smile, he said, "Don't fret, my love, whatever I may be finally seeing through that locked door, the whole kit and caboodle hasn't thrown any dust into my eyes yet!"

He had told Rachelle all she wanted to hear, and yet, on the other hand, he had told her nothing. Even so, returning his smile, she said, "There's so much to talk about, John. So many to meet and see for the first time, besides those whom we had no idea we'd be meeting again, ever."

"Yes," John agreed, suddenly looking pensive, "for instance, there's Pa. I wonder if he'll recognize me!" And, with John continuing to wonder, along with theorizing a bit too, about those of whom who would or would not recognize him among his family and friends, he and Rachelle did talk and they talked a great deal, or at least John did because Rachelle mostly listened. No, it was not on this day that John began to share a lot of his past life with Rachelle. That all began the next day when it was reported that he was feeling some better. Though there were a scant few in the household— namely his host and hostess—who questioned this because of his continuing strange behavior. For aside from his wife and daughter, no one had set their eyes upon John Fillmore-Lee all day long, except Bessie, Of course. Bessie was still running errands and delivering the few messages that came from upstairs, delivering them with an overzealous curiosity one might add, too, because the likes of such peculiar behavior coming from a guest Bessie had yet to see. Ever since he had made his dive into the privacy of his and his wife's appointed bedroom the evening before, John Fillmore-Lee had continued to remain in seclusion behind its closed door. That is, until he finally did emerge to head downstairs late that evening to be in attendance, at the dinner party that the Heyward's were giving in his and his wife's honor.

Indeed, when it came to the matter of John's seclusion, one could not say that his behavior that day had been any stranger, or worse if one desired to look at it that way, than that of his wife's. Because after Rachelle had made her retreat from the supper table the night before—having excused herself with the ultimate in voiced delicacy, naturally, the Heyward's had not set their eyes on her, either.

As for that matter, from early morning when Bessie had come downstairs with the first message, telling Eliza, "No'm, Miss Rachelle be staying in da bedroom with Mister John dis momin' , havin' her vittles with him," Eliza had had a feeling of being backed up against a wall throughout the rest Of that day. And little wonder, considering whether to go ahead with the dinner party or call it off, before Bessie had finally come to tell her, "Yes'um, Miss Rachelle say dat Mister John will be up to comin' downstairs for supper dis evenin', say to go ahead with da supper party." But, even after Eliza had received this word, had been assured that the Fillmore-Lee's would indeed be able to participate in the entertainment that she had made plans for in their honor, for her, it still did not remove that state of suspense that had seemed to cling to every wall of the house since the Fillmore-Lee's arrival—a feeling that every nook and comer were being stalked by some innominate apparition.

All the same, as Eliza went ahead and began to wade through her duties that day, she tried not to let this feeling of uncertainty get at her too much because not only did she share a meaningful look with Luke upon each message that Bessie was to deliver, she also had Luke's word that he would venture to put one or two questions to John Fillmore-Lee before the latter took his departure for home. Yes, Eliza had already decided the night before that she had had her fill of John Fillmore-Lee's unique manner, and she had told Luke so once they had gotten to the privacy of their own bedroom.

Surely, it was for wiser to do a little prying into the man's character now, at least get to know a few of his beliefs and ideas became better acquainted with his way of thinking, then it was to say nothing and have his outlandish behavior constantly startling them, Eliza had reasoned. "Why, Luke, I haven't even gotten a good look at the man's face yet. He seems to want to keep it hidden from me," she had told Luke.

"I know, doll," Luke had replied, giving a long sigh as he had finally gotten stretched out on their deep featherbed beside her. "And, it's not only you but everybody else here, too, I've observed. But, despite his obvious unwillingness to have me do so, I looked at him and I must confess there does seem to be something about his face—say a fraction of familiarity that disturbs me."

"Familiarity?" Eliza asked, and from force of habit raised up, scrutinizing Luke 's face in the night's darkness. "You mean you think you've met him before or seen him some place?"

Too late, Luke realized he had said too much. He was not quite ready to tell Eliza that he thought there was a good chance that their strange behaving male guest might possibly be her own brother, Phil. As in the case of Matthew Carson, Luke had no wish to heedlessly alarm his wife. He wanted more time to make sure of his suspicions before he said anything else about the matter.

so, desiring to drop the subject and at the same time be truthful too, Luke had replied, "'Well, I can't say for sure. One second I sense a fraction of recognition about the man. Then, the next second his manner belies the feeling altogether." And suddenly, Luke's arms had come up and pulling Eliza down to him he had kissed her long and hard, adding, "Now, what do you say we let our misgivings about the gentleman from Lexington rest for tonight, sweetheart? It's been a long day. I promise you, I'll do my best to become better acquainted with Mr. Fillmore-Lee before he takes his leave here."

Eliza's response had surprised Luke. Falling down beside him instantly, she had giggled, "you mean after a smack like that, you want to call it a day?"

Though the day had been long like Luke had said, it had not been so long that he could turn his back and ignore her invitation.

Drawing Eliza closer to him, he had told her as his mouth sought hers again, "Only the part regarding our guest down the hall, dear, you may be sure!"

Thus, because of Luke's love and devotion—the knowledge of its abidingness made her heart literally sing—Eliza met the next day's duties and bore its untimely upheavals with far more ease than had her and Luke's relationship been less, intimately, impassioned. For on top of all the unusual tension that had developed in the household since the Fillmore-Lee's arrival—strain that seemed to be growing worse instead of calming down any—there had also been the grim business of clearing away the shattered elm tree at the cemetery.

Eliza and Luke had gone to view the wreckage together and, as they stood and watched Sam and his crew gather the last of the pieces of limbs and debris up and cart it all away, the grounds had looked as bare and desolate to Eliza—if not more so than what she had visioned the place looking in her mind.

For Eliza, the huge, graceful elm had sort of been a Portraiture of life's lastingness—bestowing any element of life never-ending upon the place despite the fact that it was a cemetery; and this exemplification was made all the more real to her when in the springtime the tree began to take on new, tender buds again. Now; however, with the tree gone there seemed to be nothing but a grim disclosure of mortalness—nothing to give credence to a protraction of other tomorrows.

"Luke, everything looks so—so final and empty now," she said, resting her gaze upon the vacant spot.

"Not for long, dear," replied Luke. "I've already instructed Sam to set a magnolia in its place. They grow fast." He turned and smiled at her. "Besides, I think I prefer the magnolia over the elm, anyway. It's sort of special to me and should hold something special for you, too, considering that I proposed to you under one, remember?"

"How could I forget that," she said, smiling back at him, "when it Seems it was only yesterday." She reached for his hand, her demeanor doing an abrupt about-face. "Come on, Luke, let's go on back to the house, I have a lot to do before suppertime. That is, if Bessie isn't waiting with another message telling us our guests have decided they can't make it downstairs after all, or worse still, informing us that John Fillmore-Lee has jumped out of an upstairs window and broken his neck, leaving us no alternative but forgetting the dinner party and prepare for a wake instead!"

Luke threw back his head, his hearty laughter filling the air around them.

The hours passed, though, with no more messages of regrets being delivered from the upstairs guests. And, at long last, Eliza and Luke—flanked by the Fillmore-Lees and their daughter and Carr, too, were standing in the entrance hall greeting the Randolph's, the first of the invited supper guests to arrive. Even so, and although she was all decked out rather handsomely from head to toe in her new rose-pink Easter outfit—saving the hat with its pink satin roses naturally, it was hard for Eliza to believe that she had indeed made the company of John and Rachelle again and was in the process of making them acquainted with Bruce and Martha and also Lucy Randolph who had become more sociable since meeting Gilford Sloan. Though Martha herself had not dawdled too long with the mores of decorum. In fact, she barely acknowledged the introduction before she was shrieking, "Welcome to our part of the woods," and moving on to banter with Beth Anne and Carr—something she did at every opportunity.

All the same, so much was Eliza surprised to see her plans for the evening finally shaping up and running halfway smoothly for a change, she almost gave herself a pinch test she was dreaming the occasion instead of living it. Presently; however, she had lost all impulse of convincing herself of what was taking place. The pinches were no longer necessary. For the few short, dry responses that John-Fillmore-Lee had seen fit to share with Luke and Bruce had left no doubt in Eliza's mind about the realness of the event.

Still, after studying John Fillmore-Lee for a brief few minutes longer—that is to say as near as she was able to study him because he was still inclined to keep his head lowered to the floor—Eliza became convinced and in no small amount at that that their guest was a deep-troubled man. Moreover, he did indeed look ill; and in point of that fact and distress too, his wife standing beside him holding tightly onto his hand appeared to be rapidly on her way in catching up with him.

For all Rachelle's warm graciousness and elegant grooming which did punctuate her attractiveness that much more—she was wearing an elegantly brocaded light green gown with strands of pearls interwoven throughout her spiral-shaped coiffure—her strain still remained to be very much evident, overshadowing all those things about her, it was Eliza's opinion.

The truth was, as Eliza continued to observe Rachelle and John, she got the feeling that they both wanted to take right back up the staircase in a run. It made her wonder, all of a sudden, if she had allowed her Yankee prejudice to lead her astray for this one time when it came to the matter of using good judgment. She thought this was precisely what she had done and found herself regretting that she had not gone ahead and called off the whole affair.

Now, fearing that she had failed her guests by not being as considerate and mindful as she should have been regarding John Fillmore-Lee's narrow escape from what would have been sure death for him had the lightning actually hit him, to say nothing of

Rachelle's anxiety, Eliza began to yearn for some sign—verbal or otherwise—from the couple that would prove her misgivings were all for naught. She had no intention of calling attention to the matter herself; however, even if she had formed the opinion that John would do well by himself if he were to pamper his strength somewhat by taking the side chair that he was standing near! She was well aware that to voice concern at this late hour for the man's health would only make her appear as having a block for a head, if not right downright callous and indifferent about his whole misfortune, which; in truth, was not the case with her at all. Thus, she had parted with that idea no sooner than it had popped in her head.

Eliza wanted to do something though and thought to herself that if she did nothing else, leastwise she would like to take a stab at trying to break down John Fillmore-Lee's frosty mien. Even so, she found herself hard pressed to come up with anything that would seem like a feasible approach, and especially since the minutes were beginning to add up with neither he or Rachelle giving one single sign that told their strain was becoming any less intense. However, the chance came sooner than Eliza had trusted it would when she saw John, suddenly, draw forth his pocket watch and glance at it.

Seeing John's move as her opening—his desire to obviously know just how "slow" the time was actually passing—Eliza wasted not one second in making use of it. Turning a most charming expression upon him, she laughed, "Believe it or not, John, we did take pity and didn't invite that many strange faces. Only two more carriages to go and then all this introductory business will be finished with for this one time!" Instantly, as a number of jovial chuckles broke in unison around her, the abrupt sound of carriage wheels breaking in the drive had Eliza's head turning toward the door with her going on, "In fact, here they are now, both Father's coach and Seth's too."

The laughter had made Eliza feel good and —slowly but surely—a feeling of prevailing over her misreckoning dealing with John Fillmore-Lee had begun to wash over her. It solaced her conscience and, at the same time, brought her to conclude that an air of flippancy over one of constraint and reserve was no doubt the better way when it came to the matter of trying to reach their staid guest.

Fully expecting to meet John's chuckling smile as she turned her head back to him, Eliza's astonishment at what she did meet could not have been any more profound. Minus one fraction of mirth, there was John's joyless, weariful gaze resting fully on her at last—solemnly searching her face so intently before he turned to stare at the arriving guests now coming up the steps that it seemed as though she heard his voice crying in her ears. It disturbed her, but with these additional greetings and introductions starting immediately, there was not one second to spare for woolgathering or for that matter disconcertion, either. Indeed, for quite a spell after that, Eliza barely let John Fillmore-Lee pass through her anxious thoughts. For she had no more than turned away from greeting Caroline and Seth to embrace her father and Aunt Amy, who were following the Roalfs and whom on this occasion had been accompanied to Green Sea by the Reverend Marsh Reed and Elizabeth Drakston, than she was turning back at hearing a sudden gasp and to her horror saw Seth making a grab for Caroline as she went toppling to the floor at John Fillmore-Lee's feet!

Abruptly, all greetings and all introductions were have done with as everybody's attention was transferred to Seth Roalfs stricken wife. In fact, in due time, if those of whom who still lacked to be presented to the Lexington couple did not see fit to take it upon themselves to make their own acquaintance known to John and Rachelle or, on the other hand, if there was no effort made by John and Rachelle either, no introduction was ever to come off between the two parties. A case in point was that of Matthew Carson. Yet, for the most part, it became hardly necessary because, immediately, strangers and friends and family alike were all concerned with one common effort and working together toward that affect and that was to see the unconscious Caroline Roalf revived from her dead faint.

Without waiting for the doctor or anyone else to suggest it, Carr, well aware that Seth Roalf never went any place without his medical bag which he ever kept well-equipped against by-the-way happenings, made a dash for the doctor's buggy and had the bag back at the doctor's hand almost as quick as it had taken the startled Seth Roalf to scrutinize his wife's symptoms and contemplate the remedy. Someone in the crowd—no doubt envisioning dousing the victim back to consciousness—ran and fetched back a washbasin of cold water. Seeing the ready water, Eliza, snapping back to the crisis at hand, made haste for a washcloth and upon Seth's nod proceeded to keep soaking the cloth and applying it to Caroline's brow while he kept bust administering the smelling salts. In addition, somebody else in the group ran and got a number of fans—doubtless viewing the fans, too, as providing another stimulant which were promptly put to use. Of course, since there was not enough room for everybody to gather around the victim all at once and be loaning his or her hand to the doctor in his effort to revive his wife—crowding the case would not have been behaving very bright anyhow—a number of guests were doing nothing but standing by, or sitting, anxiously looking on as they waited for Caroline to come round. John and Rachelle were among those who had taken a seat.

The truth of the matter, when it came to John sitting down rather than stand, he had had no choice, or at least he had felt he hadn't. Although he had made a grab for Caroline Roalf himself and had, actually, broken her fall before she hit the floor and then had helped the doctor lift his wife and carry her over to the yellow sofa, his moves; nevertheless, had been spontaneously made—made on a blind impulse alone and carried out the same way. For seeing Caroline and his father and finally being able to remember them after so many years, had been no trivial experience for John's already shattered nerves to take on. Upon first glance, not only had his legs felt as if they were trying to putty under him, but his whole body had seemed to separate at the joints as well, with him near the point of buckling to the floor himself as Caroline reached him and fainted. And, even then as he sat beside Rachelle, taking in the incredulous circumstance he found himself in and at the same time marveling how he had gotten by without falling flat on his face, he still would have been skeptical about trusting that quivering feeling in his legs.

Even so, John would have been the first to admit that the incident had not been wholly devoid of availing some good in his behalf. For as much as it had robbed him in physical strength, it nevertheless had rewarded him too—restored a lot of that self-confidence which he had lost upon that moment at the cemetery when he had yielded to what time had rendered to his person. For he was certain, in spite of all the years that had passed, that Caroline had recognized him the instant he had started to extend his hand to her.

The mere thought of it happening—finally having someone to see him for who he really was, sent a surge of energy shooting to John's legs and as he suddenly heard the doctor say, I think she's coming out of it," he slipped his hand inside Rachelle's again and rose back to his feet.

John's hope was that somebody else in the crowd would

recognize him—see enough likeness between him and that picture that they carried in their memory of the young Philippe Carson that they, too, would know who he was, as Caroline had known, and everything would finally be out in the open at last. He abhorred the thought of having to disclose his own identity to his family and friends. He wanted them to discover who he was and tell him, not have it happen just the opposite way around. Further, there was something else that had suddenly become of vital importance to John. Besides wanting to be waiting—ready at hand, to meet any possible move that Caroline might make toward him when she did rally, he had also had a sudden urge to let her know, somehow, what it meant to him to have her see that he was indeed Philippe Carson and not merely some unfamiliar guest whom she had never looked on before. But, even so, to his great disappointment, John's hopes were to come to nothing on all scores. To begin with, no sooner than John had heard Doctor Seth Roalf declare his prognosis of Caroline 's faint and he had gotten to his feet, the doctor was sweeping Caroline up in his arms and taking her up the staircase out of John's sight, leaving him no chance whatever of even exchanging a look with Caroline, let alone one word. Eliza Heyward, who was swiftly proceeding the doctor up the stairs, had suddenly proposed the move, pointing out that Caroline should have the comfort of a bed, and going on to add that she wasn't going to tolerate her doing without one minute longer! Thus, hardly being given any alternative but to take back to his seat, John motioned to Rachelle and did just that, with him noting while they continued to wait along with the others for some additional word from upstairs, that there was not another member among the group who seemed to take any special interest in him whatever—that is to say no more than what they would have taken in some other distant visitor, or maybe not even as much since the temper of their wait was of the nature it was.

Even so, John felt that this self-contained attitude among those of whom he waited with was especially stressed in the behavior of his father, Matthew Carson, and it hurt John more than what he would have thought possible. Yet, to a certain degree, he was able to understand this suppressed interest of his father's, because the longer John became exposed to his company, the more it became evident to him where Matthew Carson's mind and thoughts were—with no other but the indisposed Caroline Roalf upstairs—revealing to John in bold letters how deeply devoted his family had become to the woman whom he had once been slated to marry.

All the same, the minutes were to wear on and it went without saying they were difficult minutes for John, too. In the meantime, both Luke and Martha had offered their excuse and hurried upstairs also. And, when John finally saw the foursome descending the stairs again he was doubly glad for two reasons—glad because apparently everything was going all right with Caroline Roalf and glad because he felt he could surely use the intrusion. For he knew to continue to sit in his father's presence and try to keep on holding in his emotion—that redeemed attachment for Matthew Carson that had come so readily to him—was not going to be an easy thing for him to do. In short, he had near about reached the end of all his self-restraint and was much aware of it. So, more than ready to exert any degree of action, John quickly got to his feet once again no sooner than he saw the group take to the stairs on their way down.

All the others whom were sitting, which included Matthew Carson, also rose, and seeing their anxious focus as well as the faces of those Of whom who had never taken a seat, Doctor Seth Roalf quickly came through with a report telling them even before he had covered all the steps, "She's going to be all right. I'd say her biggest trouble right now is worrying about delaying supper." Suddenly, lifting a puzzled brow, the doctor paused his step letting his eyes fall on Rachelle. Then, just as quickly a wide smile had his brow relaxing as he took the last two Steps of the stairs in one long stride and went on to exclaim, "Well! What a small world it is! Rachelle—Rachelle Fillmore, after all these years!" He held his hand out.

Rachelle smiled, letting her hand meet his. "My very own words, Seth, upon hearing Eliza made a creditable remark about you yesterday and further inquired if you and the Virginia Doctor Seth Roalf were one and the same person and learning that you were. It certainly has been quite a long time since those days at Lincoln, all the more reason why I must add, how kind it is of you that you didn't walk right on past without recognizing me!"

By no means was Rachelle yearning to hear a word or two of flattery spill from the doctor's lips, because she was endowed with little vanity, if indeed any at all. Having grown somewhat wearisome by this time with her husband's family and friends since she was on to his great disappointment over the fact that not one single one had come forth, yet to utter one word bearing on his true identity, Rachelle had made the remark for the benefit of those people alone and nothing more, even though her hope of their perceiving what she meant by it, was nil.

"Pass you up, Rachelle?" The doctor came back, cocking his eye at her in all earnestness. "Not a chance, my dear, when you've hardly changed a day. I would've recognized you any place. That is, once I'd had the opportunity to have looked your way." Quickly shifting his eye to John and raking him over from head to foot, the doctor went on as he now offered his hand to him, "And, if my eyes aren't playing tricks on me, it appears I'm placing you, too. In fact, I must admit your face, as well as a number of others among those of whom who were doomed to endure the ordeals of that Godforsaken place along with you, seems to have stamped itself in my memory over the years. It's good to see you again, soldier, and to finally learn you did survive the odds." Somewhat warily, the doctor ventured on smilingly. "It seems that guardian angel of yours still continued to work a little overtime in your behalf in more ways than one, since I last saw you. Not only on the scene of your recovery, but also in respect to this lovely, gracious lady who graces your side and your beautiful daughter as well. We all simply adore her."

"Thank you, doctor," John replied, as he finally recovered his hand from Seth Roalf's vigorous handshake. "I have to agree with you. I must have some special providence working for me, because I have scored lucky on a number of things. Especially in point of my wife here, and in the gift of our daughter." A sudden glint of deviltry lighted John's eyes. "A gift, I might add, we'll share with Carr Heyward but never bequeath to him!"

"I take it that you mean business, too," laughed Seth. "Still, I can't help wondering what Carr's thinking right now!"

Before John or Carr could comment, Rachelle, with a laugh, offered, "Oh, I think Carr pretty much understands how it is with John when it comes to the matter of his daughter. Beth Anne's been the apple of John's eye since the day she was born and doubtless this is his way of getting it across to Carr, without coming right out and saying so, that he won't stand for their marriage changing that."

Grinning at his bride to be, Carr put in, "No chance of that happening, Miss Rachelle. You and I both know I'd be a fool to even consider holding with the idea of ever trying to put myself between those two, the way they go to bat for one another on any and every issue that come up. You're absolutely right. I've known from the beginning that she's a daddy's girl!"

"And, what's so awful about that, if I may ask!" Retorted Beth

Anne. Carr only grinned wider though, letting her retort hang in the flowing laughter.

Doctor Seth Roalf was laughing too. Then, as suddenly as it had hit him on the night of the housewarming, that cold, needling sensation was pricking along his spine again—tempering the pitch of his laughter to a low ebb as it came to him that he had just heard this former soldier's given name repeated for the first time. John? He thought, the name seeming to stick in his ears like a wad of glue, blocking out everything around him but the startling thoughts and questions whirling in his head.

So, the soldier who had chosen to remain silent, refusing to say one word to anybody but Rachelle Fillmore, did have a name after all, John—such an ordinary and everyday name, too. While, on the other hand, there was nothing ordinary about his surname, whatever. Actually, by some strange coincidence, part of his last name was the same as Rachelle's maiden name, Fillmore. John Fillmore-Lee indeed! Well, he didn't know where the Lee part came from, but Rachelle Fillmore's husband was nobody but the, supposedly, deceased Philippe Carson! He'd bet his bottom dollar on it! The face in the portrait and what he remembered about this man's face as he lay in that Union hospital was just as he had suspicioned when he had questioned Caroline about Philippe Carson that night, the two faces were one and the same face—being the face of no one but Philippe Carson himself.

But what, for the love of God, had happened here? Considering all the things that Philippe Carson had had going for him, why on earth would he choose to give it all up? It made no sense at all. Surely, it couldn't have been that he didn't want to face Caroline with the news that he had fallen in love with Rachelle Fillmore. No, that made no sense either, because Matthew Carson could never have sired a son who was that weak-willed and spineless. Besides, come to think of it, it was logical to reason that Caroline herself had played a little part in Philippe Carson's decision to take another name and get lost so to speak. Because, basically, Rachelle's and Caroline's physical appearance was of the same mold—fair, flowerlike and fragile—looking. In fact, he had married a woman who bore a striking resemblance to Caroline. No, there was something else involved.

Had Caroline recognized this man for who he really is? Is that why she had fainted out at his feet? If this was the case, she had chosen to keep quiet about it, because so far she had not said one word about her discovery to him or nobody else. Maybe that's what he should do, for the time being anyway, taking into account that no one else seemed to be onto John Fillmore-Lee's true identity, not even his own father and sister. Yes, he thought that might be best, just continue on as if he did not suspicion one thing and see if he could figure out what purpose it was serving Philippe Carson to play this kind of parlor game—see what the man was trying to pull off here. For he had a feeling this charade of his was going to be mighty interesting to watch!

Fearing that he might have let his startling discovery keep his thoughts preoccupied for too long, drawing attention to the self-counsel that he was having with himself, Doctor Seth Roalf, quickly giving his own attention to the subject at hand, told Beth Anne, "Don't expect him to carry the subject any further, dear, because he knows he's already put himself out on a limb."

"I'll say he has, Seth," chimed Eliza, turning her head to smile at Matthew, "because I happen to be a daddy's girl, too."

"That's what I was driving at, Eliza," laughed Seth, doing his best to let on like that nothing was amiss with him. "And, not only you but Caroline, too, as well as a number more of the fairer sex of this neighborhood!"

As Doctor Seth Roalf received a somewhat withering look of esteem from several of his admiring women patients in the group, Luke, amused that some of them had not taken too kindly to Seth's remark, plunged in to have his say on the subject. Besides, like the doctor, Luke's nervous system was not operating at its normal level anyhow. He was suffering from the jitters. For, by this time, Luke had finally convinced himself that they all were standing in the presence of Matthew Carson's long, missing older son. Caroline's faint is what had clinched it for Luke, persuading him to make up his mind on the spot.

At any rate, trying also to go through the motion of pretending that nothing was out of line, Luke jested, "Well, I can appreciate my son's position because I, too, knew from the very moment of my introduction to his mother, that if I were to be successful in winning her, it was going to have to be a must with me that I stay in accord with her father." He was not worried one fraction about Matthew Carson taking his jest the wrong way.

All the same, instantly observing a number of the faces turning on him now with rising brows—to be sure a number more than what he had expected including his wife's—Luke abruptly let forth with a loud guffaw and waving the looks of disdain aside, went on to tell them, "Now, wait a minute and hold onto your thoughts, will you. I'm not finished yet, I have more to say."

"I can't speak for Father, but I'll wait, so please go on," Eliza retorted, churned up as much at Luke's horselaugh as she was at his remark, viewing it as coming on entirely too strong—actually out of place.

"Well," Luke continued, as he tried to keep his gaze from fastening on John's face, "Even though I did express a fact that I'll remain to stand by, I still want to stress another side of the coin in this situation of being married to a daddy's girl. It's my opinion that when the case is such, a man pockets an advantage because his father-in-law will be far less inclined to look at his faults and shortcomings, or leastwise that's the way it's' always been in my case. "

"Well put, Luke, much obliged," smiled Matthew. "But, did you ever stop to consider that maybe the reason for all that smooth sailing between us has been because I felt I didn't lose my daughter at all, but gained a son in the bargain instead!"

With her voice dropping its sharp edge, Eliza smiled, "He hardly deserved that, Father. Still, I think before we completely befuddle this subject for Beth Anne and Carr, I'm going to suggest we drop it." She turned looking down the hall toward the dining room door. "Besides, I see Pete's still waiting to start serving supper. Father, will you and Aunt Amy take the lead, with John and Rachelle next. Carr, you and Beth Anne come on. Reverend Reed, you and Elizabeth..." And, Eliza went on pairing up her guests, purposely positioning Luke and herself last in line so she would have time to dash back upstairs and take a peek at Caroline before everybody settled down at the table.

Though John had the urge to do nothing right at the moment but scream, "Look at me, Pa. I'm your true son, not Luke," he repressed the urge, letting the words lie silent in his throat as he found Rachelle's hand again and forced himself to do as he was bid.

Matthew Carson's failing to recognize John had undone him no small amount. Once again, John found his resolve to cope precariously shaky—slipping rapidly from what he thought had been his grasp of the situation only minutes before that. Having his sister not recognize him—she appeared to John to never give herself time to centralize her thoughts on any one thing long enough, to reason it out anyway—had not seemed to bother him to any great extent. However, to have his father look at him and at the same time appear not to see him either, was not something John could shrug off so easily.

There was a whale of a difference. Although he had been dearly devoted to his only sister and found he still harbored that attachment to her most affectionately within him, their relationship had still not been that side by side kind of comradeship that he had shared with his father and brother. They had been teammates, so to speak, with no disparity of spirit between them.

The mere thought of those long ago days, now pulled painfully at John's heart, causing him to feel that much farther separated from Green Sea and those of whom he found himself among as well, not to mention that it made him feel conspicuously out of place too. Though he could have reached out and laid his hand on his father's back, something John would never have thought possible so shortly before this day, he kept his hand steadfast in Rachelle's instead and yearned to escape—wishing with all his might that he were in his own home in Lexington—headed for his own dining room instead of the one he was following Matthew Carson to.

The fact was, with his stomach feeling as though it might have come up in his throat and lodged there, John was wondering how he was going to make out once he got to the table, anyhow. Certainly, satisfying his taste buds with food right then was one of his weaker wants! He kept on moving though, thinking to himself that it would not surprise him one bit if he were forced to have to make an apology, most any moment, and go running for the nearest chamber of personal convenience that he could find. He breathed in deeply one or two times, however, which did seem to brace him up somewhat and, eventually, found himself settled down in the place that Pete had indicated for him to take at the long, richly dressed table.

Since John was now able to recall back to some of the tables that his mother, Anne Carson had set on certain occasions, he noted that this table, in many ways, greatly resembled the one that she had supervised over; that is, aside from the unique flower arrangement that graced the table's center. It had caught his eye immediately because never before had he seen a centerpiece made up of wild violets. Yet, the effect was so breathtaking, with the various shades of blue blooms mixed with white looking as though they were actually growing in their low silver container, it brought John to wonder why someone had not thought of using violets long before this. And, it seemed the majority present were also sharing his view, for, instantly, much ado was being made over the violets with Eliza explaining through the many cries of delight coming from around the table that she had selected to use them because they were Luke's favorite—picking them herself this afternoon. His sister's remarks instantly aroused John's memory, taking it all the way back to that one particular period when she had almost died from the dread typhoid fever shortly after Luke's arrival at Green Sea. John though that perhaps the violet had become Luke's favorite, considering the trillions he had picked for Eliza through her illness that spring.

Gazing at the table's attractive centerpiece and thinking about all the giggles that Luke's violet picking had created among the servants at the time, John decided that maybe he could use the violets for a cause too, even if his was a cause way wide of what

Luke's had been, telling himself that with something that pleasant to look at and focus his attention on he should be less aware of all those dishes that over-crowded the sideboard, which he had been so unfortunate as to be seated near. And not only that, he also thought he might be less prone to become all wrought up over some unpleasant subject matter that could spring up.

Whether the centerpiece of violets helped or not though when, of all the subjects to come up, the conversation finally turned to him and Caroline, John was never too sure. For in spite of all his gazing at the violets and reveling in their wild velvety beauty—a splendor so captivating that it almost made John feel as though spring had slipped through the window and seated itself among them—he still was not able to keep his emotions as cool and unexcited as he would have liked it.

To a great extent ever since Matthew Carson, upon Luke's request had done the honor of citing a long blessing, John had pretty much been successful in his endeavor to set himself apart from his surroundings, keeping track of the table conversation just enough so that he would not give every appearance of having gone deaf and dumb, all of a sudden. Like the servings of food John had helped himself to from the numerous dishes that Pete and Penelope, Bessie and Sam's older daughter who was assisting Pete, had paused at his plate, he had kept his remarks and responses at a minimum, which of course had not surprised his hostess none at all. She had given no thought to his aloofness for, by this time, Eliza Heyward had come to accept John Fillmore-Lee as being no other way than the introvert she thought he was. However, the cuisine matter was quite another thing with Eliza. Though John was unaware of it, the little interest that he was taking in the appetizing dinner that she had planned and had worked at so hard in order to have everything just right—having fidgeted so much over the menu that she had almost made a nervous wreck out of herself, besides preparing many of the dishes with her own hands when she had finally come to a decision—was something Eliza Heyward could not ignore very well. To see John Fillmore-Lee almost frown every time one of her tempting dishes was paused in front of him, piqued her plenty, with her thinking that he might as well have stayed in his room on this night, too, and not gone to all the bother of coming to the table in the first place!

Actually, what really lay at the bottom of John's ability to more or less be able to detach himself from those of whom he dined with—having, more than anything else, given him the power of dominance over his will, had been the citing of the blessing by Matthew Carson. Hearing the old familiar words and phrases, which he had heard so many times in the past, fall from his father's lips once again, had brought such a conglomeration of memories rushing into John's head that it was a marvel he had had anything to say at all.

At any rate, with Rachelle having aided his effort along by nudging his leg once or twice with her knee under the table, John had managed to hold on and follow the conversation without having drawn too much attention to himself. though it was fact he had not heard half of the discourse that had thus far flowed back and forth since the meal began. But now; however, as a fraction of John's straying mind brought his attention to the fact that Carr—after having addressed Doctor Seth Roalf as "Uncle" he noted—was telling the doctor something about seeing to having his horse stalled for its overnight stay at Green Sea just as quickly as he finished with supper, John suddenly and somewhat anxious at that came back to the present. With his thoughts buried in bygone days no longer, he was finally alert to his surroundings, opening his ears wide so that not one word of Seth Roalf's response would he miss out on. To John, it was one thing to be exposed to the doctor's company—not to mention Caroline's—for a few hours. However, the thought of there being a possibility that he might have to endure the Roalf's company for an indefinite period, or for that matter, maybe for the remainder of the time he had left at Green Sea, was an apple off another tree as far as he was concerned. The mere thought of being subjected to this sort of circumstance, made John yearn all the more for that comfort in Lexington, which he knew so well and craved and which he felt, so far, had given him the slip at Green Sea.

In truth, it was not the thought of being in Caroline's company that was causing John so much concern. The fact was, since he had come to the conclusion that he owed it to Caroline, he had already decided that he was going to try to arrange to have a private visit with her before his departure for Lexington. What mostly had John so much on edge, was the thought of having to keep company with Seth Roalf. The doctor simply made John feel uncomfortable—unmanned his self-confidence. And, John felt if there were anything he was in need of, it was less stress and tension as a whole, not only for then and the remainder of his stay at Green Sea, but for all time to come!

To John's anxious relief, though, the doctor did not go along with Carr's idea of having his means of transportation deposited away for the night, telling him, "That's thoughtful of you, Carr, but since Caroline wants to go on back home after she's rested for a spell, maybe we should humor her and not go ahead and plan on our staying overnight. I think she'll be up to making the trip back, once She's had a good, long rest." Though the situation continued to give his spine the cold creeps, Seth, still trying to affect a normal attitude, smiled and went on, "I insisted on the long rest, not only for her sake but for mine too. I wanted to give myself plenty of time to feast on all these good dishes that Eliza's tempting our appetites with this evening."

"Well," laughed Carr, "if you think that's the best. Still, Elms in a fairly long stretch from Green Sea, and especially for someone like Aunt Caroline, who's always reminded me of a delicate china doll, anyhow. I'm not surprised one bit that she fainted!" His laugh had faded into an expression of seriousness.

"Neither am I, Carr," Martha joined in. 'And, I go along with your thinking that she'd be better off to stay put right where she's at. But, don't blame, Seth, if you hear that she faints again on the way back. He suggested her staying in bed till morning, but she wouldn't listen to him or, for that matter, to Luke, Eliza, or me either!" Martha's flaring voice, rising a note higher on each word that she had uttered, prompted Doctor Seth Roalf to come forth with more pleasantry. "'Watch your blood pressure, Martha,'" he wisecracked. "We wouldn't want to be carrying you upstairs, too!'" "Now that would surprise me," laughed Carr.

"Don't mention it, Carr," said Bruce, lavishing a doting smile on Martha. "For me though, petrified would be more the word, because Martha's never fainted in her whole life, that I know of."

"You're right about that, dearest, and you may believe me when I say I have no intention of starting," avowed Martha, sidestepping Seth's and Carr's remarks entirely as she kept busy pushing the food in. "Besides, never knowing what minute Caroline and Eliza were going to swoon over, I learned to bear up and not flag, a long time ago. I never will forget the day that we got Caroline to come round by fanning her with Early Cole's old, battered hat. Early helped Eliza and me revive her. In fact, I imagine that was one the few times in Early's life that he really worked in earnest. He fanned and fanned frantically, even for some time after Caroline had come to. Remember Eliza?" "Early Cole fanning Aunt Caroline to?" Questioned Carr before Eliza had time to respond. "Who's Early Cole?"

"No one you'd remember, dear," said Eliza. "He left the neighborhood a good while before you were born, just packed up and vanished in the night, along with his three sons. Knowing Early for the freeloader he was, he probably headed for the hill country to sponge on his relatives for the remainder of his days. In any case, Early Cole dropped out of sight overnight."

"And, if I do say so, without Early and his mare, Maybelle, in many ways, the neighborhood hasn't been the same since," volunteered Matthew. "Early was a character, Carr, a strange breed of man, that's who he was. Though it's too much to go into now, and especially since we have guests present who have no idea in the world who we're talking about. Remind me sometime later on and I'll be happy to tell you all about him, including his stunts. Well, some of them anyhow."

"I'll certainly do that and soon, Grandfather," said Carr, "for I have a feeling it's going to be a mighty interesting story." Then, with a wide grin, he added, "I think we've already left Miss Rachelle, if her lost expression tells me anything."

"Well—I."

"Oh, she's a good listener and so am I," interrupted John, grateful for the twist in conversation. "Please, continue on with this

Early Cole. My interest is stirred now." Anyhow, John thought, surprised to hear that Early had vanished long years back and, at the same time, also wondering if they could tell him anything about Early and his indolent sons that would go one better than what he was already recalling in his mind about them.

"Yes," Rachelle smilingly rejoined, "please go on. As John says, I am a good listener even if my expression does, sometimes, indicate the contrary. It wasn't that I was losing out on the subject of Mr. Cole, Carr, though I did appear to be. Actually, what made me seem lost, I was trying to work out the family connection relative to Seth and Mrs. Roalf being your uncle and aunt."

"Oh, that!" Carr cheerfully grinned again. "I knew there was something you were puzzled over. I'm sorry, Miss Rachelle, I guess it does have you stumped."

Quickly, Eliza put in, "Perhaps I should explain to Rachelle, dear." And, immediately, she plunged in, going into a long rigmarole as the meal continued to progress along about how the unfortunate circumstance of Carr and Jane Anne having no living blood uncles and aunts, had been softened and more or less appeased—in fact nearly diminished altogether—by not only the close ties that the Heywards had ever maintained with the doctor and Caroline but with Bruce and Martha as well. And, even though she failed to pause one second in order to give Rachelle time to respond to her question, she went on to ask had not Rachelle, at some time or other, observed the fact that Carr also addressed Martha and Bruce as aunt and uncle too, going on to point out though that she and Martha were first cousins, actually.

Then, apparently feeling that she still had not amply clarified the situation for Rachelle and, while the later sat almost paralyzed in her gaze with astonishment and John began to feel as though he wanted to cringe out of sight under the table and had a feeling that Doctor Seth Roalf felt likewise, Eliza turned to the doctor who was seated on her left and added, "If Seth here will forgive my doing so, Rachelle, I'll go a step further." She looked back across the table at Rachelle. "'You see, we all don't only love Caroline for herself alone, but are concerned and have become somewhat overly protective of her, I fear, because of the terrible blow she suffered over the tragedy that befell my older brother at Gettysburg. They were engaged and had planned to be married in June of sixty-one. But, that same month, he was called to the battlefields of Virginia instead. Thinking he'd be back home in no more than ninety days when he left, with the war all over and done with—they postponed their wedding till fall. She—never saw him again..."

Eliza's voice had grown weaker and weaker until it had finally trailed off altogether, whether from emotion or the fact that she, at last, realized it was going to be awfully hard for Seth Roalf to forgive her if she didn't shut her mouth, only Eliza knew.

Luke, whose eyes by this time had become almost as transfixed on his wife as Rachelle's were, suspected it might be a little of both. Even so, he was still hard put to understand why Eliza had felt it a must that she prattle on into details as she had. It was a side of her nature that he found himself unfamiliar with and certainly one that he was not taking much delight in, despite his overwhelming love and devotion for her. The awkward silence begins to mount, hanging over the room like a menacing cloud, since Rachelle had come forth and murmured a faint, "I'm sorry". However, Luke was to observe and with some relief at that, since it appeared there were not going to be any more comments coming from anybody for the time being, that the silence seemed to be holding a certain amount Of good, after all. For it was causing everybody to give more attention to their plates, with the result being that they were soon swept clean of the main course and Pete and Penelope were back in the invading silence removing them in order to make room for the dessert course—their presence relieving the situation somewhat—before the awkward hush had had time to become too pronounced.

Even so, it still seemed there was a reluctance on the part of everybody to offer anything toward getting the conversation started back again till, suddenly, Seth Roalf cracked, as Pete took it upon himself to start to remove his dinner plate, "Don't take it too far away Pete, I may be calling for seconds a little later on!" His tolerance and understanding, by no means, escaping Luke Heyward's notice.

"Any time, Doctor Seth, just send me word," returned Pete with a grin as he took the doctor's dinner plate and stacked it atop a number of others that Penelope had already collected and placed on a tea cart.

It seemed the doctor's remark had suddenly worked wonders in the way of bringing the dining room's atmosphere back to its customary norm and especially to that which had ever prevailed over Eliza's dinner parties. For now Bruce was laughing, "Does that go for me too, Pete?" Then, before Pete could respond and as several more chuckles sounded round the table, he gleefully went on, "In fact, I'd call for seconds this instant if I wasn't saving room for Eliza's dessert. She always has something special. Tell me, Pete, what's it going to be this time?"

"'Don't you tell him, Pete, it's a surprise!" Eliza hastily exclaimed. Now, even she appeared to be completely recovered from whatever it was that had, so shortly before that, quelled her tongue to silence.

With the dinner plates all collected and stacked on the tea cart and Penelope preceding him and cart through the door, Pete, still wearing his grin, finally told Bruce over his shoulder, "Sorry, Mr. Bruce, you heard, I have my orders. You'll be seeing in a little bit though. It's all ready."

"Well, I should hope because surprises make me all the more eager and impatient too. So don't keep me waiting long." Bruce laughingly hollered back as Pete disappeared through the doorway.

And, the wait was not long. The resound of Bruce's echo had hardly faded down the hallway before the rattling sound of another tea cart being pushed through the door had everybody's head turning and Beth Anne merrily singing out, at the same time, "Oh, how delightful, strawberry shortcake with whipped cream! Look, papa! Those strawberries look just like the one on your left cheek!" She giggled. "I mean they remind me of that strawberry birthmark that's hidden in your beard!"

Instantly, with the impact of a sweeping tornado, the room's recaptured airy lightness was gone, vanishing like a flash and leaving a stillness so deathlike—soundless as a tomb—that Pete was moved to halt the tea cart and go no further. Looking expectantly at the several startled faces that had turned upon John Fillmore-Lee as the latter's hand had, involuntarily, found his left cheek and rested there, Pete stood in his tracks and waited. Why he continued to wait he did not know, but suspense held him fast from taking another step from where he had paused

Beth Anne, whose giggle had died abruptly, was also held fast in suspense. Though her uncertainty was even more intensified because she was wondering why her remark had made such a shocking impact. She saw nothing improper about referring to one's birthmark. Yet, considering the reaction it had caused she suddenly began to fear that maybe she had bungled convention a little bit, since she happened to be in mixed company and at the table to boat. Even so, this after-thought still did not stop Beth Anne from taking on the notion that if this were indeed the case, that no doubt about it, she was marrying into a bunch of stiff necks!

At any rate, thinking that maybe she should offer an apology for her "scandalous" remark—it appeared to Beth Anne that that was what everybody was waiting for—Beth Anne was ready to do just that, but before she could open her mouth, Matthew Carson's faint unsteady voice was suddenly breaking the silence to mutter, "What did you say, child?"

Beth Anne's head did a fast turn toward Carr's grandfather whom she had come to greatly admire and whom on this night sat at the head of the long dining table at Green Sea. However, to her astonishment, Beth Anne did not meet Matthew Carson's gaze. She saw that he was looking straight at her father instead—his white expression questioning—his intense blue eyes probing. And then, all of a sudden, while Beth Anne still kept her mute silence and sat in bedazed wonder along with everybody else, Matthew Carson went on to mutter, "Phil?" and started pushing his chair back from the table, making an effort to rise.

Even though he was instantly overcome with emotion, that Nat only had his heart welling over but also fluttering a wild dance, too, Philippe Carson was not long coming out of his chair either, telling his father in a broken voice as he dashed around the table to throw his arms round him, "Yes—Pa—it's me, Phil! But—take it easy—Pa don't get upset—everything's going to be all right." Yes, in the spacing of a mere split second—that fraction of time that it had taken his father to utter his name—Philippe Carson had, automatically, cast aside his long borrowed, adoptive name, John Fillmore-Lee and reclaimed his own.

Pulling back somewhat out of his overly long and soul-stirring embrace, Matthew, obviously overcome with this jarring surprise, said, "But, why didn't you let me know, Phil, who you were—here I've been sitting all this while.."

"I know, Pa." Phil interrupted, wiping at the tears falling on his cheeks with the back of his hand. "I waited, because I was hoping that some of you would finally get around to recognizing me, and you did, Pa!" Phil quickly gave his father another hug and then stood back, appearing to be unaware of most everybody in the room now gathering around him to stare in unbelievable wonder, as he himself gazed into Matthew Carson's own teary face.

Matthew gazed back, thinking to himself that it had been more like guessing with him than it had been recognizing who his son was. Even so, in point of Beth Anne's remark it had been a guess that had certainly seemed worth the risk and definitely one that he would have taken at all cost and, especially whether from that time on he would have been dubbed an old crazy dotard or not, in case he was wrong.

Though he tried not to let on that it was that way with him, Matthew Carson's heart was dying a thousand deaths at seeing what time, and obvious pain and suffering had done to this vital, handsome son whom he last remembered. Pulling his handkerchief from his pocket he said, as he lifted his glasses and wiped at his eyes and nose, "Yes—I guess I did, son, and I might've recognized you a lot sooner had not my attention been centered on Caroline. We've all been a little concerned about her state of health lately. But—getting back to you. I don't quite understand your appearing up again like this, after all this time. I searched and looked for you everywhere—left no stone unturned, I thought." Matthew's eyes were still searching—his expression still taut. And, it was likewise with the rest of Phil Carson's relatives and close friends who still stood silently around him, waiting patiently to greet him while this exchange of words was going on between father and son.

"Of course you don't understand, Pa, how could you," Phil readily accorded, "when I'm hard put myself to even imagine that all this is actually happening to me, let alone make myself believe it. As absurd as it is, Pa, I didn't come home because I couldn't remember who I was, or where home was at to come to. It's been that way With me for the past twenty-one years; that is, up until the day before yesterday when I was taking a walk after I arrived here and made an effort to seek cover beside the tombs in the cemetery, when I was overtaken by the storm. I had barely gotten squatted down, though, against the lashing rain before I realized I was getting soaked and should try getting on to the house and had started to rise, when, all of a sudden, a peal of lightning had me spinning back to the ground into unconsciousness, an incident I'll ever look on as something that God willed because, when I came to, I could remember again—all of it, Pa. Everything started coming back to me again as clear as a bell ringing!"

"Heavens and earth! What are you talking about, son?" Matthew gasped, in open mouthed astonishment as his hand grabbed the edge of the table for support. He had heard of cases where there had been a temporary loss of memory. But, never in all his days would he have dreamed that amnesia could be this severe. Twenty-one years! It was incredible, to say the least!

Seeing that Matthew Carson's nervous system had just about reached its end of endurance when it came to supporting him much longer in a standing position, Phil hastily came back, telling his father as he reached to give him assistance in settling back down into his chair, "Here, Pa, sit back down and I'll try to start at the beginning and tell you everything just like it happened. Rachelle will fill in the part where I lay at death's door in a Union Hospital for days. I don't remember that part, nor will I ever, I was too near gone. But, I think I can tell the rest exactly as it happened."

Finding Amy's bolstering nod of courage from where she still sat in her chair a few feet down the table from him, as placidly and composed as ever, Matthew, suddenly not only having gained more strength but patience too, replied, "Yes, certainly, son. I'm more than anxious to know what happened to you. But first, here's your sister, Luke and all the others who wants a word with you. Then, you can tell us."

"Sure, Pa." Phil said, and turning to seek out Eliza first, he tried to be at home with her and all the others, too, who were gathered around him as near as it was humanly possible for him to do so. Their smiles, and their embraces and handshakes were also warm. But even so, the air was somewhat strained, with one greeting hardly varying from the other, including Eliza's, until Phil found himself face to face with Martha. Then everything changed.

Grabbing hold of him and giving him a bear hug that Phil was certain would have posed some special effort even for man to better when it came to muscular force, she shrieked, "Well, speaking of the dead rising!" Then, before Phil could catch his breath she had pulled back and with a gale of laughter that came close to making his ears ring, she went on to say as she let her gaze hang on a direct line with his, "I want you to know Phil Carson, that in regard to that one Biblical trust, your presence is going to be a great inspiration to me from this day forward and, especially, when I'm inclined to let my mind sank in doubts from time to time!"

It mattered not one fraction to Martha that her minister, the Reverend Marsh Reed was present. Martha was being herself. Even so, her mother, Amy was suddenly all aghast, crying, "Martha!" as she wondered, as she had a hundred times if once, who in the world had her daughter inherited her lack of delicacy from.

If Martha heard Amy's distinct, reproof, though, she did not show it in her manner. For she went on with her unconventional bantering, saying to Phil at one point, "Boy, do you have a lot of catching up to do," until Phil, breaking in with a laugh, told her, "Martha, you haven't changed a bit." Martha's refusal to be tamed in his presence had Phil feeling game and surprisingly relaxed, all of a sudden.

"Of course I haven't changed, nor do I expect to." Martha quipped. "Still, for this one time, I think you've been at the mercy of my tongue long enough, so let's you and me and everybody else get back to the table and on with our eating before that strawberry shortcake swims away in that whipped cream! Besides, I don't want to wait another minute to hear what you have to tell us, especially about that pan where you ended up in a Union Hospital, because I surely can't feature those Yankees putting forth any effort at all to save a southerner, much less one from South Carolina!"

Despite all this thick crust and sauciness, which had indeed near-about made her invulnerable to anything she had ever encountered—pleasant or otherwise, this last remark that Martha had made was to dig at her somewhat when she realized she was sitting only a couple of feet from the "Yankee" who had more or less saved Phil Carson's life, not to mention the part that Seth Roalf had played in it. The fact that Phil had been disguised as a member of the Union forces at the time, helped little. She still felt as if someone had taken her down a peg or two.

At all events, it appeared that everybody was ready to follow Martha's suggestion. Eliza readily gave Pete the nod to come on and start serving the dessert and, outside of Phil taking long enough to stop at Amy's chair to embrace her and exchange a word or two, in less than no time everybody was settled at the table again.

Quite surprised to now find himself feeling perfectly at ease for a change, Phil said, no sooner than he had settled in his chair, "It happened at Gettysburg." And, along with Rachelle's help and, while they all leisurely went through the dessert course, to say nothing of the several servings of coffee that followed it, Phil told them his startling Story—all of it—omitting nothing. As each and all still remained at the table giving him their rapt attention, with some partaking of the coffee and others passing it up, he told them everything, about the joys of this twenty-one-year period, as well as the pain and the trials that had been his to suffer too, going by the name of John Fillmore-Lee. Finally, Matthew said, as he drew forth his handkerchief and wiped at his teary cheeks once again, "The one small thing that could've possibly located you for me and doubtless proven your identity to yourself, that birthmark on your cheek, I failed to mention it once, in all the searching I did. I feel I failed you, that when you needed me most, I let you down."

"No, Pa," Phil hastily came back, "I won't have you harboring such thoughts. You've never let anyone down in your life, least of all me. In my opinion, I let you down, and not only you and other members of my family who's here, but my sister and my daughter as well. I can see that now. Maybe if hadn't been so pigheaded, worrying about what someone might say or think about me if my plight became known, letting my pride become the one all-absorbing factor in the matter, I would've found my way to Green Sea a lot sooner than I did." Phil reached for his coffee Cup and finishing emptying it, went on to add as he set the cup back in its saucer, "Still, on the other hand, maybe it was best my coming home happened just as it did. As I've just explained about my business partner, Gilford Sloan. Even though he's been convinced of my true identity since he visited here a few months ago and has been trying to convince me and prepare me for this visit, before that lightning bolt knocked me into unconsciousness, Green Sea still seemed no more like home to me than had I been walking through an unknown wilderness."

"But now it's different, you do know. Heaven be praised." Amy cooed affectionately.

Looking down the table and finding his aunt's face, Phil smiled at her and said, "Yes, thank God, Aunt Amy, I know," and for a moment, even though a silence fell, it were as if the whole room was overflowing in a hymn of praise and thankfulness. And then, with the entity of this same prevailing gladness, coming through in her voice, Beth Anne, unable to keep her sudden discovery to herself one second longer, was crying ecstatically, "Papa, I just thought of something, I'm Carr's first cousin!"

"Indeed you are, darling." Phil smilingly averred. "I just thought of that myself." "Makes everything all the more crazier," laughed Carr, and as other chuckles from round the table emerged in with his, making the occasion seem united in spirit and gratitude all that much more, Carr made so bold as to send his future bride a devilish wink— the likeness between himself and his grandfather, when the later had set out on that journey to New Orleans a half century earlier astoundingly pronounced.

Chapter Six

Never was there an Easter Sunday like it. Nor in the days following Easter anything like it ever in the whole community and neighboring countryside. Further, no one subject or happening could have affected a wider distinction in people's emotions once this sensational news of Philippe Carson's return befell the hearer's ear. Even so, this kept nobody from rushing toward the place that gave rise to the news as quickly as they could make ready to get there. With their fixed expressions of shock, misgivings and doubt, joy, thankfulness, or just plain nothing—a blank mask, still planted on their faces, they flocked to Green Sea in droves. Not only did they swarm to Green Sea for the purpose of convincing themselves that this staggering news was for real and not some mere hearsay, but also to satisfy their curiosity about that inevitable change that time brings to man and, especially in this case where for a long period of twenty-one-years the subject had been thought of as being deceased!

Even a large number of those whom had seen and greeted Philippe Carson at church on Sunday morning, did not hesitate at following him back to Green Sea after the Easter service. It made no difference at all that they had not been invited. They came anyway. And, from then on and well into the following week, Green Sea gave every appearance of having suddenly converted to a railroad station. The only feature missing—the one traveling conveyance that truly kept the scene from looking like the real thing in every respect— literally authentic to the letter, was the train! Traveling conveyance of all types, loaded down with guests, kept coming and going in a constant stream, keeping the stable yard and lane too, continuously overflowed with vehicles and their different "breeds" of pulling power. No sooner than one rig took its departure if another one was not already there to take its place, it was soon sighted coming up the oak-lined drive naturally, with custom being as it was, refreshments and eats were ever in order.

So, with not one single pot or container of food left in Pete's kitchen that was not scraped clear to the bottom by Monday morning, despite the bulk that had been prepared for the weekend, and with uninvited company still pouring in—making it plain that the situation might even become worse before it got better—Luke saw no alternative in the way of keeping food on hand but to stage a full-fledged barbecue. After talking it over with Eliza and with her agreeing, too, that a barbecue seemed the only sensible way to solve the problem, Luke then approached the main brace of the plantation, Willie and Allen, something he had ever done when it was a job of work where time and skill were both important. The rest of the tenants, which included Charlie and Sam and a number of their offspring, were only too willing to lay aside whatever task they had planned to work at that day and loan their assistance too. And, with the women also bonding to the job with an enthusiasm that would equal that of Christmas, by noontime the result of their efforts was speaking for itself through the severing smell that was coming from the barbecue pit where a whole half-grown yearling and hog were roasting.

In the meantime, Pete had thrown all his energy and skill to baking bread and when this aroma combined with that from the barbecue pit got to sifting through the air, it certainly did everything but throw a wet blanket on Green Sea's stream of visitors. Their urge to head in that direction was whetted that much more, causing even a greater number of callers to come bounding up the drive—some even padding up the drive on foot!

It seemed the impact that Philippe Carson's reappearance at Green Sea had made, was going to have no stoppage point. Nor did it appear there was going to be anybody left in the neighborhood who was not going to make the most of the event by way of their stomachs. Well, those that enjoyed a hale and hearty stomach, anyhow! In truth, when it came to taking an event and turning it to their advantage, it appeared even the Reverend Marsh Reed was no exception—actually on top of the heap, so to speak. Despite all that pounding and flailing away the reverend had done over the miracle of the event on Easter Sunday—sounding like the congregation had assembled that day for the purpose of celebrating the resurrection of Philippe Carson instead of the Resurrection of Christ—not only had Marsh Reed practically taken up residence at Green Sea in the meantime, but he had also continued to cry to this one and that one about the good that ever befalls believers, until he had finally succeeded in gaining the promise of several backsliders meaning that they would be nowhere when the next Sunday morning rolled round but on the front seat of the Baptist Church; and that they would be there with a liberal sum of money to put in the collection plate besides!

Matthew Carson was another whom had hardly left Green Sea,

or, for that matter, his son's side since the two were reunited with one another. Unlike the reverend though, Matthew's case was different; in that, his presence was expected. Indeed, had Matthew Carson not been present, the public would have been most astonished because besides being the father of the long "out of sight" Philippe Carson, Matthew was Green Sea, in a manner of speaking. He identified with the place, was linked with the Plantation as much as ever in the minds of the people despite all those years he had resided at Drakston Hall.

At any rate, in addition to being the ultimate when it came to news, no neighborhood happening had ever attracted more attention or stirred more emotions than Philippe

Carson's sudden homecoming. Not even that shocking accident that had taken the late Frank Drakston to his untimely death, had crowned its impact in magnitude. And yet, when it came to emotions being aroused because of it, it is safe to say that nobody's had undergone any more upheaval—high and low—than Lucy Randolph had as she had sat and taken in Phil Carson's startling story. However, the stunning realization that the man from Lexington was no one but Philippe Carson in the flesh, and the moving details of his experiences, had not been the main cause of Lucy's perturbation, even as much as the facts of the telling had moved her. Mostly, it had been what Lucy had learned about herself that had disturbed her and, at the same time, had also started a bubble of excitement coursing through her veins as well.

Having found herself wishing that it were possible Nat could also turn up and wondering as she had what their meeting would be like if he could, thinking to herself would she faint like Caroline had, Lucy Randolph had been startled cold to realize that aside from being grateful and happy to see Nat Carson alive again, the occasion would hold nothing more for her. For finding that her heart was doing nothing but running along at its normal rate—not one retained quiver quickening its beat—not one wistful tug pulling at it, Lucy had suddenly become aware that she was enamored of the late Nathan Carson no longer. Yes, that smoldering passion that had ever dwelled within Lucy's being for Philippe Carson's younger brother—not only living on even after his death and keeping her emotions jailed in its fervid grip, but also ever flaming anew each and every time her thoughts had turned to him—had finally smoldered to its last and final spark.

149

To realize that she no longer yearned for the deceased Nat Carson—finally holding nothing more in her heart for him than feelings of mere friendship when she had been prepared to go on being devoted to his memory for the remainder of her days, had been a difficult and desolating fact for Lucy Randolph to take in much less accept until, all of a sudden, another important factor had captured her awareness. Gilford Sloan's sensitive, trouble-battered face had edged its way into the picture. It had brought Lucy up sharp and at the same instant had made her realize something else and that was, there had been a lot more involved in all that easy freedom that she and Gilford Sloan had enjoyed in one another's company, when the latter had visited the low country in February, than what she had been aware of at the time.

And so, having abruptly transferred her thoughts from the long deceased Nat Carson to the much alive Gilford Sloan and letting them rest on that short, peaceable interlude that she and Gilford Sloan had reveled in at the time—the sharing of ill-fated dreams finding them much the same, not to mention the near paralleling of views and impressions and the much delight that she had taken in his heartwarming letters since his return to Lexington—Lucy's heart had taken a sudden upward swing. And later on that same night when she departed for Oak Grove, Lucy Randolph had finally been made aware Of two more startling facts. Not only did she know that, at last, she had taken possession of her heart once more—no longer leaving it behind buried at Green Sea with Nat Carson, but she would also put no restraint on it whatever when she and the compassionate Gilford Sloan had the opportunity to be in one another's company again.

For Eliza Heyward, it was good that due to her heavy responsibilities she could only snatch a moment or two here and there to reflect upon the situation. For had she had the time to have, literally, weighed all aspects that were now involved in the turn of events, there is no question that her own senses would have been awakened to even greater tension and surprises, too, than Lucy's had been. Now, there was not only the question of who the heirship of Green Sea's vast holdings rightfully belonged to hanging over Eliza, but there was also that strange side to her nature that she had to deal with besides—a side that caused her, at time, to dwell in a state of extreme turmoil. Even so, it was a part of herself that although she had never come to fully understand, she had come to accept and even, on occasion, revel in. Though she walked the paths of this alien world alone, sharing these premonitory experiences with no one, not even her adored Luke. And, it had ever been thus and especially since that mystical encounter long ago when she had looked upon Green Sea's serene, snow-blanketed grounds and had seen the peril surrounding Luke as clearly as if he had been standing before her.

Strange as it was, Eliza's deep reasoning logic had embodied her with a strong conviction to keep her silence about these psychical encounters that she met with, no doubt sparing herself the ordeal of being scorned and looked on as an oddball by the greater majority of people—even cast completely aside by many. At the same time, something else of great significance had also played a big part in her having the ability to cope with this clairvoyant power which she possessed and that was, her tendency to always view it as being solely the work of God's hand, at the time, rather than something related with her oneself.

At any rate, Eliza's way of viewing the matter had still not spared her the agony of feeling a certain amount of guilt when that apparition, which she had felt following on her heels for days, had suddenly materialized into her long missing brother. And, an Obviously declining and grey-bearded brother at that. It pained Eliza deeply to look at Phil Carson, because she had to acknowledge when she did that she had always been almost certain that he was still alive and dwelling some place. Though she had no idea where. All the same, when she and Luke had finally gotten around to discussing this most unexpected and shocking incident of their lives, so far, Eliza was still unable to bring herself to disclose anything about her feelings or clairvoyant experience to Luke, regarding the matter of her brother or anything else that her psychic sense had convinced her of over the years.

To have disclosed it would have been breaking that pact that she had more or less made with her God long ago, would it not, she told herself—a promise to keep those visional experiences to herself because in the glade that day when hopelessness and despair had gripped her, He had let her see that Luke was well and safe. How could she betray a confidence like that? She couldn't, she had finally concluded, and had gone on and, with her troubled mind seen to the things that, as mistress of Green Sea, were demanded of her.

After shaking what seemed like several hundred hands and acknowledging that many introductions for the greater part of two full days, Rachelle Fillmore Carson was having some difficulty in adjusting to being addressed as "Mrs. Carson," and at her husband's insistence was finally persuaded to ensconce herself in the quiet of their assigned bedroom so that she could get some much needed rest. Though Rachelle would have been the first to admit that both her hands and feet felt as though they were drawing close to a paralyzed state when she finally did move from Phil Carson's side, not to mention the failing of her strength in general, this nevertheless would not have kept her from trying to continue to bear up under the strain, if the matter had only been left to her alone. For besides wanting to be present so that she would not miss out on meeting a single one of these former friends and acquaintances of her husband's who were still pouring into Green Sea by fits and starts, Rachelle also wanted to be there in case Caroline Wilton Roalf might feel up to dropping in again. Since Caroline Roalf, or her husband for that matter, had not shown her face at Green Sea another time —word had sifted that she was feeling a great deal better —Rachelle thought that maybe she was more inclined to be just plain curious about Seth's wife than she was jealous. Though she would not have taken a bet on it!

At any rate, because divulging this fact of not wanting to miss seeing Caroline Roalf—in case she did put in an appearance again, would have been the ultimate of confessions for Rachelle, she went ahead and yielded to Phil Carson's wishes, telling herself as she did though that even if it was going against the grain with her that it would be sort of nice to have a calmer atmosphere to do her thinking in—mull over those wearing questions in her head. For example, when was her husband going to get around to mentioning Caroline Roalf's name again? And further, if Caroline Roalf did fail to come back to Green Sea, would John go to Elms to see her before he departed for Lexington? It seemed her mind could not cease to stop wondering!

Surprisingly to Rachelle, she soon knew the answer to both her questions. She had no more than gotten herself out of her clothes and into her dressing gown and, with the bed pillows supporting her back had plopped down on the bed in a comfortable propped up position, setting her mind to her questions as she sipped a cup of hot chocolate that Bessie had just left on the night table, then her husband had her head turning toward the door as he softly opened it to peek inside.

"Come on in." Rachelle smiled. "I'm not asleep yet. For the present, I'm only following part of your orders, to get off my feet."

As Phil pushed the door wider and came on in, she went on, "This hot chocolate is very satisfying. If you'd like a cup, I'll ring for Bessie before she heads back downstairs. She's just across the hall."

"Not now, dear, maybe later," he replied as he sat down beside her on the edge of the bed. I was just anxious to know if you'd gotten settled down yet. Now that you have, I bet you'll agree that I was right. Surely lying here sipping a cup of hot chocolate has to be a far sight more relaxing on your nerves than having them exposed to all that racket downstairs, not to mention your physical strength as a whole."

Smiling at him over the rim of her cup, Rachelle said, "Well, I suppose I can stretch my toes a great deal farther than what I was able to do in those slippers I had on. It feels good, too."

"Your toes!" He laughed. "And, I should think that by this time you'd know that it's not just your toes that concerns me!" He dropped his laughter and suddenly grew serious. "I want you to take it easier and rest because I 'm concerned for your health in general. There's the long trip back home we have to consider, I want you to be up to it. And that's not all. Our daughter's wedding is also coming up in the near future. We have to plan and prepare for it."

"Thinking of going home already?" Rachelle quizzed, disregarding his last remarks because she knew that nothing had prompted them but that fierce ingrained dignity and pride of his— something that she had detected running in his blood from the first, and something that she had never seen him lose no matter what. Certainly, she knew that more than there being a tendency in him to want to crow or be a showoff, so to speak, it had been these proud-spirited qualities that had actually fired the outburst.

"It appears to be that way with me," he finally confessed, "though I've decided we probably shouldn't be taking our leave before the latter part of next week sometime. I've been thinking about Sloan a lot. I'm anxious to see him—tell him about all this— about all the incredible things that's happened to me since our arrival here." He grew silent for a moment, his eyes wondering across the room. "It's not the same though, Rachelle. I can't seem to overcome feeling out of place. I guess I've been away too long."

His seemingly low spirits got to Rachelle. Even so, trying to hearten him and, at the same time, trying to get across to him, too, that if he were expecting to take up where he left off it was not going to be that way, she laid her hand on his and told him, "You must keep in mind, dear, that nothing stays the same. There's always some degree of difference, even from day to day, though as a rule we're blind to it, which is good. Change is a part of life. Not only is it inevitable, but it also makes no exceptions, regardless of whatever it is that's involved."

"True enough," he agreed, "still I should think that it wouldn't be that way when it comes to the matter of emotional attachment. Closeness between family members, and friends too for that matter, should be more durable to my way of thinking." Suddenly, to Rachelle's surprise he was turning a grinning face back to her and going on, "Now that, last remark necessarily, isn't meant to imply that I was thinking about Doctor and Mrs. Seth Roalf."

"Well, why did you come up with it then?" Rachelle asked, a slight trace of indignation edging her voice in spite of her determination to keep it out.

"Oh come, Rachelle," he said, still grinning at her, "I know the Roalfs' absence here these past few days has aroused your curiosity just as much as it has mine!"

Rachelle was put out a little, all of a sudden, to realize that her regarding Caroline Roalf had not been hidden from her husband at all. Knowing she was hooked though, under his gaze, she bore with it and said, rather shyly, "It does pose some questions doesn't it, especially since word is stirring that Mrs. Roalf is feeling a great deal better..

"Yes, it does," he said quickly falling to seriousness again. "Still, on the other hand, maybe we shouldn't jump to any conclusions; like, maybe they're avoiding us on purpose. Caroline appears to be terribly frail to me. Most likely, it's Seth Roalf insisting that she stays put for a while, taking no chances that she gets overly excited and faints dead away again, and who can find fault with that, if that is the case. I know that's what I'd do if I were in his shoes. It's frightening to see someone looking as lifeless as Caroline looked, and especially if the victim is your own wife. For a few minutes there, she looked as if she might have been on the verge of taking her last sleep! In point of Seth Roalf himself, he could be very much occupied with a difficult confinement case, or attending to some other patient's troublesome problem.

Suddenly, Rachelle was feeling very comfortable again. Though Phil Carson's remarks had solely concerned the Roalfs, they had made no less impact on Rachelle than had he been whispering words of love in her ears. Now feeling very safe and much unthreatened by anyone in Phil Carson's devotion for her, it mattered not one iota to Rachelle if Phil did call to Elms. In fact, all of a sudden, Rachelle were wishing that her husband would call on Caroline Roalf and felt no uneasiness whatever about broaching the subject to him.

"But, you will see Caroline before we leave here—I mean, have a talk with her, won't you?" Rachelle questioned.

Phil smiled. "You think it's best, don't you?"

"Not only do I think it's best, but, all of a sudden, I'm also thinking it's your duty," she replied.

"So do I." Phil Carson said, as a meaningful look passed between him and his wife.

Thinking about how jubilant in years passed that he had made for Elms unique and impressive door knocker whose shape and leaf design was supposed to symbolize the Elm tree, taking the wide steps and overlarge porch in bounds and leaps in order to announce his presence as quickly as possible to Caroline Wilton—who as a rule was standing directly behind the door waiting for him if she was not already planted smilingly on the porch, Philippe Carson found it to be rather ironical that he was now standing back in the same spot gazing hesitantly at the door knocker as his hand hang idle at his side.

Still, knowing that he had gone too far to turn away and leave without making his presence known and also that he could not continue to keep on standing there and doing nothing, he lifted his hand to sound the knocker but suddenly became startled to see the door being pulled open by Caroline herself before he even touched it.

For a fleeting moment neither did nothing but stare at the other. Then, Caroline was smiling at him and, to Phil, it seemed to wipe the greater part of the awkwardness that gripped him away.

"Come on in, Phil," she said as she stood aside, her hand still on the doorknob. "I promise I won't faint at your feet anymore."

Indeed, from all appearances Phil was confident she wouldn't. For with her apple-green dress bringing out the green highlights in her eyes and the trace Of color that had risen to her cheeks framing her face in a warm glow, she looked far from being the ill woman whom everybody seemed to think she was.

He returned her smile, saying, as he stopped across the threshold, "I'll not fret about that possibility, Caroline, if your looks tell me anything. In case you do though, I'll also make you a promise and that is, I promise I won't let you hit the floor too hard!"

Closing the door behind him, Caroline laughed and gesturing for Phil to proceed on into the parlor she told him, "Fair enough, sir, and thank you kindly for the compliment. They come in short measure these days!"

"You'd have a hard time in convincing me of that," he shot back at her as he took his seat in the deep-blue velvet wing chair that she had indicated. He suddenly felt good, relaxing considerably in the pleasantry which they had ever enjoyed in one another's company— pleasantly that seemed to be as natural and easy as always.

Seating herself opposite him in the mate to the chair he sat in, Caroline sent him another charming smile and said, "You haven't changed a bit, the same gallant knight you ever were."

"In some respects, maybe not," he agreed. "But..." he stopped. His manner and gallantly were one thing, but discussing his countenance with Caroline was quite another. He had no taste for getting into such a subject.

Taking his cue, Caroline went no further with it, letting the subject drop. Instead, she promptly asked of everybody's health and well-being at Green Sea. Then after offering to ring for refreshments, which Phil graciously declined and joking went on to point out that he was fasting for a few hours, she took on a sudden look of seriousness and said, "Seth said you'd come."

"He did?" Phil asked, and then felt foolish. Her remark had thrown him.

"Yes, he did," she soberly came back and added nothing more.

Seeing that she was more than ready for the conversation to swing from their trivial repartee to that which had apparently brought him to Elms to start with, Phil came straight to the point, saying quickly, as his eyes fell upon her right hand, "The doctor must be a very understanding man. I see you're still wearing my ring."

Likewise, she made no attempt to evade nothing, telling him on the instant, "'He is that. That's one the reasons I married him. Another was I wanted children. Though, unfortunately, we weren't blessed with any." She made no reference to the ring, nor did Phil mention it anymore.

"I'm sorry, Caroline," he said.

"Well," she said, her expression turning more cheerful, "I didn't miss out altogether, you know. I did have Seth Junior. He was only a tot when I married Seth. I mothered him and took a lot of pleasure from doing it, so I suppose my disappointment once not having one of my own was more or less compensated through him. You may have already learned of this but in case you haven't, Seth Junior is married to Bruce and Martha's older daughter, Maggie. He decided to follow in his father's footsteps and study medicine and is serving his internship in Virginia. Both he and Maggie have been living there for some time now. He'll soon have his doctor's license though, so they'll be coming home right away. He wants to practice medicine here at home with his father."

"No, I hadn't heard about that yet." Phil said. "Thanks for filling me in. I've already concluded that if I'm to sensibly engage in conversation that pertains to this community and its people, it's going to be essential that I catch up on all the things I've missed out on."

"I suppose so," she murmured, falling to silence once more as she let her gaze leave his face and drop to her lap.

Seeing that if he were to make any progress at all along the line of achieving what he had hoped to achieve when he had set out for Elms, which had been to make a few important facts clear to Caroline, Phil, deciding that he had better get on with it plunged straight to the point again, saying, "Caroline, I truly couldn't remember who I was until the other day at the cemetery. I wanted to tell you this in private and also tell you that I never once held one reservation about you or our relationship, in case you've wondered about it since my return to Green Sea. I loved you and wanted to marry you. As for what happened to me, I have no answer or explanation for it. Certainly, it couldn't have been that I subconsciously wanted to walk away from my life here and, unknowingly, allowed my misfortune in battle to be the means of gratifying this subconscious want. Even though I'll admit I've entertained the possibility of such a thing happening and questioned it in my mind many times over the years, in no way will I ever believe it. And now, since I can see and know all the things that I had going for me here, I'm positive of it. Anyways, my hope is that you'll believe me when I say this and, if there were any doubts in your mind about it, come to view the whole matter as I do and that is, that it was an unfortunate circumstance that was beyond our control."

His usage of the past tense in connection with the words love and marry did not slip Caroline's attention. Still, surprising to her was the fact that it caused her little pain, if any at all. Granted, she lacked a mile being as disturbed as she had ever anticipated she would be in the event that it should happen. The fact was, Caroline Roalf was suddenly more piqued at herself than anything else—piqued to realize how one's own emotions could deceive one for so long. Even so, it made what she had to say to Philippe Carson easier than had it been to the contrary.

With her gaze finding his face again, she said to him, as a little playful smile began to take shape around her mouth, I won't deny, Phil, that I have done a lot of wondering about the matter the past few days. Still, that doesn't mean that I have doubts about any part of what you've just told me. Thinking back to how it was between us that last night before you left to join Lee's Army in Virginia, I hardly see how I could doubt you, do you?"

He wished that she had not mentioned that and was much surprised that she had. Since she had brought it up though, he saw no reason to try to evade answering her, or for that matter answer with some vague and empty response, either. So, instead of answering her question outright and leaving it at that, he put his eyes on a level with hers and came back with a question of his own, saying, "Did you ever regret it?"

"No, I didn't," she firmly declared, "because with your going away and the possibility of our never seeing one another again hanging over us, I felt that it was right for us, at the time," surprising him once more.

"I felt the same way and still do. But, I want you to know that I did worry a great deal about it for some time afterwards." He said.

"Until you were certain nothing was going to come of it," she affirmed, her smile becoming more prominent.

"Something on that order," he came back, smiling back at her and, although they let the matter of their last night together lie where it was dropped at and did not refer to it another time, before either of them realized it, they had talked away the whole afternoon and Caroline was saying all of a sudden, as she rose to her feet and reached for the match box on the mantel, "I guess we'd better light the lamp."

"Here, let me, dear." Phil offered, jumping to his feet and taking the match box from Caroline's hand. And, as he put a flaming match to the wick and sat the lamp globe back down over the lighted flame and a soft glow fell upon them, a hush also fell between them—a hush that not only seemed somber but also one that seemed to be saturating each of them with a deep reluctance to speak.

Her lack of not being fully aware of how much her feelings had changed over the years for Philippe Carson was not a vexing matter to Caroline any longer. For in the last few hours she had come to realize that regardless of empty memories, or whatever the case was with either him or her toward the other, she was totally defenseless against his charm and would stay that way, no matter what. Caroline was certain of this. And, standing and watching Philippe Carson step back to the mantel and silently go about placing the match box back in its place in a most lingering way, she thought that perhaps he was feeling likewise toward her and also was mentally acknowledging it.

Finally, after another long silent moment had passed—a moment in which Philippe Carson had turned his head back toward Caroline and gazed at her intently, he broke the hush, saying, "I suppose I'd better get a move on and head back for Green Sea. Not only is it almost dark but it's going to soon be suppertime."

"You could dine here, Phil," she readily offered. "Even though I'm not expecting Seth back until bedtime or maybe later, I'm sure the cook will be calling supper right on schedule, as usual. I'd love having you join me. Dining alone can become rather boring, you know."

"That it can, dear, and I'd love our dining together too," he smiled, "but I fear if were to accept and stay, they'd have a search party out looking for me before we even thought about dessert, let alone devoured the rice and meat!"

Caroline laughed, "Well, considering that possibility, I guess we'd best forget it.

But thanks for coming anyway. We've had a most pleasant visit just the same, or I know I have."

"A most pleasant visit that was filled with good talk. I don't believe we've skipped over any one person whom we know or left out any one happening that's occurred, or, for that matter, balked at any one subject," he averred, as he turned to step across the room to where his hat was hanging on a hat rack beside the door.

With her face growing pensive all of a sudden, Caroline, starting to move toward the door too, said, "I'll see you to the steps."

"No, dear," Phil readily came back, bringing her to a stop as he reached for his hat and clapped it slapdash far back on his head like she had seen him do countless of time in years gone. "You stay inside and out of the chill. I can find my way out." Turning back to face her he went on with a grin. "Besides, you're much prettier standing there where the light can reflect on your beauty and that apple-green dress than you'd be out there in that growing dark, anyway."

She appeared not to have heard the flattery in his remark, focusing all her attention on only one word.

"The dark," she murmured softly, her gaze straying past him at nothing. "It seems out goodbyes are always being said in the gloom of darkness. I recall the last time I followed you out to the steps, or maybe I should say a little way beyond the steps. It was so dark that time, I couldn't even see your face."

With a fading grin, Philippe Carson crossed the room to where Caroline Roalf stood and told her, as he reached for her two hands and held them, "That's strange, I was thinking the very same thing. That's one the reasons I suggested you stay where you're at this time and not follow me out. One can call it anything they like, but I don't mind telling you that I have a feeling about things like that, repeating ill-fated steps, so to speak. So, such being the case with me, what do you say to our not taking one step that would put any uneasiness in my mind that our parting this time might be ill-fated like it was last time." He inclined his head and let his lips brush her cheek. "Take care, dear. I'll be leaving for Lexington in a few days but hope to make it back to Green Sea, if not before Beth Anne and Carr's wedding, shortly afterwards. Maybe then the four of us, you and Seth and Rachelle and I, can get together and have a good visit like you and I have had here at Elms this afternoon."

"'I'd like that, Phil," she said, her gaze suddenly leaping back from nowhere to center on his face in lively expectation. "You've suddenly made that twilight out there seem like morning sunshine!"

Likewise, her remark made Philippe Carson's face grow lighter, too. "Bye, dear one," he smiled, and then after gripping Caroline Roalf's hands in a most affectionate manner, Philippe Carson let them fall from his and turned his back to her, finding his own way out like he had said he would.

Even so, for all the good that was to come from all that care and discretion that Philippe Carson exercised in his parting with Caroline Roalf—leery about either her or him taking one step that would be a repetition of some move they had made in that long ago parting, he might as well have saved his steps and measures and let Caroline have followed him as far as she had wanted to. For despite all the wariness and also any high hope or enthusiasm that he may have departed from Elms within regard to Caroline Roalf in the future ahead, destiny was to rule against it; in that, Phil was not to see Caroline again for several months. And, the grim fact was when he did see her, Caroline Roalf was lying in her coffin!

Actually, in point of fact, despite all the trouble that Philippe Carson had already seen in his lifetime, he was to come to look back on this period in his life as being the bleakest he had ever endured. Even those few short happy months that were vouchsafed to him and Rachelle before their daughter's wedding and the few short weeks that they had afterwards, not to mention the wondrous miracle of him gaining his memory back in the period, were to save Philippe Carson from viewing the entire year as being the most trying and dismal he had ever experienced. And, in the forthcoming months, his sister Eliza Heyward was moved to share his view.

All the same, the year did bring forth their children's wedding and, in all fairness, to boast of a more gala affair the whole of Lexington was forced to keep a quiet tongue the weather not withstanding. The June day was perfect. Still, for all the day's sunny brightness, the smiles seemed that much sunnier with none appearing to top Eliza's when it came to wideness!

To realize that her beloved son had not become entangled in a lecherous Yankee's net after all—losing his senses under her deceitful luring, and was marrying no other than a Carson and one of her own blood at that, had generated a cheerfulness in Eliza that seemed no less charged than had she been connected to some generating apparatus. The one and only factor that kept the occasion from being of the most enjoyable of her entire life was her staying knowledge of Stuart Drakston's presence. As much as she tried to ignore Stuart and go on about her business of enjoying herself—making it a point to smilingly convey her happiness over the affair to this one and that one, regarding the smile not only did it drop by several degrees once or twice when she was subjected to Stuart's presence a little too long, but it vanished altogether one-time when she suddenly spied him and Jane Anne obviously lost to all and anything around them but one another's presence parked off together under a distant apple tree!

The incident ruffled Eliza to no end. And, one may be sure, she hesitated not one instant in making a move toward the scene—her mind centered on nothing but making a fiery tongue-lashing invasion! However, by the time she gained her way through the throng of milling guests to where she could get another clear view of the battle site, to her dismay she saw the enemy had vanished, fleeing to other whereabouts and taking her daughter with him, she was positive! Nonetheless, since the problem was no longer right before her very eyes and because, too, way deep down she truly did not want to stage a fight with Stuart Drakston on her son's wedding day, Eliza promptly pushed her mentally-charged ammunition to the back of her head and put her smile back on, telling herself that she would go ahead and accept the inevitable for that one day as she turned and let the smile widen at the person brushing her elbow.

Of course, Eliza was not the only one on this particular day who was forced to fight taxing emotions. With a great deal of frangibility running in the veins of mankind as a whole, naturally along this line she had company—namely the Simpson family, Phil and Rachelle's closest neighbors. Though it was fact all three Simpson's father and mother and son had suffered a powerful letdown when it was known that Carr Heyward had won the hand of the vibrant Beth Anne; and also, that Scott Simpson lacked a long way from being completely recovered from the defeat, he still appeared to be more reconciled of the matter than his parents were. Even though both older Simpsons were their usual gracious selves and did manage to keep their joyful nature intact throughout the day, it still was not enough to conceal the great disappointment that they were feeling.

Still and all; however, when it came to emotional upheaval, the wedding did not become a testing experience for everybody. There were many guests present who appeared to be totally free of any concern or care, having come for one purpose only and that was to eat, drink, and make merry! Then, there were others present who appeared to have stacks of cares—loving cares that is and Lucy Randolph on the arm of Gilford Sloan had slowly but finally freed her emotions and placed herself in this group! Still, Gilford Sloan was giving every impression that he was holding a lot of tender affection, too, and apparently he was because that coming November he was to make Lucy Randolph his bride on Thanksgiving Day.

The bride on this day though was Beth Anne Carson and a more joyful or lovelier bride the eyes had yet to look upon. Nor did handsome Carr Heyward pose any hardship to look at, either. Thought his fortitude did seem to be near the toppling stage once or twice due to the continual ribbing of his many friends and fellow classmates from the nearby military institute. Even so, Carr was aware that he had nobody to blame but himself, because thanks to his magnanimity—and popularity too—the number he had invited to his wedding on his own, was staggering. It brought other Lexington guests and those of whom who had come from South Carolina and other parts of the country, too, to wonder if the whole academy had not turned out for the affair. Cadets swarmed everywhere, especially around the numerous buffet tables that were set up in the dining room and on both porches too—front and back—with all sorts of delectable spread out on their white linen cloths, including Boston baked beans, which not only turned Eliza's smile into a little grimace when she saw them, but also made her conscience weigh somewhat heavy with guilt besides!

Although he did appreciate the swarming attendance of his friends, their raillery was another thing and something that Carr was not prepared for. Not so with his bride though. She took it all in stride, either shrieking with laughter at the cadet's jokes or bowing to the other ungraceful extreme of sticking her tongue out at them and making a face, much to the chagrin of her refined parents, to say the least. None the less, with the help of his grandfather, Matthew Carson who actually devised the plan and his old-time friend Luke Green who along with his parents Tom and Betsy Green had journeyed from North Carolina to attend the wedding, Carr finally outsmarted his friends and had the last laugh.

When all was ready for Carr and Beth Anne to take their departure for the train depot to catch the train for their secret honeymoon destination—Carr was determined that his friends would continue to guess what part of the country he was headed for—instead of going out the front entrance and pay the brunt of what he knew was going to be a thundering send-off in the coach, which the cadets had waiting and which they were gathered around with its amassment of bells and ribbons and other odds and ends that startlingly displayed the length of their imagination, Carr grabbed Beth Anne's hand and guided her through a side entrance and on down the lane toward the stables a little way to where Luke Green was waiting with the Green's Coach.

Having already planted himself in the driver's seat and waiting with the reins in his hands ready to go, Luke, ever grinning like his father before him, chuckled, "Hurry up and get aboard lovebirds, before they get wise to what we're doing."

Now, nearly out of breath from trying to match Carr's long swift strides, Beth Anne pulled back somewhat, crying, "But, what are we doing, Carr, for heaven sakes! Won't you tell me?" In his haste Carr had explained nothing, leaving Beth Anne wondering if they were headed to North Carolina with the Greens rather than their honeymoon destination.

"We're escaping these devilish cadets, that's what we're doing." Carr came back, picking Beth Anne up in one swift move and plumping her down in the back seat, then going on to add as he hopped in and plumped down beside her, "I've been under their fire too long as it is. Bend down, darling, so the devils won't see us through the window, and don't worry about our luggage or anything else, Luke and grandfather have taken care of everything.

Now, seeing what Carr was up to, Beth Anne instantly became game. As the coach started to move off, she snuggled down beside Carr out of sight, snickering, "You mean, Grandfather Carson is in on all this?" Having greatly admired Matthew Carson from the first moment of their meeting, it now thrilled Beth Anne to the very tip of her toes to think of him as truly being her own grandfather, too.

"He sure is and you're going to learn a lot more about our Grandfather Carson that's going to surprise you. One thing that you'll come to see is, he won't be old when he reaches a hundred," averred Carr, as Luke Green drove on down the lane and on by Carr's rowdy friends as nonchalantly as if he were doing nothing but merely taking his own leave for home.

Having heard the cadets for some few minutes now whoop and yell their heads off for Carr to take his bride and come on out, Phil Carson, growing rather weary of their racket, said, "Pa, don't you think it's about time we let them know there's no longer a groom and bride here to be cheered aboard their waiting coach?"

Before Matthew could reply, Amy piped, "Yes, pray do something, Matthew, because I'd say from the sound of their clamor, they're becoming a little out of hand."

"If you say, dear," smiled Matthew, rising from his chair where he sat in the living room with his wife, his son and Rachelle, and several more relatives and close friends, and going on to step to the door and on through the hallway and onto the front porch hardly any less agile than had his years been cut by a third. And moreover, as he paused his step and promptly let a mischievous gaze fall over the impatient gang before him and asked, "Boys, by any chance, did any of you happen to hear that train whistle just now?" The voice that had cut through their whoops and yells had sounded stout as ever.

Instantly, from the looks of the falling faces before him, Matthew knew that going into a long, wordy account of what had developed while the cadets had been so joyfully occupied, was totally unnecessary. So, deciding that one simple Statement would suffice, he told them, "That's right, boys, he and his bride are already on their way from these parts," affirming their keen suspicious that they had finally been caught with their pants down—so to speak—with a wide grin before he turned back to go inside amid the several disgusted groans rising after him.

In less than no time, Carr's much thwarted friends had stripped their bedecked coach, which in the first place had belonged to Phil Carson, of all its gaudy trappings and after depositing it back in the carriage house had headed back to their lodgings at the academy, leaving Matthew Carson to be about the only one present who failed to gain a great deal of contentment from their leaving.

With his devoted Amy accompanying him, Matthew had gone to Lexington weeks before the wedding and, having made the acquaintance of these young men as he had visited with Carr several times at the academy before Carr's graduation, which he had also attended, he had become quite taken with a number of them. And so, ever desiring to see a good sprinkling of spice fall on any gala affair, Matthew had appreciated their presence and savored every moment of liveliness that they had loaned to the day's event, even if he had plotted against them just for the sake of being in on a little devilment.

Still, as Matthew sat in the calm wake that his grandson's animated friends had left behind them with his family and friends once again, contributing a nod or word here and there to the flow of conversation as his mind tended to follow in the path of the absent cadets as well as dwell on a dozen of other things, he soon discovered that not only did the more quiet atmosphere provide the workings of his mind with better thinking power, but also caused his eyes to concentrate more lingeringly on their object too, leaving him awed at what he was finally detecting about his son's wife, Rachelle Fillmore-Carson!

Even as much as he was moved upon his arrival in Lexington when his eyes had first taken in the many accomplishments of his handicapped son, to say nothing of the astonishment that gripped him—and delighted him too—at seeing that Lucy Randolph had at last mustered up enough good judgment from somewhere to emerge from her long grief and ensconce herself where she belonged, which in her case was on the arm of Gilford Sloan, none of it affected Matthew like he was moved now at seeing how much Rachelle Carson resembled Caroline Wilton Roalf!

Why, aside from the eyes—Rachelle's were hazel while Caroline's were blue-green they could have been taken for sisters, maybe even twins since their build and make-up appeared to be so nearly the same, Matthew thought, and wondered if his son was aware of the striking likeness between the two women. And, while he continued to wonder about it, Matthew Carson was finally persuaded to marvel no longer about life in general, telling himself that no matter what the jarring experiences may fall his way in the time that was left to him, he would accept it without question and take life's mysteries as being nothing but what they were and that was, something way beyond him and all other human understanding to see or perceive ever.

Of course, due to her rapidly failing health, Caroline Roalf did not attend the Lexington wedding. Neither did Doctor Seth Roalf, but the Roalf family was represented anyway by the two younger Roalfs, Seth Junior and Maggie, which resulted in Caroline hearing about the affair firsthand and in full details no sooner than the couple returned to Elms. Though she heard the telling while she lay abed.

Yes, by this time Caroline Roalf had mostly taken to her bed, with only two people, her husband and Luke Heyward knowing why she was there and that it was actually her deathbed. It had only been a few days earlier when Luke had learned the seriousness of her condition.

Having sighted one another along the river road, Luke and the doctor both had slowed their buggies and pulled up alongside one another, with the doctor greeting Luke no different than he always had. Yet when Luke went on to inquire of Caroline, instead of responding like he normally did, Seth Roalf abruptly shifted his gaze and stared absentmindedly into the swamp, looking to Luke, all of a sudden, as if a water moccasin might have been charming him out Of all awareness. And, he held his abstracted gaze until Luke, unable to bear the uncertainty another second, called, "Seth."

Breaking his fixed stare to look back at Luke the doctor said, "She's dying! That's how she is!" The hostile tone of voice something new to Luke's ears.

Now, it was Luke who was staring in stupefaction, too stunned to do anything but hold Seth Roalf in his gaze, which did seem to shift him back to his ordinary calm. 'forgive me, friend," he quickly said. "I didn't mean to spring it on you like that, but

Caroline has a severe blood disease and I'm helpless to help her.

"How—how long have you known—Seth?" Luke finally croaked.

"For quite some time now, and suspected it a lot longer." Seth replied. "But, good Lord, Seth!" Luke explained, his aversion to such distressing news now showing up in his own voice, "That's too much of a burden for anyone to carry that long without confiding in friends! Why didn't you tell me? Are you certain?" Seeing how hard the news had hit Luke, the doctor took no offense at the last question, telling Luke, as calmly and unemotional as he could, "I didn't tell you because I've had a lot of trouble in bringing my oneself to acknowledge the facts. And yes, since one can't live without red corpuscles in the blood, I'm positive of my diagnosis. Caroline has pernicious anemia, which so far has no known cure."

A silence began to grow on the doctor's last words and, for some little while, neither man made one single effort to do a thing about it.

Luke took out his handkerchief and slowly began to wipe at his face and down beneath his shirt collar. And, as Seth Roalf just sat quietly and observed him, he would have betted that the handkerchief had been drawn forth for the purpose of suppressing Luke's tears more than anything else, even though the June day was rather warm, with the road being dry and dusty too.

Finally, stuffing his handkerchief back in his pants pocket, Luke, appearing more composed if not resigned to the news, said, "l didn't mean to question your ability, Seth, I'm sorry. It's just that one of the best friends I've ever had is carrying an awful burden and I want to help but realize, at the same time, that there's little I can do, if anything, to make the burden lighter, despite my remarks to you a while ago."

"Oh, forget that. But you're wrong, you can help a lot," said Seth.

"How so?" Luke asked.

"By being available, like you said, when I feel the need to talk. It'll help shift the weight a bit. But listen, Luke, I've decided I don't want Caroline to know the grim facts of her condition. So we'll keep it strictly between us. I hope you understand."

"Of course, Seth. You bet."

"Well, I'd better get on. I have a patient waiting. So long, Luke."

"So long, Seth." Luke echoed, and after a long solemn long look passed between them, both men picked up their reins and started moving on, going in opposite directions from one another toward their destination.

And so, even though like Eliza, Luke could not have been happier about the wedding—sporting a broad smile through most the day, by no means should this have suggested that his feelings, as a whole, were proportional in gaiety to hers because this was not the way it was with him at all. Luke's thoughts had made too many grim journeys that day back to South Carolina where they dwelled with his old friend Seth Roalf, and, yes, Caroline too, for his heart to take very much cheer from anything. His knowledge of what they both faced had dampened every smile that he had flashed.

Even the company of his other longtime friend, Tom Green, and that staying hilarity that Tom kept going continuously, had done much in the way of keeping Luke's mind from closing the distance between Lexington and the trouble that prevailed at Elms. But Luke was thankful for one thing, though, as shallow as it was when it came to changing matters eventually. Observing Eliza's happiness, he was grateful that Seth Roalf had bound him to secrecy, sparing him the ordeal of conveying the tragic circumstance of Caroline's condition to her. And yet, to his shocking astonishment, and while Caroline remained to linger on with a gradual decline in strength besides, Luke found himself barely two months later on one August morning breaking news of the worst kind to Eliza without having had a moment's notice to prepare either her or himself for the blow it rendered.

Bearing the yellow telegram from Lexington, which had just been delivered and which he was certain was going to convey nothing more than the hour that Carr and Beth Anne would be arriving in Charleston the next day, Luke's step was light. As was his habit with all personal mail, he had stopped at opening the telegram until he and Eliza could read it together. Now entering the kitchen where he knew he would find her helping Pete place their dinner on the kitchen table, he smiled and said, as Eliza anxiously eyed the yellow envelope in his hand, "Here it is. They're making sure we'll be there." He hurriedly began to tear the telegram open.

But suddenly, instead of hearing Luke read the words that she was all set and waiting to hear, Eliza heard nothing coming from him but a faint intake of breath. Then, seeing his sunny expression joyless and sorrow—torn and while she herself began to feel as if she had tumbled into a tub of ice water all of a sudden, she heard her own shallow breath trying to question, "W-hat is it, Luke? It—is from Carr, isn't it?"

Looking up from the telegram and staring at Eliza in shocked disbelief, Luke stammered, "No—it's from Gilford Sloan. It's—about Rachelle. She's... Luke had stopped at saying the words.

Seized with fear, Eliza pressed on, and sensing what the reply was going to be before she heard it, "She's what, Luke? What does Mr. Sloan say about Rachelle?" "'He says she passed away early this morning, dear," Luke finally muttered, and passing the telegram on to Eliza he reached for the table chair that he was standing near and fell into it with a heavy sigh.

Now, with her worst fear confirmed, Eliza also turned and sought a chair. And, as she let her eyes fall to the shaking piece of yellow paper that she numbly clutched with both hands, she said brokenly, "But—it was only a few days ago that—that we had a letter from her, Luke. She—she seemed to be fine then."

"I know, sweetheart, and no doubt she was when she wrote it," said Luke. "But, we must remember that she was indisposed there for a long period in late winter. It prevented her from traveling to Green Sea at the time. Besides, one's state of health can change awful rapidly, you know."

Recalling that long ago day in New Orleans when her mother's life had suddenly come to its end, Eliza said, she leaned forward and laid the tragic message on the table, "Yes, how well I know." Then, while she dabbed at her welling eyes with the hem of her apron, she went on and shared some of her fear with Luke, saying, "But, what on earth will Phil do, Luke? He seemed so devoted to Rachelle, and he's already gone through so much. In fact, relative to his wellbeing, it's my opinion her death is about the worst thing that could've happened."

"Yes, it's bad," agreed Luke. "But, Phil's come though and survived a lot. So, let's hope this tragic, untimely death of Rachelle's won't prove to be the one exception with him. He does have friends there and that'll help. And, there's the children, too, they'll. "

"No, Luke," interrupted Eliza, her firm reluctance to go along with what he was saying surprising him, "don't count on those newlyweds helping very much. Friends? Maybe. But no newly married couple."

As Luke stared back at Eliza and was forced to concede that her remark was full of logic, she surprised him a second time by going further and declaring, as she gave her eyes a final dab and let her apron drop, "I know what he can do! He can come home, back to Green Sea, that's what!"

Again, Luke mentally admitted to himself that her words made a lot of sense, even if they were being spoken under a great deal of emotional stress.

"I go along with you there and maybe, in time, he will come back," said Luke. "Apparently, it's crossed his mind since according to Mr. Sloan's message there, his plans are to have Rachelle's remains interred here at Green Sea rather than in Lexington where her parents are buried. A most wise decision to my way of thinking, because as you've pointed out, Green Sea is his home. He rightfully belongs here."

"Well, I'm going to count on it, but right at this minute, I'm thinking about something else. "

"And what's that, sweetheart?"

"I'm thinking how I wish that there was some way that I could make that train trip that they're undertaking less painful for all of them. I know all about such agony, I'm saddened to say. In fact, it's so much like that day in New Orleans so long ago, it gives me the shivers to think about it."

"I know what you mean, but it's better we put a stop to that kind of thinking." Luke reached and gave her hand a tender squeeze. "Instead, what do you say to our getting up from here and centering our minds on all the things that's awaiting to be done before that train does arrive. We want to have everything that needs to be done as near in order as we possibly can. That's one way that we can help them in this trying time.

Finally breaking her stare upon the telegram to lift her eyes in Luke's direction, Eliza said, "But you haven't eaten one bite of dinner yet," appearing to be aware for the first time that, while she and Luke had been talking, that Pete had discretely gone ahead and placed their dinner on the table before slipping out the door to his own quarters in the small grey house behind the mansion. The Heyward's trouble had troubled and affected Pete too. He wanted to get away and think about this woman, whom he had recently seen so alive and well and, now so soon, would be seeing coming back to Green Sea in death.

"I know I haven't eaten and neither have you." Luke replied. "Speaking for myself though, I'm going to pass it up this time because, as usual with trouble, my stomach's already revolting against the idea of food."

Before she realized what she was saying, Eliza came back, as she let her eyes go wondering through the kitchen door to the open space beyond, "Well, I'm going to start praying that your stomach will soon overcome that weakness, Luke, because if it doesn't, it won't be long before you're reduced to skin and bones. For, when it comes to trouble, we're going to see a lot more before this year is out, including the shaking of this very earth that's under us!"

Though her remarks had started Luke and sent him falling back down in his chair, stunned, he fixed an incredulous gaze on her and said, "Good Lord, dear, I pray not! And, what's all this about the earth shaking? I realize you're deeply disturbed, but to hear you make such foreshadowed remarks is frightening, to say the least."

Seeing now that in her rashness she had not only upset Luke but almost alerted him as well to the clairvoyant side of her nature, Eliza, trying to be truthful and, at the same time, persuade Luke to brush her remarks aside, told him, "'It's just a feeling I have, Luke, but try to put it from your mind. I guess hearing this sad news about Rachelle, pushed it out. Whatever the case though, it's like you say, if everything's to be in order when they arrive, we can't waste another minute sitting here doing nothing but talking!" She jumped up and started toward the kitchen pantry. "'First I'll check the pantry and then the smokehouse, to see what items we have on hand and those we 'Il have to buy at O'Henry's. I'll send the list by whoever goes to Drakston Hall to give this terrible news to Father."

With his incredulous gaze still continuing to follow her back, Luke said, "I'll go break the news to your father, dear, so give the list to me when you've finished."

Spinning around to look at Luke, she cried, "Oh, thank you, Luke! I'd rather Father would hear it from you than anyone I know! " Then, she spun around again and was gone, leaving Luke still fastened in his chair by the dread predictions she had made—the closest that she ever came to telling him or anyone else that she could indeed, see things that were not revealed to the average eye.

Chapter Seven

On this last day of August, 1886, the grim and unbroken trial of Rachelle Carson's burial, scarcely two weeks before, still hang heavy on Eliza's mind. And now, as she stood in the hot August sun and started to stoop down to gather up the shrunken, faded out flowers lying atop the new mound of earth—the colorful summer blooms that Philippe Carson had painstakingly picked himself and placed on his wife's grave before taking his departure from Green Sea, Eliza suddenly straightened back up, leaving the shriveled, discolored flowers yet untouched.

She had the sudden feeling that something was stalking her. And not only that but something uncanny besides—some creepy and unheard-of thing that she would not even be able to recognize if, by chance, she even were to spot it. It was a strange feeling. She felt she wanted to see whatever it was, and at the same time, felt that if she did she would deeply regret it. She went ahead and looked anyway though, turning all the way around in her tracks. She saw nothing though. That is, nothing but the same country landscape and habitat that she was accustomed to. A far-off cotton field hanging like a white blanket on the distant horizon. ripening corn in the vast cornfield nearby. The gleaming weathercock atop the mansion's highest peak in the distance. The lush, green timberlands that lay on the left side of the road leading to the burial ground—thousands of heavy timbered acres that stretched for miles toward Drakston Hall. The huge tombs close by. The shrubs. The summer flowers growing around the graves. And last but not least, the thriving magnolia tree that Luke had planted last spring. She gazed at the magnolia tree for some few minutes, trying to quell her uneasiness. Failing to do so; however, she gave up and turned back to the task awaiting her—reflecting over recent events as she labored at her work.

She regretted that she and Rachelle Carson had not known one another longer and knew deep in her heart that because of their brief relationship, the tears that she had shed and those that were smarting her eyes now, were more for Philippe Carson than the woman whose grave she grieved over. No rain had fallen for weeks and as she wept and worked at cleaning off the grave, she noticed that the loamy soil around it was still packed solid with her brother's footprints.

In truth, she had to admit that she was greatly relieved and she thought that Luke had been too, when Phil suddenly made up his mind to accompany Beth Anne and Carr back to Lexington! No, pertaining to what Phil should or should not do, in point of how he handled his life in the future, not one word of advice to him had she let pass her lips the whole time he was at Green Sea. No sooner than her eyes had fallen on him at the train station in Charleston, she had known then that it would be useless to try, that she might as well talk to the wind. He was totally crushed, seeming to be unmindful to everybody and everything going on around him except the one thing that completely absorbed him Rachelle's sudden death. And, his manner had pretty much remained that way. Even when the conversation had turned to Caroline once, how seriously ill she was, Phil had appeared as if they were discussing a stranger, making no comment whatever.

The fact was, she very much doubted if Phil, Beth Anne, or Carr would ever have made it to South Carolina for Rachelle's funeral to Start with, had it not been for Gilford Sloan's staunch support. Mr. Sloan's dependability and devotion were absolutely indisputable throughout the whole ordeal and she would ever be grateful to him.

Of course, Gilford Sloan had poured an awful lot of attention on Lucy Randolph, too, but she had certainly harbored no objection to that. Nor did she believe anyone else had either.

Even though she had not talked to Phil about it, she surely hoped that he knew he was welcome to come back to Green Sea and make it his permanent residence if he so desired to do so. After all, no matter how things stood at present, by birthright, Green Sea belonged to Phil. Regardless of whose names the deed was in now, the fact remained he was heir; that is, if the traditional way of dealing with things like that was still in order and she supposed it was because she had never seen or heard anything else to the contrary. Still, on the other hand, if Phil ever let this matter of his being heir presumptive, so to speak, cross his mind, he had given no indication of it so far. In fact, the one time that the subject had come up, and it had been left to Luke to bring it up then, Phil had laughed it off as being of little consequence to him, saying, back to Luke, "So what? Besides, taking into account, Luke, that your heir and my only child saw fit to fall in love and marry one another, I can't see that it will make one bit of difference in the long run." Then, turning more serious, Phil had added, "What's more, it's my view your name deserves to be on that deed more than mine does."

Yes, she and Luke had been in Lexington at the time, attending Beth Anne and Carr's wedding, with the four of them, Phil, Rachelle, Luke and herself all having a nice quiet visit together one night after supper. Now, with Rachelle gone, there would be no more visits like that to look forward to, ever.

With this last thought obliterating her all concern for deeds and heirships and taking her spirit down so in languishment that she was suddenly seeing all earthly existence as being no more enduring than delicate dew-spun spider webbing in early morning, Eliza recognized that to dwell over Rachelle's grave one moment longer would be very foolish if not down-right irrational, reasoning that the thing to do was to get on with what she came there for and leave!

So, quickly lifting her apron and drying up her tears Eliza bent over and scooped up the dead flower debris in her arms and went tearing down the hill with it toward the woods. But, as she flew through the brick-pillared entrance and hurried on to the edge of the woods, heaving the dead debris in the underbrush, that same strange feeling that had gripped her earlier seized her again. And yet, in the same breath and before the feeling had even had time to clear her toes, it finally hit her and in a great surprise at that what it was that was troubling her—that ghostly, mystifying thing that had crowded her so. It was the heavy stillness that permeated everything. Never before had Eliza seen or experienced anything like it. Not one sound did she hear. It was as if some quiet hand had reached out and gathered up the whole universe in its palm and was slowly squeezing on its stunned victims.

She saw birds perched on tree limbs, looking like the work of some still-life artist, so silently and still they sat. Not one insect did she hear making a sound. There was no whizzing or buzzing noise of any kind. No snapping of twigs, no rustling of leaves—nothing. The presence of that throbbing vibrancy, which had ever been a part of the woods and thickets that bordered the land and which Eliza had always taken for granted as much as the air that she was breathing, was in the picture no longer, making it seem, to her, as though the very pulse was stripped from everything.

Although the day was hot, Eliza shivered and hugged herself with her arms. Baffled at this seemingly death that had fallen over everything, she quickly turned away and started making her way on toward the house, feeling more down in the dumps than ever. Since she felt she could not get to the house fast enough, she decided to take the short cut through the cornfield instead of following the cemetery road back.

Now, buried deep in the middle of the large cornfield, hurrying along between two towering rows of corn, Eliza wondered about the possibility of a storm gathering, in spite of the fact that she was well aware that the brilliant sky above her did not even hold a hint of a cloud, much less that of a gathering storm. Still, as a rule, a calm did; indeed, precede a storm, did it not? But, nothing like this fearful stillness, she thought, and wondered again if she were the only one who had detected that there was something different about the day.

She wished that Luke were at the house so she could feel out his opinion about it, but he was way off in the north cotton field, with every hand on the place, trying to gather all the prime cotton that was ready to be picked while the dry weather lasted. No, she had not seen Seth about her jittery nerves. Though it had been suggested to her more than once lately. Well, maybe she should but she was not quite ready to admit that her nerves were shot to pieces—not yet! She could broach the matter of the stillness to Pete, he was at the house. No, on second thought, she didn't want to do that, either. The blacks always seemed to be too much in awe of the unexpected as it was. She would only alarm him and maybe needlessly at that.

Well, she continued to tell herself, it looked like, short of finding some boring chore to get into, that she was going to be walking and wondering for the rest of the day and, in her opinion, neither would be what she would prescribe for calming one's nerves. As far as that went, she had never been overly fond of housework, anyhow. She much preferred being outdoors gardening, working in tobacco, or even picking cotton. Picking cotton!

Started at the idea that had popped in her mind, Eliza's scurrying feet paused briefly. Now, why in the world had she not thought of doing that in the first place? She asked herself. No, Luke was not going to like it, but once she was there, there would be little, or really nothing, he could do or say about it, and especially in front of the hands! Besides, her nerves were her nerves, were they not? They didn't belong to Luke! If she wanted to pick cotton, she was going to pick cotton! Yes, just as soon as she told Pete what to cook for supper, she was going to get a cotton sack and make haste for the north cotton field where Luke was at!

Resuming her scurrying steps on down the middle of the two

rows of corn, Eliza presently found herself out of the corn's deep fronded foliage and hitting the orchard. Then, covering the orchard and passing by the old dilapidated and moss-gown slave cabin's, she was finally at the barnyard and, despite her eagerness to get on to the north cotton field, was brought up sharp again by the same lack of activity that she had witnessed earlier in the woods.

She saw that all the farm animals housed there—that is, those aside from the several mules and horses who had been taken to the cotton field that morning to pull the cotton wagons, were doing nothing but standing stationary in their tracks; and seemed to be standing gingerly at that like some gravitating force was pulling hard at their feet, keeping them rooted to the same spot. And, Bullitt's behavior was no different. Instead of perking up and making an all-out effort to reach her upon first glance like he always did, he just stood motionlessly in the same spot and stared at her. Though she was well aware that he was feeble as well as physically impaired, this did not stop her from thinking that something other than those factors were inducing the stallion's behavior. She was positive of it. She knew his manner would not have changed so drastically in such a short while.

Now puzzled more than every by Bullitt's behavior, Eliza moved on toward the several chicken coops and the pens that enclosed them. She stopped, observing that no activity was going on there, either. All the chickens seemed to be either sitting on the ground or quietly standing around. One Barred Plymouth Rock rooster she noticed in particular—surprised and really thrown to see that he had finally found some place else to sit beside on the backs of her hens!

The rooster's ardent nature had ever agitated Eliza and, because of his constant harassing her hens, not only had she dubbed him a true blue Yankee long back but had threatened to put him in the cook pot a hundred times if she had one. so, continuing to observe the rooster as he sat quietly on the ground, she suddenly decided that it was high time she got on with his execution, especially since he seemed to be so subdued for a change. Yes, and stewed slowly in a big copper pot along with wild rice and ham hocks he was going to make a right tasty dish, too, she quickly concluded, and turned away, setting her course in quite a bit of haste to find Pete.

Of course, Eliza knew that even with Pete taking his and Hannah's supper from the pot that she and Luke would hardly make a dent in its savory contents. But she also knew no problem was posed because she would share with Bessie and Sam as usual. They did not own the first chicken. As a matter of fact, chickens were not the only thing that Bessie and Sam were without. Whereas all the rest of the tenants owned a flock of chickens, raised their own hogs and garden patch, had their own milk cow, a team of mules, and a horse and buggy, too, for Sunday traveling, Sam and Bessie hardly owned anything—not even a decent chair to sit in. Still, with their happy-go-lucky attitude, Eliza had a strong suspicion that she worried a lot more about Sam and Bessie's impoverished circumstances, than Sam and Bessie did themselves and; indeed, held little trust that the situation would change, because, in her eye, Sam's lack of ambition had become too well-rooted in his youth, when he had done nothing but mostly lie on the front porch at Green Sea and snooze.

Now rounding the comer of the little grey house that she and Luke and the children had spent so many years in, Eliza stopped in the few feet of shade that the sloping roof provided from the sun and hurriedly called out, "Pete, are you in there?" She did not fancy the idea of missing Pete if he were not inside and be forced to trot back in the boiling sun to find him.

Pete was inside, and also blinking his eyes, Eliza noticed, and looking somewhat sheepishly to boat as he promptly pushed the screen door aside and said, "Yes'm, Miss Eliza, I'm here."

Pete had heard Eliza express her views too many times concerning Early Cole's siestas for him to act any Other way but shamefaced. Eliza herself never took a midday nap. Even so, she refrained from further embarrassing Pete by remarking about it now, merely saying instead, as she pushed back her bonnet and wiped the sweat from her face with her apron, "I thought you might be." Hmmm, the heavy stillness was having its effect on Pete, too, she thought, continuing on, "Listen, Pete, I think it's about time I made good my threat of killing that old Barred Plymouth Rock rooster. You know, the one I call Yankee. He's never been nothing but pure aggravation. So why don't you stew him up for supper, along with those ham hocks that's left, in that big oversized copper kettle? It'll take something that large to cook it all in, and especially when the wild rice is added. We haven't had any chicken bog for a long time, so it should be to everyone's liking for a change."

Instantly, Pete's eyes stopped their blinking, flaring wide with delight.

"Hot ziggity! Miss Eliza," he cheered at the top of his voice.

"That old rooster's neck is good as wringed off already!"

Eliza smiled, "I thought it'd be a chore that you'd enjoy carrying through with. But, if you have any questions, Pete, ask me now because I won't be back to the house till dark. I'm going to the north cotton field to help with the cotton." Sudden astonishment covered Pete's face.

"Not with the picking, Miss Eliza?" He ventured to question.

"Why, of course," she replied. "What else, pray tell?"

Pete shook his head, venturing a little further.

"But, what about Mister Luke? He won't like it, and especially on a day like today. That sunshine is powerful hot out there."

"Oh, a little sunshine's never hurt anyone, as long as they keep something on their head," she said, jerking her bonnet back in place. "Besides, it's important that field of cotton is finished today for I believe it's going to storm and soon at that."

"Well, yes'm, that could be, too, Miss Eliza." Pete agreed, but still stood and shook his head to Eliza's back as long as he could see her when she suddenly turned and started back toward the stables to get her riding mare.

Though—to be sure—Eliza was to bear the brunt of quite a wordy lecture from Luke about being in the hot sun, not to mention the hard job that she was taking on, when she reached the cotton field with a cotton sack boldly tied around her middle and started stuffing cotton balls inside it like sixty, still, by the same token, she also brought his and several more heads shaking likewise to Pete's in amazed unison at her unwillingness to listen and take heed to his advice, regardless.

Of course, nobody on the plantation knew better than Eliza herself what she was in for. She knew well enough, from experience, that picking cotton in the hot sun was no picnic—no sipping a mint julep on a cool, shady veranda. Yes, she was determined to lend a hand no matter what, and, needless to say, this natural down-to-earth quality of hers—an ever ready willingness to pitch in and help with any job that needed to be done, was the primary characteristic in her nature that endeared her to each and every domestic worker, tenant, and hired hand at Green Sea, not to mention the long ago slaves who still dwelled there. Once she determined that a job should be finished by a certain time and saw that there just might be no way to bring it about without bearing a hand to it herself, a hundred objections by Luke could not stop her. Luke knew this and so did everybody else at Green Sea. And, even though no one person had ever gone so far as to talk about it openly, there was something else that all were aware of, too, and that was, the no mistaking of the invigoration that her presence brought to the job site once she did make her arrival. A new pluck and stamina never failed to grip the workers instantly, and this day was no different.

Under several approving smiles, someone began to hum a melody and before many minutes had passed, and while cotton balls begin to come off the cotton stalks a lot faster, other workers had joined in, with the melody bursting into song at the same instant. Even so, and although everybody seemed refreshed and worked with a new vigor that held for the remainder of the day, the sun had long disappeared from the evening sky and dark was rapidly falling before the last cotton row was picked over. And then, by no means had the workday come to its end.

The workers were paid by the pound. So, besides the usual evening chores that still had to be seen to, like milking the cows and feeding the chickens and slopping the hogs as well as feeding and stabling the horses and mules, there was the job of loading the picked cotton on the wagons and hauling it back to the cotton house to be weighed. And, by the time all this was done, with everybody's quota of picked cotton for that day weighed and the poundage set down and credited to them in the plantation account book and all the other jobs seem to, not only was it way past dark but way past everybody's suppertime too. Nobody grumbled though. For stretching a workday on a plantation till way after dark was something that most certainly Was not out of the ordinary, and especially when it came time to harvest one of the many different crops that was worked

Though Bessie still continued to be the Heyward's main—and most the time only—maidservant, she had gone to the cotton field to pick cotton today like everybody else at Green Sea. She had left the cotton field with Eliza, trekking along beside the later in the growing darkness.

Now having emerged from under the canopy of live oaks and walking around the mansion toward the back, Bessie said, "Lordie, Miss Eliza, I heap more w'nt to make beds an, sweep, den pick cotton. I'm plum ready to drop."

Saving her surprise to the last minute, Eliza said, "You'd better not drop, not before you cook Sam's supper, anyhow."

"Lordie be, how I know dat." Bessie readily agreed with a

flagging sigh. "Dat man e'ts like a hog! No fillin' him up, hit seem. First thing he say wh'n he com' in de door, wot yu got cooked?"

They had reached the back-porch steps.

Now ready to spring her surprise, Eliza said, "Well, tonight you'll be able to give him the surprise of his life by telling him, chicken bog! Yes, that's what I said, chicken bog!" She went on as Bessie's whole body appeared to shudder with shock in the reflecting light from the kitchen window." Come on in. It'll only take Pete a minute to dish it up for you, if he hasn't already."

"'Lordie, Miss Eliza, yu good to Sam and me. Chicken bog! Wait til Sam heer. He be so surprised, he may fal' d'ad fur sure," chuckled Bessie.

Going on up the steps with Bessie trailing her, Eliza laughed, "Well, I shall hope he won't go to that extreme." Then pulling in her laughter, she went on to say as they crossed the porch, "I want to think I do right by you, Bessie, for you've been standing by me a long time now, far longer than even Julia did."

Experiencing a rare wash of earned vanity to finally be told that she ranked alongside the able Julia, whose name she had heard often enough through the years, Bessie agreed rather pertly, "Yes'm, a long time."

Entering the kitchen, Eliza was not one bit surprised to find Pete, at that precise moment, pulling the simmering chicken bog and one or two more cook pots, which she was certain held a variety of fresh summer vegetables, away from the heated eyes of the big iron stove and setting them off to one side. As usual, Pete had timed his cooking right on the dot. It made no difference that the meal had been delayed far longer than the normal hour, he still had come through on time. In fact, when it came to measuring time, or taste for that matter, in the art of culinary, Eliza thought that Pete was totally unmatched— even topping that of the able Prudence and Daisy, whose reign over Green Sea's kitchen had ended long years back. They ruled no kitchen but their own now, leaving Pete to hold claim of being sole chef at Green Sea.

"It smells good, Pete." Eliza said, and telling him to see about a kettle for Bessie and, with Pete's toothful grin following her in acknowledgment and the gleeful Bessie looking on too, she hurried on through the kitchen and on upstairs to the warm bathtub of water that she was sure Pete would also have waiting for her.

Though she would have loved soaking her aching bones longer,

Eliza hurriedly stepped from the tub and gabbed a towel. Giving herself a quick rub down, she pulled on her fresh underclothes and in the nick of time was smoothing out a cool summer lawn dress over her narrow hips—finding that the sweetness of a warm bath and clean clothes were indeed most bracing as she whirled to the mirror. Hearing Luke's foot hit the back porch below at that very second, though, Eliza forgot the mirror, merely gathering up a few loose curls that dangled around her face and tucking them in the heavy bun at the nape of her neck as she went fleeing from the room and on to the long staircase—her face still glowingly pretty in spite of the fact that she had left it untouched.

Eliza had covered the last stair step and was stepping upon the floor in the foyer when suddenly a movement—a motion she was unable to detect, brought her to a standstill. She turned around and gazed back up the staircase. Seeing nothing; however, that might explain it, or hearing nothing either, she turned back around and went hurrying on through the long foyer, wondering as she did if maybe a field mouse or, worse still a vicious rat, had found its way inside and scurried across the floor under her. Certainly, it was not an unthought-of possibility because, regardless of all the cats they kept, it did happen sometimes, she reminded herself, and was also mentally noting that she would have to warn Pete to be on the lookout for either, and especially in the kitchen when again, all of a sudden, the same identical motion stopped her for a second time. Though this time her sense of detection was keener. It seemed as though something had, actually, pulled at her—giving her a feeling of being ill balanced for a split second and, it was for a certainty, she promptly told herself, no mouse or rat either, for that matter, was capable of doing that!

Now dismissing all thought of mice and rats from her mind, Eliza, having stopped near the door at the end of the foyer—the door was opened directly into the dining room, and a window into its outside wall. Absenting the window, it came to her that along with the motion she had felt a moment earlier, that she had also heard a faint clattering sound, something like a window creaking its frame when a hard wind was blowing. The wind! That's it! A storm was finally making up and doubtless a severe one at that, she thought to herself, and rushed across the floor to the window to peer into the starlit darkness, positive that she was going to see treetops tossing and storm clouds rolling.

But no storm clouds rolled. The night sky was as clear and star-studded as it had been when she and Bessie were trudging along through the falling darkness toward the mansion. Nor was there one tree branch stirring, she observed. Not one thing to see that spoke of a gathering storm. The outside was as still and motionless as it had been all day—a calm that now, in one heartbeat, bespoke of phantoms—mocking phantoms, because, without wind, one did not hear windows creaking in their frames. And yet, at that very second, she wanted to scream that she knew better but found herself too horrified to utter one sound. For even though everything on the outside was dead-still with no wind stirring whatever—inside too for that matter, Eliza felt the windowpane that she had her nose pressed against as she peered outside, give a hard quiver; and in less than another second and while the whole window began to shake violently, a long broken line was streaking down its middle, cracking the windowpane in half right under her very nose!

Petrified, Eliza jumped back, glaring at the broken glass in the shuddering window. Then, in the same instant, she whirled around and started to run for the back porch instinctively seeking the comforting presence of Luke, as she always did when troubled or frightened, as quickly as her feet could take her to him, However, to her further horror, she became aware that no matter how hard she tried to move her feet that she was making no progress at all. Not only did some powerful gravity seem to be holding her back, keeping her rooted to the same place that she was standing in, but it was also as if her mind were unable to make contact with the rest of her person, too. It seemed willed to go in one direction while the rest of her seemed bent to head into another. But suddenly, just as she grasped the fact that the floor under her was no longer level, tilting horribly, she heard Luke screaming her name and yelling at the same time, "Earthquake! Get outside! Everybody, get outside, quick!"

With the full impact of knowing now what was, actually, happening scaring her to death—striking fear in her that the earth could open under all of them any second, Eliza became panic stricken, unable to decide what direction might be the less hazardous for her safety. But even as she frantically glanced around the swaying room, Luke was already making a dash through the doorway toward her. He grabbed her hand. Then, with the huge mansion sounding like every foot of timber in it was groaning in agony, plus glass flying all around them from breaking windowpanes, to say nothing of the big crystal chandelier over their heads giving all indication that it was going to shatter upon the floor any instant too they both started laboring forward toward the kitchen—the nearest exit to the outside, with Eliza having the feeling that she was being dragged uphill with every inch of progress they made.

All at once; though, the severe tremor, which seemed to be taking the huge house and suspending it in midair from its foundation, passed over as quickly as it began and the floor rapidly tilted back. But, even so, the reprieve was a short-lived experience for Eliza and Luke. For no sooner than their racing feet had gained the kitchen, it was the same thing all over again, though this second severe shock was worse than the one before it. Instantly, its powerful force made Eliza's and Luke's gait become more like scrambling on one's all fours than running. In addition, the kitchen table and everything on it was sent on a savage slide clear across the room immediately. Laden down with a big platter of chicken bog and several more side dishes, plus their eating utensils and dinnerware,

Eliza heard the table hit the opposite wall with a loud, sharp bang just as she finally made it through the outside kitchen door and, literally, slid across the porch and down the doorsteps into the yard.

Eliza was positive that supper and dishes alike had all gone to the floor together. Still, the thought was only spontaneous with her, because the idea of supper being dumped on the floor amid broken dishes was not to cross her mind another time that night. In fact, for several hours and far on into the night, her main and only concern was whether she herself, her loved ones, or anybody else in the world would ever see another sunrise. Indeed, even when she witnessed it breaking in the clear dawn of summer's eastern sky next morning, she still remained to be totally convinced that the world was going to stay intact and not shake to pieces—bringing its end for all time, because the shocks were still coming, one as late as 8:30 A.M. that same morning!

At any rate, wild-eyed and speechless with terror, Pete, heeding Luke's shout for everyone to get outdoors quick, was already in the yard. Though like Eliza and Luke he was having trouble standing erect because of the passing earth waves from the violent shocks.

Seeing the solid ground under their feet in the bright starlight actually swell and, at the same time, fearing with every breath that the violent disturbance was going to crack through the earth at any second, they all three swiftly passed a mute look of desperation between them—each one probing the other's face for some sigh that would give them a grain of hope.

They saw none. The look was unrewarding.

Then abruptly, Luke was saying, and not very blasé at that, "Let's all hold hands!

Here, dear, get between Pete and me!"

As Eliza hurriedly placed herself between the two men, stumbling somewhat as she made a grab for their outstretched hand on either side of her, she suddenly cried out, her frightened gaze searching ahead of her in the nights' darkness, "I hear someone crying out there! I think it's Bessie! She didn't have time to get home, I know she didn't! She may be hurt! We have to find her!" She pulled forward on Luke and Pete's hand.

Trying desperately to put some degree of calm in his voice even if he did have better sense than to try to make himself feel that way, Luke said, as he restrained Eliza's pull on his hand and let his own troubled gaze follow hers into the distance, "Wait, dear. It does sound like Bessie's voice, but I believe she's more confused than she is hurt. I passed her going home just before I reached the back porch, so I'd think she couldn't have made it any further along than say, the grape arbor, which in my opinion is about as safe a place as she can be. But, first, let me try to make certain that her voice is coming from there. We wouldn't want to set out in the wrong direction, if we're going to try to locate her."

Pausing his remarks and, straining his ears more closely against Bessie's moans and cries, not only did Luke distinctly hear her say through her sobs that she was indeed lost and could not find her way, but he also learned that it was Bessie's most earnest belief that the world had ended and she had gone to purgatory for her evil ways, which made Luke wonder, for one fleeting second, what evil doings she was talking about. Because to his way of thinking, if Bessie thought that she was going to strike out on Judgment Day, hardly anyone else could expect to miss Hades' pit.

Still, Luke let the thought drop, entertaining it for one brief second only because there were too many other things absorbing his attention—awesome and terrifying things like the strange sounds filling the air—eerie sounds that were enough to make one's blood curdle. To Luke, it was one thing, and certainly had enough, to have the sound of straining timbers, falling boards and bricks and shattering glass in his ears, but to hear water in a deep well swishing around like a whirligig gone wild, was something else again. He felt like clapping both hands over his ears and keeping them there, but stopped at going through with it because his behavior could cause Eliza's own fright and dread to heighten, not to mention that of Pete's, who in addition to looking as if his eyes were going to bulge out of his head any instant, also appeared to have been shocked into a state of frozen muteness. So far, it seemed neither Eliza or Pete had taken notice of the alarming disturbance inside the well and, Luke certainly had no desire to say or do anything that might draw their attention to it.

Suddenly, as he wished with all his might that, at least, the well in the yard would become calm and quiet again, Luke went on to exclaim, his voice more disquieted as ever despite his effort to control it, "She's there all right! Sam too! I hear him calling to her! Wait a minute, I hear other voices besides Bessie's and Sam's! I believe it's Willie and Allen, sweetheart, and that they've rounded up every soul on the place and's heading this way. It certainly sounds that way! Hear them?"

If Eliza heard or did not hear the voices which Luke was referring to, she did not say, saying to him instead, "Oh I'm so glad, Luke, that Sam's with Bessie, but what are we all going to do? Is the world ending—going to shake to pieces before all this stops? And, what about the children? Do you think they're..." Hard, raking sobs finally broke in Eliza's throat, cutting her question off before she could finish asking it.

Actually, some of Eliza's wretching sobs were due to her ever anxiousness to want to put as many miles as possible between her daughter and Stuart Drakston. She knew well enough that Jane Anne would have been nowhere right then but beside Luke and herself, had she not suggested that maybe Jane Anne should accompany the family Of the deceased Rachelle Carson back to Lexington—going so far as to point out to Jane Anne that a fourth accompanying party, no doubt, was just what the family needed at that stage of their grief, that her presence would help appease it. Of course, Eliza was well aware that if her suggestion was carried through with that Jane Anne's summer vacation at home would be cut short by two full weeks. Still, that did not matter to her as long as it meant one time less that Stuart Drakston would set his eyes upon Jane Anne—an occurrence that seldom happened for Stuart except at church on Sunday—a time that he and Jane Anne both looked forward to and treasured and a time that Eliza had grown to almost detest!

Upon Eliza's sobs, Luke's head came back fast in her direction. He shared her distress and anxiety, wondering, too, if the earthquake were circling the entire earth and Carr and Jane Anne were experiencing the same terror they were. He stopped at thinking anything worse for either of his children—could not bear the thought. Though likewise to Eliza he was well aware that, at least, his daughter would have been beside him had he not, as usual, gone along with her suggestion—a plaguing fact to Luke this time, because he had not had the courage to say "no," when he had known all along what had truly put the idea in Eliza's head in the first place. All the same, he still yearned to comfort his wife—tell Eliza the things he knew she wanted to hear—things like he knew their children and all the rest of their loved ones were all right and, that everything there at Green Sea was going to be, too.

And yet, with the sound of the well water whirling in his ears bad as ever, to say nothing of the earth continuing to quiver like jelly under his feet, Luke found he was unable to mouth not one optimistic word, replying to Eliza's first question only as he squeezed her hand and said, "We're joining the others down at the grape arbor, that's what we're going to do, get away from all these buildings." He threw back his head and gave a sudden yell for Willie and Allen not to come any further toward the house, telling them to stop where they were at and keep the others with them. Then, turning to Pete, he added, "Pete, we'll go by your house first. When we get there, I want you to try to make it inside and see about Hannah, try to persuade her to come along with us, if you can. Apparently, she's already gone to bed and is unaware of what's happening."

Still too afraid to utter one sound, Pete sent Luke a mute nod and, without further delay and also giving every appearance of walking on glass, they all started moving forth—with Pete having a fleeting thought that Luke might have rephrased his last remark regarding Hannah, because there was not one person at Green Sea who did not know that, of late, the aged Hannah had come to behave as though she were hardly aware of anything.

Having become arthritic as well as feeble in mind and body, she seldom ventured nowadays outside the little grey house where she had lived with Pete for so many years and, in truth, none of them expected her to do so now—budge one inch from her chair or bed, whichever she happened to be occupying, no matter what Pete said to her.

All the same, being Luke, he had to try, try to make Hannah understand that, undoubtedly, she would be exposed to greater danger inside the house than if she were outdoors, even if he did have little hope that she would listen to anything that Pete might have to say.

Presently, however, they were there and as Luke waited with Eliza a short distance from the house, where there would be less exposure from falling timbers and breaking windowpane, while Pete was inside, he was given another start to suddenly see Hannah coming through the doorway on Pete's arm. Though Luke could tell by the lamplight shining behind her that she appeared to be dazed.

"Wait here, dear, I'll give him a hand with her." Luke said to Eliza, and hurrying along toward the doorsteps he stretched out his hand to Hannah, telling her, "We're going to have a prayer meeting down at the grape arbor tonight, Hannah. We wanted you to be with us."

If Hannah thought anything strange about Luke's idea of holding a prayer meeting down at the grape arbor, she made no mention of it, saying to him instead as she willingly gave him her other hand, "I fell ou' of bed!" Bringing Luke to think that in all probability she knew why he had decided they should start sending up prayers despite her obvious stupefaction, and especially when Pete looked at him over Hannah's head and confirmed her statement about falling from her bed, by nodding his head again.

Hearing Hannah's remark, Eliza rushed toward them crying, "Oh, no, Hannah, are you hurt? Luke, do you suppose she has any broken bones?"

"I don't think, dear. At least she's walking and doesn't seem to be in any pain. Here, take my other hand and let's try to make it on and join the others as quickly as we can." Luke told her and felt a mite relieved, all of a sudden, to realize that he was putting a considerable length of distance between himself and the sloshing water inside the well, at last.

With Eliza making a grab for his hand, they all started forth once again—warily placing their steps some distance from the outside buildings in the bright starlight. None the less, despite the countless times that Luke had heard the phrase "Heaven and Earth" uttered in his lifetime inside church and outside of it too, on this night, for the life of him, he could see no correlation whatever between the two. The heavens above were too serene, the earth below too turbulent and creepy-like, bringing one to fear it as much as they would hold in dread some vicious animal, snarling angrily at them in the dark and, in that respect, he knew he was not counting himself out, by no means!

Even so, Luke shepherded his small group on through the eerie darkness, having hopes that when they did reach and join those of whom he had advised to stay at the grape arbor that everybody— including himself— would gain a little reassurance by everyone being together. However, stumbling among them some few minutes later he knew immediately, to his dismay, that that was not going to be the case, no time soon anyway. For if any one person in the group was gaining any solace from the presence of anyone else, as far as he could tell in the dark of night, he could not see it. The whole bleary scene seemed to be nothing but a hubbub of confusion and uncertainty, with nobody appearing to be aware of anything but their own terror.

While some in the group were on their knees lifting up impassioned prayers and cries to their Maker, asking Him to make His peaceful, giving earth quiet again, others likewise to Bessie— who Luke spotted clasping a cook-pot tightly to her bosom and assumed it was the one he had seen her carrying earlier, were proclaiming that Satan had descended among them and ended the world, plunging them in Hell! In addition, a number more were giving every sign of having become totally senseless. Mumbling incoherently to themselves, they just jumped from one spot to the next, looking as if they may have been playing a game of leapfrog. It seemed even Willie and Allen had chucked their usual levelheadedness and succumb to the madness too. Luke heard their voices chanting the "Amens" and wondered if they were giving sanction to the prayers being offered, or going along with all that nonsense that Bessie had conceived and started and still continued to sing about the World having ended and landed everybody in the abode of the damned

Suddenly, feeling Eliza's hand in his tighten convulsively, Luke knew that not only for her sake but everybody else's as well, he had to gain control of things—if he could outshout Bessie—and be quick about it to boot!

Thus, feeling if he could only get through to her that everybody else might also heed his voice, Luke, straining his lungs to the limit, shouted, "For the love of God, Bessie, won't you get hold of yourself

The world hasn't ended! We're in the midst of an earthquake!" Then, as frenzied cries and lamentations began to quell abruptly—Bessie's included—he continued on, trying to explain to the terrified figures before him what was, actually, taking place in the earth beneath their feet, with a voice that was carrying a lot more confidence than he truly felt for the ground was still quivering under them.

Finally, when Luke thought that he had told his rapt, indistinct listeners enough, or what he dared tell them of what little he did know about earthquakes, he reverently added, "Now let's all kneel calmly on the ground here in prayer. I'll lead you." And, there close about the grape arbor they remained for the rest of the night, praying and singing hymns. Indeed, with the shocks remaining to be in effect well into the daylight hours of the next day—three more severe ones following the four that took place before midnight—Luke had no thought of suggesting they seek some other place to keep watch.

Granted, it was a scary and torturous night for all concerned. And yet, when it came to fright or mental pain, particularly among those of whom who kept vigil at the grape arbor at Green Sea, nobody's were more intense than Eliza Heyward's. For all the while she was praying and singing the hymns along with Luke and the others, praying that the earthquake would soon pass over and leave no loss of lives, she was also silently agonizing over the burial ground at Green Sea and lifting prayers in its behalf too asking that, at least, that plot of earth would be spared the violent disruptions, if no other. She thought she could not bear it if the graves or tombs were to become unsettled or disheveled in any way, and especially the grave of Rachelle, which was so newly banked.

Even so, that was the very first place that Eliza headed to when it became evident, late the next morning, that the shocks were finally ceasing. Luke accompanied her and, considering all the boards, bricks, and shattered glass they saw lying around the outlying buildings and the mansion, too, not to mention the glaring fissure they came upon in the cemetery road, which was at least a foot wide and several inches deep, they both not only deemed it no less than infinite mercy to see upon their arrival at the graveyard no sign of disturbance whatever, but also a heavenly miracle as well. And, this blessing was revealed all the more once they trekked back to the mansion and inspected it, because evidence aplenty of last night's earthquake was to meet their eyes there. Chairs were overturned—tables and other furnishings too. Bedsteads, especially those equipped with rollers, had moved several feet from their stationary place, with one or two even going on to wedge against opposite walls. The library floor was covered from end to end with books and other items that had spilled from the library shelves. In addition, there was not one room in the entire house that did not have some broken items scattered on its floor, to say nothing of all the broken china and glassware, that littered the dining room and kitchen floors. Portraits had fallen off walls. Numerous windowpanes were broken or had completely fallen out. The pantry off the kitchen was in a total jumble. Among other piles of disorder, the contents of several broken jars of canned fruits and vegetables had spilled into the new barrel of flour that Pete had only opened the day before—spoiling the entire barrel. Still and all, the one thing that shocked and surprised Eliza the most was to see last night's supper still setting atop the kitchen table, despite her sureness that it had gone to the floor when the table had banged the opposite wall. And, what surprised her even more was the fact that nothing on the table had broken or upset, merely jamming together as the table had hit the wall and stopped.

With his gaze feeding rather hungrily upon the spread table, the cold and caky looking chicken bog in particular, Pete said, "It still looks like it's all right to eat, Miss Eliza."

"I suppose, Pete, but I don't care for one bite now. A cup of coffee will do me. You go ahead and eat though, and see about something for Hannah too, I'll make the coffee," she said, and suddenly started clearing her way through a rubble of pots and pans that had dropped on the stove in order to lift the eyes off so she could start the fire.

"Yessum, if you say, Miss Eliza," Pete happily accorded, not in the least surprised at Eliza's lack of appetite or her eagerness to keep busy until she had had news of family members and friends alike.

Messengers had already been dispatched to Drakston Hall and the other nearby plantations. And Luke, hoping to get a wire through to the family members in Virginia, was making haste himself toward the telegraph office in Charleston. However, the nearer Luke came to his destination the more his hope of reaching anyone by wire dissipated. And, once he entered the city's limits and let his eyes scan the ruin and devastation around him, he knew his mission there was an out-and-out hopeless one, that Charleston's contact with the outside world was completely cut off and would be for days, at the least. Because it was startlingly obvious the city was setting near where the center of the earthquake had concentrated, if not directly upon it.

Everywhere, telegraph wires were dangling uselessly from their supports, having been severed by falling poles or other objects that had collapsed and fell on them. Buckling into a rubble of scrap iron and broken tiles, railroad tracks had been made all but useless. It looked as though every building in the city had either been damaged—some severely—or totally wiped out by fire. While nothing remained of a large number of them but piles of shattered masonry and smoldering ash, a great many others were swaying dangerously over the obstructed and panicky filled streets—streets that literally cried with hysteria and grief as scores of frantic survivors searched for loved ones amid the gaping fissures, broken water mains, toppled gas lights, and jumbles of other debris, which made Luke feel as if he were witnessing the ravages of Sherman's Army all over

Suddenly sicken at all the rack and ruin that he had ridden into, Luke, wondering about the Cooper family, had just turned his mount's head in the direction of the Cooper mansion when out of the dust and ash that chocked the city's streets, he saw Brent Cooper emerging toward him.

"Brent!" Luke yelled, and sailed off his mount's back to throw an arm around Brent's shoulders. "I was just wondering about you-all. I trust all the others are safe too."

"My God, Luke! Where did you come from? I didn't even see you!" Brent exclaimed, bringing his haggard-looking face up from the rubble under his feet to stare at

Luke in shocked wonder, and then adding in a gust of excitability, "Yes—yes—bless the Lord, we're all safe! It wasn't as severe out where we live, but there's so many others who weren't so fortunate. Our house was damaged some, but it's nothing compared to the ill luck that hundreds of others are suffering. You know that open area that's just beyond the battery a little way—well, it's packed full of out townspeople, scores of survivors who's gathered there out of fright, or simply because they've been left homeless and have nowhere else to go. And, on top of many of them being injured and moaning with pain, there's the bodies of several of the 27 people killed instantly last night that were taken there still lying on the ground waiting to be buried. Thought their bodies are covered with sheets, it's a ghostly sight. Mollie and I and several more of our

191

townspeople have taken food, blankets, and other items down there. She's there now, helping do what little can be done for the survivors till some degree of order is restored. I decided I'd better get on back to the bank to see about things there. It's still standing, thank God, and the vault held too! But, tell me, before I go rattling on any further, did it strike at Green Sea?"

With an expression that had grown tighter and tighter through Brent's spun-out reply till it was now pulled as taut as a violin's string, Luke said, "Rocked the ground about all night it seemed, plus another bad shock early this morning, the most frightful experience of my whole life, I think. We had no injuries though, I'm grateful to say, Or no serious damage either, nothing like this anyway. We're concerned about the children though, and the rest of the family who's away, wondering if it struck where they're at and if all's safe. That's why I'm here, rode in first thing to send a wire to Virginia, but I see that's out."

"Yes, and unfortunately they won't be able to wire you either. Because if we can't send a message, we certainly can't receive one." Brent said, and went on to add, as he gave the ruins around them a long penetrating look, "Still, it's my opinion, Luke, that it was Charleston's earthquake. Granted, the ground may have shook in Virginia and several other places, too, but doubtless Charleston received the worst of its fury. Jesus! I believe this city is sitting right on top of where the trouble lies!"

"Well, after riding in here and seeing all this—" Luke waved a hand over the wreckage they stood in—"I'm going along with you there, Brent. But, what about these survivors who's gathered down there, the homeless and the injured in particular? Is anything being done toward providing some sort of shelter for these victims? I'd be willing to loan a hand, bring back some help from Green Sea if necessary." "I think the state's militia will be taking charge of things, Luke. I understand they've been alerted and should be pretty near organized and ready for duty by now, but, you bet, I'll keep your Offer Of assistance in mind." Suddenly, Brent was waving a hand over the wreckage too. "Looks like Sherman's paid us another visit, doesn't it?"

Luke's tight expression loosened somewhat. Smiling faintly, he said, "My own thoughts as I gazed down this street a short while ago, and doubtless there's hundreds more besides us who's viewing it likewise." He turned and gathered up his horse's reins and jumped astride its back again. "I'd better be on my way, Brent, I know Eliza's on pins and needles, waiting to hear if I got through to Carr or some the others. Give my best to Mollie and be sure and let me know if I can help out."

"You bet I will, friend, and tell Eliza that I'm positive Carr'll be getting in touch soon and not to worry," called Brent to Luke's departing back. And so, Brent Cooper stood and watched Luke raise his hand in acknowledgment to his words and then let it drop to take the reins again—picking his way around the wreckage lying in the street—he suddenly regretted that he was unable to relive his first meeting with Luke—regretting deeply that he had lacked the wisdom to see on that day long ago that one was lucky to meet with the likes of Luke Heyward, just once, in the whole of a lifetime. As it turned out, the conversation between Brent Cooper and Luke Heyward had carried a lot of conviction—coming remarkably close in sizing up the situation for what it was.

First, in point of whose earthquake it became, indeed Charleston was to claim legal title by being so unfortunate as to have the Woodstock Fault, which of course faulted and gave way, lying directly beneath the city—a property that Charleston's inhabitants would as leave they never heard tell of, much less have the name of their city linked permanently with it because of its violent disturbance. And second, in addition to the vicinity of Charleston—the chief focal point of the disturbance, the earth did shake in other places and shake plenty at that—stretching to distances that even astounded the geology experts who made the survey. Not only did the energy produced from the shocks affect everything within a 250-mile radius Of Charleston, but vibrations were felt as far away as some points in New York State, Massachusetts, and even the state of Wisconsin—nearly one thousand miles away! Moreover, a number of southern cities reported chimneys falling and also hearing sounds similar to that of a cannon ball exploding. It was reported the entire state of Florida quivered and Bermuda reported that tremors were also felt there.

However, with its more than a hundred lives lost and property damage estimated at several million—and astonishing amount for that day—it was Charleston that was to make newspaper headlines around the world; and was also stated to become a major point of interest for future tourist seeking to see the city and its several historic landmarks—namely St. Michael's Episcopal Church, which sank some eight inches or more into the ground during the earthquake.

At any rate, it was a most grim and frightful experience for all concerned and, not a very pleasant period of time for anybody who lived in the region for some time to come, because aftershocks were to continue on for almost a full year.

All the same, if Luke Heyward ever thought about the dire prediction that his wife had made to him relative to the earth shaking, a short while before it did shake, he stopped at reminding her of it, or, for that matter, made no mention of it to anyone else. And naturally, it remained to be a sealed subject on Eliza's part, too. Still, it is plausible to reason that in Luke's case he was simply too involved with other matters—sorrowful matters—at the time to have the will or freedom to do very much conversing with anybody and least of all the grieved Eliza, even had there been things on his mind he would have liked to unloaded. For the burials of both Hannah and Caroline Wilton Roalf—Doctor Seth Roalf was indisposed from grief and fatigue combined—fell upon Luke Heyward to arrange and see to only a mere week after the earthquake and a mere two days apart!

In any event, it was both a grievous and scary time indeed.

Chapter Eight

Another hot day abounded and, wearily, Eliza climbed the front porch steps and flopped down in the nearest chair available—a wicker rocker, which as ironical as it was she had never sat in it before and which most surprising to her she found quite relaxing, in spite of the fact that feeling relaxed anywhere, of late, was something she had held in prospect the least.

Once again, although the task had weighed heavy on her emotions, Eliza had finally done what she felt she must not put off doing any longer—visit the grave of the recently deceased, which on this occasion had not only been one grave but two, Caroline Wilton Roalf's and Hannah's.

Having chosen to make her journey by horseback on this day, Eliza let her riding crop, which she was still clutching in her hand after leaving her mount at the stables, fall to the floor beside her chair. Then, in the next instant, she was reaching for her wide-brim straw hat and letting it follow suit as she gazed down the drive and wondered where Phil Carson was heading to. She had just spied her brother's dejected figure disappearing through the entrance to the plantation. Surely, not toward the cemetery again, she thought. On the other hand, Phil maybe had decided to go to the tobacco barn where Luke and the hands were grading and packing the cured tobacco. Or, who knew? Maybe he had decided to walk clear to Drakston Hall again to have a visit with their aged father. To everybody's shock last week, including their father's, Phil had done just that, and she certainly would not put walking there for a second time, or even a third time for that matter, past her brother's doings for ever since his arrival at Green Sea, two days after the earthquake, his manner had been unpredictable—not only projecting a keen perceivable restlessness but also an open indecisiveness about making up his mind whether he preferred Green Sea over Lexington or vice versa. Though she thought Green Sea would be his choice in the end.

Yes, just when she had thought that she could not endure another minute without knowing if the children had escaped the earthquake, Phil had walked through the door, bringing word that everything was fine in Virginia; that is, aside from everybody being anxious to hear from family and friends at that end of the line. The way she understood it, no sooner than Gilford Sloan had received the chilling news and conveyed the message to Phil, Phil had set out for South Carolina immediately, making it to Green Sea in record time despite broken railroad ties, twisted tracks, open fissures, or anything else he had encountered along the way. She would never forget her relief at seeing him. By the same token, neither would she ever forget the obvious strain and tension that Phil arrived under. Though she had told him that Rachelle's grave and the entire cemetery as a whole had come to no harm during the earthquake, he was not in the house five minutes before he was on his way to see for himself. Still, she could understand Phil's concern because had not she herself done the very same thing the moment the ground had seemed to quieten after the earthquake?

Actually, she reckoned Phil was doing remarkably well at that, if one stopped to consider all the trials that he had to shoulder lately. For instance, on top of all his other fears and anxieties, there was the sorrow of Caroline's death to go through hardly no time after his arrival at Green Sea—a grim time for all concerned, and a very agonizing experience for Phil, she knew, though he still had not mentioned one word regarding it to either Luke or herself, Apparently, it was something that he preferred to keep locked inside him, choosing to air to nobody—the matter of his open grief over Caroline's casket as loved ones and friends alike were viewing her body for the last time.

Phil had seemed to be totally unaware that others were waiting in line behind him as he continued to stand there and weep. Finally, just as she herself had started to step forward and go to his assistance, Elizabeth Drakston, stepped forth and gently slipping her arm through Phil's, had guided him on down the church isle and through the door to the churchyard where she and Phil had joined those of whom who had already filed by Caroline's casket. And, Elizabeth had continued to remain by Phil's side throughout the rest of the burial service—a praiseworthy gesture on Elizabeth Drakston's part and one that she herself planned on not forgetting though in all honesty she knew that she still was going to have little use for Elizabeth Drakston, the person!

Caroline's parting with this world had been as peaceful and quiet as her nature. She had merely ceased taking another breath. Though she very much doubted that Caroline had known of their presence due to her languorous condition, both Martha and she were there with her, keeping vigil, at the end. Everybody had known; however, that death was imminent with Caroline. But, even so, its reality when it did finally ring true, for herself, had been something else again. It had gone hard with her and going to Elms today for the first time since Caroline's death had been no different.

All the same, she was glad that she had, at last, made up her mind to go even if she had felt a driving compulsion to give her mount full rein all the way there and back. Like Martha had told her, more than once lately, that she acted as though she were running away from something; and she supposed Martha was right, or she would have journeyed to Elms long before this and also not behaved as if she were trying to set a speed record while going about it, besides, still, she must concede that she had left Elms feeling a whole lot better than she had expected to feel, and certainly less gloomy than she had when arriving; in that, she had seen that Caroline's wish for Elms to run on—be there—would indeed come about.

Yes, after having visited Caroline's grave first, which was on Elms' ground surrounded by both her parents who were also gone now and a number of other long deceased Wiltons, she had gone on by the house to pay her respects to Seth, Seth Junior, and Maggie and, during this time she had visited with them, had seen as plain as the back of her hand that Maggie Randolph Roalf had what it takes to carry on—to preserve and keep Elms alive despite the fact that Caroline was no longer there and had left no direct Wilton heirs to inherit it.

A dynasty had ended though, had ceased with Caroline's death. Now a new one was beginning in the Roalfs, because aside from a few sentimental tokens that Caroline had specified in her will were to be handed to Martha and herself, she had willed Elms and all its holdings to be shared equally between her husband, Doctor Seth Roalf and his son, Doctor Seth Roalf Junior. Of course, Caroline's generosity had made both doctors wealthy men and particularly in the case of Seth Roalf Senior who owned the bordering Davis properties as well.

Well, the way she herself felt about it, no one was more deserving than Seth. Since coming to the low country to join the late Doctor Davis in his practice, Seth had given of himself, round-the-clock, to the whole community, serving its rich and poor alike with no mark of difference whatever. Still, at the same time, she could not help wondering if Caroline, through her will, had not been trying to tell Seth something—perhaps prove to him that he had her love despite the fact that she had loved Phil too?

Well again, if this had been the nature of things with Caroline and Seth, there should be no doubt in his mind now that Caroline was totally devoted to him because, regardless of what her feelings were for Phil, she could not have made her feelings for him, any plainer than had she shouted her devotion for him from the pulpit in the Baptist church.

Seth did seem well enough today, and she believed that he would continue to be. She wished she could think the same about Phil. Of course, with his busy medical practice, Seth had more going for him, more in the way of keeping his mind distracted and off his grief than Phil did. And too, this was Seth's second time around, if that meant anything, grief-wise. Maybe it did. Then again, she supposed something like that depended on the nature of the person involved. Whatever the case, she wondered if the day would ever come when any of them—Caroline's family and friends alike—would not miss her dear presence? So far, it certainly had been thus with herself and she thought it would never be no different. Further, that ever squabbling between Martha and herself had to stop now because, with no dear Caroline to calmly intervene and smooth things between them, it was anyone's guess what might happen if their squabbling was not brought to an end. Dear Caroline —

All at once, letting her reflecting drop aside, Eliza was pulling her shoulders up and slipping forward to the edge of her rocker. The approach of a fast-moving buggy, which had missed turning over only by a hair as it had just whirled into the drive off the river road, had caught her full attention. Blinking hard at the tears that had started gathering in her eyes a second earlier, she tried to make out who was driving the buggy but failed due to the distance and her blurry vision. Still, as her gaze stayed with the rapidly moving vehicle—she was too rapt in its approach to even think about the whole scene that reminded her of that day long ago when Martha, with Caroline hanging on for dear life, came tearing down the drive bringing news of Gettysburg.

However, knowing that Bruce had finally laid down the law to Martha about her wild driving—threatening to put her mare and the buggy, too, under lock and key if she did not stop traveling at such breakneck speed—Eliza was casting all thought of Martha and her reckless driving aside when, just at that instant, she saw that indeed, it was Martha and no other, as Martha suddenly pulled the galloping horse from the main drive onto the circular drive, which lead to the front steps; and not only almost flipped over again but came spinning on one wheel right on by the steps where Eliza was sitting and finally bringing mare and buggy to a stop some several feet distance away.

Instead of jumping up and running to inquire if Martha were all right like she had ever done when her cousin had overleaped the bounds of good common sense and gotten in trouble, Eliza did nothing, merely saying to herself "I might've known" as she still kept to her rocker.

Even though Eliza was frightened for Martha's safety as well as being afraid, too, that Martha might be carrying bad news, she nevertheless had also become so piqued with Martha for scaring her half to death that she had made up her mind, this time, not to let her cousin have the satisfaction of knowing that she cared one way or the other—telling herself that besides staying put and doing nothing, to act as though Martha had done not one thing out of the ordinary, that having a guest spinning by their front door on one wheel was a regular occurrence with them and she thought nothing of it. But then, as Eliza continued to sit and watch Martha begin the ordeal of trying to get the horse to back up and got a more distinct view of Martha's face as the latter did edge a little closer back—a face that was so drawn and tight that it looked as though someone had actually taken steel thread and stitched it that way—despite everything, she found herself jumping to her feet and crying out, "Martha, what's wrong? Pray tell me, it's not bad news again!"

Finally, at that same moment, having paralleled the buggy with the front steps at last, Martha, throwing the reins to one side and jumping to the ground, barked back, "I can't do that because it is bad news and plenty bad at that!" Tearing on up the steps while Eliza's face drained whiter and whiter of color, she roared on, "I tell you, Eliza, nothing in our entire generation has ever happened like it before! Even Frank's marriage to Elizabeth, whom none of us had ever heard of at that time, was scarcely a drop in the ocean compared to the blowing news that reached Bruce and me only a few hours ago!"

"Then, there's no death in the family?" Eliza managed to croak as Martha tore on by her and flopped down on a wicker settee, which matched the rocker that Eliza had been occupying and which was part of a wicker setting group that was arranged close together on the porch.

Having thrown off her bonnet and grabbed a palm leaf fan, which she was sailing back and forth like mad, Martha, abruptly letting the fan stop, screeched somewhat fiery,

"Death? Whatever made you ask a question like that? And, sit back down before you fall! You're white as a sheet!" Seeing that Eliza had decided to hear her bidding and hold whatever comment that she may have made, Martha went on as she resumed her fanning, "No, there's no death, I'm thankful to say, or at least, I'm not aware of it, if there is. Besides, I'm surprised that you'd ask such a question as that with our lot being as it's been lately regarding that sort of thing!" Her irritation with Eliza was obvious.

With her alarm now rapidly evaporating while Martha's vexation, obviously, grew worse; Eliza came back rather moderately, "Well, you said it was bad news." "It is!" Martha flared. "And, if I could only get up with a certain Mr. Silverspoon, I grant you, it would be worse! In fact, I'm here to tell you that Mr. Silverspoon's worldly time would certainly be in jeopardy, if not ended for good!"

Overcurious, Eliza ventured to ask, "Silverspoon? Who's Mr. Silverspoon?"

"Who's Silverspoon?" Martha stormed, her face looking as stormy now as the tone of her voice. "Haven't you heard one word that I've said?"

Though she had no wish to grate on Martha's bad temper, making it worse, Eliza could not hold herself from retorting back, telling Martha, "Well, so far, there hasn't been much to hear! Only that you'd do away with a certain Mr. Silverspoon if you could catch up with him, a name that you must remember I've never heard tell of before till you uttered it, just now!"

Relenting somewhat to the inevitable, Martha said, "Well—yes—true enough, I'm sure a more ridiculous name you have yet to hear, Mrs. Silverspoon! I tell you, Eliza, it's enough to drive me up the wall. Carrying a name like that, she's bound to be the laughingstock of her surroundings, forever!"

"Martha, I don't have the first idea who you mean, let alone what you're talking about. First it seems you're ready to do away with some man who goes by the name of Silverspoon. Now, it appears you're all tolerance toward Mrs. Silverspoon, worrying about the possibility of her becoming a laughingstock to whomever she's around because of the uniqueness of their surname. Who are these people and why have you become so upset with them? Simmer down, won't you, at least long enough to explain it to me." Eliza said, feeling thoroughly confused by this time.

"Oh, botheration!" Martha stormed again, tossing her fan in the air—which fell several feet from her—and throwing up her hands. "It is for a fact; you haven't heard half of what I've said! What's the trouble, is your hearing failing on you? It's Laura! How many times do I have to repeat it! She's married, Eliza! Married! Married an actor by the name of Cornelius Silverspoon, of all damnable names! He performs with a traveling troupe that, I understand, presents Shakespearean drama only." Martha had suddenly stilled her hands in her lap and lowered her voice too. "I gather he's descended from a line of Shakespearean actor's way back and, at the present time, is performing in *The Tempest*, one of Shakespeare's plays. In the play, he portrays the son of a duke who usurps his brother out of his title. I'd say Mr. Silverspoon is cast in the wrong role.

Instead of playing the son's part, he should be playing the part of the usurping duke, the part would fit his character perfect!" Martha's excitement was mounting again. "At any rate, the troupe gave only three performances, stayed in the city just three days! Three days, mind you, but it seems it was enough to do the trick! He saw Laura, Laura saw him, and that was it!" Suddenly, Martha's hands came back up in a helpless gesture. "Now, you know, and go right ahead and laugh all you want! I certainly have no objection because, aside from the fact he's an actor, hearing that she's taken on a name like that is enough to make you laugh and laugh the rest of the day, at that!"

Surprised so, that she felt no less jarred then had the porch ceiling caved in on her, Eliza might have told the excited Martha that laughing was the least thing she felt like doing right then. She also might have pointed out that none of this spill had Martha repeated to her before. She let it all pass though, Martha's contemptuous remarks and all—saying nothing as she sat and stared back at Martha with an incredulous gaze till she finally asked, wondering all the while if she had indeed heard it right, "Where is Laura at now? And where and when did she marry this man?"

Suddenly, to Eliza's astonishment again Martha started sobbing, wailing back, "I might've known you'd come up with something like that!" She jumped up and ran to one of the porch columns, turning her back to Eliza as she leaned against it sobbing.

Nonplused, and after having eyed Martha's back for some little while and intently at that, Eliza finally said, "I'm sorry, Martha, but again you baffle me. Obviously my question's upset you and I fail to see why because, to me, it was neither improper or errant, I was only concerned and I should think that being thus is not only creditable of one but seemly as well and, that it should be taken in that manner and no other way.

Certainly, the way you lashed back at me was presumptuous and uncalled-for!"

"Of course," sobbed Martha, sniffing hard at the sobs that threatened her voice, "and I don't suppose that it's ever occurred to you that while you're going about this proper and well-deserving probing that you're also gathering, at the same time, all those little details that's so important to you and that you're ever combing for, has it, Eliza?" "That's grossly unfair, Martha." Eliza defended, now having a sudden suspicion what lay at the root of Martha's impetuous behavior.

"Well, undue or not, it's the truth and you know it." Martha came back and went on in a voice, that had grown mightily in strength again. And, something else, Eliza, when are you going to start realizing that all daughters aren't cast in the same mold as Brent and Mollie Cooper's? I don't believe that Grace Cooper has ever made a move in her whole life that she first did not consider it from a conventional standpoint, wondering if it would meet with popular custom or not. Still, I must say that all this primness certainly seems to have harmed her none at all when it came to catching a husband! Though she did go about it as decorous as an old prim lady would have, she still had no trouble swagging that doctor who came to town, what's his name?"

"Cyrus Blake, and the most eligible bachelor in the whole state of Mississippi, the rumor goes," Eliza offered.

"Yes, and as fitting as you please and no sooner than he hanged his shingle out, Grace had him hooked as solid as any fish has ever been hooked on a fishing pole. And, that's not the half of it. Did you know that Bill Cooper's in Mississippi right now at the Blake family estate, Foxwood rushing the doctor's sister? Harriett, I think her name is. Mollie was telling Elizabeth and Elizabeth told me," said Martha, a begrudging tone now filling every word she spoke.

"No, I hadn't heard." Eliza said.

"Well, it's a fact and all I've got to say about that is, lucky Coopers! Anyway, I'm ready to answer your question now regarding Laura. She's in Chicago, where she wrote from and where she says she and this Silverspoon were married. What date the marriage took place she, conveniently, forgot to say. Now, you can ask Marsh Reed to start offering prayers in behalf of her lost soul because I know that's what you're thinking she's in dire need oft"

"Well, you're wrong. For my mind's so busy right this moment with trying to figure you out, centering it on anything else would be attempting the impossible, I fear!" Eliza retorted, bringing Martha whirling back around to face her.

"What do you mean, figure me out?" Martha cried, her temper flaring again like a hurricane blowing up. "When did I become such a riddle to you, for heaven's sakes!"

"Just now, when you were talking about the Coopers. Martha, you sounded so envious, and especially in point of Grace's marriage, it's a wonder your eyes haven't turned green! One would think the way you're always worried about Laura becoming an old maid like her Aunt Lucy, that you'd be happy to hear that she's gotten married. Now that it's happened though, it appears marriage is not what you wanted for her, after all. I'm simply unable to comprehend your attitude."

"So, I'm making a fuss about nothing, is that it?" Martha bristled, her brown eyes beginning to smolder like live coals.

"I said nothing of the sort, Martha, and why don't you sit back down and stop this nonsense!"

"Oh, so now it's nonsense, and, no, I shall not sit down!" stormed Martha. "The rest of what I have to say I can manage it on my feet, thank you, then I'm going home because I can see if it's sympathy I want, which I'm not ashamed to confess was my main purpose for coming here, I'm wasting my time! Since it's my daughter and not yours who's eloped and with a stranger at that, to you it's a matter of no significance whatever, merely fiddle-faddle stuff, isn't it?"

"Martha, what's come over you, for pity's sake! You can't mean what you're saying. You know I care very much about what happens to Laura."

"Well, if you do care, your attitude about the whole matter is not very convincing, I can tell you that! You just called it nonsense and you can't deny it, so don't seesaw with me, Eliza, if you expect me to believe what you say!"

"I'm not seesawing. You took my remark the wrong way, that's all," said Eliza, growing a little weary of being driven into a corner by Martha's foul mood. "You feel let down and it's made you oversensitive."

"Well, maybe." Martha allowed. "But, I just wonder to what extreme you'd go to if Jane Anne were to elope with a total stranger, though, I know there's no chance of that happening as long as Stuart's alive."

Martha had pelted on the wrong nerve.

"Would as leave a stranger as Stuart Drakston." Eliza fired back. "Further, I'd prefer you leave Jane Anne out of this conversation. She's happy, content, and doing well in her studies, which goes to show that I knew what was best for her. We miss her, make no mistake about that, but with her happiness at stake, Luke and I both are willing to suffer the privation of her company and make the best of it."

"Bah!" Martha sneered, her flaming gaze looking down at Eliza in contempt. "You mean you're willing, because from all signs, I'd say, Luke certainly isn't. Furthermore, just how long do you think Jane Anne will be disposed to go on playing the lead role in this little deceptive charade that you've worked out? Not very long, I can tell you, once she's completed her studies next spring. Not only is she and Stuart more in love than ever, but I know for a fact that she's promised to marry him then, whether she has your permission or not! The fact is, Eliza, Stuart's trying to persuade her to marry him now instead of then, so he can take her to England with him and Elizabeth when they sail at Thanksgiving time. So, don't think for one moment that he's ever given up the idea of making Jane Anne his wife!"

Thinking that the part about England was the best news that could possibly come her way, Eliza was more than willing to push the insults aside in order to learn more about the forthcoming trip, saying, as she looked up at Martha with naked interest, "Who told you they were going to England, and just how long do they plan to stay over there?"

"Stuart told me himself!" Martha blazed, and ignoring the last part of Eliza's question, she went on to add, "Now start praying that the ship will sink! I wouldn't put it past you as much as you hate him!"

Feeling that Martha on second thought had deliberately kept back the information that she had sought pertaining the length of the purposed journey, Eliza shot back, "Whether his ship sinks or stays afloat the consequences will be no different when it comes to Jane Anne marrying him because she won't! She'll continue to listen to her father and me. So, such being the case,

Stuart Drakston would be wise to find himself someone else to pant after!"

"Oh, you're impossible, Eliza. And, since I can see that I'm getting nowhere with you on this subject either, nor have any hope of ever making you see that you're wrong about Stuart, I'm going home right this minute! Further, it's going to be a while before I set foot here again I can tell you!" Blazed Martha once more. And, running down the steps and jumping inside the waiting buggy, she grabbed up the reins and jerked the horse to another wild start tearing down the drive as recklessly as she had torn up it and leaving Eliza's call for her to please be more careful falling unheard into the rumble of the flying buggy wheels.

Having realized that she and Martha both, on this occasion, had let their tempers put a stop to their clear thinking altogether, Eliza had jumped to her feet and tore down the steps after Martha. And now as she stood in the dust of Martha's wild leave-taking, knowing that she might as well have directed her pleas to the side of the house for the good they have done because the buggy was doing another wild spin in Martha's effort to hit the river road, she found herself crying the deceased Caroline's name, saying over and over as she clasped a hand to her bosom in fright, "Oh, Caroline, whatever will become of us!"

Though she saw the buggy settle back down and safely make the turn, most likely saving Martha's neck, she still kept her eyes fast upon the rising rolls of dust that Martha was leaving behind her till there was no more left to see.

And, while all this stormy parting between his sister and cousin was taking place, Philippe Carson—having just crawled from the back of a farm wagon that he had hitched a ride in, was ambling up the well-manicured drive that lead to Drakston Hall's front door. His head was down though. And, as usual, so were his thoughts. However, as he ambled along with his eyes fixed on the toes of his boots—thinking about the abrupt turn his life had taken again and trying to decide what direction to go in since Rachelle was no longer at his side to give comfort and guide him in her wisdom—he not only began to take notice of the dust and grime caked on his expensive leather boots but, for the first time in weeks, let his mind become concerned with what he saw and was brought up sharp by it, suddenly stopping in his tracks to let his eyes travel up the front of his summer linen suit as well.

Now seeing that his suit with its wrinkles and layers of dust was in no better condition than his boots, actually looking more like a hand-me-down than the recently and costly purchase it was, Philippe Carson hesitated at taking another step toward the elegant mansion setting before him. Gazing long and hard at the mansion, which to him looked as bright and clean as Monday's wash and certainly too grand for his unkempt attire on this day, he was seriously thinking of turning around and heading back in the direction he had come in when, suddenly and out of nowhere, he heard a voice calling his name from a far distance.

Turning to scan the wide tree-splashed lawns and flower-decked terraces around him, not to mention the formal rose garden itself and the many more shrubs and flowers that required the work of two gardeners in the summer months full time, he finally, to his surprise, spotted Elizabeth Drakston emerging from the tall rose bushes waving to him and, at the same time, indicating that she wanted him to come forward and join her where he saw her taking her seat on a nearby stone bench—one of several that spotted the dazzling landscape.

Though Philippe Carson believed that he and Frank Drakston's widow had not spoken more than two dozen words in the short time that they had known one another and those had been said through mere courtesy alone, he nevertheless had felt for some time that it was essential he talk with her and, on every visit that he had made to Drakston Hall lately, had been waiting for just such an opportunity as this to arise. The fact was, since it had looked like he was never going to catch her without having an audience present to hear every word, he had almost convinced himself to forget about it.

But now, grateful and greatly relieved too, that Elizabeth Drakston was finally making it possible to be alone with her, he started forth, cutting across the grounds that separated them and wondering as he did if she had sensed his need to talk with her all along.

Now as he approached her, he smiled and said, trying to act as offhand about it had they been old friends and meeting one another for years, "They won't stay pretty for long, Miss Elizabeth, if you don't get them in water right away," referring to the basket of cut roses that she had set down on the bench beside her.

For a split second he saw she seemed perplexed, uncertain as to what he meant. Then, just as quickly, and to his relief too, she was glancing down at the roses and then back to him saying, as she sent him a smile in return, "Well, we'll enjoy them while they do last." She pulled the basket close to her side. "Have a seat, Mr. Carson. I think your father and Mrs. Carson have just retired for their afternoon nap, I thought you wouldn't want to disturb them."

"No, certainly not, and thank you for letting me know," he said, flapping down on the bench with the same air of casualness that he had tried to effect in greeting her, though he was sure she was wise to every taut nerve he felt. "As a matter of fact, having just taken notice of how soiled my clothes have become, I was standing there wondering if I should try to make it through the front entrance, anyhow."

She laughed, "Oh, come now, Mr. Carson. I should hope we don't appear to be all that elegant and fussy."

Her laugh was easy and unfeigned, he noticed, instantly making him feel that she was more friend then stranger to him and that there was no need for him to try to pretend anything with her that he did not feel.

Now surprised at how rapidly his nerves were settling down; and also experiencing the first real sense of lightness that he had known for weeks, he said, "You don't think so? Then take a look at these boots, will you." He pushed his feet forward. "Would you say these and Oriental Carpets go together? To me, they look no better than field brogans. And it's not only the boots. I bet if my suit's got one layer of dust and dirt on it, it's got one dozen." He, automatically, brushed at a trouser leg.

"Oh, you'll pass front door inspection, Mr. Carson, so don't fret so," she laughed again. Then abruptly turning serious she went on to ask, "But, tell me, you didn't walk all the way from Green Sea in this heat today, did you?"

"No, not every step of the way, by a long shot. I hitched a ride part way with some fanner back across the river." He turned his head to look at her. "I suppose you're wondering why I'd be so foolish as to set out walking here in the first place when I could ride just as easy."

"No, not in the least. I understand," she said.

"Of course, and I'm sorry," he said, actually thinking of her as being the widow of Frank Drakston for the very first time. The truth was, he had let his thoughts dwell so little on his late cousin since gaining his memory back, a pang of guilt shot through him, forcing his eyes to look away from her in another direction.

"Thank you," she murmured softly. "It was a long time ago."

He turned to eye her again. "But there was a time of unrest, you say, before you did learn to accept and adjust to the condition of things," he said.

"Yes," she replied, a long period of nothing but despair and hopelessness, it seemed. But I don't like to use the word accept in connection with my husband's death because I truly don't think I've ever accepted the untimely and tragic factors that were involved in it. As far as adjusting to what my life became afterwards, yes, I adjusted and you will too, given time."

"Time," he echoed. And then, after a long moment of silence and while he gazed off into the distance once more, he went on, plainly showing the skepticism he felt, "But, when there's so much to deal with, as in my case, I'm wondering if it'll work for me. Actually, in a manner of speaking, I'm dealing with two lifetimes, all at once, grievous happenings of past years that just caught up with me at Easter of this year, plus all the misfortune and sorrow that's fell my way since then. Sometimes, I feel it's a little more to bear with than I have strength for."

"But, you are enduring," she said, "and that shows great strength, not lack of it, Don't sell yourself short, Mr. Carson, when you've already braved so much in your life and come through."

"Well, maybe, Miss Elizabeth, and take my word for it, I won't forget your kind words, but my feeling is, I could certainly be a lot more steadfast, particularly when it comes to restraint and self-control and I'm sure there are a number of people in these parts who wouldn't think of disagreeing with me, either." He was finally touching on the subject that he had long felt he must talk to her about

Instantly grasping the literal meaning of his reply, she said, her candor surprising him as she wasted no words, "Mr. Carson, don't regret or ever feel embarrassed by the fact that you wear your heart on your sleeve. Better that a man be this way I should think, than project an air of coldness and disregard when, actually, underneath the hard, cold exterior there's a warm human being. I think, a number of men tend to do this, no doubt holding the notion that it would be weak and unmanly of them to show their emotion. My late husband was a man of such nature.

He was capable of great warmth, but the public never saw it or, was ever even aware that he possessed warmth, for that matter. To tell the truth, with his mother, Stuart and me being the exception, Frank very rarely exposed the good side of his nature to anyone." She suddenly fell silent. Then after a long moment of seemingly reflection, she went on, "Of course you knew Frank, and here I am rambling on about him as if he were someone you'd never heard tell of. I'm sorry, Mr. Carson."

"No, please go on," he quickly said, no need to apologize. It's been so many years now, it makes it difficult for me to see and place people as they were in those days, anyway."

This was only partly true, merely pertaining to those persons whom Philippe Carson had not known very well in the first place. Certainly, the late Frank Drakston was not one of them.

"Well," she said, appearing reluctant to go on with the subject as she fingered at a rose petal, "there's not much more to say except, if you were referring to that painful incident that occurred at Mrs. Roalfs burial and I believe you were, I think you're taxing yourself needlessly to let how others may have looked upon it to concern you to any degree. Certainly, you or no one else should think of yourself as being a jellyfish or the likes of some other fragile creature because of it and, this was what I was trying to convey when I brought my late husband's name into our talk."

He had detected a note of regret in her voice for having mentioned her husband's name at all. It was obvious Frank Drakston had had her complete devotion. Still, he did not want the subject closed before he had a chance to explain himself further and also thank her for having come to his aid.

"Of course, you're right," he said. "But, it isn't my open grief over a dear friend's passing that I'm concerned about, It's the hope that I didn't disparage the relationship that I enjoyed with my late dear wife in the minds of this community by it, that's all. I loved my wife deeply, and I thank God that I can separate the devotion that I hold for her from any affection that I might have found I still held for Caroline Roalf."

"I think what really threw me was seeing the engagement ring that I gave to Caroline so long ago, still glowing on her finger. It brought everything back, rushing at me as vividly as the light of day, all the things that were, those we lost, and those that won't ever be. Everything about those days, I saw in that ring—the glory, the grief, and the torment all heaped together, a glowing hue of finality. It hit me hard. Anyway, that's about as near as I can explain what happened to me, and since you did take it upon yourself to come to my aid, I've been wanting to tell you this; also thank you for coming along when you did. I'll ever be grateful to you." "It pleases me that you've told this to me, Mr. Carson," she said. "But, as I've already pointed out, this painful experience that you speak of isn't all that inconceivable to me. At some time or other in our lives, just as you did, we all find ourselves vulnerable to happenings of this nature. Why even here, after all these years away from England, I meet with situations sometimes that seems to transport me back to the days of my childhood in London." She looked up and catching his eye, smiled, "Especially when I first look out my bedroom window some mornings and see swamp fog rolling in."

"Yes," he agreed, his features growing lighter too. "Our low-country is pretty much like London in that respect, isn't it?" Then, with a sudden interest that she had not seen in his gaze before, he went on as he keenly studied her. "But, even without fog, I'm sure these parts didn't seem much like home to you when you first came here. I mean, there was a vast difference to struggle with and adjust to, was there not?"

"Not as much as one would think," she replied, folding her hands in her lap and gazing down at them, "a few customs maybe but that's all. Through Frank, I became acquainted with southern culinary, something I relish very much I must admit, long before I saw Drakston Hall. He taught me how to prepare many of his favorite dishes. As far as being troubled, or having to struggle with managing the domestic or business side of things here, for the most part, I've been shielded from that responsibility from the first. Except for the few years that Frank's mother lived away from Drakston Hall, following her marriage to your father, she's mostly seen to managing the household duties. And, fortunately, Drakston Hall itself and all its people, your father was here to shoulder Frank's duties after his death. Of course, with Father Matthew's heart—

Elizabeth Drakston had honored Matthew Carson with this title for a good many years now—not being as strong as it once was, Stuart has relieved him of this responsibility in recent years.

Along with his law practice, Stuart has managed the plantation ever since he and I returned from England where he attained his higher education." She suddenly lifted her eyes back to his gaze.

"Speaking of your father, you do realize, do you not that he's counting on you to come back to these parts as soon as you're able to settle your business affairs in Lexington? This was my main reason for waving at you to join me. I've been wanting a chance to tell you that he's going to be awfully let down if you don't decide to come back."

"And, it's my sudden conviction that if my father should happen to meet with anything like that, that Miss Elizabeth is going to be awfully unhappy too," he smiled as a hint of merriment appeared in his eyes.

"You're right about that, Mr. Carson," she smilingly confessed, completely unabashed. "Not only do I consider your father the best friend I've ever had but look on him as being a second father to me as well. What's more, Father Carson has become my closest confident, business matters or otherwise, since my own father passed on a few years back. So, little wonder I hold him in high regard and am concerned for his every happiness. He's truly a remarkable and fine man, one of the best."

Still studying Elizabeth Drakston and heartened by what he saw, Philippe Carson said, as his gaze grew brighter still, "Thank you, Miss Elizabeth, I agree but, at the same time, let me say that I can see the type of friends my father has, would serve as credence of his honor, any day, if nothing else would. So, that being the case, coupled with the fact that I wouldn't want either one of you to undergo any disappointment or distress on my account, I think I'm going to head back for Lexington in a few days and get busy settling my affairs there!"

"So, you are coming back! Oh! Your father's going to be awfully happy to hear that news, Mr. Carson!"

"Well, let's say I'm going to start working on it," he grinned, suddenly feeling better by having said he was, "I might be able to sell out my half of my newspaper business to my partner, Gilford Sloan, of late he's mostly been running it by himself, anyway. And, when Carr finishes law school and he and Beth Anne come back to live at Green Sea, if Beth Anne has no objection to letting the house go, I'll sell it to Sloan, too, if he wants to buy it, which I think he will. Anyhow, Luke has already asked me to come back and help him manage Green Sea, says he's not getting any younger and the job is getting to be more of a burden every day. So, even if it's the first of the year before I get my business organized, I promise you, my father will get his wishes."

"Oh, how wonderful, Mr. Carson," she cried, jumping to her feet and sweeping up the basket of cut roses. "Let's go tell Father Carson! I can't wait to see his face!"

Rising to his feet, Philippe Carson said, "Let me carry those for you, Miss Elizabeth." And, taking the basket of roses that she held out to him and slipping it on his right arm and then offering his lame left arm to a slightly flustered Elizabeth Drakston, he started forth toward the mansion once more, stepping much lighter than he had stepped many a day.

He had finally, in the last few minutes, made his decision, and he had a feeling he was not going to regret it.

Chapter Nine

Home for the Thanksgiving holidays, Jane Anne Heyward drowsily opened her eyes from a long night's sleep. For a split second—in her drowsy state—she thought she was back at school with nothing to look forward to that day but just another long session of classes that, of late, were not only becoming more and more boring to her, but downright meaningless as well. Because embarking upon any type of professional career, once she did graduate, was the one thing that Jane Anne was not counting among her future plans. Suddenly; however, with her eye catching sight of the pink ruffled canopy hanging over the huge mahogany fourposter that she was lying in, Jane Anne blithely realized that she was truly in her own bed at home instead of lying in the drab dormitory cot that she occupied back at school!

Now savoring the luxury of knowing that she was free from all boring school duties for several days and, that her time was also going to be hers to mostly fill as she saw fit—with the one exception, of course, being Stuart Drakston whom she well knew was off limits to her—Jane Anne remained abed for some little while, basking in the wondrous delight of her charming pink and white decorated bedroom and, at the same time, allowing herself to muse over present events as she did.

All the same, in as much as Jane Anne Heyward had come to treasure these holiday visits at home and was delighted at finding herself there on this day, she was still soberly aware that this particular visit home and forthcoming Christmas holidays, too, were going to fall way short of what others had been because Stuart Drakston was going to be nowhere around—the Baptist church being no exception.

Yes, that ever expectation of seeing Stuart and maybe, if she were lucky, sit beside him in church and feel the loving touch of his hand upon hers, was only going to hold through this day and the next. Then Stuart would be gone. For Stuart and his mother were scheduled to sail for England Thanksgiving Day. Having promised his mother that they would sail no later than Thanksgiving, when all the harvest was in, Stuart was keeping his word even though he had known that she herself was planning to come home on both holidays,

Of course, Stuart had asked her to accompany him and his mother to England, naturally as his wife, more times than she even liked to think about. For months, he had begged her to marry him, telling her in his letters all the places of interest in London he wanted to take her to as well as all the other exciting things they would do, Stuart had made it all sound so marvelous and she was certain that everything would be no less delightful than the picture he had painted to her on paper, she simply could not treat her parents in such a manner, no matter how much she loved Stuart or wanted to sail with him.

She had made a promise to her parents too. She had promised to finish school and she must keep that promise. This fact, she had pointed out to Stuart time and again. And finally, he had written to her that he would try to understand, that her happiness meant more to him than any personal desire he may have of his own. She wondered about that though, wondered if Stuart had been completely honest when he penned these lines to her. Certainly, in no way did she doubt his love for her. Still, by the same token, she was sensible enough to realize that Stuart had just about gone the limit of his patience with her and this whole matter. Well, her patience was wearing thin, too, and for that very reason, with or without her mother's consent, come summer she was going to marry Stuart Drakston and she had written him to this effect. Frankly, she thought her promise to marry Stuart in the summer was the one and only thing that was sustaining his patience with her anyhow. He knew, as likewise to the promise that she had made her parents, that once she promised to marry him that she would keep her word to him at all cost. But summer was a long way off in the future. It had nothing to do with today—a time that had turned into a crisis as far as she was concerned. For Stuart's long leave—taking of these parts was rapidly drawing near and she had, as yet, to lay her eyes on him. And, see him she simply must do before he left, but how?

Drawing the pink quilted bed coverlet up higher under her chin, Jane Anne continued to lie abed, unmindful now of her surroundings and everything else while her mind got busy at trying to work out some plan that not only would give her an opportunity to see Stuart Drakston before he sailed but a private moment with him as well. And yet, after it seemed like her mind had come up with a hundred or more plans and still not one of them measuring up to an ounce of sound reasoning, one simple thought sliced through her head and it was settled. Tonight at church! That was it, she thought. It was prayer meeting night! Her anxiety over whether or not she would get the chance to see Stuart and tell him how much she loved him before he sailed had caused her to completely forget that it was prayer meeting night. Of course, there was no doubt in her mind that Stuart would be there. He never missed prayer meeting. Neither did her parents, for that matter. So, her chance of seeing Stuart on this very day promised to be more than favorable, indeed!

She would use the morning hours for visiting with Mother and Papa, bring them up to date on all the news at school as well as let them tell her about all the local happenings around here. Most the afternoon she would while away riding her mare, Starface, Then, shortly after supper, she would be on her way to church, practically holding her breath till her eyes fell on Stuart again. Though, as usual, she must not forget to pretend indifference on account of Mother. It had been a long time since they had had words over Stuart and in no way did she want to disrupt this harmony which they had come to enjoy so much again.

Once again, the warm November sun had infused the air with a delicious feeling of Indian Summer. And, as Jane Anne Heyward rode her mount out of the stable yard that early afternoon and looked down the long drive ahead of her, wondering in what direction she should turn once she reached the archway—north toward Drakston Hall or south toward the ruins of the old Early Cole place—she realized, all at once, that she wanted to head in neither direction and turned her mount's head instead back the other way toward the area of the outer buildings and the old abandoned slave settlement below the stables.

Centering along the wagon path that led through both these areas and then continuing to center along it still until she had come to where it ended at the edge of the woods—having skirted the entire length of the vast field of com stubbles that marked the land now, she was pulling up her mount to make the turn back when the opening of the old timber trail caught her eye. Though it had been ages since she had ventured to ride along its winding, stubbly ruts, there was not a hook, bend, or curve in it that she still did not remember, having ridden there many times with Carr and her father.

Knowing that the lay of the land along the trail was one of the most scenic within miles around, the sudden urge to see it again on this lovely fall day became too compelling for Jane Anne to resist.

So, picking her way around the edge of the field, she soon had reached the area of the burial ground and circling it was, presently, meeting with the timber tail and all the primeval splendor that adorned it. Even though it was late November, with the maples and the birch and the hickories all having already disrobed against winter's long sleep, the red and purple dogwoods were still as fully clothed and seemed to be as wide awake as ever, their brilliant leaves dancing in glowing profusion in the shafts of sunlight falling through pine boughs, The red oaks, too, she observed, appeared to be as stubborn about buffing it as the dogwoods were. But, of all the breathtaking delight that Jane Anne was meeting with as she guided her mount on up the pine-scented trail, it was the shiny-green holly with its bright red berries that overwhelmed her the most.

She became so enchanted with the Christmas-like beauty of the blazing hollies—losing herself in fanciful scenes of banked fireplaces crackling and glowing amid holly-strung mantels, bedecked halls, and snow-frosted windowpanes—that the fact approaching sound of another horse galloping through a medley of flying leaves, dead pine cones, branches and wigs did not fully penetrate her thoughts till Stuart Drakston was already pulling up his mount alongside hers and shouting, "For gosh sakes! Jane Anne! What in the world are you doing way out here? I can hardly believe my eyes! If you didn't look so gorgeously real, I'd swear they'd played a trick on me!"

"Stuart!" she cried, pulling her mount to a standstill. "Imagine your being here too! I didn't know you hunted in these woods!" His attractive hunting attire as well as the stock of his shotgun protruding from the saddlebag had not escaped her as her astonished gaze—attended by much elation too—fell on him and held there.

Jumping from his mount and dashing over to stand beside hers, Stuart, flashing a wide grin as he looked up at her, said, "I don't very often. Wacky of me, too, I should think, considering the lovely game I'm discovering they hold! But, never mind me and my stupidness. I want to know what you're doing way out here in these woods all by yourself. You must be a good two miles from Green Sea, and I must tell you I don't feel very good about that. What if your mount should go lame, only one of a number of things that could happen?" His grin had faded into a look of concern and seriousness.

"I suppose I have ridden further out than I should have," she said, taking her eyes from him to look around her. "But the trail is so pretty, and the hollies, I simply can't resist them. It may be Thanksgiving, but here on the trail it seems like Christmas to me."

Seeing that the look on her face was carrying something far beyond his own feelings of appreciation for the hollies beauty, Stuart promptly laid the pitfalls of her riding alone aside and said to her instead, "Christmas and Indian Summer, and my beloved to grace it. What more could a man ask for? Tell me, sweetheart, how long have you been home anyhow?"

Turning her aesthetic face back to him, she said, "I came last evening. We were dismissed from classes a day early."

"Of course!" He shrugged his shoulders. "And, here I've been beating my brains out all day, trying to think of some way that I could see you before I leave. Never once did I think of that possibility and the fact that you'd be here to attend prayer meeting tonight."

With her joyful expression suddenly turning cheerless, Jane Anne came back, rather faintly,

"So, you will be leaving."

"Everything's set for it," he replied, turning somber also. "In point of Mother, I feel like I've been stalling the trip too long as it is. Anyway, the sooner we get started now, the sooner we'll return." Abruptly, doing an about face Stuart was grinning again and going on, holding out his arms to her, "Sweetheart, come on down off that horse and let me hold and kiss you like I've been aching to do for ever so long. I have no idea how you feel about our meeting like this, but I want to think that maybe fortune saw to turn its wheel in our direction. So, what do you say to our not wasting another second of the time that's been allotted to us?"

Jane Anne needed no further prompting. All at once, she was gathering her smile again and sliding from the saddle into Stuart's arms, meeting his lips as hungrily as he met hers.

Finally, although both their hearts were still beating a wild rhythm, Stuart, pulling his mouth away from hers, pleaded huskily, "Say you'll come to England with me, sweetheart. School or no school, I need you now. I've waited so long."

"I know, my darling," she whispered back, letting her head fall against his heaving chest. "But..." She broke off, finding that the ecstasy of his arms around her made it impossible for her to go on and voice another word against going with him.

All the same, since she was demurring his pleas no further, Stuart became ecstatic with hope on the spot, saying quickly, "Why don't

we find some place where we can sit down, darling, and discuss it?"
Suddenly, breaking their embrace to look around them, he went on,
his voice now singing on a high note, "Over there! Over there look's
like a nice spot! Come on, sweetheart!" And, with their hands locked
together, seconds later, they were plopping down on a high mound
of dead leaves and pine straw that fall winds had banked under a
glowing dogwood tree nearby.

And, they did talk. Or Stuart was doing most the talking while
Jane Anne dreamingly listened.

Savoring every word, every look, and every kiss that Stuart
Drakston was planting on her hand as he pleaded his cause in earnest,
she became as placidly contented in the warmth of his love as it
appeared their two drowsy, half-awake horses had become in the
warmth of the Indian summer afternoon.

But then, Stuart was saying, "I would prefer your choosing the
place where we'll say our marriage vows, darling. We could arrange
to have Reverend Reed marry us at Drakston Hall before we leave,
or wait and have a justice of the peace marry us when we arrive in
New York. For that matter, if you'd like, we could wait till we're
aboard ship and let the captain marry us."

And Jane Anne, awaking to reality, was dreaming no longer,

Say their marriage vows at Drakston Hall! She thought. Why!
She could never bring herself to do that to her parents. She was
appalled to think that Stuart would suggest such a thing. Nor did she
want to marry him in New York, or on board any ship either,
surrounded by strangers. Certainly, no two ways about it, she wanted
to marry Stuart. But, she wanted their marriage to take place at Green
Sea, with friends and family members in attendance and this was
particularly so in the case of her parents—being married the
traditional way like coming down the stairs on the arm of her father
wearing the same beautiful bridal gown that her mother had worn the
day she had married Papa.

Somehow, even though she deplored the thought of thwarting
Stuart's hopes, she had to get this message across to him—let it be
understood, whatever the cost, that if they were ever to win her
parents approval and enjoy a lasting and sound family relationship
with them once they did marry, that what he had proposed, for the
umpteenth time, was not possible. She must finish school first.

But, forthwith, Stuart Drakston said, "You're not going to marry
me anywhere, at Drakston Hall, in New York, or nowhere else,"

reading Jane Anne's message as clearly as a sign board in her tortured expression even before she could part her lips to speak.

Still not so sure that her resolve might shatter completely if she let her hand remain in

Stuart's grasp, Jane Anne, easing it forth and drawing it back to her lap to lock with her other hand, finally said, "But, you must believe that I want to marry you, that nothing would give me greater joy."

"Well, I should hope that you know, if I'm to believe that, that you'll have to put me first, for a change, and come with me!" Stuart shot back, his frustration with her taking his generous mouth and sitting it in a firm, straight line as he turned his head away from her and looked off down the winding trail.

Granted, Jane Anne did know—knew that Stuart's disappointment and letdown were so keen that to try to explain her reasons or anything else right then would be futile. Besides, she was wise enough to see that it was no ideal time to start talking about promises and school. It could lead to their first real quarrel and she did not want that, particularly since Stuart was going away with her having no idea when she would see him again.

And yet, as the tension and silence began to mount between them and continued on mounting—with Stuart giving every indication that it could continue on that way for his part, Jane Anne decided that it might be best if she did go ahead and comment on his outburst, but in a tone and manner that would not upset him further, she cautioned herself.

So, gingerly choosing her words, she softly told him, "I hold you in my heart as firmly as I hold, or could ever hold any other, darling, but I can't marry you now. Come summer, however, I will marry you if you still want me."

"Want you!" Stuart spouted back again, yanking his head around to face her once more, "Christ Almighty! That's the whole trouble now! Here lately, I can't seem to remember that there ever was a time that I didn't want you!" He saw that he was shocking her by the way she suddenly dropped her eyes but on he went, venting his frustration, "Yes, yearn and actually ache for you! I love you." His voice had begun to grow calmer. "And, loving you means that not only do you affect my feelings emotionally but physically as well. That's about as plain as I can say it. But surely, you must be aware of this—was aware of it when we were sharing that kiss a few

Louise Gore Sayre-David

moments ago, a kiss I must confess to you was certainly no remedy for easing the kind of pain I'm suffering from! Though I do swear to you, by the Almighty above, I did relish it—seared to the sky in rapture, I must admit to you, too, that snatching these long between kisses here and there, by no means, appease my desire for you. My passion and yearnings are aroused all the more." Abruptly stopping to pick up a pine needle and sticking it in his mouth, he said no more, reasoning that he had gone far enough.

Never before had Stuart Drakston ventured to be so bold in expressing his feelings to anyone. And now that he had stopped talking, he began to feel as though he had stripped off every piece of clothes that he was wearing and exposed himself in raw nakedness to Jane Anne. Still, by the same token, he knew he was fighting and fighting desperately for a love that, of late, he had begun to feel was rapidly slipping away from him, despite his threats to Eliza Heyward that he would never cease his fight to win her daughter.

Knowing that his bold disclosure had already shocked Jane Anne, Stuart had no idea what her next move was going to be. Feeling as he did right then, had she risen and without saying one word or given a backward glance, walked to her mount and rode away from him, he would not have held it against her.

Certainly, on no account, was Stuart Drakston expecting Jane Anne to suddenly lift her eyes and say, "Yes, I am very much aware of every burden that this unhappy situation is putting on you. Not only have I been mindful of it each and every time that we've been granted the privilege of snatching a kiss, but I was also intensely aware of it a little while ago. And don't think, for one moment, that at times I don't almost despise myself for not having the courage to go ahead and marry you as quickly as possible, so that our love for one another can finally be culminated. As I tried to tell you a moment ago, I know nothing would give me greater happiness." Surprising Stuart and, at the same time, making him feel like a louse besides. For Jane Anne had made him conscious of the fact that he was not the only one who had suffered, or was suffering, from the pain stirred emotions. And, that was not all. He could see by the way she was shyly looking away from him again that it had taxed her modest nature plenty to come forth and tell him what she had.

Now aware that the situation was no picnic for Jane Anne either, Stuart, actually regretting that he had spouted off about his feelings in the first place, said, "Oh, forget about it, darling. Summer's not all that far away anyhow. I'll make out." Then putting on a half-smile, he went on, "Have I told you yet just how adorable you look today in that green riding habit? Is it new?" "Close to it," she smiled, looking at him again. "This is the second time I've worn it."

"Well its very pretty," he said, "and so are you, my darling, and for that very reason alone, I think I'd better see to it that you get back on your mount and ride out of here. What do you say?" He reached for the pine needle that he had stuck in his mouth and gently toyed around her nose with it.

"Whoa! That tickles, Stuart," she giggled, rubbing above her upper lip with her forefinger.

"Don't do that."

Letting the pine needle idle somewhat, he said, "I didn't know you're ticklish."

"Well, I am, or at least I can't stand the feel of that pine needle around my nose," she laughed.

"Well, I like to hear you laugh. It'll give my mind a happy thought to turn to while I'm gone. So just for that, here goes once more," he said, and now laughing also, he, innocently, began to move the pine needle back and forth under her nose once more.

"Oh, please, Stuart!" She cried through a shriek of laughter. And, making a move to grab his hand she lost her balance and fell backwards on the pile of leaves and pine straw, still giggling hilariously as he followed her down and continued to tease her.

For the whole of one full minute or more, their play was as innocent as two frolicsome kittens—jollying, harmless intimacy. Then, suddenly, there was a maddening sense of touch and, in less than one second more, with arms locking and mouths joining and hands starting to explore, their playful innocence had become as dead as the lifeless pine needle which had started it all and which Stuart had now cast aside.

Now the weeded trail was no longer just that. It became their Eden—their dreamland where dreams did come true and the fruits of love were blissfully savored and devoured. No sense of the forbidden here though. Nor no pangs of conscience either. Only the delightful joy of finally being able to give—to receive. Less he shatter this delightful dream and have the glory of it lost to the both of them forever, Stuart took great care with the fragility of its existence. He moved with caution. Gentleness. Tenderness. Ever reminding himself to control his eagerness because this was virtuous flesh he was dealing with. All the same, although instinct alone guided her, Jane Anne helped him and their bodies were soon joined—a first coupling that had taken a bed of dead leaves and pine straw and turned it into a Utopian paradise as far as they were concerned.

They lay for some little while in a state of blissful euphoria—bodies still joined—the Indian summer warmth wrapping them in their love as snug as a flannel blanket. The fact was, so much were they submerged in the heaven that they had made for themselves that, when it finally dawned on Stuart a search party could be forthcoming if conditions did not change, both were only two winks from going fast to sleep!

However, up to this point—when the thought that Jane Anne could be missed had hit Stuart and made him aware that they did; indeed, remain on the planet Earth and were still vulnerable to its realities instead of being in paradise—the whole of Jane Anne's sensibilities had concentrated on him and his needs alone. She had completely forgotten about her own and knowing that she had, at last, satiated his burning passion for her was simply the ultimate in happiness as far as Jane Anne was concerned; or so she thought. And, like as not, the state of her yearnings and desires would have remained unchanged—solely wrapped in Stuart Drakston's and unawakened for some time to come, had he not made sure that he was going to savor the sweetness of her mouth just one more time before announcing that they must stir and make ready to leave.

For now as Stuart put his mouth to hers and finally drew back somewhat, whispering with every syllable falling in regret, "My darling, we must go," Jane Anne fiercely pulled him back telling him, "No, Stuart, not yet," startling Stuart Drakston and, in the same breath, plunging him into an overwhelming wonderment too, because Jane Anne was already stirring and stirring rather frenziedly at that and it had nothing at all to do with any leave-taking. Finally seeking the same need—demanding it with little cries—of Stuart Drakston that he had sought of her; he did not let her down.

And now again with passions and needs and yearnings of both calmed and served at last, it was a tranquil hush all over again, but a silence of wide-awake wonderment for both of them. No heaviness of eye this time. Nor no lethargy either. Only an awed astonishment as they lay in their soundless calm and marveled about the wonder they had shared—a marvel that to Jane Anne, and Stuart too, had already begun to take on a whole new meaning—an experience that now in essence was only a precious gift from God that He in His wisdom had seen fit to vouchsafe man and woman for the purpose of sealing their love for one another.

And so, viewing this marvelous experience in this light, and the fact that during this second coupling they had delighted in its occurrence simultaneously, Jane Anne and Stuart saw no weakness of the flesh or any wrongdoing—for this short while anyhow— connected with the act, It was simply in entity a God-created function—a hallowed thing to treasure and hold between them. Nothing more, But, even so, one simple little word was to soon change all this and let them see just how much they had deceived themselves and this was especially true in Jane Anne's case.

At any rate, allowing himself to be concerned once again about such matters as the hands moving on the clock and all the additional trouble that could be heaped on their heads if he and Jane Anne were caught in the woods together, Stuart, quickly rolling over on his side and gathering Jane Anne closer, said, "Darling, we must marry and marry now without delay. I see no other course for us." Striving to make every second count, he had dispensed with all his usual endearing bibble-babble and come straight to the point, hoping that Jane Anne would grasp the meaning of what he was trying to convey without spelling it straight out.

To Stuarts' dismay though, Jane Anne appeared to digest only one word in his statement and perceive nothing in it,

"Marry!" She was instantly crying. And up out of his arms to a sitting position she came like a shot, appearing to be startled as her eyes darted here and there around them. And she was startled. The word had not only brought an abrupt end to Jane Anne's golden sojourn in Eden but had also made her sit up and take a look at the way things really were with them.

Why, Stuart and I should be married already but we aren't—we aren't, she mentally cried to herself as her heart went plunging to the bottom of her stomach. This pile of dead leaves and pine straw where she had fallen from grace was certainly no marriage bed, and, not for one second, had God smiled on what had happened here this afternoon. No matter how much she loved Stuart, she should not have strayed from the teachings of God's word, let alone every moral principle that her parents had raised her by. But she had strayed and so had Stuart—strayed just as easily had their ears never heard one word about ethical conduct on His commandments. Why, she was hardly one notch from being on the moral level of those girls who dwelled in Charleston's red-light district, and Stuart was not far behind the men who paid visits to it!

Suddenly; spying that all important garment that she were painfully wishing she had kept on, but had discarded so eagerly glaring like a unfurled flag where she had sailed it off to one side, Jane Anne, letting all thought of red-light districts and prostitutes go, said as she cowered shamefully under Stuarts' gaze, "Will you please turn your head so I can get on my underclothes!"

"Of course, dear." Stuart said, understanding her modesty but not the tone of her voice. Even so as he jumped up and turned his back to Jane Anne and began to tidy up his own attire somewhat, like brushing off a number of clinging leaves and pine needles and buttoning the fly to his riding breeches, he chanced to go on and say, "Darling, if you'd like, I'll ride on back to Green Sea with you. In fact, I think that's the only honorable way to handle this matter. And, when we get there, if you'd prefer that I tell your parents about our decision to go ahead and marry now before I sail for England, I will. Though I can tell you, I'll be praying every second that I'm face to face with your mother, that the good Lord will give me the wisdom to say the right words. "

"You needn't bother yourself!" Jane Anne flared, the growing sting in her voice whirling

Stuart back around to look at her. "And, what a pity for both of us that you waited till now to think about honor. Why not one hour ago, pray tell me!" Giving a final pat to her riding habit, she straightened up to face him.

Bewildered—he had ventured to wonder for a split second if Eliza Heyward had suddenly spirited herself among them and was whispering in Jane Anne's ear, Stuart just stood and held Jane Anne's gaze. Finally, he asked, "What do you mean, not bother myself? Do you plan to tell them?"

"I do not!" She flared again.

"Then, if not you or myself, who will? Stuart pressed. "They must be told, you know." "Nobody's going to tell them, that's who!" Jane Anne brusquely declared, her guilt pushing words out that even she herself was amazed at. "Besides, you're talking about a decision that you alone arrived at. Never once, this afternoon or any other time, have I said I'd go ahead and marry you before you sail for England. I said I'd marry you next summer and next summer doesn't mean now!"

"But—but everything's changed now." Stuart said, feeling trapped. "And I should hope that you'll see that it has and also feel, as I do, that our marriage should take place immediately and not way into next year, if then. I don't want to leave you—not now—especially not after what we just shared. Can't you see that?"

"I think I see that you planned, from the first instant that we met here this afternoon, to do ‗to do everything you did!" Jane Anne heatedly replied. "And, you know, Stuart, we should've waited—waited till we were married!"

Stuart was now simply aghast, unable to believe his own sense. And, had he not been the gentleman he was, he might have pointed out to Jane Anne that the second go around for them had taken place all because of her demands, not his. By the same token; however, Jane Anne might have told Stuart that not only was her guilt forcing remarks out of her mouth that she did not mean, but it was also causing her to feel as if the trail were nothing now but some devouring jungle that she must claw her way out of and flee for all time!

None the less, in point of Stuart, his senses were not so much befuddled by Jane Anne's lashing that her misery was totally lost to him. Hardly before her stunning accusation had had time to make its impact, he was perceiving her distress and also gathering a hunch what was producing it, which brought him to mentally agree with her last remark instantly, despite the fact that he was dismayed because she had accused him of planning the whole incident.

Yes, the forbidden fruit should never have been plucked. It should have remained hanging on the tree in its virginal state, and Stuart was now regretting, deeply, that it had not. Still, what was done was done and no way could it be undone. To try to offer comfort in that respect would be little at best, if not hopeless, and he knew it. And yet, he also knew he had to try.

So, agonizing over the whole episode, Stuart, stepping forward to take Jane Anne in his arms, said, "Don't be upset because we aren't married, darling. Our loving one another and wanting to be together is the important thing. Try to look at it that way. I vow to you with all my heart that I'll ever love you and that we'll be married as quickly as possible."

To Stuart's dismay again; though, Jane Anne would have no comforting.

Brushing his arms off and stepping back from him, she was

crying on the instant, "No, we won't be married and don't be touching me anymore! I'll never break my promise to my parents!"

Beginning to wish that he had never gotten the idea to go squirrel hunting in the first place, much less turned toward that neck of the woods once he had entered them, Stuart said, "Your father would give his approval to our marrying now or any other time and you know it. And, regarding your mother, I think your promise to her to finish school is not holding you back from marrying me, at present, any more than your knowledge of her hatred for me. In fact, I think this is the main thing that's bothering you and why you've become so upset." These valid points he had felt he must bring out.

"Well, you're wrong." Jane Anne cried again, her deep-grey eyes now beginning to mist over with tears. "What's bothering me is the fact that I know now my mother was right and I was wrong! I'm going home!" And with her last words croaking on a sob, she suddenly made a break for her mount, running so fast that she gave every appearance of being winged.

Telling himself that this had to be a nightmare, Stuart raced after her, gaining her side just as she, literally, sailed—Jane Anne was a skillful horsewoman—into the saddle.

Seeing that there were going to be no shilly-shallying about Jane Anne's departure by the way she was making a grab for the reins, Stuart, quickly making a grab for the mare's bridle as well, pleaded, "Please, darling, let's not part like this. I'm truly sorry about everything. Won't you please give me a chance to make it up to you." He attempted to reach for her hands with his one free one.

But still no part of Stuart Drakston would Jane Anne have.

Letting her guilt continue to keep her ears and her heart closed to every tender gesture he made or loving word he offered, she sobbed back, as she brushed Stuart's hand away and gave a hard yank on the reins, "Enjoy yourself in England," crushing Stuart Drakston so completely that had she trampled him with her mount the pain would not have smarted him no harder. All the same, as Stuart stood and winced under Jane Anne's grinding dejection and let his eyes fall on her speeding off down the trail, he never once entertained the idea of taking them off her for good, till he had seen that she had made it well within the protection of home first.

Yes, even if Stuart Drakston was aware that handling a horse was one of Jane Anne

Heyward's chief talents, no way would he have turned his back and left her to leave the hazard of giving her mount full rein over ground of scrub and undergrowth alone. The scrutiny of his eye she would have regardless.

And so, after letting Jane Anne get a good lead on him, Stuart turned and mounting General, he started down the trail following her—his ears alerted to every hoofbeat of Jane Anne's mount—his eyes watchful ahead of him. And yet, despite all this keen alertness and the fact that every pore in his body was still seeping with mortification, Stuart still managed to find time to wonder as he slowly centered along how such a pleasure-giving experience as Jane Anne and he had shared could erupt so violently painful so quickly.

Here, minutes later, he thought, Jane Anne at her own free will was fleeing his very presence.

It was almost unbelievable, considering how they had yearned, for long years, to be together. However, he must remember that the girl fleeing ahead of him was not the same girl whom he had met earlier this afternoon. No longer was Jane Anne innocent and unknowing to the ways of the flesh and, no two ways about it, he was deeply regretting it too.

What was it Jane Anne had said to him? Oh, yes! She had told him not to touch her anymore! What's more, she had also told him that she had finally discovered her mother was right as well as having made it clear to him before that that she would never break her promise to her parents! She had truly meant her mother as he had felt compelled to point out to her. At any rate, it looked like Mrs. Heyward had won and he had lost, lost Jane Anne because of his own willingness to let his passion master every ounce of prudence he possessed, or it certainly seemed that way.

Come to think of it, maybe it might have been better for all concerned had he not set out to win Jane Anne Heyward for his wife in the first place, played the field like Whit had done. The fact was, if Jane Anne had meant what she said and from all appearances she did, he was going to have no choice about yielding to Whit's lifestyle anyhow, unless he wanted to continue on living contently, which of course he did not even if that had been precisely what he had done ever since the day he had declared his love to Jane Anne.

Ironically, it was only yesterday that Whit's letter, saying pretty much the same thing, had reached his hands. Even though Whit had tried to take his feelings into account, picking and choosing his words carefully, his message nevertheless had still come through loud and clear. In short, Whit saw no chance of Jane Anne ever going against her mother's wishes and marrying him, next summer or any other time.

Well, he supposed, from all accounts, Whit's estimation of the situation was pretty near accurate, if not true as gospel. And, he reckoned again that that was one of the main reasons that Whit was trying to persuade him to journey on to Europe once he got his mother settled down with Grandmother Stuart in London. The ship that Whit served on had been cruising in the Mediterranean Sea off the French Riviera coast for sometime now, and Whit had suggested that they meet in Monte Carlo, a gambling center located in Monaco. Of course if Whit's letters told him anything, this gambling casino was not the only attraction this little country could boast of!

Well, even though he was positive that it was going to take a lot more than gaming houses and opera and ballet houses, not to mention Monaco's fairer sex, to get his mind off his troubles, Whit's idea might be worth trying after all. Certainly, it would be great to see Lieutenant

Whitney Carson, in any case, and enjoy his cheering company again if nothing else. In fact, since this chance meeting between Jane Anne and himself had turned out to be so agonizing unpleasant for both of them he thought the sooner he took departure from these parts, the better it might be for everybody involved, especially in Jane Anne's case.

Yes, if Mother did not mind leaving for New York on the six o'clock train this evening instead of tomorrow evening, that was exactly what they would be doing come six o'clock. She had expressed her desire to do some shopping in the city anyway before they boarded the ship. So, leaving this evening would give her an extra shopping day. Their baggage was already packed and setting in the hallway ready to be loaded on the carriage, so that would present no problem. In addition, he had already settled all his law business and closed up the office till he returned home. All the plantation business was also in order and up to date. Thus, he saw no reason for waiting around another whole day before they got started. There was another important factor too, actually the most important and that was, Drakston Hall was not going to be deserted, with only the overseer and the tenants and the servants around to look after things. He was grateful to say that Grandfather and Grandmother Carson would still be there to see that aside from his low practice things would run as normal as ever. As a matter of fact, Grandfather Carson was an amazing specimen of man anyhow. His mind appeared to be about as young as ever. And, it went without saying that his physical appearance was younger looking by fifteen years than his actual age. He still had fainting spells occasionally though, but nothing so severe that a drink of brandy did not seem to turn for the better in a few minutes, if not cure.

Suddenly, feeling as though some probing hand was reaching through his rib cage and squeezing his heart, Stuart Drakston was giving no more thought to anything except the rapidly disappearing figure of Jane Anne Heyward as she was making her approach toward the area of the outer buildings and barnyard at Green Sea.

Having already reached the end of the trail a short while before this and discreetly guided General behind a tall bay bush from where he had continued to let his eye follow Jane Anne's movements, Stuart now reached forth and pulling the glossy-leaved branches wider apart, he peered intently at Jane Anne across the field, hoping to see if she would, at the very least, look back just once before the outer buildings swallowed her up from sight. Nothing of the kind was forthcoming though, vanishing his hope almost as quickly as he gained it. For Jane Anne did not do anything aside from what she had done since the instant of their parting and that was, to look straight ahead till she was there no longer for him to watch.

Now feeling no less put down again than had Jane Anne walloped him one with her riding crop, Stuart was more determined than ever to board the six o'clock northbound train out of Charleston. And yet, he seemed unable to make a start toward it, continuing to sit there and gaze on across the vacant field. All the same, with it presently coming to him that staring at nothing was gaining him nothing and certainly getting him nowhere, he finally pulled on General's reins and said out loud, as he turned the stallion back up the trail in direction of Drakston Hall,

"Goodbye, darling."

None the less, Stuart Drakston had only covered a very short distance before he felt bound to reach for his back pocket and draw forth his handkerchief. For despite the warm Indian summer sun still filtering through the tree boughs, the trail had become awful misty to his eyes all of a sudden. But, even so, his vision was still far clearer and in better fettle at that moment than Jane Anne Heyward's was. Because her eyes were so red and swollen by this time from all the tearful buckets of guilt and remorse continuing to wash through them, that had they met with the fury of a maddening bee the results could not have been much worse.

However, as luck would have it, fortune seemed to suddenly cast a smile in Jane Anne's direction, not only saving her from what surely would have been a distraught and fluttering Eliza Heyward hovering over her and even an emergency eye examination by Doctor Seth Roalf, but a lot of probing questions from both her mother and the doctor as well.

Normally this beautiful fall day was not the kind of weather that Luke and Eliza Heyward would have chosen for buckling down to the task of tallying the yearly plantation records and bringing them up to date a must that ever followed harvest. They usually chose a dismal, rainy day for the job. But, no sooner than their daughter had voiced her desire to go horseback riding this afternoon, they had suddenly decided that since they always stuck close to the house anyway during her visits home that working on the records was precisely what they were going to do despite it being an ideal afternoon to be outdoors. So, after seeing Jane Anne bounce off gaily down the steps and head toward the stables, they had turned and immediately made for the oak paneled library where the records were kept.

Deep into the record of each tenant and summing up his liabilities for that year as well as his share of the profits from the various crops that had been grown and marketed, not to mention tallying the gains of the plantation as a whole, the hours had come and passed on without either Luke or Eliza noticing the clock once. And, even now as Jane Anne's feet hit the hallway, they did not think of checking the clock to see what time it was, only noting the fact that she was back by raising their heads from their ledgers to look toward the doorway.

Showing her disappointment that Jane Anne was not bothering to seek anyone else's company but her own and giving every indication that she just might do something about it, like calling her daughter back as the sound of the latter's feet went racing on for the staircase, Eliza said, "She's going on upstairs."

"Obviously, dear, and let her be," smiled Luke, reaching across the huge desk where they both worked on either side to lay a hand on Eliza's. "We wouldn't want to give her the feeling, while she's here with us, that we're crowding her. She gave us the pleasure of her company all morning long, so let her fill the rest of the day as she sees fit. She'll seek us out if she wants to talk." His smile stretched to a teasing grin. "Besides, we still have work to do on these ledgers, Mrs. Heyward."

Plainly showing that she was now nettled somewhat as well as disappointed, Eliza said, as she pulled her eyes away from the door and dropped them back down upon the ledger before her,

"So we have, Mr. Heyward, and I'm simply detesting the thought of it too."

So fortunately, with Luke Heyward broadly hinting that he preferred they not be interrupted as well as his wife staying where she was at till the work they had started was finished, it not only gave Jane Anne time to sort of get a grip on her emotions before coming face to face with her mother, but also time to do something about her tear-washed appearance to boot. Still, Jane Anne's recovery was not so great that she felt up to leaving the seclusion of her bedroom.

Indeed, when Eliza Heyward at long last emerged from the library and trekked upstairs to see what was delaying her daughter from making her appearance downstairs, instead of finding Jane Anne dressing for supper as she expected to do, she found her daughter dressed in her night clothes and already in bed—buried as deeply under the elegant fourposter's bedcovers as its several down mattresses could accommodate her. Though she appeared to be more frightened than sleepy, something that Eliza Heyward was making little sense out of as she hurried on to the bed and said, her brow creasing in deep concern, "Dear, you're not coming down for supper?"

"I don't feel like eating, Mother." Jane Anne replied, appearing as if she wanted to shrink out of sight by pulling the bedcovers as high under her chin as she could get them without covering her head completely. "I have a headache. Till Papa I'm sorry and not to worry."

"Of course, and I'm sorry too, darling," said Eliza, laying a hand on Jane Anne's brow. "But, thank heaven you don't seem to be feverish. You probably overdid yourself this afternoon. Where did you ride to anyway?"

"The trail," whispered Jane Anne, her hands tightly clutching the bedclothes under her chin.

"Good heavens, not the old timber trail!" Eliza exclaimed. "That place is hardly more than a jungle after all these years, I'm sure. No wonder you're all in. I can't understand, with all the other nice places to ride, why you would even think of venturing into that wild place!"

"I—I just wanted to see it again," murmured Jane Anne. "It's so..." She broke off. Eliza's piercing scrutiny had become too keen to risk volunteering another word about the trail, and especially telling about the glowing hollies, which she had started to do, because they grew too near the boundary of Drakston Hall's timberlands. The risk would be too great.

Nevertheless, despite Jane Anne's balking at further disclosure, Eliza pressed on anyway, saying, as the ridges in her brow grew deeper, "Yes, yes, go on, What about the trail?"

"Pretty." Jane Anne finally rejoined. And then, before Eliza could open her mouth to fire another question at her, she went on to plead, "Please, Mother, I don't feel like talking now, maybe later. My head hurts too bad."

Unable to keep her disappointment over the subject being closed out of her voice, Eliza said, "Well, as I've already stated, that's not surprising to me at all considering all the hazards you subjected yourself to this afternoon on that trail! Still, what's done is done, and I do reckon the sensible thing to do would be to let your mistake rest and try to do something about your headache instead. So, for a starter, I'll run and get a basin of ice water. Sometimes laying a cold washcloth on your forehead will help. Eliza laid the cloth on Jane Anne's forehead, "Now close your eyes and try not to let your mind be concerned with one single thing and that includes attending prayer meeting tonight! For this once, we're going to forget all about it and stay home!"

"You and Papa could go anyway, Mother, I'll be all right." Jane Anne murmured. "Bessie never leaves to go home till bedtime, so if I should happen to need anything, she'll be here. Besides, Pete and Sam both will be around too, so it's not as if you and Papa were leaving me all alone."

"Why, that's thinking nothing but plain nonsense! Your father and I would never go traipsing off to church and leave you home sick in bed no matter how many others are around. Besides, I'm positive our absence won't cause the church to cave in, or send anybody into hysterics, either! The fact is, some in the congregation could even welcome it! Anyhow, I'll be going now and let your father know that you're indisposed and we'll be staying home for a change. I'll be back a little later though to look in on you, and if you're not more comfortable by then we'll have to give you a dose of Seth's headache medicine. It'll not only relax you but put you to sleep as well, something you no doubt need!" And, with all this ringing in Jane Anne's ears, not to mention her other remarks about mistakes and hazards that were not only still pulsing in Jane Anne's head like the smart of a needle but also causing her to want to cringe further and further from her mother's sight as well, Eliza Heyward turned from the bed and went sailing from the room for a second time.

Knowing however that any lack of relaxation or sleep, on her part, had had nothing whatever to do with landing her where she was at, and that swallowing Doctor Seth's headache medicine for the purpose of inducing these comforts was certainly the last thing that she now wanted to do due to the wild and breathtaking decision that she had, just moments before this, finally arrived at, Jane Anne made certain that she sounded more than convincing when she said, upon seeing her mother sweep back into the room once again with the medicine and a teaspoon in one hand and a glass of water in the other, "Oh, Mother, not that icky stuff, please! It makes me feel groggy, for days, every time you make me take it. I feel much better anyway, so I'm sure I don't need to take it this time. Let's just continue on with the cold cloth on my head. It seems to be working just fine."

Deep down, Jane Anne knew that the reason the ice-cool washcloth seemed to hold such a potent healing power was simply because the pain was more in her conscience than it was in her head, anyhow.

"Well, if you say, dear." Eliza said, her brow relaxing for the first time in an hour. "But, I'll leave it here on the night stand just in case. Now, let me refresh that washcloth for you. Like I said, it does seem to do the trick now and then and I'm grateful that this time appears to be one of those times because a sickbed, during vacation, shouldn't be anyone's lot to bear with." After refreshing the washcloth in the basin of ice water once again and placing it back upon Jane Anne's brow, she went on to add, "Now since you seem to be feeling a lot better, I'm not going to disturb you anymore for a spell. Oh, your father said to tell you not to fret one bit about his missing church tonight, that he was sort of bushed anyway from all that book work this afternoon and was looking forward to an early bedtime, for a change. To tell the truth, I am too. Anyhow, we'll both be back to look in on you and say goodnight. I'm warning you though that I'll be bearing a glass of warm milk whether you have an appetite for it or not. In the meantime, you just try to keep on resting and letting your mind be free of all thinking and who knows, maybe you'll fall asleep, despite the headache!"

"Y-es, maybe so. Thank you, Mother," Jane Anne murmured, knowing full well that falling to sleep was one thing that she was not going to do. Nor was she going to even try, though she usually adhered her mother's bidding to the letter.

Yes, since her overwhelming guilt had had time to grow calmer, giving her mind a chance to go back and not only re-examine every word and every move that she had made but also those that Stuart had made as well—moves and words that had, ultimately, led to the betrayal of her morals on this day, Jane Anne as likewise to Stuart had now come to see that there was only one course left for them and that was, to delay their marriage no longer. Far besides the fact of her no longer being the innocent virgin she had been—now knowing a rapture that she had experienced with Stuart that was beyond description and one that she could not deny that she wanted to delight in again, there was also her mother's fierce and lasting disapproval of Stuart to consider—a disparagement that she knew—deep down—was going to continue on. Moreover, her keen, penetrating intelligence had also brought her to conclude that Stuart was no more at fault, if as much, for their immoral behavior this afternoon than she was, reasoning that to have allowed herself to see it otherwise had been pure ridiculous, if not out-and-out childlike and silly. Besides, she had convinced herself that the quicker she married Stuart, the quicker the wrong they had committed would seem less so.

And so, now near aching to reach Stuart Drakston's arms and his forgiveness for being so cold and indifferent to him when they had parted as well as announce her important news that she had decided to go ahead and marry him immediately, Jane Anne hastily flung back the bedcovers and gently let her feet hit the floor—cautioning herself all over again to be very quiet in her moves as well as fast. Because if her mother were to awaken and decide to check on her, there would not only be no seeing Stuart tonight, but no marriage either!

Granted, this decision to flee the security of her parents' roof and in the dark of night at that, to say nothing of their loving devotion, had not been an easy decision for Jane Anne Heyward to come by. Still and all; however, her love for Stuart Drakston was real and solid too. Therefore, choosing to put her devotion to him above that which she held for her parents had been inevitable and, this she had known and done. But, even so, the pain of having to choose between them was still with her. In addition, she felt that she was as treacherous and falsehearted as Judas, the betrayer for no more than one hour earlier, when both her parents had looked in on her to check on her headache and say goodnight, besides assuring them that her head had finally eased off, she had also told them, "Now all I want to do is go to sleep."

At any rate, doing her utmost to not succumb to these pangs of conscience that pulled at ever nerve, threatening to disarm her determination to reach Stuart any second, Jane Anne hurriedly felt around on the nightstand for the match box and relit the lamp. Then, pulling out the top drawer to the nightstand and drawing forth pen and paper, she scrawled a fast note and left it lying in plain view atop her pillow. Knowing that it would have been a waste of time, not to mention effort, to have tried to explain her reasons for secretly sneaking off in the dark of night, she had made the note brief— merely stating where she had gone and her reason for going—to marry Stuart Drakston as quickly as they could find someone who had the proper authority to conduct the ceremony! Visioning her mother's reaction upon reading this last startling statement, Jane Anne could not help shivering as she turned and noiselessly crossed the floor to the huge wardrobe that graced the opposite wall.

Opening the wardrobe and seeing all the attractive clothing that she had hanging there, such as the silks and the satins and the taffetas and laces, Jane Anne regretted that she was forced to bypass all this pretty array of clothing and reach toward her plainer riding habits, since she was going to be astride a horse for some little while before she reached Drakston Hall. And, what made it worse was the fact of knowing that, aside from what she would be wearing on her back, she would be taking nothing else with her, leaving all those lovely outfits where were. Because there was no way that she could even take one dress garment with her and reach Drakston Hall with it in proper condition. So, endeavoring to make the best of the situation, she reached for the same green riding habit that she had worn this afternoon. At least Stuart had admired it and told her how becoming it was on her, she thought to herself and also let herself take heart by thinking that maybe she could send back for some of her things on the morrow.

Throwing the green riding habit on the bed, Jane Anne's next move was to rush toward the lingerie chest where to her delight, she was not hampered none at all in making her selection. All the laces and frills she desired to don were there at her disposal and, to be sure, this one gain regarding her clothes plight she made good use of. And presently, with all this feminine daintiness clinging to her hide and making her feel better still, she was smoothing down the riding habit once again on her body and picking up her shoes.

Now about as all set as she saw possible to make herself for the journey ahead of her, Jane Anne stopped and listened for any sound that might be stirring in the house. Hearing nothing, she stepped to the lamp and blew it out. Grateful that the night sky was graced with a full moon, she waited momentarily to get her bearing from its light filtering through the window before making her move toward the door. But promptly she was there and already through the door and closing it softly behind her. Then, willing herself to close her mind to everybody and everything except the one objective that she had her heart set upon and that was, to reach the man whom she had so callously spurned a few hours earlier, Jane Anne crept toward the staircase and, readily, with shoes in one hand and feeling her way with the other she was stealing down its many steps in her stocking feet.

Finally gaining the foyer on the first floor, Jane Anne then turned to take the back route out through the mansion, creeping on down the long hallway and on through the dining room and kitchen where she promptly found herself at the outside kitchen door. Reaching for the doorknob, she gently turned it and forthwith—and so far without incident too—she was on the porch and softly pulling the door shut behind her. Then, shoeless still and also with her heart in her mouth to boat, she stole on across the moon—shrouded porch and down the steps.

Having now hit the yard, Jane Anne paused just long enough in her tracks to set her shoes down and slip her feet inside them before beginning a rapid beat for the stables. As she entered the barnyard and was hurrying on toward the stall where Starface was housed, she softly called the mare's name and also had a few reassuring words for the mare's neighbors as well in order to prevent them from becoming disturbed and start neighing, giving her presence away. For there was not one animal on the entire plantation, horse, mule, or otherwise, who did not seem to recognize her voice from all others.

So, confident that Starface and all the other horses too, did recognize her voice and that they would not be alarmed by her presence, Jane Anne grabbed a bridle from a long row of many hanging on an outside stable wall and hurrying on inside Starface's stall, she slipped the bridle over the mare's head and led her outside where she next threw a saddle on her. However, she did not mount the mare at this time. Less parents, or some the tenants or workers who lived close by on the plantation, be awakened by the sound of Starface's hooves on the drive as they made their getaway, she took the mare by the bridle and led her all the way down the long drive, even clearing the archway, before she mounted her. But then, finally with the moment upon her, Jane Anne sped forth into the darker night, riding hard so that she would arrive at Drakston Hall before all the lights in the mansion had been extinguished and everybody was in bed for the night—two wills laboring and enduring in concert with one another—the will of a girl to reach her destination and that of her mount to get her there.

Shortly, however, as she lowered her head further still against the nights biting chill lashing straight into her face and all around her from the flying speed of her mount, Jane Anne were wishing that she had, at least, brought along a wrap for herself.

Carrying a small lighted table lamp along with him to see his way back with as he went from room to room putting out all the lights throughout the great house, a nightly bedtime chore and the last of his daily duties that he performed at Drakston Hall, the ageless Albert had just extinguished the brilliant glow of the huge Waterford chandelier that lit the grand hallway and was turning to go to his own quarters in the mansion when a fast, pealing blast of the doorbell not only spun him back around but brought a scowl to his face besides.

Now, normally, Albert never let the ringing of the doorbell, or for that matter any other working or function that was connected with his duties, inflame him one mite. Nor had he ever because he truly enjoyed his work. For one thing, serving as chief butler in the three or four houses and two mansions that Matthew Carson had so far dwelled in, not to mention his role of valet, had seldom left Albert for want of something interesting to watch or think about. For there had been many unexpected and stimulating comings and goings in these dwellings through the years. In addition, the abrupt moves from one residence to the next, to say nothing of the four years that he had stuck by Matthew Carson's side during the war, had seemed more adventurous by far, than they had tiring or worrisome. Then, over and above all these advantages that had been and still were beneficial to Albert's well-being, there was the prestige permanence linked to his position, something that Albert had and did and appeared to never stop taking into consideration; that is, in the eyes of the other household servants and especially those servants whose station in the household was lower than his, Though he himself had taken orders and still did on occasion, Albert nevertheless, as a rule, barked out more instructions and orders in one day than he had ever received all told. The fact was, Albert had served in his elevated position so long that he had, many years back, come to think of himself as being indispensable to any house or mansion that he presided over as chief butler. And, in truth, as far as Matthew Carson was concerned, Albert's view of himself was pretty much on target; Amy Carson would have agreed with her husband. Of course, Albert's competence and know-how had been infixed under the guidance and subtle teachings of the late Anne Carson, Amy's sister.

All the same, this was one time that Albert's enthusiasm for his work had run out. He was dog-tired, making it impossible for him to generate one spark of interest in anything except taking his weary bones on to where he had started and that was to bed. And yet, as another urgent peal of the doorbell vibrated in Albert's ears and he shuffled forth with his frown still intact to answer it and, impatiently, yanked the door ajar and peered out, he was so overcome with astonishment—not to mention curiosity— at seeing Matthew Carson's beautiful granddaughter standing there that, instantly, neither his weariness of body or the time of night nor did not matter to him anymore. In fact, Albert's aching bones and tired out body had suddenly become such a mere nothing with him that this could very well have been his first duty of the day as far as he was concerned. For being aware of Eliza Heyward's determination—hardly anything escaped Albert's eyes or ears—to put as many miles between her daughter and Stuart Drakston as possible, he knew that Jane Anne Heyward making a sudden appearance at Drakston Hall all by herself and in the dark of the night at that, after she had not visited there for years, was certainly no small matter of importance.

Still, despite any special rights that his lofty position granted him, Albert also knew there was a limitation to these privileges. In short, a sensible and wise house servant did not overstep. Especially when the matter or the subject at hand did not concern them, regardless of how much they knew about it, wanted to know about it, or was astonished by it.

So, dropping his frown immediately and letting one of his most pleasant smiles disguise his surprise so deftly clever that one would have thought that he was in the habit of opening Drakston Hall's door to Jane Anne Heyward every night at bedtime, Albert, letting the door swing wide open and stepping aside said, "A most pleasant, good evening, Miss Jane Anne."

Holding the lamp higher so as to light the hall better and giving a little courtly bow, he graciously gestured for her to enter.

Staying in the same spot though that she had paused in, Jane Anne hurriedly sang back,

"Good evening, Albert. No, I'll wait here for the moment, but would you tell Mr. Stuart I'd like to see him."

Now that he was getting a good look at the marked anxiety on Jane Anne's face, Albert was certain that nothing would have given him more pleasure than to have been able to trot to Stuart Drakston with her message. But knowing that was impossible he said, somewhat hesitantly, "Master Stuart ain't here, Miss Jane Anne."

"You mean he isn't back from prayer meeting yet? I thought it was later than that." There was a note of sore disappointment in her voice.

"Yes'um, it is late like you say and Master Stuart would've been back by now, sure enough, if he had gone to prayer meeting. But he didn't go tonight."

"He didn't go tonight," echoed Jane Anne, sending Albert a look of bewilderment. 'Well, do you have any idea where he might have gone? It's important that I see him tonight, just as quickly as possible."

"I'm real sorry to hear you say that, Miss Jane Anne, because Master Stuart ain't nowhere around these parts by now. He's already left, won't be back till after the first of the year, sometime. I tell you, I sure hated to see him go too. And the same goes for Miss Elizabeth. I miss them already just thinking about it."

"Gone?" Jane Anne gasped, staring at Albert now in disbelief, "You mean to say Stuart's already taken his leave for England—today—tonight? No, Albert, you must be mistaken! Stuart would never have left—with—without…" She suddenly stopped. She must not weep in front of Albert She had to hang on to her composure.

"No, no mistake, Miss Jane Anne." Albert averred. "Master

Stuart and Miss Elizabeth left for New York on the northbound six
o'clock train this evening. Master Stuart come in from squirrel
hunting and said he was ready to take his leave right then, said he
didn't want to wait around any longer. He seemed awfully upset
about something and being all worked up and on edge is just not
Master Stuart at all, no ma'am. But we all pitched in and hurried like
Miss Elizabeth asked us to and they did get off this evening like
Master Stuart wanted instead of hanging around another whole day.
Master Stuart thanked every one of us though and took time to shake
our hands, too, and say goodbye. Even though he did seem awfully
troubled and time was running short, he didn't forget to do that.
That's the way he is though. That's why all of us here at Drakston
Hall hated to see..." Finally seeing how hard his flowing prattle was
hitting at Jane Anne, Albert had abruptly decided to cut it off and
went on to say instead, "I'll run and let your grandfather and Miss
Amy know you here, Miss Jane Anne. I'll only be a minute or two."

"Oh, oh no, Albert," she quickly came back as Albert started to
turn away. "I have to go, so there's no need to disturb them. Besides,
I—I really shouldn't be here anyway." And, suddenly, upon her last
word, she had spun around and was running for the steps.

"But, Miss Jane Anne, it's late and it's getting chilly out there
and you're not even wearing a wrap," cried Albert, hurrying through
the door and on across the porch after her. But, as he held the lamp
higher still and peered forth into the darken night to offer his protest
against her leaving for a second time, he saw there was nothing
without sight or call to make it to but the sound of thundering hooves
making a fast getaway on the drive.

"Fool girl," he grumbled out loud. "Even if she's lucky and saves
her neck, she'll catch her death of cold before she reaches Green
Sea." And, putting on his scowl again, Albert turned and shuffling
back inside and closing the door, he started forth once more for the
comforts of his bed.

However, Albert would not fall asleep for quite some time,
because Drakston Hall's late caller had set his brain working far too
much to feel heavy-eyed, anymore. And, not only did he let himself
become so deeply concerned over Jane Anne Heyward's visit to
Drakston Hall on this night that he could not sleep, he hardly let
himself think about anything else for the next several nights and days
too—unless it was Stuart Drakston—due to the grave news that
Doctor Seth Roalf Junior and Maggie were to bring to Drakston Hall

late the next day, news that made Albert shiver when he overheard the young doctor convey it to Matthew Carson. Jane Anne Heyward was seriously ill with pneumonia!

Though hearing that Stuart Drakston had gone home and rearranged his departure schedule a whole day early had plunged Jane Anne into the darkest kind of despair—a despair so intense and humiliating that it had come near shattering her all self-command on the spot, she nevertheless had pulled herself together and been just as determined to get back to Green Sea and destroy the note that she had left for her parents, before they looked in on her again and discovered it, as she had been determined to write it and leave. In addition, the warmth of her bed waiting at Green Sea had offered what Jane Anne most desperately craved at that instant—a snug and safe place where she might quell her fears and cushion the bruises of her heart. Thus, she had fled Drakston Hall to seek it. And she had sought it and in record time to boot. Furthermore, she had also been able to retrace all these steps and moves without anyone having discovered her, or the note that would have disclosed what she had been up to.

Nonetheless, even after Jane Anne had finally found herself back inside her bed and had also had the relief of knowing that she had pulled off her unpromising mission without anyone being the wiser to its purpose, including Albert who would keep his mouth shut anyway, she had still discovered that in spite of the soft, protective depths that she was buried in that her misery was being no less subdued, nor were the hard chills that had started to grip her.

Forcing herself to get up, Jane Anne had felt her way to the blanket closet that sat at the foot of the tall fourposter and pulling forth several more blankets had piled them on the bed. But despite the blanket's added warmth, her chills had continued on and, by morning, she was suffering from fever as well and Doctor Seth Roalf had been sent for immediately. And, although the doctor had suspected pneumonia no sooner than he had paused at saying the dread word until that afternoon when additional signs of the dread disease began showing up—signs that made it all too clear to Luke, and Eliza Heyward what their daughter was stricken with even before Seth Roalf got around to confirming it. For by this time there were coughs, blood-stricken sputum, and oxygen shortage—all undoubted symptoms of the killing disease.

And still, when Eliza heard Seth Roalf finally utter the word, she was unwilling to accept his diagnosis, refusing to believe that her beloved and gentle-hearted daughter was rapidly approaching death's door.

Sending the doctor an incredulous look, she cried, "But that can't be Seth! Pneumonia is a cold weather—winter disease! How could Jane Anne have gotten pneumonia in the kind of mild days we've been having? And besides, she was out riding this time yesterday, feeling fine!" Eliza, Luke, and the doctor were all standing in the upper hallway, having just left Jane Anne's bedside.

Knowing Eliza's fear for his own was no less, Seth Roalf feeling no offense whatever at her outburst, said, "I know, dear. But, sometimes, as in Jane Anne's case, the onset of pneumonia is very rapid. And, although you're right about it being a cold weather disease, it can still strike in mild weather too, even in the hot summer months. I've seen several such cases."

"How bad is it, Seth?" Luke finally asked, his voice sounding as solemn as he looked.

"Well, so far, only one lung appears to be infected, which we all know makes the prognosis look a lot more promising than if both lungs were inflamed. Still, no matter what the case is, pneumonia is a serious disease and, not for one second, must we forget that it is. I'm sorry."

Appearing as if the word had become too much for her to try to repeat anymore while she stood on her feet, Eliza, falling into a straight chair beside the wall, creaked, "Pneumonia—it kills and she's so young. What—will we do L-uke?" A sob finally pushed its way out, causing her shoulders to heave under its force.

As Luke moved to Eliza's side and silently and gently laid his hand across her shoulders _his way of trying to wipe away her tears and, at the same time, let her know too that he had no answer to give her—Seth Roalf, seeing it as his duty to answer for Luke, said, "I know what you'll do, Eliza, you and Luke both. You'll do what's required of you, as you've always done, that's what you'll do. Since I'm a friend to you both as well as your family doctor, I won't deny that I've got a tough fight ahead of me to save your daughter, and I'm going to need your help while I try to do it. Though I don't want to mislead you, I am hopeful and I want you both to be, too, As you've just stated, Eliza, Jane Anne is young, So, the way I see it is, that's a plus in her favor instead of a hindrance." Seeing that, Eliza, had brought her head up and was giving him her full attention, the doctor went on, "Now, I have to leave for a while, but I'll be back shortly. I'm turning the care of all my other patients over to Seth Junior until I have Jane Anne over the worst of this illness. Watch her closely and, if you detect any increase in her temperature whatever while I'm gone, give her another dose of that same medicine that I've just given her. In fact, double the dose. It's the larger bottle setting there on the nightstand. I'll be going now. The quicker I leave and get the care of my other patients settled with Seth Junior, the sooner I'll be back here." Starting to turn away, the doctor turned back and added, "Oh, something else. I want someone sitting with Jane Anne constantly. If we keep abreast of any change that might occur for the worse in her condition and administer treatment on the spot instead of after it's already taken hold, the better it'll be for her all way round."

"Of course, Seth, anything you say," said Luke. "And, Eliza and I both appreciate your decision to come back and stay till you see Kitten through this. We won't forget it." Taking his hand from Eliza's shoulders, Luke offered it to the doctor.

Meeting Luke's gesture, the doctor replied, "Wouldn't think of doing less, my friend," and dropping Luke's hand he rapidly made for the staircase and his fight to save Jane Anne Heyward was on.

And, some fight it turned out to be. Before it had ended not only had it put Doctor Seth Roalf's medical skill to its severest test ever, but it had also nearly drained the doctor's body stamina to the breaking point as well, plus, bringing both Luke and Eliza perilously close to turning into walking zombies. But, the worse for wear, was the victim of the fight herself. The scorching fevers and her inability to take nourishment and keep it on her stomach, not to mention the strain of coughing and trying to breathe, soon had Jane Anne looking like a shadow of her former self. The fact was, in addition to all the pain and suffering Jane Anne bore, to say nothing of the fear and strain that her parents and other family members and Doctor Seth Roalf were under, this was an illness that seemed to affect the whole neighborhood, or at least those of whom who were mature enough to realize the odds against one struck down with double pneumonia. For what Doctor Seth Roalf had dreaded most had become fact. By the second day, the pneumobacillus had worked its way into Jane Anne's other lung and no one, including the doctor, expected her to pull through. Hence, the greater majority in the community had become absorbed with this dread expectancy, waiting with bated breath and praying, fervently, while they waited that it would not happen.

By the number, these neighbors and friends came to Green Sea to keep vigil. Though they did nothing in particular, aside from merely sticking fast to their chairs once they arrived, they still dropped everything and came, nevertheless. Also, there was very little discourse between them while they sat. They deemed it rude to converse as they normally would have because this was a time of trouble and not a social gathering. Every now and then, someone would brave a hushed remark and it would be acknowledged in the same subdued manner. But, for the most part, they just simply sat in solemn, mute silence and stared at one another or at nothing until they thought they had discharged their duty for that one particular visit and took their departure —their decision likely as not having been motivated by the fact that a new flock of callers had walked in and found a scarcity of vacant seats.

Among those numerous callers was the patriarch of the family, Matthew Carson and his ever-loyal Amy, Jane Anne's step-grandmother. They did not stay long though. Seeing his adored, softhearted granddaughter struggling to hold onto her life's breath, pained Matthew too deeply. His emotional make-up was simply not geared to handle it, or the tortured look that both Eliza and Luke were wearing. So, shortly after his arrival, Matthew was mutely giving Eliza's hand a tight squeeze and heading back to Drakston Hall where he fully expected to hear the worst at any time. Eliza was glad that her father had chosen to leave—glad that he had chosen to escape what appeared to be imminent.

Bruce Randolph was another who came, but unlike Matthew Carson he stayed. Of course, Martha came with Bruce and she stayed too. Martha had decided, for the time being, to forget about those high words that she had flung at Eliza back in September about coming back to Green Sea. But, even so, her convection that Eliza was wrong about Stuart Drakston was still intact and she had no intention of swaying from this belief. What's more, not only was she still harboring the notion that Eliza had affected an indifferent attitude about Laura eloping with the actor, Mr. Silverspoon, but she also felt that Eliza had been anything but condolent toward her when she had gone charging to Green Sea that day with the news—had failed to support her emotionally—something she had craved and needed and had counted on receiving from Eliza but had not gotten it.

Of course, on the subject of Laura, Eliza had desired her the best of everything, but no amount of warmness that she had affected toward Martha in trying to convince the latter of her sincerity, had moved Martha once from her stand. At the same time, in point of Stuart Drakston, Eliza was just as hard-set in her belief that he was not the man for her daughter as Martha was convinced that he was and also that Eliza had let her down. In brief, Eliza had turned a deaf ear to every argument that Martha had offered in Stuart's behalf. Thus, this unbending attitude on the part of both cousins had been the state of their relationship far near two months now—the first real falling out that had ever happened between them. But, even so, they both had the burden of carrying their fight alone because their husbands had flatly refused to become involved. Relative to their own relationship, Luke and Bruce both had gone on about their business, hunting and fishing together and seeing one another as often as they ever had.

At any rate, feeling a hand softly touch her shoulder as she sat at Jane Anne's bedside, Eliza was cheered somewhat, and at the same time nettled a little too, to see that the hand upon her shoulder belonged to Martha. As pleased as she was to have found that it was Martha who was standing at her elbow, she could not help thinking that it had taken no less than a sickbed crisis to get her there—something that chafed her plenty. Still, troubled as Eliza was, she had no will to let the thought fester, Indeed, her heart was too full. So, pushing it from her mind, she lifted her hand to where Martha's still rested on her shoulder and gently squeezed the latter's. She was too laden with worry to do more.

Meeting Eliza's gesture by leaning over and kissing her on the cheek, Martha said, "I'll sit with her, Eliza. You go on and get some rest."

"I— I—can't leave her, Martha." Eliza croaked. "I can't take my eyes off her till that fever breaks."

Moving a step forward and peering around at Eliza's drawn face, Martha came back, mincing no words as usual, "Well, from the looks of you, I hardly see how you're going to be able to do that unless it breaks in the next minute or two, because if you sit here much longer than that, you're going to be toppling to that floor. Mercy's sake, Eliza! Don't you think I'm capable of doing everything for Jane Anne that you're doing? Now, you just get yourself on up from there and out of here. I promise I'll wake you if there's any change at all.

Now, come on, Eliza, and give me that chair. I've been on my feet most all day and I want to sit down now, not next week."

If Martha's pointed remarks had reached Eliza's ears, she gave no sign of it. Still sticking fast to her chair, she said, "I'm scared, Martha. Look at her breathing, it's so labored."

Martha looked and she observed and not only did she have no taste for what she was observing, but she also found herself deeply moved by it. All the same, thinking that it might be better for all concerned if she continued to stick to her normal high-geared mien rather than give way to the feeling churning within her—a feeling that made her want to fling both her arms around Eliza and bewail the latter's burden as well as Jane Anne's suffering to high Heaven—she said, "Doesn't surprise me one bit, Pneumonia's like that. I've never seen or heard of a case that wasn't the very same way,"

Finally turning her head to look Martha full in the face, Eliza said, appearing to take heart somewhat, "That is so, isn't it, Martha? I really hadn't thought of it that way. But, that is the way it works and some do pull through, despite it being so dreadfully bad."

With Jane Anne in the fevered, semiconscious state that she was, they both knew there was no need to be concerned with what their words might imply.

"Of course, that's the way it works." Martha affirmed, her voice sounding so decided that one would have thought that she was a practiced physician. "Still, it wouldn't take me by surprise if that scent from all those mustard and onion poultices that you have her wrapped up in isn't bothering her breathing some. I know it's certainly bothering mine and, aside from the wear and tear of quite a few years, there's nothing wrong with me, or at least nothing that I'm aware of. Certainly, I don't have pneumonia like she does!"

"Seth says the poultices aren't going to harm her if they don't do any good, either." Eliza said.

"Well, I'm not so sure Seth Roalf knows what he's talking about when it comes to that question because I'd take a bet, and a high one at that, that she'll never taste another onion as long as she lives! And, you know full well, Eliza, that some dishes just can't be seasoned to taste worth the pains of fixing it, if there's no onion flavor. Can you imagine what cornbread stuffing would taste like without onions? I wouldn't even attempt to try." She stepped forward and picked up a half-filled glass of brown liquid setting on the nightstand and, after holding it under her nose for a brief second, she went on, "And, pray

tell me will you, what's this? It even smells worse than those onions and mustard poultices. The fact is it smells just like a rotten egg!"

"It's herb tea," informed Eliza, her voice coming on a bit forceful.

"Herb tea," echoed Martha, setting the glass back down. "Well, it's formula must be something new, because the herb tea I make doesn't smell like that."

"Neither does mine," said Eliza, "Prudence and Daisy made that. They said it's an old recipe that Hannah told them about and asked that it be written down before she passed on. She told them that it was known to have pulled more than one through a number of illnesses, including pneumonia. Luke told Seth he wanted to try it, said he trusted Hannah's word. So with Seth agreeing, Luke took it upon himself to coax Jane Anne to take that much of it. That was about two hours ago; and you know, Martha, although it may be my imagination because I want it to work so much, I do believe her fever has stabilized. It doesn't seem to be climbing like it was."

"What's in it, or didn't they say." Martha quizzed.

"Yes, they mentioned several things, root bark of dogwood for one."

"Dogwood!" Martha snorted. "More like chicken droppings if the truth were known! But, if you think it's helping her, that's the important thing, no matter how awful I think it smells. How often do we give it to her?"

"Only twice a day and it has to be piping hot. I'll take the rest of that back to the kitchen to be reheated. They said it could be heated up several times without losing its strength," said Eliza as she finally rose to her feet.

"Now that I don't doubt." Martha said, sliding into Eliza's chair before she had hardly cleared it.

Picking up the herb tea, Eliza said, "I know you're tired Martha, but you will watch Jane Anne closely and if there's any change come and wake me?" Martha's quickness to seat herself had made Eliza somewhat qualmish about her cousin taking any steps that she was not forced to take.

"Yes, I promise I'll sit right here and wake you immediately if I detect any change whatsoever in her condition. Now, for a second time, I'm suggesting that you go on and get some rest before your face kisses the floor." Martha replied. And, her watch was as good as her word. Not only did she keep an attentive eye on Jane Anne, but she was to sprang to her feet and do whatever she could in the way of trying to make Jane Anne more comfortable every time her ears picked up the slightest groan.

Mollie and Brent Cooper arrived, with Mollie taking the second shift, relieving Maltha. And, there were other friends who also sat during this crisis. Lucy Randolph was one who did not come though. Nor did Charlotte or Bill Clarendon. Lucy had already taken her leave for Lexington, Virginia to marry Gilford Sloan when Jane Anne was taken ill. Charlotte Clarendon had become a total recluse by this time, and in point of Bill Clarendon, the world he dwelled in had become so widely separated from that which the Heyward's dwelled in, that had he made his appearance, they would have been shocked speechless. The fact was, the last time that Eliza and Luke had set their eyes upon Bill Clarendon, was the night of the housewarming celebrations at Green Sea, some several years back.

Nevertheless, the change for the better that Martha and everybody else were praying and looking for in Jane Anne's condition did not take place till almost two days after Martha's first watch began. And what's more, it happened to be Martha who detected it.

Martha and a grim-faced Luke Heyward had just exchanged a few sober words about the unchanging state of Jane Anne's raging fever and Martha was turning her attention back to her diligent vigil when, suddenly, she noticed that one or two stray hair locks on Jane Anne's forehead appeared to be damp.

Hoping against hope that she was not letting her anxiety cause her to imagine she was seeing something that was not there because she wanted to see the fever drop so badly, Martha tentatively reached forth and gently brushing the hair locks back, found to her relief and joy that she was indeed seeing straight. Four tiny beads of sweat breaking out on Jane Anne's forehead had it wet as rain! Heart quickening, she turned back to Luke, whispering excitedly, "Luke! Her fever's broken! She's beginning to sweat, come and see!"

Though Luke suddenly looked no less surprised than had Martha announced that she was going to land her fist in his face, he spared not one second in planting himself nearer his prostrated daughter, dashing around the foot of the bed from where he had been standing and observing her to bend over her and peer more closely into her face. Then, as likewise to Martha, appearing as if nothing less than making contact with what he saw would convince him that it was, actually, there, he softly let his fingertips fall into the beads of sweat.

Straightening back up, Luke turned his weary, bloodshot eyes, which were filling with tears, upon Martha and said, "God's looking down on her, Martha."

"Y-es—yes, He is, Luke." Martha said, her voice breaking with emotion.

And yet, despite their devout faith in their remarks, an earnest belief that made their words to each other as true to them as the daylight filtering through the window, that still did not mean that either Martha or Luke had forgotten that this was only the first win toward conquering the illness they were battling. Because this was pneumonia they were dealing with—a fast-killing and virulent, complex illness where a half dozen things could go wrong.

Thus, all treatment was to continue on—the whole cure, the poultices, Doctor Seth's medicines, and the late Hannah's herb tea remedy too, until several days later when it became evident that Jane Anne was; indeed, going to pull through. But, even so, her illness had laid her so low there was no thought of her returning to school till after the New Year holiday, around the same time that Stuart Drakston was taking his leave of his Grandmother Stuart's resident in England—his Grandfather Stuart had been dead for quite some time now—to join Whit on the French Riviera.

And so the year had ended—a year that not only had brought a devastating earthquake to Charleston and the regions surrounding it, but had also brought so much grief, terror, and fear to Eliza herself that she was more than grateful to let it pass so she could embrace the start of another. However, despite all the ill fortune that had fallen in this year of 1886, a lot of good things and much good will had occurred too. For this was the year that the first rivet anchoring the Statue of Liberty in New York Harbor, was fastened—a gift to America from the people of France. The statue, which is one that symbolizes the forgotten in the world and which symbolize the privileges and total rights of a free people, was finally dedicated on October twenty-eighth, in this same year, by President Grover Cleveland.

Chapter Ten

As drab-looking as I feel, Eliza thought, as she peered through the kitchen window at the grey-hued, misty February dawn. But then, as she turned from the window and reached for the coffeepot—she had risen earlier than normal and was not waiting for Pete to arrive to start breakfast—she gave no more thought to the weather, dismissing it from her mind altogether. For despite the drabness that she had sighted outside and also her discomfort at having to deal with the most awful head cold that she thought she had ever experienced—her reason for being up this early—she knew she would not have traded the morning for the freshest one in May simply because, she was enjoying more peace of mind and contentment in these quiet, tranquil winter days—no matter how dismal they looked—than she had known for a long time. And, as she sat the coffee on the stove to make and began to busy herself with other things about breakfast, she now reflected on this period of happiness that she was luxuriating in.

For one thing, with outside work on the plantation being at a minimum—since the tobacco plant beds were already prepared and sewed, there was nothing much left to see to till ground breaking time but having the ditch banks cleared and wood cut and stacked at the tobacco barns for the caring of the tobacco next summer—Luke had more time for leisure. And not only were they taking advantage of this free time by seeing that they idled away a lot of it in sweet companionship alone, but they were also sharing it with family and friends as well. Besides having called on Bruce and Martha several times in recent weeks, she and Luke had also dropped in at Drakston Hall at least twice a week lately to chat with her father and Aunt Amy —something she must admit that she had done with more freedom than what she would have dreamed; in that, there had been no need whatever for her to be concerned about having to make small talk with Elizabeth Drakston, too, or for that matter, Stuart Drakston either, while she visited there. Yes, this was the first time, in many a long year, that she had the privilege of knowing that she could go to Drakston Hall and not have to worry about encountering a Drakston once she had arrived there! To tell the truth, visiting with Martha these days was also more relaxing and enjoyable. For ever since

250

Martha's visits to Green Sea during Jane Anne's illness there had seemed to be an unspoken agreement between Martha and herself to keep Stuart Drakston's name out of their conversations. Yes, stubborn as a mule, Martha had held to her word about coming back to Green Sea until she had heard Jane Anne was near death. Foolish of her to be so pigheaded!

She did not know how long Elizabeth's and Stuart's visit abroad would be, but whatever its length, she knew she would not be pining for it to cease before it did! The fact was, it would suit her just fine if they both decided to stay abroad permanently. However, even if by some remote chance that were to happen, she certainly would never want to take up residence at Drakston Hall! Never! Her father might do this and choose to call it home, which he did. But that was something she had no desire to ever do, even if its finery did outshine all the other low country mansions,

True, she had journeyed to Drakston Hall a great deal lately, and, to be sure, her visits there had given her a lot of pleasure. By the same token, however, that did not mean that she had let all her free time be used up in visiting at Drakston Hall. No, indeed, not by a long sight. In addition to all those visits that Luke and she had paid at Oak Grove, they had called on several other neighbors and friends, too, and had also gone to Charleston shopping three or four times and called on Brent and Mollie Cooper besides. Moreover, they had also attended the Saint Cecelia Ball in Charleston, as guests of the Coopers, in January. And, some delightful, romantic affair that had been! The beautiful waltz music and lovely decorations. The pretty ball gowns. The young, lovely debutantes. Some spectacle they made, making the Grand March on the arms of their fathers or brothers.

Well, she herself was many years past having the right of that kind of privilege, marching in a Grand March. But, all the same, she had had a grand time anyway. At Luke's insistence, she had bought a dazzling new blue dress to wear and, even though she had been no young debutante that night, she still had felt that she was pretty; and especially when Luke had whispered, "Bless Strauss for setting your beauty to music, my love," every time the orchestra had played Strauss' lovely waltz, Roses from the South. Strauss' lovely waltzes were so hauntingly beautiful; she could have danced all night. The fact was, Luke and she nearly did and right through the soles of their shoes at that!

However, the important thing was, it looked like that even when groundbreaking time did start this spring that Luke was not going to be forced to spend every day in the fields as he had always done, cutting those outings that they were enjoying so much completely out. For it was only yesterday that Phil had finally come back home for good. Yes, having gotten all his business affairs in Lexington settled at last, Phil had come back to Green Sea to live out the rest of his days. From now on he would help shoulder the responsibility of managing Green Sea, converting it from one family operation to a dual co-operation between Luke and himself.

The business arrangement between Luke and Phil had been worked out and agreed upon months ago. Though Luke had argued and contended that since the burden of management and all operating expense on the plantation were to be shared equally between them that all profit should be too, Phil would not listen or have it that way, making it plain to Luke that he would consider only one-third of their share of the earnings.

Phil had also refused Luke's offer again to deed back the half-part of Green Sea to him that their father had deeded to Luke, explaining once more to Luke that he saw no need for that since his only child was married to the present heir of Green Sea. Through her marriage to Carr, Beth Anne would reap the fruits of her birthright anyhow. And further, her first-born son would be in line as legal heir to Green Sea as well. But, surprising to both Luke and herself, after some few minutes of silence, Phil had gone on to say that if Nat were living they all might try to work out something in the way of having a new deed written that would include him so that his heirs, if there should be any, would share in the holdings of Green Sea too.

Well, Nat was not living, His life had been cut short long ago. So that being the case, Luke had finally closed the subject by telling Phil that if he should ever change his mind to let him know and they would take care of it.

Phil, literally, was bursting with news yesterday—all sorts, from Carr's scholastic ratings at the university and Beth Anne's homemaking in Lexington and God knows what else, to the quiet, sentimental rites that had finally banded Gilford Sloan and Lucy Randolph together as husband and wife. The wedding was solemnized at Phil's house in Lexington on Thanksgiving Day. And, from what she could make of Phil's account of it, not only had he had the honor of serving Gilford Sloan as his best man, but he had also seen to most the wedding arrangements himself and had had everything ready and waiting even before the bride to be made her appearance in Lexington. It appeared that Phil had been just as eager to see Gilford Sloan and Lucy Randolph tie the knot as they, no doubt, had been to get on with it.

However, Phil had not told the most exciting part of his news to the very last, actually saving it to almost bedtime. Then as nonchalantly as you please and without blinking an eye, he had announced that Beth Anne was with child and likewise to himself that Luke and she could look forward to becoming grandparents in September. September 1887, twenty years from the same month that Carr himself was born. How time passed one by! At any rate, Phil had appeared to relish the fact that his announcement had jarred both Luke and herself speechless. Momentarily, however, they had recovered and then all three of them had started laughing together. Their laughter had been brief, though, because no matter how thrilling and exciting the news was, it nevertheless had made each one of them mindful of other things too, such as time and its rapid pace and how vulnerable one became to it. Yes, for all their happiness over the thought of becoming a grandparent, it had not saved a one of them from mentally acknowledging the fact that time was rapidly, but surely, sweeping all three of them toward old age.

Still, the inevitable must be accepted and when it came to the matter of her age, she thought she had and did with grace at that. No question about it, she knew she was grateful to be able to count every day and every week and every month and year; and also more than grateful for a lot of other things too. One thing for sure, she knew she would ever continue to thank her God for sparing her beloved and only daughter from what had looked like sure death a few months ago. It was one of His miracles and nothing else that Jane Anne was well again and back in college, completing her final studies before graduation this coming spring. She —

"Better do something more than what you've been doing for that cold, dear, or you're going to be bedfast," said Luke from the doorway just as another fit of sneezing had gripped Eliza and suddenly suspended her musing in midair.

"I second that, Luke," chimed Phil as he, too, came breezing through the door on Luke's heels and fell down into a chair at the kitchen table while Luke made his way on to the big iron stove and began to turn the hickory smoked ham that Eliza had frying in an overlarge iron skillet.

Catching her third sneeze in her handkerchief and giving her nose a real hard blow, Eliza, stuffing the handkerchief back inside her apron pocket, said, "You two didn't have to get up just because this dreadful cold got me up. It's still almost an hour before the usual rise and shine time around here. Pete's still sleeping and you two should be too." She turned and reached for the egg basket.

"You expect us to sleep and the aroma of coffee making and ham frying, filling our nostrils?" Laughed Phil, as he rose from the table with an empty coffee cup and stepped over to the stove. Pouring himself a cup of coffee and going back to the table and taking his chair, he went on, as he began to swill the coffee down, "Luke, anything special about the outside routine that you'd like me being in on today?"

"None that I can think of," replied Luke, now in the process of dropping several beaten eggs that Eliza had handed to him into the ham drippings. "Hope you'like your eggs scrambled."

"I'll take'em anyway you fix'em." Phil said and added, "Well, if there's nothing I can do here, I think I'll go to Drakston Hall and spend the day with Pa and Aunt Amy, bring them up on all the latest news. I know Pa'll be anxious to hear all about Lucy Randolph and her marriage to Sloan. Of course, I want to tell him he's going to be a great grandfather too!"

"Well, if you recount all those wedding details to them like you told it to Luke and me last night, it'll take you all day," said Eliza as she and Luke together began to set the makings of a full course breakfast on the table, that included a dozen items or more as always. "The truth is, I'd like to be there when you relate it all again and would, if I wasn't afraid I'd give Father and Aunt Amy this awful cold. Instead of going with you though, I guess I'll have to stay here and entertain myself the best I can with piecing quilt scrapes together. Give them my love and tell them I'll try to see them in a few days."

I'll tell 'em sis, and I'm sorry you can't join me," said Phil. "How about you, Luke? I'm always in the mood for company. Care to come along?"

"I think not, Phil, not today. I promised Bruce that I'd take a look at one of his brood sows one day this week. So, if I don't change my mind, I think I'll be heading for Oak Grove a little later on this morning to take a look at her," said Luke, and taking his chair he bowed his head and began saying a long grace.

However, although Phil did ready himself and carried through with his plans that day, Luke never did make it to Oak Grove. Neither did Eliza get many quilt scrapes pieced together. For it was only a few hours later when Luke was in the process of leaving the drive and turning the buggy in the direction of Oak Grove, that the local mailman pulled up alongside him and handed the day's mail to him instead of stopping and putting it in their mailbox, which he had just passed a little further back from the archway. A deep-yellow envelope from the telegraph office blaring on top of the other pieces of mail, explained the gesture without any words.

The mailman never moved one Inch further or said one word till Luke had ripped the telegram open and was letting his eyes scan its contents. Then, he said, "Hope it's not bad news."

Barely comprehending what the mailman had said, Luke, finally lifting his eyes from the telegram, muttered, "N-o. No, it's only a message from my daughter in Virginia, telling me what time her train arrives in Charleston. She's coming home today."

"Well, that's good to hear." The mailman said. "I never like to handle these telegrams. They scare me, give me goose pimples till I know they're not carrying bad news."

"Me too," said Luke, and returning the mailman's wave as the latter moved on along his route, Luke turned the horse and buggy around and headed back up the drive.

Finally letting her probing gaze shift from the telegram back to Luke—Eliza had read through as many as three times or more, Eliza said, "Wonder what's happened, Luke." Of course, she had known what the telegram said even before her eyes fell upon it, for Luke had revealed its message no sooner than he was coming through the doorway. But, even so, that had not stopped her from reaching for it and reading and rereading it over and over.

"I really have no idea, dear." Luke replied, the pallor and anxiety that the telegram had brought to his face, adding years to it.

"But, this says here that she's leaving college for good, and her with only a few months left before she graduates. It doesn't make sense, because she's been doing so well in her studies. Besides, I could scold her good for scaring you half to death, and me too, when I just now saw it in your hand." Eliza flared.

"Now calm down, dear. No doubt she came to her decision to leave college all of a sudden, therefore sending a telegram instead of writing because it's a lot faster." He looked at the clock on the mantel. I'd better get going. She did say the three o'clock train, didn't she?"

"Yes, and I'm getting up from this chair and going with you. I just can't sit here and wait, not knowing why she's doing such a foolish thing!" Flinging quilt scrapes every which way from her lap, Eliza started to get to her feet, but was stopped by Luke's restraining hand on her shoulder.

"No, dear," he said. "I won't have your risking your health out there in that damp weather like that. Just try to sit here and continue on with your sewing. I promise I'll be back as soon as I can. I warn you though, even if the train is on schedule, it'll still be between five and six o'clock before we get here." Bending over and planting a kiss on her cheek, he hurriedly turned away.

However, even though Eliza resettled herself in her chair and began to gather up the sewing that she had flung aside, she promptly let her feelings about the matter fall loud and clear on Luke's back by saying, as he was clearing the door way, "Darn the weather and these blasted sniffles too!"

For all his worry, Luke could not help letting his mouth curve into a faint smile.

The deep-grey mist still held and, as Luke kept his horse at a steady pace through it toward Charleston, his face became just as marked with concern as the day was drab and dreary around him.

Trying to reason out as to why Jane Anne was coming home, he had all sorts of frustrations and was now asking himself once more, what did give with Kitten? The message on the telegram was so businesslike, not like his daughter at all. There had not been one word, not even a hint, as to why she was suddenly leaving college. Had she been dispelled for some reason, like a disagreement perhaps between her and one of her professors? No, it wasn't that, not Kitten. She was too reserved and modest for that kind of behavior. That was only preposterous thinking on his part because if his daughter had a grievance, she would never air it.

What then? Was she ill? He had stopped at remarking about that possibility due to the fact that he had not wanted to alarm her mother. Still, they had almost lost their daughter as recently as last November with pneumonia, an illness that had kept her indisposed for weeks. So, it was feasible to think that maybe she had resumed the rigor of college classes, not to mention the added work of making up her lost studies, too soon. He prayed this was not the case though. And yet, he knew this girl child of his, knew that she would not be leaving school unless her reason for leaving there was serious and, no question about it, her health was the only thing that he could think of that might be serious enough to bring her home. Well, here were the train tracks and over there, just a little way, was the depot. Thus, he supposed, one way or another, he'd soon be finding out!

Pulling his horse to a stop and looking either way down the long line of train tracks, Luke was surprised to see that a rolling trail of black smoke was already sifting to nothing above the southbound rail bed in the gray-laden distance.

Now more concerned and anxious than ever to realize that the southbound train had already arrived and taken its leave of the Charleston Depot, Luke hurried on across the train tracks, wondering what his daughter must be thinking that no one was at the depot to meet her. Setting his horse at a rapid pace, once he had cleared the tracks, he was presently in the parking lot at the depot and pulling horse and buggy to a fast stop, The questions that had plagued him every step of the way—actually delaying his traveling time and causing him to be late so preoccupied his mind had been with them, he had forgotten for the moment. Now nothing mattered with him but sighting his daughter's face and, forthwith, he was doing just that as he came dashing inside the train station through the nearest entrance way and spotted Jane Anne standing over against the opposite wall surrounded by several pieces of baggage.

Although Jane Anne appeared to be well, Luke thought that her face did seem to be unduly strained and troubled. He dismissed the thought though and cried, "Over here, Kitten!" His gladness at seeing her coming through in his voice.

However, fully expecting his daughter to come running and fly into his arms as she had always done, Luke's joy was thwarted somewhat when Jane Anne did nothing or said nothing till he had gotten within arm's reach of her. Then, completely throwing Luke, she reached out with one hand and letting her fingertips caress his cheek, she said, "Dear Papa, so full of all that's kind and good."

Almost at a loss for words, Luke, bringing his hand up to clasp hers, murmured, "So are you, my dear child."

"No, Papa, I'm not good like you are." She said, still making no move to embrace him. The fact was, instead of flinging her over-large reticule aside as she normally did so that her arms would be free to wrap around him, Luke observed that she continued to let the reticule keep swinging from her other arm and swing between them to boat!

Baffled by this seemingly desire of Jane Anne's to stand aloof from him in spite of the keen devotion that he saw in her eyes, Luke said, "Nonsense, my child, you're nothing but goodness all the way through. But we'll talk on the way home, because I'm afraid that mist out there is going to grow worse and we want to be well on our way before it does, if not already home. So you just stay put till I get your baggage taken care of. Then, I'll come back for you. I think I can get it all strapped to the back of the buggy." He grabbed up a suitcase in either hand and called to a depot attendant to bring the other two remaining ones.

With a voice that sounded as low in spirit as her face looked, Jane Anne replied, "As you say, Papa."

It was not long before all the baggage was loaded and Luke was back inside the buggy with his daughter seated beside him, heading out of Charleston. He still had no idea why Jane Anne had abruptly decided to quit college and come home. Though he was curious and anxious to know, he refrained from asking, hoping that she would say; and soon at that, at her own discretion. He was not one to pry in other people's affairs anyway, with those of his daughter being no exception.

However, the buggy kept on rolling with Jane Anne hardly mumbling a word since she had settled herself inside it. And, it kept on rolling until finally—just when Luke was beginning to wonder if she were going to engage in any more conversation at all to say nothing of disclosing her reason for leaving college—she up and asked how her mother was doing, taking him by surprise since she had waited so long to ask but pleasing him, too, to see that she was, at least, overcoming some of her aloofness.

"She's fine, dear," he replied, "except for having a terrible head cold. That's why she didn't come with me. Of course, she wanted to come but I wouldn't hear to it because, this is regular pneumonia weather, and the good Lord forbid anyone else in this family falling prey to that affliction. Better pull the buggy robe up closer around you, Kitten, so you'll stay warm. I don't mean to fuss like a mother hen, but I can't forget it was only a few months back that we almost lost you."

"And what a blessing in disguise that would've been!" Jane Anne blurted, instantly taking advantage of the opening that her

258

father's last remark had created and, at the same time, bringing his head toward her in a hard jerk besides, "In fact, I wish I were dead, Papa!"

"Y-ou—you what?" Luke gasped, automatically taking such a hard grip on the reins that it brought horse and buggy both to a sudden standstill in the middle of the roadway.

"Wish I were dead, Papa, I truly do," Jane Anne repeated, demurring not one fragment of a second. "I would've been, too, had I had the courage to have taken my life like I planned to do!"

"No! Don't!" Luke exploded, his features distorting to nothing but plain horror. "I won't listen to the likes of that kind of talk! You must pray and ask God to forgive you, no later than this very day, for harboring such a notion as that, much less wishing you were dead!"

Unswerving, Jane Anne came back, "But I mean it, Papa." And suddenly, bringing both hands up to her face and burying her head inside her open palms, she was letting all the misery that consumed her come through in racking sobs, smarting Luke Heyward's heart so that no longer was he thinking of prayers, forgiveness, sin, what was right, what was wrong, or anything else of that nature. Nothing mattered to him now but the obvious agony that his beloved daughter was enduring.

"Here, here, darling," he croaked, letting the reins fall from his hands and encircling her heaving shoulders with his arm. "Whatever it is, it can't be all that bad. Please try to get hold of yourself. I'll help you work it out, and we will, believe me."

"But we can't, Papa, we can't," Jane Anne sobbed, harder than ever. "There's nothing you, I, or anybody can do. I hate myself!"

"Try me, dear, and see," begged Luke. "Don't you know that's what fathers are for. I promise I'll listen and remain calm and won't harshly judge you no matter what you tell me."

Suddenly bringing her tear-washed face up out of her palms and turning it up toward her father, Jane Anne sobbed, "Not even if I tell you, Papa, that I'm going to have a baby out of wedlock! It's true, Papa, I'm going to have a baby and I have no husband!" Her head fell back in her hands.

For a heart-stopping instant Luke thought that despite his promise to Jane Anne, he had let the scream constricting in his throat break and spill in the buggy. Then, the next instant, he knew the scream was still there inside him, yowing and swelling—a terrible aching lump so profound and deep inside his throat that he was certain if he did not to something to quell it, and soon, that it was going to take his life's breath. Taking in one or two big gulps of air and breathing deeply, he tried swallowing the painful obstruction away. But, even so, there was no relief for him at all until, aner some little while, he became aware of a voice calling to him—a voice pleading in a soundless hush—the warm, sweet-tempered voice of his adored daughter pleading, over and over, "Papa, please speak to me! Papa, please speak and say you're all right! Please, Papa! You look so pale."

Finally finding his voice as he gulped in another big breath of air, Luke muttered, "Never mind about me, dear, I'll be all right, let's talk about you. So, that's why you've suddenly decided to come home, you're with child?"

Instinctively Luke's eyes fell to his daughter's abdomen, but not one glimmer of her shame did he see. All bulge was well-concealed under the full-cut folds of her heavy winter cloak, something that he took as a blessing, right then, because he had his doubts that he had recovered enough to withstand the shock.

"Yes, Papa, that's why I'm here." Jane Anne replied, lifting the back of her hand to her cheek and wiping at a stray tear, another something that Luke observed and was grateful for, even if it had taken the shock of his own pallor to cease her sobbing.

However, suddenly gathering the idea that he may not be up to handling the fact; that is wisely, of knowing who the baby's father was either, just at this point, Luke stopped at asking, saying to Jane Anne instead, "And the baby's father, I take it that he refused to marry you." Turning her head back to her father and looking somewhat stunned, Jane Anne said, "No, nothing like that, Papa. He would marry me. I know he would."

Now looking somewhat stunned himself, Luke said, "I don't understand. If he would marry you, then why aren't you married?"

"He doesn't know about my condition, Papa. In fact, I didn't know myself until a few days ago. Since..." She broke off, hesitating to go on as she turned her head from her father's gaze once again.

"Yes, go on." Luke pressed.

"Well—since Uncle Seth told Mother and me both that my illness may affect the regularity of my periods, may even cause them to stop for a while, I thought that's what had happened until I noticed ..." She broke off again.

All the same, there was no pressing from Luke this time for Jane

Anne to finish what she had started to say. For her remarks had been too painfully similar to those that he had heard her mother make so many years ago—a time in his and Eliza's marriage that he thought he had completely forgotten. So trying to steer the conversation away from that question in point and, at the same time, try to make clear that he was far from understanding his daughter's loose conduct or her ignorance either, he said, "But, surely you were well aware that an involvement of that nature forever, and without doubt, carries its penalties. Certainly, you can't be so foolish as to think otherwise." In spite of himself Luke Heyward had not been able to trim the edge from his voice.

"There was no involvement, Papa. Not the kind you're thinking about anyway. It happened only once, just once, and I became pregnant!"

Now completely thrown and exuding his exasperation with every word, Luke exclaimed, "What! For crying out loud, dear! Don't tell me that you find yourself in this holy mess because of a chance encounter with some man about town, whom you allowed to seduce you, without giving one thought to properness or your moral principles, much less considering the consequential aspects that's normally involved! I can't believe it!"

"Stuart did not seduce me, Papa!"

"Stuart!" Luke gasped in surprise. "Stuart Drakston you say?" He wondered if his hearing had deceived him.

In a voice that was very much heavy with her disappointment, Jane Anne replied, "Yes, Papa, Stuart, and I'm surprised that you'd think there were some other."

"But how—where? Luke questioned, sending his daughter an incredulous look. "You never see Stuart Drakston except at church. Besides, Stuart's in England, been away from these parts for months."

"We met by accident on the old timber trail the day after I arrived home for Thanksgiving. I would've been married to him, too, and with him in England, had I not been so foolish like you say," said Jane Anne. And, continuing on, she related the whole episode to her father, or most of it, and finally concluded her account of the happening by saying, "When Albert told me that Stuart wasn't at Drakston Hall, having already taken his departure from Charleston to New York that very evening, I didn't know what to do. I cried all the way back to Green Sea. Though I know better, I felt he'd deceived me."

"And you haven't heard from Stuart since that day?" Luke asked, not now so sure that the situation had changed from bad to worse considering his wife's attitude where Stuart Drakston was concerned.

"No, I haven't heard one word, Papa." Jane Anne said.

"But, the fact is, neither of you have written, isn't that so?" Luke pressed. "You do know where to reach him in England, his grandmother's address, do you not?"

"Yes, I memorized it years ago, Papa, when Stuart and his mother were living there while he attended Oxford, but I couldn't bring myself to write, not after he left a whole day early and without trying to see me again besides," said Jane Anne.

"Well, pride is a good thing, dear, and I take joy from the fact that you possess it. However, sometimes when our own behavior makes for a situation where it's much wiser to stick it in our pockets, as is the case here, we must use prudence and do so." Luke said, and setting his wits to work on an idea that had just popped in his head, he picked up the reins and began to turn the buggy back toward Charleston.

Puzzled by her father's remark, not to mention his abrupt decision to turn back in the direction that they had come from, Jane Anne said, her voice somewhat frayed with anxiousness,

"Papa, why are we turning back?"

"We're going back, dear, because I think it's high time, and also most urgent, that you get in touch with Stuart Drakston as quickly as possible; and the fastest way I know is by cable. How you word the cablegram is your affair but send it to him you must. You can be thinking about what you want to say while we make our way back to the telegraph office." Knowing the blunt of his command must be weighing something awful on her, he reached for her hand and added, "It's the only thing, dear, that I can think of that might help the situation. We must reach Stuart if we can. However, regarding your mother's reaction when she hears about all this, I can only say, pray that the good Lord will cast His merciful eye upon all of us because, woe betide, the brunt of her fury!"

Strange as it was, all the edginess and frustration that Luke Heyward had felt and had been unable to keep out of his voice, despite his effort to control it, had suddenly evaporated. Only compassion flowed in his blood stream now. And, his sympathy was not solely for his daughter but for Stuart Drakston too. For he had suddenly begun to view his daughter's plight not from a standpoint of her weakness or the frailty of Stuart Drakston's will power, but from a standpoint of his own shortcomings—his failing to take a verbal stand against the fallacy of his wife's reasoning where Stuart Drakston was concerned. In short, though this was an odd time for it to hit home, Luke had finally seen that Eliza's fault finding with Stuart was and had ever been baseless and nothing more than mere avengement and that he should have spoken up, long back, in Stuart's behalf instead of side-stepping the matter. Still, hindsight was normally no worth at all and certainly, was of no advantage here, because it was too late, Luke was thinking.

So, wanting to make up for his own failings and silently praying that Jane Anne's mother would, at the very least, use logic about the matter, Luke squeezed his daughter's hand and said, "Don't despair, dear, we have to trust that, somehow, it'll all work out."

To Luke's dismay though, the situation was to worsen.

The gray-laden mist had turned to steady rain and as Eliza anxiously pressed her nose against the windowpane, for what must have been the umpteenth time, and gazed out into the somber looking twilight, her relief at finally seeing the buggy coming up the drive was so overwhelming that it seemed as if she were emerging from a quagmire of quicksand. Whirling from the window, she literally sailed across the room and on through the door and adjoining hallway to the front porch—trading the warmth of her hearth for the damp, chilling outside with no less alacrity than had she been headed for the cheerfulness of a June flower garden.

Totally disregarding the fact that her case of sniffles was still raging, Eliza went sailing on across the porch and was coming right on down the steps out into the rain when Luke's voice, calling from the buggy as he halted it at the steps, stopped her. Now that Luke had made her aware that she had no business out in a pouring rain, she whirled back up the steps, her heart by this time dancing a fast pitter-patter in her excited anxiousness.

However, as Eliza stood on the porch and anxiously peered through the falling rain at the two figures alighting from the buggy, it came to her, in spite of her excitement, that Luke's voice had sounded a little more impatient with her than what she would have expected out of him. And moreover, although she was well aware that traveling in such nasty weather was certainly no cakes and ale, she nevertheless was a bit surprised that the two faces that she was peering at were looking so grim and overwrought. Still, with Luke and Jane Anne both making a dash for the porch at that same instant; and then having Jane Anne's greeting and another scolding from Luke about her exposing herself to the weather falling all at once and together besides, Eliza promptly concluded that it was not the right time or place for her to let unnatural looking expressions, or a tone of voice that had sounded far from the ordinary, trouble her head.

But even so, no sooner than Eliza had blithely and lovingly taken in Jane Anne's greeting and scrapped her husband's scolding by ignoring it and jubilantly led the way inside, chattering like a magpie, it came to her again and quite disconcerting at that, as the trio gathered around the blazing hearth and Luke and Jane Anne were shedding their wraps, that a grim-looking face was not the only thing about her daughter that was looking unnatural!

Instantly, with her lively chatter falling into low gear, Eliza was eying Jane Anne more closely as the latter turned to hang her wrap upon a wall rack. Then, with one or two sputters and a final gasp falling between words, Eliza was doing no more talking. For as Jane Anne turned to step back to the hearth, the physical changes that Eliza saw developing in her daughter's once subtle, girlish figure had stunned her to mute silence. To her horror, she saw that Jane Anne's wasp-like waist had about disappeared. The wide girth that she now carried was all but swallowing it! What's more, Jane Anne's bosom had enlarged so, that Eliza was astonished to see that the buttons on her daughter's blouse were still holding, because they looked like they might pop off and start flying in all directions any second!

Now in the abrupt, pervading hush—a hush so still and electrifying that it had brought Jane Anne and her father both to a motionless standstill—it was Eliza's own face that was taking on the unfamiliar, a strange and mysterious look that even she would have been hard put to make out, let alone identify herself with as she continued to keep her probing gaze fastened upon her daughter.

Finally, when it seemed like the permeating tension was going to explode and blow the whole mansion and everybody and everything in it to nether world, Eliza said with a dead calm, a calm that sounded too coolheaded for one geared so highly emotional, "So, that's why you've come home. Stuart Drakston's seed's swelling in you!"

Unlike her husband, Eliza had not wondered for one single second who had impregnated her daughter. She was as positive of her remark had she been occupying a ringside seat on the timber trail in November past, not only jarring Jane Anne and Luke, too, to their very toes with her keen insight, but also startling them with the raw way she had put it, For talking this coarse was strictly out of Eliza's character. But, even so, the veracity of her words had cut out any attempt on her daughter's part to evade the issue.

Thus, with nothing left to do but acknowledge the unavailable, Jane Anne, dropping her head in humiliation, muttered, "Mother—please try to bear with me until—until..." Out of fear of sending her mother into a rage by mentioning Stuart Drakston's name, Jane Anne had stopped at saying what was in her thoughts, because she was certain that Stuart, within hours of receiving her cable, would be sailing home to wed her. Never once did she conceive that there was a good chance that it would be weeks—maybe months—before Stuart even saw her cablegram.

Still holding on to her composure, Eliza said, "Until you what, have your bastard? Well, I'm waiting and also trying to wait with patience to hear what you have in mind to do then. I certainly can't see where the birth of this baby you're carrying will change things for the better one bit, if that's what you mean. The fact is, this shame and disgrace that you've brought upon yourself and your family as well will be even worse then, and I should think you'd be aware of that and would've been mindful of it all those times you slipped off behind our backs, your father's and mine, and lay with Stuart Drakston like a common streetwalker!"

Feeling that she must renounce this terrible charge immediately, come what may, Jane Anne said, although she was still unable to brave her mother's eye, "No, Mother, please believe me, that's not the way it was."

"That's not the way it was," echoed Eliza, and then she fell silent again, studying Jane Anne for a brief moment—a time of waiting in which the years began falling away and, suddenly, the mystery of her calm was no more as long-healed wounds flamed raw again, galling and painful, so hurtful that despite all her resolve not to give in and let the torture of it devour all self-control and strength of mind, she heard herself screaming as she went on, "He raped you! That's what happened, he raped you! I knew all along and tried to warn you that your body was all he was interested in! The miserable fox! I swear to God, I'll murder him."

Stunned, Jane Anne's head hang no longer. She flashed a look toward her father, but seeing that he appeared to be as shocked as she was herself, she knew that if any clearing up of the matter was to be done, to say nothing of crushing her mother's explosive threat, it was going to be up to her to try to bring it about.

Thus, with her all abiding love for Stuart Drakston moving her to action, Jane Anne rushed to Eliza's side, crying, "No! No! Mother! You mustn't believe that about Stuart and say those awful things about him! He never raped me! He would never be so base minded as to do that. You must believe me." She warmly attempted to throw her arms around her mother's shoulders.

No embracing would Eliza have though.

Recoiling back from her daughter, she stormed, "Don't you tell me what I must believe or not believe, you little—you little tramp! Get out of my sight!" And, swiftly bringing her hand up, she fired Jane Anne's face hard, actually reeling the latter backwards.

Though he was horror-struck at his wife's behavior, Luke sprang forth, saving his daughter from falling with one hand and using his other to grab Eliza's hand before it ever cleared midair, all in one move, Then, letting his one hand still cling to Jane Anne's side, he turned to Eliza and dropping her hand and giving her the hardest look that he had ever let fall upon her, he said, overstressing every word, "Get hold of yourself, and now. Never will I condone such talk or behavior under this roof, from you or anyone else. Do you hear me?"

Apparently, Eliza heard him. Abruptly, falling down into her chair, she began to wail. But if Luke was concerned with her tears, he did not show it.

Turning to Jane Anne who was crying also, he softly suggested, "Maybe it might be better, Kitten, if you went on upstairs to your room. I had Pete to lay a fire up there hours ago, so I'm sure it's as cozy and warm up there as is it is down here. I'll have your supper sent up to you, too, since I know you must be exhausted and need to rest." He leaned forward and kissed the cheek that her mother had fired red with her hand before Jane Anne obediently turned away.

When Jane Anne had finally cleared the staircase and Luke could no longer pick up the sound of her footsteps, he too turned away, leaving his wife alone with her tears without even so much as sparing her another look or word—the first time in his and Eliza's marriage that he had stopped at making any effort whatever in trying to dry Eliza's eyes and ease her sorrows.

Pete went ahead and laid the bountiful and special meal that he had prepared for Jane Anne's unwarned homecoming at the usual hour. But, aside from Phil Carson occupying his customary place at the table and showing his appreciation for Pete's efforts by indulging himself as usual, the meal might as well have never been spread. In addition, another near useless task was the tray of food that was carted upstairs to Jane Anne's room. For when it came to tucking away all the tasty edibles that Pete had filled the tray with, a sparrow would have made a better showing than what Jane Anne did.

On his return from Drakston Hall around the supper hour, Phil Carson, to no minute surprise to him indeed, had found that he had entered a tense and troubled home. Not only had he found his sister and her husband occupying separate hearths, but the way they both looked had made Phil think that the worst had happened and to one the children at that, until on second thought he had told himself that surely, if that were the case, they would be grieving together rather than grieving in private alone. For Eliza was still weeping; and Luke, sitting by the hearthside in his study, had all the features of having cried for days, so somber and sagged in spirit he looked.

However, upon learning the full particulars that accounted for all the weeping and gloom, not to mention the incident of Eliza frying Jane Anne's face, which was the main thing that had driven Luke to seek a hearth that was divided from his wife by nearly the length of the whole house, Phil Carson was so relieved to actually know that no one was dead, or dying, that he immediately surprised everybody by taking on a complete unconventional attitude about the whole matter. In addition to promptly letting Eliza and Luke both knew that this was not the worst thing, by far, that could have happened to their daughter, he also bounded upstairs to greet Jane Anne and give her a warm welcome home.

Of course, because of his newspaper business having forced him to deal with the many inconsistent habits and customs of society, to say nothing of man's fallible ways, over so long a period of time, Phil had learned, long back, to quickly absorb the shocks and keep an open mind. So more or less being used to reacting to the upsets and improprieties of the established mode in this manner, Phil's free and easy attitude about the crisis that now prevailed in the Heyward household was; in truth, not too offbeat from his usual manner. In short, Phil's outlook on life had drifted somewhat from the old standard. It was now more unprovincial and worldly than either Luke's or Eliza's. However, something else that had a great deal to do with his attitude now was the fact that, it happened to be Eliza and Luke's daughter who was in trouble rather than his daughter, Beth Anne,

Nonetheless, Phil's endeavor to restore the family harmony was a sincere effort and, to some degree, he finally did succeed in making Luke see that Jane Anne's plight was not all that bad.

Scoring likewise with Eliza though, was an apple off another tree!

To no avail could Phil convince Eliza that the most sinful and disastrous thing possible, not to mention disgrace, had not happened to her family. She kept wailing over and over that not only was the entire family disgraced for life and that no family would ever be able to take pride in their name ever again, but Jane Anne's and Stuart Drakston's sin, had also banned the entire clan from worshipping the Lord in church as well! Gazing incredulously at Eliza's pained and tear-washed face, Phil finally said, "Eliza, you know better than that. You're talking plain nonsense."

"No I'm not!" She wailed back. "How can any of us attend church and keep our minds on what we're supposed to be in church for when besides all the whispers that'll be beating against our ears, there'll be churchgoers in every hole and comer who's supposed to be believers as well as our friends counting on their fingers like crazy!"

Disbelieving his own ears, Phil shook his head.

Presently, endeavoring to make his point again, he said, "So what? Let 'em count. Though I do want you to understand that I don't approve of Stuart's and Jane Anne's behavior, I'll guarantee you that long before that baby arrives in this world that those finger counters, whom you speak of, will already have latched onto some newer type of gossip to spread and bug over in this community. You must remember that what makes news one day, makes for old and dull copy by the next, or that's certainly been my experience. But, most important, Eliza, you mustn't let this unhappy circumstance tear you and your family apart. More than ever before, you need each other now and don't forget that. Now, I'm going on up to bed. It's been a long day, too long. But please, keep in mind what I've just said." And, adding nothing else to his remarks but a warm goodnight, Philippe Carson made his retreat, a retreat which Eliza Heyward was scarcely aware of and one which was just as well considering the progress that he had made towards changing his sister's views.

For all this was made evident no later than Sunday morning at breakfast when, taking both Phil and Luke completely unaware, Eliza up and announced that she would not be attending church services that day. Nor would she be going to Wednesday night prayer meeting, either. In fact, she had no idea when she would go to church again! The truth was, she may not go anymore, period! And, no sooner than this jarring announcement had fallen like a bag of rocks on both Luke's and Phil 's heads—jerking their heads up from their plates—she went on to inform them—actually demanding—that in the meantime they were to tell the Reverend Marsh Reed, or anyone else who should so happen to inquire of her, that she had come down with the flu! Moreover, they were to tell nobody, absolutely nobody, and over and above all that included

Martha Randolph, that Jane Anne was home!

As Luke promptly protested to the fact that Eliza was stretching the truth in point of her health, although he would have been the first to admit that doubtless the flu would not have undone her no worse than what the ravages of her cold were doing, she flared back, "No, I say it's the flu! I should know my own feelings, should I not?"

Coming to Luke's aid, Phil said, "Well, in that case, Eliza, maybe none of us should go to church. Influenza is not only serious, it's highly contagious, too."

"Of course, don't you think I know that?" Eliza flared again, drawing forth her handkerchief to catch a cough. "But I don't need Seth Roalf's attention yet and neither do you or Luke. So such being the case, you both might as well go on and attend church and, once you arrive there, do as I've asked besides!"

Seeing that it would be only a waste of breath to put in another word on the flu subject, much less challenge Eliza's obvious decision to go into hiding, Phil and Luke exchanged a meaningful look between them and said nothing else. And shortly, by her own choice, Eliza found herself once again bearing the brunt of what she felt was her daughter's betrayal alone, The crux of her feelings for Stuart Drakston was so powerfully revolting and unmitigated that wording it by name would have tested the powers of Solomon!

Assuredly, because neither Luke or Phil had no desire to lie or cause a panic in the neighborhood, Eliza's absence at church was not explained by announcing that she was down with the dread influenza. Those who did inquire of here were simply told she was suffering from a terrible cold, which indeed was fact, but only one of the several facts that made up the whole story Therefore, it never occurred to either Luke or Phil that they were stating only a half-truth.

In point of Jane Anne, since no one had been expecting her to arrive home and chance had seen that she and her father had encountered none of their friends or acquaintances on the day of her arrival—at the train station, telegraph office or any place else—it had not been necessary for Luke and Phil to say anything in that respect.

At any rate, even though Eliza's absence at church was accepted with grace and understanding and without the raising of no more than two or three eyebrows as well, that was not to say that after hearing Luke and Phil repeat the same story for the third consecutive Sunday that Martha Randolph was still accepting it for gospel because she was not. And, on the following Monday, she suddenly decided to do something about it.

Of course, she was well aware that March had blown in raw and bitter, too bitter for one whom had been ailing for over three weeks to brave as yet, Martha shot back to Bruce when the latter aired his own opinion over her assuming that something was amiss at Green Sea besides Eliza being down with a cold. Yes, certainly she knew that Doctor Seth Roalf Sr. had called to Green Sea, and one among the many orders that the doctor had, supposedly, laid down to Eliza was for her to continue on favoring her cold as well as her nerves in seclusion, saying on the whole that it would be better for everybody concerned. But pray, would Bruce tell her just how long a cold was supposed to last? Certainly not a lifetime!

No, something else was wrong at Green Sea besides Eliza having a cold. She could feel it in her bones. So if Bruce wanted to think that she was a meddling busy-body, which he had hinted at, snooping into other people's business, that was up to him. But, less him catching her and tying her down with a rope, she was setting out for Green Sea this very minute, regardless!

And, firing off this final say over her shoulder at an exasperated Bruce Randolph, Martha almost made the boards in the century-old mansion at Oak Grove shake as she tore through it and on to its front steps where her buggy was already parked and waiting for her.

Leaping inside the buggy like she might have been in the full bloom of her girlhood instead of a woman way past her prime, Martha jerked up the reins and went tearing off on her mission, on this occasion, at such a violent speed that when she finally whirled through the archway at Green Sea, all four wheels on her buggy literally cleared the ground! But, never mind Martha was not deterred from gaining her goal by this mishap. For despite the danger involved, Martha's nerve and her adroitness with the reins stayed intact. No sooner than the buggy righted itself, she went tearing right on up the drive at her breakneck speed until, at last, in her normal fashion, she skidded to a stop at Green Sea's front steps.

Nonetheless, even when she leapt from the buggy and was forced to cover the rest of the distance to Eliza's side on foot, Martha was not inclined to decelerate her pace. That is, not until she slammed headlong into Luke Heyward as she started to run up the steps. So hell-bent was Martha on reaching Eliza and hearing firsthand the source—Martha was positive it was no cold _of the latter's trouble, she had not even sighted Luke who, in his descent of the front steps, had been started to a sudden stop by Martha's perilous approach.

The strain of those ensuing weeks had left its mark on Luke Heyward's face. Chiseled across his brow and down along his jaw line were deep, saw-like creases, that previously to his daughter's arrival home, had been lost to one's eye. But now these lines had come to light, blazing as fixed in permanence as an etching engraved on hard granite, and for good reason, too.

At first, Luke had taken heart that his daughter's plight might be set to rights somewhat, once her cablegram had reached Stuart Drakston's hands. His trust that Stuart Drakston would not beat a retreat from his daughter and would meet his responsibility to her had been a subtle and definite belief within him. In point of fact, he expected Stuart Drakston to rush home and marry Jane Anne, immediately. But when the days began to fall one upon the other, until they had made up three weeks or more and still no word from Stuart Drakston had reached Green Sea, Luke's faith in him had begun to tatter drastically. As much as he deplored to even entertain such a thought, he was not so sure now that his wife's disesteem of Stuart Drakston was and had been well-founded all along.

However, although this cablegram problem was disappointing and weighty enough on Luke—causing a lot of distress as well as a lot of scathing remarks to fall in his home that certainly he himself, his wife and his daughter could have done without—there were other problems weighing on him, too, that he considered to be even worse and far more aggravating. For example, his wife's decided and unbending attitude when it came to holding the belief that their daughter was telling the truth about her pregnancy. In brief, whereas Luke believed Jane Anne's account of her chance meeting the on the old timber trail with Stuart Drakston, or as much as he would allow her to disclose about it, Eliza obstinately refused to accept one word of it, affirming that Jane Anne had secretly met Stuart Drakston for months till finally, after Jane Anne had tried several times to reach her mother and got nowhere, Luke took a stand and forbid the subject to be aired in his presence anymore!

So, consequently, with Jane Anne in the middle, relations in the Heyward household had hardly improved, The fact was, instead of abating, the rift between family members had intensified. Nowadays, Jane Anne seldom left her room. Eliza continued to keep her hearth alone and, Luke did likewise; that is, to a certain extent. For even though he was very much put out with his wife's behavior toward their daughter, that in no respect meant that he was totally ignoring her because he was not. He loved and cherished Eliza still and was greatly concerned for her happiness. Therefore, despite the variation in their way of thinking about their daughter's pregnancy, he sought Eliza's company often enough to inquire of her health and well-being. But even so, there was never a moment in those times that Luke spent with Eliza, that he was not also hoping to spot something about her that would tell him that she was relenting in her feelings toward Jane Anne. So far; however, he could see no change, which, of course, did not improve matters at all and especially when it came to bringing his and Eliza's relationship back to its normal attunement.

At any rate, Luke also made a point to look in on Jane Anne several times a day. And in addition, there was the breezy, debonair Philippe Carson to keep company with too—the one gratuity in the whole circumstance of things as far as Luke Heyward was concerned. If there were any one thing, of late, that was helping to make Luke's day, it was the cheering presence of Philippe Carson and his encouraging words, something that Luke was grateful for many times over. But, even Phil, with his cheering effort and casual attitude, had not been able to take wrong and set it to right, or, for that matter, make it sound right regardless of how much he tried to polish it.

So, on this day of Martha's wild and frenzied arrival, the inharmony in the Heyward family was still churning and churning plenty. For besides the gulf between Eliza and Luke being wide as ever, her fury with Stuart Drakston was mounting every day, which made Jane Anne's despondency all the blacker, to say nothing of Luke's disappointment and sadness over the whole unhappy situation.

And now as Luke grabbed hold of Martha Randolph to save her from landing flat on her face, he made an effort to brace himself against the shock of hearing more bad news as he cried, "What on earth's the matter, Martha?" For he was positive that no one would go tearing at the blind gait that Martha was tearing at unless some terrible misfortune had fallen.

Reeling backwards and gaping up at Luke in surprise, Martha cried back, "I'd like to ask you the same thing, Luke Heyward, now that we've encountered one another someplace else besides inside the Baptist church, surrounded by the whole neighborhood!"

"What! You mean to tell me that you'd go tearing at the kind of pace that you've come tearing up here at, running that mare there to her limit and almost falling down here on these brick steps in your own haste, when you have nothing of importance to convey?" Incredulity spread from Luke's brows to his cheekbones!

Already irritated with Bruce for objecting to her coming to Green Sea in the first place, Martha did not go for the look.

"Well, I suppose whether I have anything of importance to say depends on what I find out here!" She shot back. "And, to set your mind at ease about my mare, she's like I am when it comes to speed, she enjoys going at that kind of pace!"

"I wonder," said Luke, more for the benefit of his own ears than Martha's. "I'd say she's about paced out."

"In your hat!! Luke Heyward!!" Exclaimed Martha. "That mare's good for twenty more miles, if not further. But, I didn't come here to discuss horseflesh with you. I come here to find out what's going on. Now tell me, why hasn't Eliza been to church for a month? No cold hangs on that long!"

Still holding the tendency to be addressing himself rather than talking to Martha, Luke looked out beyond the live oaks and said, "Hers has, but it's because she doesn't have the heart to get well, and you'll find out why soon enough."

"Oh, my Lord, Luke! Don't tell me that Seth Roalf's come here and told Eliza that she has some dread disease like Caroline had. I simply couldn't take it, not so soon anyway."

Quickly bringing his gaze back to the near distraught Martha,

Luke cried, "No, no, Martha! Nothing like that, thank God. But I warn you, I don't want her upset anymore than she already is."

"Well, for crying out loud, Luke, why would I want to upset Eliza? I came here to see about her, not upset her."

Martha looked sorely put out all of a sudden.

"Not intentionally, Martha, I'm sure," said Luke. "But I know how you and Eliza are, once Stuart Drakston's name comes up. You're immediatcly at sixes and sevens with one another."

Stumped, Martha quizzed, "But, why on earth, pray tell me, should Stuart's name come up?" Luke set his eyes on a straight line with Martha's.

"For the reason that he's very much involved in the trouble here, if not the leading cause of all of it. That's why." Luke said.

"Well I never heard such nonsense, the cause of Eliza's illness, and him thousands of miles from these parts!" Martha flared. "What's come over you, Luke? I've never seen you this ill considerate of Stuart, me, or anybody for that matter. Perhaps Bruce was right. Maybe I shouldn't have bothered about checking on Eliza at all."

"I'm sorry, Martha, I don't mean to be unpleasant. The truth is, I'm glad you're here. Go on in and visit a spell with Eliza. I think when you do, you'll begin to understand why you see me the way I am right now." Luke reached out and covered her hand. "All right?" He questioned.

With her facial expression now locked in bafflement and disconcertion together, Martha said,

"Of course, Luke, if you say; and I promise, I won't upset her."

"Good," replied Luke, the tone of his voice marking his usual tenderness. "You'll find her in our bedroom. "

Feeling lighter—but no less confused because of the charge that Luke had pinned on Stuart, Martha went dashing on up the steps and, presently, found herself facing the bedroom door that Luke had indicated. Deciding not to wait to be invited in once she had signaled her presence, she gave the door a light tap and turned the doorknob.

Though Eliza was not abed and was curled up in a rocking chair beside the hearth instead, Martha thought that a bed would have been more appropriate, no sooner than Eliza's head turned to the sound of her footstep. Martha was positive that she had never seen Eliza looking so sallow or so downcast.

Now regretting that she had not followed her hunch that

something more serious than a cold was troubling Eliza and come to Green Sea sooner, Martha rushed on across the room and squatting down in front of Eliza's rocker, said, "Eliza, forgive me. I should've come to seen about you long before now. After the first week though, I was sure you'd be at church the following Sunday. Then when you didn't show up that Sunday on this past Sunday either I told Bruce I was coming to see you, cold or no cold."

Appearing to be totally unmoved by Martha's presence, to say nothing of her offered apology or explanation for not calling sooner, Eliza said, as she gazed indifferently across the room at nothing, "My cold's gone, Martha, been gone for more than a week now. Cold's don't last forever, you know!"

"Well as I live and breathe! Those were my very words to Bruce, Eliza, no later than one hour ago when I told him I was coming to Green Sea to see about you!"

"Really?" Eliza said, finally bringing her gaze back to look at Martha with a more attentive eye. "Then, if you knew there was no chance of your catching a cold, why did you wait so long to look in on me?"

Feeling no less hooked than a snared fish floundering around on a fishhook, Martha cried, "I just told you why, Eliza. I've already explained that I thought you'd be back at church every Sunday that's passed since the first Sunday you were absent because of your cold."

"And, I'm going to be absent from now on, and you and everybody else might as well get used to it. I won't be there this Sunday, next Sunday following, or no other Sunday! In fact, Martha, I have no intention of attending church anymore!"

Though Martha was already squatted down on the floor, she thought her face was going to kiss it anyway. Determined however, to hold on and get to the bottom of the whole puzzle, she pulled on that durable spirit of hers and repeated, "Not going to church any more. But why, Eliza? Don't tell me that you've let some of that madness that Marsh Reed's forever letting spill, in the second hour of his sermons, get to you!" Martha's deep-brown eyes probed into Eliza's intently.

"Oh, don't be absurd, Martha, of course not! I'll confess something to you. When Marsh Reed takes the pulpit, I usually give him about thirty minutes of my attention. Then, rather than letting my thoughts dwell on what he's saying, I let my mind busy itself with piecing quilt scrapes, making wash soap, or doing some other task that's ever waiting to be done around here!"

"Well, I wondered because when it comes to estimating time; that is, figuring out the proper moment to close his Bible and shut up, Marsh Reed's green as a gourd! The thick wit should realize that anything worthwhile he's had to say, that by the first hour of the service, he's already said it twice over and should stop. But no, on and on he goes, never realizing that those of whom he hasn't put to sleep by then, don't give a good tinker's damn about what he's saying anymore because they already see themselves going to hell anyway! For a split second there, Eliza, I thought you'd begun to see yourself in this group! I'm glad to hear that you don't!" Her gaze still probed Eliza as earnest as ever.

"No, not yet, Martha." Eliza said, still showing a tendency to be blasé to all and everything around her. "Still, that doesn't mean that I'll be changing my mind about attending church or showing up in any other public place, for that matter."

"But why, Eliza? You say your cold's gone, and you say it's not Marsh Reed's preaching, so what is it? I don't understand any of this. What's come over you? You must tell me, if I'm to have any idea of how to go about trying to help you." Little wonder that she had found Luke's behavior not up to its usual pleasantness, Martha thought.

"You can't help, Martha, not now. When you could've helped, you chose not to."

Feeling that Eliza not only had her cornered again but had grossly offended her as well,

Martha, recoiling somewhat, said, "Eliza, I've already apologized once, for not having looked in on you and practically here on my knees at that, before now."

Abruptly, and for the first time, Eliza appeared to be cognizant of Martha's humbled mien, saying, as she finally gave Martha a full eye at last, "Martha, squatting down there is your own doing, not mine. I'd never require anybody to fall on their knees to me, and least of all those of whom I feel close to and you well know that, or should. So before your legs refuses to support you when you do take a notion to rise, I'd suggest you get up from there and take that other rocker setting there. Besides, I wasn't thinking about my cold, anyway. Forget the cold!"

Reminding herself to be patient because she now felt that on top of everything else Eliza had added insult to injury, Martha straightened herself up to a standing position. However, as she stepped over to the other rocker to comply with Eliza's suggestion, instead of plumping down in the usual easy fashion that she ever adhered to when visiting at Green Sea, she perched down on the edge of the seat and said, holding her back straight as a ramrod, "Well, if it isn't the cold, I can't imagine what you're referring to, Eliza, because I can't recall of ever having failed to give you my support and especially when the circumstances entitled your right of it."

"What you're saying then," retorted Eliza, "is my stand regarding your nephew, Stuart Drakston is not worthy of your support so that's why I've never received it. Well, I should hope, Martha, that my reasoning is not so outrageous and preposterous that I'm still not going to be deserving of your sympathy, even though my daughter was forced to leave school nearly a month ago and come home because she was already swelling out of sight with Stuart Drakston's bastard!"

The situation had affected a way to pay off old scores with Martha and Eliza had made use of it. But, if Martha had taken it as a counterblast or had any desire to repay in kind or even had noted it for that matter, either her promise to Luke Heyward, her astonishment or maybe both, was keeping her tongue tethered on this occasion.

Finally, aner a long moment and with her eyes still flared as big as hen eggs, she did manage to sputter, "W-hat!"

"Yes, I can see, Martha, that this news is rather hard for you to take in, but have no doubt, it is true. Actually, though I doubt you will believe me, I can understand your astonishment, since you're so inclined, and always have been, to hold your nephew in such high esteem. Still, you should've known, as I knew all along, that all Stuart Drakston was ever interested in, was to get my daughter off in the bushes somewhere! And, he did finally succeed, making good his threat to me." Eliza said, taking Stuart's threat to continue seeing Jane Anne and making free with it to suit the occasion as she saw fit.

And, this injustice to Stuart, Martha had noted. And not only was it making her blood boil, but she was also near gritting her teeth over it, clasping her jaws firmly together to keep from giving Eliza a bawling out over it. What's more, she also wanted to fling out that the making of a baby required both male and female. Still, her levelheadedness told her that if there were ever a time for her to be tactful and hold her temper it was now. The situation was too precarious.

277

Besides, and again, there was the promise that she had made to Luke to take into consideration.

So, rather than verbally spilling her vexation on the spot, Martha told herself, for this once, to bridle it as she asked, "But how is the world, Eliza, did they—I mean how did Stuart manage to get—to coax Jane Anne off in the bushes some place? He so seldom ever gets the chance to hold her hand."

"Oh, he managed all right. Her belly demonstrates that!"

"But how?" Martha pressed. "Where—When? Has Jane Anne said?"

Sending Martha a glare that was anything but warm, Eliza snapped, "You wouldn't be trying to suggest that he didn't, by raising these questions, would you, Martha?"

"No, of course not." Martha vowed. "I'm well aware of what their feelings are for one another. It's just that I can't see how they—how Stuart was able to get Jane Anne off alone some place, and especially long enough for something like that to take place!"

"She said they happened to meet on the old timber trail at Thanksgiving time when she was out riding. But from the looks of her, I'd say it was nearer to September, and you will, too, when you see her," said Eliza. And upon spilling that opinion, she began to let quite a few more of her beliefs about the matter fall on Martha's ears, as well as relating Jane Anne's account of the episode along with all the other particulars in the case that had ensued in past weeks. Then, she ended by exploding, "Planting his seed in my daughter and then hotfooting it out of here. I could murder him"

Still warning herself to be cautious and not lose her temper, Martha, letting Eliza's last words fall any place they may, gingerly inquired, "You say Jane Anne sent the cablegram to Mrs. Stuart's address in London and, so far, Stuart has failed to even acknowledge it?" "That's what I said, the mongrel!" Eliza snapped again, contempt for Stuart Drakston bringing a blaze to her eyes.

If Martha noted it though, or the name calling, she gave no sign, still continuing to let Eliza vent her anger with Stuart in any way she saw fit, The fact was, Martha was so busy gathering her thoughts and becoming excited in the process, that Eliza could have said most anything she desired right then for all Martha cared.

"Eliza," she cried, "Stuart's never laid his eyes on that cablegram. I'd stake my life on it! He's..."

"Oh, botheration, Martha!" Eliza angrily interrupted. "You're the limit, always trying to shield him, no matter what. I swear I believe if you'd see him do murder, you'd have an alibi in his defense!"

"No, but never mind about that." Martha cried again, literally bursting to go on with what she had started to say. "Stuart's not even in England! He left London more than two months ago!"

Fastening her stormy gaze upon Martha's exultant features, Eliza said, "Well, if that's true, why isn't he back here? And, how come you know so much about his globe-trotting, anyhow?"

Instantly, not only was Martha having second thoughts about the cablegram matter that were wiping all excitement from her face, but she was also feeling that her will to overlook Eliza's ill humor and derogatory remarks was just about to flag. In short, she had had an overfill.

Quite emphatic, she said, "I know about his travels, Eliza, because we're family. Stuart and Elizabeth both writes home to Uncle Matthew and Mother and me rather frequently. Now, to get to your first question. Stuart isn't back here because, when he left England nearly two months ago, he didn't head back to America. He met Whit somewhere on the Riviera. Then, when Whit's ship sailed, Stuart persuaded Elizabeth and his Grandmother Stuart to meet him in Paris. He wanted them to see the sights of Paris, too. And, from what I can gather from Elizabeth's letters, I received four yesterday all in one lump, she and her mother did get such a thrill out of seeing the sights of Paris, that Stuart suggested they all see more of Europe before returning to England. All the letters were written in different countries. The latest though was written and mailed in Vienna, Austria. Elizabeth remarked that she was enjoying Johann Strauss' concerts so much that she could stay there forever. She didn't say when they planned on heading back to England. For a moment there, all I was thinking about was, that Stuart hadn't even seen that cablegram. I didn't stop to reason that it still may be weeks, or months, before he sees it." Martha's voice had grown to be rather pensive by this time.

"So, Stuart Drakston's off waltzing in Vienna, Austria, while Jane Anne's ensconced within the four walls of her bedroom growing bigger each day with his bastard! Eliza raged. "Think of it. With him thousands and thousands of miles from home, there's no way the family name can be saved now!"

"I'm truly sorry, Eliza. But, maybe it's not as bad as we think.

279

They may have already left Austria by now, and Stuart could be back in London reading that cablegram this very minute." Martha encouraged.

"That's easy for you to say, Martha, because it's not your daughter who's carrying a baby out of wedlock. You have no idea how I feel. Nobody does."

"True enough, Eliza, we may understand and have sympathy with someone else's suffering, even weep for it, but no way is it possible, not even for love or money, for us to feel it. Perhaps this is wise and good though. For if things were to the contrary, no doubt we would buckle under the strain of our burdens far more often than we do. For instance, consider your present worry, hurt and distress. Certainly, you wouldn't be holding up as well as you are, if you were also plagued with the pain of my own distress, of late, too."

Scrutinizing Martha with a gaze that was rapidly losing its rage to concern, Eliza quizzed, "What do you mean, your distress? What are you worried about? Is there something that I don't know, Martha, something that you think I should be in on, and I'm not? Please, if it's some dread news or that someone in the family has come down with something like Caroline had, have the goodness not to tell me! I don't think I could take that, too."

"I'll venture to say," agreed Martha, amazed at how often the workings of hers and Eliza's mind paralleled with the other. "No, nothing of that nature, Eliza. It's Laura."

Uncovering herself from her ball-like position and putting her feet on the floor, Eliza said, finally appearing to have something else on her mind besides her own trouble, "Yes, what about, Laura?"

"I don't know, Eliza. That's just it." Martha replied. "I haven't heard from her for almost two months." Every day, I tell myself, surely I'll hear from her today." Something near panic suddenly blazed in Martha's eyes.

"Where was she living at when she last wrote?"

"San Francisco, California, if one could call following that damn Silverspoon from city to city, living!" Martha replied, and then with her eyes taking on a flicker of hope she went on to add as she probed Eliza anxiously, "But that is a long way from here. A letter would be a long time coming, wouldn't it, Eliza?"

"Yes, a long time, Martha." Eliza assured, and then with a meaningful look passing between them, they were simultaneously rising from their rockers and opening their arms to one another.

Chapter Eleven

Having just seen his mother, Elizabeth Drakston and his maternal Grandmother Stuart safely back through the front door of the Stuart residence in London and, genially, acknowledged both their wishes to be excused immediately for the purpose of seeking some quiet and rest in the privacy of their bedrooms, Stuart Drakston sat down the small valise he was carrying and made for the stack of mail that had caught his eye lying atop a side table in the hallway. The Stuart's aged and longtime butler, whom had managed the Stuart residence and watched over it while the trio had been traveling abroad, had collected the mail each day and neatly stacked it upon the table as it had been delivered—a bulk of nearly two months' accumulation.

Rapidly sifting through the numerous letters, statements and advertising matter and the like and sorting out everything that was sent first-class, Stuart suddenly stopped and stared at the yellow envelope that he held in his hand. Then, in the same breath, as he realized the envelope contained a cablegram from Charleston, South Carolina, he felt his heart give a leap. However, the start that had caused Stuart's heart to jump had not come about because thoughts of Jane Anne Heyward had flashed through his mind. The fact was, having finally begun to make some headway in past months in letting his thoughts dwell on something else besides Jane Anne, she had not taken precedence in them now. What had eclipsed her and everything else in Stuart's mind was the one place in the whole world that he loved most, Drakston Hall and the uneasiness he was feeling over it and those of whom who also dwelled there, especially his Step grandfather Matthew Carson and his paternal Grandmother Amy Carson, both of whom he loved deeply and had bid farewell to months before—a farewell that Stuart could not help looking back on and lament in his heart now as well as regret because he feared that it had been a farewell for all the time between either of them and himself. Most likely his final parting with his step-grandfather Matthew Carson, he was thinking.

So bracing himself for the bold black letters that he was positive were going to spell out his fears, Stuart ripped the envelope open and, unbelieving, stared at the message that his eyes met instead.

Even had he still been holding hope that Jane Anne Heyward would have a change of heart and think better of the cold way that she had parted from him on the trail in November past, possibly writing and telling him that she would accept his proposal without delay, the short and perplexing message that he was staring at would never have passed through his thoughts, in that respect, because it simply was so unlike Jane Anne. There was no mention of love. Nor was there any expressed desire to marry him. There were only the words "Stuart, I need you desperately" and that was all. Still, the impact of those few words upon Stuart Drakston's nerves was no less unsettling than had the cablegram been stretched out a yard long. For as he stood there staring at the message, wondering what to make of it, he not only found that his heart was leaping at a rather unsteady pace again, but he also observed that he was not as steady-handed as he normally was, which, of course, brought him up sharp to the way it was with him regarding his feelings for Jane Anne Heyward. In brief, he saw that despite all his ableness in recent months to press on with his idea of setting his life on a different course—a course that so far had seen hi, going the dizzy rounds of Monaco with Whit and reveling in the adventure to boot, that Jane Anne Heyward still—more or less—set the pace of his every heartbeat and ever would.

He had learned about Jane Anne's near death with pneumonia just before he had taken his departure from England to join Whit on the French Riviera. His Aunt Martha had conveyed, in detail, the trials of Jane Anne's illness to him in a long letter, but not before she had explained that it was certain Jane Anne was making a full recovery. For that long-sightedness on the part of his Aunt Martha, he would forever be grateful. He deplored to think the hopelessness that most surely would have been his to learn had he been aware that Jane Anne was battling this critical affliction.

At any rate, outside of finally hearing through another letter from his Aunt Martha that Jane Anne had indeed recovered and gone back to school at the turn of the new year—although this cheering news had not been his to rejoice in until his mother had brought the letter to him in Paris when she had joined him there—word of Jane Anne had been next to nothing.

Still, the puzzling part was it appeared that Jane Anne had not been in boarding school in Richmond, when she had sent the cable because it had come from Charleston. And what's more, he saw now that the cablegram had been sent almost two months ago. Heavens and earth! What did it all mean? Wait! Maybe Jane Anne had followed up with a letter to him when she had gotten no reply to the cablegram.

In frantic eagerness, Stuart was suddenly churning through the remaining bulk of mail, intently observing each piece. However, as the last item fell through his hands and he looked at the number of letters that he had come upon and sorted out, knowing that not one single one in the heap was penned in Jane Anne's elegant, distinct hand, he felt a frustration run through him that was not too much unlike a hard slap in the face. Still, aware that there were two letters in the heap addressed to him in his Aunt Martha's unmistakable bold hand, he perked up somewhat for he was positive that when it came to knowing the ins and outs of the whole neighborhood, nobody ever had a more thorough knowledge of these doings than his Aunt Martha.

So, still holding fast to the cablegram, Stuart quickly found Martha Randolph's two letters and made for the adjoining living room where he fell down into the nearest chair he came to. But, as he quickly tore into the first letter and started scanning over it, his trust that he was going to find something, some hint or some word or maybe something spelled straight out, that would tie in with the cablegram began to vanish. And, come to nothing it had, by the time that his eyes had scanned the second letter. For it seemed that his Aunt Martha, on both occasions, had had nothing on her mind but Cornwallis Silverspoon's globe-trotting and had been determined to use every particle of space in the letters to vent her beef over it. She had not even mentioned Green Sea, let alone said one word about Jane Anne. Neither would the letters which she had also written his mother and which his mother had yet to read, he decided, so put out he felt.

All the same, Stuart's disappointment in his Aunt Martha was no more deep-felt than the disappointment that started to build in him toward Jane Anne as he pushed the two letters aside and fixed his eyes back upon the cablegram.

Diligently weighing each word that the message contained, Stuart began to wonder about Jane Anne coming back home so soon after resuming her studies. What had prompted her return? She could have cabled him from Richmond just as easily as Charleston. Had Jane Anne finally decided to put their love for one another, as well as their needs, first for a change? Had she finally seen that getting a Master of Arts degree wasn't all that important, after all? No, nothing of the kind, Stuart Drakston, and you know it, because being impulsive and given to making overhasty decisions just isn't Jane Anne's nature. Besides, Jane Anne was adamant about completing her college studies. That had been made clear to him when chance had brought them together, in November past on the old timber trail. The old timber trail! God in heaven! What had happened to his thinking? Jane Anne couldn't have decided she needed him because—because —

No, he would not, could not, let himself think of that possibility. They had been together, like that, for such a short while. And most important, he must remember that Jane Anne was—had been a virgin! No, he mustn't jump at conclusions, because it was nothing short of being wild, to say nothing of gross, to think of Jane Anne as being in the family way, he refused to entertain such absurdity in his head another second. Still—

Stuart Drakston's eyes had long left the message that he was trying to read into, the shocking thought that he may have impregnated Jane Anne Heyward last November had reeled his vision upon the room's opposite wall. But even so, his eyes had no perception of the wall being there, or, for that matter, did they see anything else in the room. For confusion, doubt and sheer terror—all of it mudded together—was crippling his sense of perception as well as his ability to think straight to almost nothing.

In truth, Stuart was using his eyes and rather acutely at that but strictly through a mental sense, having become oblivious to everything except the one thing that his mind's eye was centered upon and that was, that sweet—and stormy—interlude that had occurred between Jane Anne Heyward and himself. The old timber trail and its halcyon atmosphere was all that was present to his mind now. The place that had embraced the sweetness of his and Jane Anne Heyward's lovemaking and heard the echoes of their rupture as well. The place that had also housed the stormy scene following it! Fresh and alive, it had become. Every word and every gesture and every movement as it had fallen,

And yet, as vivid and real as Stuart's mind's eye was picturing the happening and, with him knowing, too, that it was bare fact instead of some creative fantasy that his mind was merely fabricating, he still balked at seeing anything as serious and momentous as Jane Anne Heyward already being several months pregnant with his child, arising from it. Indeed, to him, the very thought of that possibility was simply too frightful to even consider, let alone accept.

But, no matter how hard Stuart tried to push the thought aside and read something else in Jane Anne's message as he continued to sit there and contemplate the matter, that all important pregnancy question endured on, leading the dance in his whirling thoughts until, finally, he was forced to see what he must do regardless of how much he dreaded doing it. For even thinking about coming face to face with Eliza Heyward in a situation of that nature, was much the same as having a nightmare. In fact, Stuart was not so sure that he was not already in the grip of one so horrifying the thought was though he did realize he was fully awake and it was broad daylight to boat.

And, the terror Stuart felt over meeting Eliza Heyward persisted in holding, griping him so that when his mother entered the room some hour or so later and inquired what the trouble was upon seeing his disgusted expression, rather than risk laying bare the intensity of his feelings to her in a verbal response, he up and handed her the cablegram to read for herself instead.

Elizabeth Drakston read the message through. Then she read it again, and then again and again, reflecting upon each word. Finally lifting her eyes and peering long and hard at her son she put another question to him.

"Stuart, have you gotten this girl in trouble?" she asked, making no attempt to mask her directness or her seriousness. The truth was, the similarity between Stuart's expression now and the one that Elizabeth remembered him wearing on the day that he had returned from squirrel hunting insisting on their departure, was too close for her to dismiss.

Mustering his courage, Stuart was as equally direct, saying, as he made every endeavor to end his mental battle with a wrathful Eliza Heyward, "I don't know, Mother, but there's one thing I do know, I'm going to find out just as quickly as I can get across that ocean that separates us!"

"I see." Elizabeth said. "Even if it means going to Green Sea and let Elizabeth Heyward put a bullet through you? That is what you're saying, is it not?"

Even if it had meant breathing life back into a painful memory for herself and her son as well, and possibly cause him to raise questions, too, that she had no will to answer, Elizabeth had felt compelled to phrase these remarks.

But, if his father's untimely death was running afresh with Stuart, he chose to make no reference to it as he rose from his chair and said, "No, not literally am I saying that, Mother, because I'm going to trust that things won't develop to that extreme when I do make my appearance at Green Sea. Considering all the circumstances involved in this matter, something that I've been busy doing from the second my eyes fell on that cablegram, I see my going to Green Sea and inquire of Jane Anne as being the only honorable way to handle this matter. "He felt that to divulge any more than he already had, would not be in good form.

Elizabeth Drakston saw it differently though.

Pressing on, she said, "I'm wondering, Stuart, if principles and honor were not involved here, as you've just made a point of pointing out, would you still chance fronting the danger of Eliza

Heyward's wrath and her loathing of you?"

A glimpse of disapproval edged into Stuart's gaze.

"Of course I would," he said, "because Jane Anne Heyward happens to be the only girl I'll ever truly love." Determined that there would be no questions ever concerning the sincerity of his declaration he decided to take it further, adding, "I should hope that if I'm able to reach Jane Anne's side and my meeting with her should happen to result in marriage that nobody, and least of all the members of our two families, will ever entertain the idea, no matter how the nature of things are at the time, that I carried through with it solely for appearances sake and because it was the right and proper thing to do. For nothing will be further from the real facts involved in the case."

Elizabeth got the drift of what her son was saying loud and clear. Still, she was resolute too—resolved that she would not wonder ever if a cat's-paw was being made of Stuart. Though she held Jane Anne Heyward in high regard and thoroughly approved of her, that still did not quell that one all important question which was troubling her and which, so far, Stuart had sidestepped and hedged around.

So, squaring her shoulders and meeting Stuart's gaze head on, Elizabeth said, "In spite of what you've just stated, Stuart, I'm curious, and I fear my curiosity will stay intact until one important factor in this matter is cleared up for me. Now, to the part that's leaving me.

Considering all the difficulty that's been imposed on you by

Eliza Heyward when it comes to your seeing her daughter and, if this message here from Jane Anne means what we both suspect, do you mind enlightening me as to how, and also when and where, the object of our suspicion came to be?"

"No, I don't mind, because I know that I can speak in confidence to you. Besides, you are my mother so I should think that that gives good reason for your interest and also justifies a clarification in the matter as well." He averted his gaze somewhat. "Jane Anne and I met by accident on the old timber trail the day before last Thanksgiving, the day I went squirrel hunting, and the same day that you and I took our departure for New York. Jane Anne had arrived home the day before, but I didn't know that. She was out horseback riding that afternoon and had decided she wanted to see the old timber trail again. Though, at the time, we both felt that our meeting had been planned by Providence, unfortunately that happened not to be the case with either of us by the time we parted. At any rate, as much as I love Jane Anne, I've regretted a thousand times over that our meeting that day took place at all. The fact is, I haven't had any contact with Jane Anne since then, and I'd come to think that everything was over between us until about two hours ago when I found myself holding that cablegram there."

Immediately dropping her penetrating gaze, Elizabeth moved to the nearest chair available and fell into it. Now that she had been furnished with the one detail in the situation, which had concerned her most and which she had insisted on knowing, she suddenly felt chagrined and wanted to kick herself for not having been more broad-minded and less doubting—more ready to go along with Stuart's decision to rush to Jane Anne's side without pressing him for every substantial and literal fact, involved, or nearly so.

Even knowing—deep down—that it was mostly fear that had driven her to press Stuart as it had made little difference to Elizabeth and comforted her less, because she felt that she had not only diminished herself in his eyes but had also caused him to endure another battering which he did not deserve.

Feeling near ill over the whole mess, a sore and sad mess that could have been avoided in her eyes, Elizabeth suddenly found herself wanting to give Eliza Heyward a clout right in the face.

Knowing that was impossible though since an ocean separated them, she vehemently blurted, devouring each word with a certain amount of glee, "Right this moment, I feel that I could take joy in wringing Eliza Heyward's neck totally off her shoulders!" Startling Stuart profoundly, but what shocked him even more was seeing that her thirst to have a go at Eliza's neck was no stuff and nonsense. She truly had blood in her eyes.

Of course, although his mother or no one else in the family had ever made mention of it to him, Stuart had always known that Elizabeth and Eliza Heyward both would just as leave slam the door in one another's face as open it. Still, as much as he was grateful for his mother's fervent support now, his logic told him that considering the circumstances looming over him not to applaud her dislike of Eliza Heyward or nourish it, In his opinion it would only make matters worse and certainly not only offer no solution for improving their relationship but further deteriorate the relationship between the Drakston's and the Heyward's as a whole.

So, trying to pretend that Elizabeth's remark had merely surprised him and imported nothing significant to him, at all, Stuart smiled and jested, "Gracious! Even Henry VIII preferred the swift blade of an axe, Mother!" Then, drawing his smile in, he went on, "Anyway, I trust that you see now why I must book passage for Charleston, South Carolina immediately. I'll only book passage for myself though since I don't expect you to embark on such a long voyage so soon after our return here. You continue on with visiting Grandmother Stuart and I'll come back in a few weeks to accompany you home. All right?"

Elizabeth was all of one second weighing Stuart's suggestions.

With the cablegram still in her hand and appearing, all of a sudden, to be back to her normal collected cool, she said, rising instantly to her feet once more, "No, it's not all right. Book passage for me, too, I'm coming with you. It's time I headed back to Drakston Hall, anyway.

I've already been away too long as it is."

Her words brought a wishful look to Stuart's eyes.

"You miss being there, too, don't you, Mother?" he said.

"Yes, I do, and why should I not," admitted Elizabeth. "Besides the fact of your father lying there in Drakston Hall's burial ground, I believe more of my years have been spent there than here." Abruptly she was offering him the cablegram back and changing the subject by saying, "Here, you may want to hold on to this."

Taking the cablegram and sticking it inside his shirt pocket, Stuart said, "Yes, and not a bad idea I don't suppose. It could come in mighty handy when I reach Green Sea, help in explaining my presence there." He turned and started rushing for the doorway.

Stuart's remark penetrated to the core of Elizabeth's heart, but not one breath of her pain or fear for him did she let him see as he whirled back around to say to her, "Oh, I almost forgot, Mother. You have several letters from home here on the hall table, two from Aunt Martha, I noticed. I warn you though before you open hers. If they're similar to the two she wrote to me, be prepared to bear with her displeasure over Cornwallis Silverspoon's acting career and his roving and wandering, as she put it. She wrote of nothing else." Despite his remarks and the pessimistic view that he had held earlier, he was secretly hoping that the letters would contain some word of Jane Anne.

"Thank you," smiled Elizabeth. "I'll buckle on my armor right now."

Stuart smiled back. "See you later," he said. "I'm on my way to see when we sail."

Stuart suddenly pulled on General's reins. The stallion halted his gait and, within seconds, his thundering hoofs had stopped altogether, bringing Stuart to a dead, but anxious, standstill in the middle of the river road. Looking down the stretch of road ahead of him, Stuart estimated that he was finally no more than one quarter mile from the place that he had set out to reach almost a month earlier. He could see the archway at Green Sea looming in the distance.

The bright May sun felt hot on Stuart's back. And yet, as he gave the costly Panama hat that he had slapped on his head, at the last second of his departure from Drakston Hall, a push back from his brow and reached to his back hip pocket for his handkerchief, he knew the excessive amount of sweat that he was having to deal with was due more to the state of his nerves than it was to the warmth of the low country weather, or for that matter, any other thing. Sweat had already played havoc with his hair, drenching it thoroughly and was rapidly soaking his white lien shirt as well. He could feel it running in rivers, or so it seemed, down his back and along his sides. He deplored arriving at Green Sea with his shirt soaked wet through and now were wishing that he had taken the carriage instead of choosing to ride General. Nonetheless, even as he was regretting his choice of travel, sitting there wiping sweat from his brow, he was forced to acknowledge something else to himself— his main reason for choosing to ride the stallion to Green Sea in the first place.

Who was he trying to kid, he thought. Surely not yourself, Stuart Drakston. General may have needed a good workout as he had explained when his mother had raised the question as to why he was riding horseback to Green Sea instead of going by carriage. But, as much as that response had held water, that had been only part of it and not the paramount part to boot! General was a sterling, certified guarantee to a fast getaway, if the situation came to that! Nothing more. Nothing less. A long sight faster than a carriage would be and, that was for certain, actually the size of it. But, blurting out that part to his mother was out of the question. At any rate, that was the main reason he was riding General; and also, why he happened to be stalled now wiping sweat and worrying about the state of his appearance.

No, that last thought was not quite right, either. It needed a little mending too. Granted, he was wiping sweat and was concerned about his appearance. But again, that was only part of the picture. The truth was, in as much as the sweat was playing its part, he was playing for time because he had become indisposed toward facing the ordeal that he was certain awaited him, if his hunch about Jane Anne's cablegram to him prove to be the case. And that fact in itself was simply ironic when he stopped to consider how much he loved Jane Anne and how hard he had pushed himself to reach her,

Still, regardless of one's bravery or courage, he believed no man ever had approached a raging battle without standing in dread of meeting it to some extent. For, as ridiculous as it was, that happened to be the way he felt about facing Eliza Heyward because dealing with her rancor of him, no doubt, was going to be strikingly like meeting an order of battle—plain warfare! He was certain of it and he dreaded it and if feeling thus made him any less of a man, he was minded to say, so shall it be!

In truth, taking into account all the hindrances that had delayed him in his effort to reach Green Sea, he was actually surprised to find himself this close to the place. From the first, since the moment he had set out to book passage, it seemed every step that he had taken had been impeded by something.

To begin with, finding a transatlantic liner that was making ready to embark for the United States had been futile. One full week he had waited. Then, once he had found himself aboard ship, no worse crossing did he think he had ever endured or hoped to experience again. The Cunard liner, which he and his mother had finally boarded at South Hampton, was whipped by severe winds and seas throughout the entire voyage, cutting the ship's speed by several knots, which in turn delayed its docking time in Boston by nearly a whole day. And on top of all that, there was another whole day delay in waiting for a southbound steamer to take them to Charleston. Throughout the whole trying voyage though, his mother never raised one complaint, patiently making the best of every delay and hardship that they had met with, including the steamer's inconvenient three A.M. arrival time in Charleston this morning. However, he was not so sure that his intolerance of all the adverse circumstances associated with the journey as well as his flagged spirit, which in spite of himself he had been unable to hide from his mother, had had a great deal to do with her abiding attitude.

At any rate, with his destination finally within his sighting distance, his long journey was nearly over-done with. By the same token; however, it appeared his courage was too! Still, he must not falter. He must keep his footing and push on because he firmly believed that he had not taken the shadow for the substance, so to speak, and misread the meaning of Jane Anne's cablegram to him. Granted, there was a possibility that he had misinterpreted the message, but he did not think so even though it remained to be all he had to go on since, as he had expected, the letters that his Aunt Martha had written his mother had contained no news of Jane Anne, either.

Well then, if he was so confident that he was not laboring under a false impression, why had he not cabled Jane Anne back and let her know that he was making all effort to reach her? It had been simply because of that one outside chance, as remote as he thought it was, that he could be wrong and his cablegram might have fallen into the wrong hands, causing a big ado that would have demanded an explanation. In addition, he had decided that if he must face Jane Anne's mother, that it might be better for all concerned that she stay unaware of his intentions. In brief, he had not liked the idea of Eliza Heyward waiting in readiness for him!

The truth was, since it was now getting on towards the dinner hour, he was inwardly praying that Eliza Heyward would be so busily occupied in her kitchen that he would not have to face her right off. Even though Pete was chef at Green Sea and knew his trade inside out—why not? He had mastered it under Eliza Heyward's supervision—it was a known fact that Eliza Heyward did an awful lot of puttering in the kitchen too. As a matter of fact, it was no rare occasion to hear her culinary talent tooted by both women and men alike. Indeed, it was said that no one, absolutely no one including Pete, could measure up to Eliza Heyward's skill when it came to preparing southern fried chicken.

Well, whether southern fried chicken, collards, or whatever, he prayed something had taken her to the kitchen o this day, or if she were not already there that she was on her way, because he had not come this far to let his dread of facing her turn him back. He must move on.

Tremulously, Stuart nudged General in the sides with the toes of his boots. Knowing the signal, the stallion promptly fell into an easy gallop.

Heaven be praised! It's Mr. Heyward instead of her! Stuart thought, as he came face to face with Luke Heyward hardly a second after, with heart in mouth, he had pressed upon the doorbell at Green Sea.

Yet, as Stuart whipped off his hat with one hand and offered his other to Luke Heyward and said, somewhat excitedly, "Mr. Heyward, sir. So nice to see you again sir," he instantly was wondering if he had rendered his thanks too quickly over the fact that he was facing and addressing Luke Heyward instead of the latter's wife. For even though Luke was meeting his hand, Stuart sensed that he was doing so reluctantly, and certainly his greeting of merely repeating "Stuart" and adding nothing else was, not only wide of his usual pattern of greeting but had also sounded cold and unamicable as well.

However, the thing that surprised Stuart most was the change in Luke Heyward's appearance. His short, trim mustache that had been black six months ago was almost white now. Due to his having his hat on—it was obvious to Stuart that Luke had been on his way outside and had turned the doorknob the same instant that he had sounded the doorbell—Stuart was unable to tell if Luke Heyward's hair had changed that much or not. He could see; however, that the change in the man's face standing before him was indeed as drastic as his mustache. Luke Heyward's face was void of any lightness at all. Only strain and worry showed and his once bright, wide-awake eyes seemed dull and distracted now, two caves of despair that made

Stuart's insides wince and at the same time brought him around to recognizing something and that something was, that he had let his fear of facing Eliza Heyward so absorb him that never once had he let one single thought concerning Luke Heyward's feelings trouble his head! He had completely forgotten that Luke Heyward was part of the picture too! Completely forgotten how dear Jane Anne was to Luke Heyward's heart.

Suddenly, as he pulled in his hand from the brief handshake that Luke Heyward had given him, Stuart felt as though saying another word was going to be utterly impossible for him. For the question that had brought him there, the question that he had so desperately pursued and yearned to know, had lodged as big as a hen egg in his throat, squeezing and constricting every nerve and muscle in it.

Still, in spite of his discomfort, his shattered nerves, his guilt, his shame his regrets, Luke Heyward's downcast features and everything else, Stuart's hunger for knowing whether Jane Anne was there or not prevailed. So griping onto his hat brim with both hands, he ventured to say, "Mr. Heyward, sir, I'm here to inquire of Jane Anne. Is she here, sir, by any chance?"

Suddenly, like lightening, Stuart saw something very close to anger sweep across Luke's face as he said, coming back with a question of his own, "Pray tell me, Stuart, where else would you expect her to be?" Not making it any easier for Stuart and also confirming what he had suspected all along.

However, thinking that Jane Anne Heyward could be carrying his baby was one thing. But having it confirmed and especially in this manner was another pair of shoes to Stuart. He thought of Jane Anne's cablegram in his pocket, but he did not attempt to pull it forth. Nor did he attempt to try to color the deed by offering one excuse or regret. He felt that anything he may have said toward trying to polish the situation, including his tardy arrival, would not only be unfitting but downright silly.

So, holding onto his hat brim tighter than ever and calling on every ounce of courage he had left, he said, "May I see her, sir, if only for a few minutes? I've come a long way."

"If she's willing, I have no objection to your seeing her." Luke said, stepping back inside and letting the door swing wider. "You may come in and wait in the parlor if you wish while I go see."

Stepping across the threshold and on past Luke into the foyer, Stuart, feeling no taller than a snake slithering in the grass, muttered,

"I'm much obliged, sir, thank you?'

Luke closed the door and now appearing to have taken on a more temperate attitude as he turned back to Stuart, he said, "I think she'll see you, but it'll probably be a few minutes before she comes down." He gestured for Stuart to go on inside the parlor, he hustled on off toward the staircase.

Still clutching his hat, Stuart crossed the foyer and stepped inside the parlor. However, feeling no more welcome than he had been some criminal who had stormed the front door, he did not sit down. He simply stood where his feet had paused and tried to collect himself somewhat by concentrating on his surroundings, observing as he looked around him that the room looked no different than it had looked some four years earlier. It looked just as warm and inviting, not to mention immaculate, as it had looked then. Still, when it came to its homeliness reaching him and making him feel more at ease, he might as well have been standing in the desolation of some cold, wind-swept barren desert and gazing at it. He lifted his eyes to the portrait of the late Anne Carson hanging over the sofa and began to study it. Knowing that she had been Matthew Carson's first wife and Eliza Heyward's mother, which consequently made her Jane Anne's direct maternal grandmother, he searched her likeness closely, trying to see if he could detect something about it that reminded him of Jane Anne. He saw nothing, concluding that Jane Anne was all Heyward but, at the same time, did decide that there was a striking resemblance between the likeness in the portrait and his Grandmother Amy Drakston Carson, something that he had been blind to till now.

He had a sudden urge to check on General and had just stepped over to an outside window that would give him a view of the hitching post where the stallion was tethered and was starting to pull the curtain aside when he heard a footfall. He turned his head and, instantly, his hand let go of the curtain and the stallion was forgotten. For there stood Jane Anne across the room from him and her whole appearance, even her lovely, dear face, had changed so that the shock of it was rendering him nearly senseless! Little wonder that her father had been reluctant to meet his hand and brief with his greeting as well! The fact was, he saw now that he was lucky that Luke Heyward had greeted him at all!

He had no idea what degree of alteration he had expected to see in Jane Anne's appearance.

Actually, that was something else that had eluded his mind too. But, even so, envisaging Jane Anne as she looked now would never have occurred to him, because she already looked full-term with child if she looked one day! Even though she was wearing a flowing floor-length green dressing gown, which was pretty and becoming on her, it did nothing toward concealing the swollen state of her pregnancy or that bloated look that seemed to cover her as a whole. In addition, her complexion, which had always looked flawless, was all splotchy and discolored and her hair was all dull looking and entirely without sheen. But what pierced his heart the most, he thought, was that beaten look in Jane Anne's deep-grey eyes. And, not only was there no light in them whatever, but they looked as though she had cried for months.

Stuart never remembered throwing his hat aside—it landed on the sofa and crossing the room to where Jane Anne stood. Moreover, the instant of finally knowing the touch of her, once more, was lost to him too. For the bold sight of Jane Anne's pregnancy and what appeared, to him, to be an overall deterioration of her health as a whole, had upset him so that he had little knowledge of what he was doing or saying.

Certainly, Stuart knew that he was trying to explain to Jane Anne that her cablegram was nearly two months old before he had seen it. But he had no knowledge of the fact that his voice had broken on a sob and he was repeating himself over and over, saying, as tears spilled from his eyes and fell on Jane Anne's face, "I didn't know, darling, I swear to you I didn't know," until Jane Anne came back, telling him, "Don't, Stuart, please don't weep. It's not your fault that I'm in this awful mess. I should've gone on to England with you as you begged me to do. I did decide later to do just that and rode all the way to Drakston Hall that night to tell you that I'd marry you anywhere, anytime, but you'd already left for New York."

"What!" Stuart exclaimed. "You mean to say that you tried to reach me that same night?" The irony of the whole unfortunate ill-timed affair dried his tears immediately.

"Yes, and I was devastated when I learned that I was too late," murmured Jane Anne, feeling so at peace and untroubled in Stuart's strong arms that she actually felt slumberous all of a sudden. She huddled closer to him, resting her head against his chest as she went on to add, somewhat sleepily, "But, it doesn't matter, Stuart, not anymore. What counts is that you're finally here. I love you so."

But although his heart was gladdened by Jane Anne's last words, it did matter to Stuart and it mattered plenty!

"Christ, darling," he said, hugging Jane Anne as tight as her protruding middle would allow him. "How I could've blotched everything as I have, is above my head to figure out. But I'll do my best to make it up to you, Jane Anne, even if it takes the rest of my life. I don't know how or what way I'll make it good, but I swear by the Almighty above that I'll try."

"You might start by making sure your bastard, which she's carrying, will at least have a legitimate name when it's born!" Exploded Eliza from the doorway. "And get out of this house and take her with you so I won't have to face the likes of her shameful lot another day!"

"No!" Roared Luke, fast on his wife's heels. "I invited him in and in this house he stays until this matter is discussed, and if I might add, discussed sensible and with taste at that." He laid a restraining hand on Eliza's arm and directed a hard, disapproving look straight at her.

Luke was thoroughly put out with his wife because he had asked her, upon informing her of Stuart's arrival, to give the couple a little time together before she confronted Stuart. But Eliza had ignored his request and had brushed on past him in the hallway and stormed into the parlor.

And, if she was taking note now of Luke's disapproving glare on his restraining hand, not to mention having heard his declaration, it was not demonstrated as she raged on, "Having the brass, Stuart Drakston, to set your foot on these premises when you've blackened our good name for all time! I say get out of my sight and take her with you!"

Looking aghast and holding on to Stuart's arm with a grip that would have measured up to the might of a bulldog, Jane Anne cried, "Please, Mother! Won't you, at least, give Stuart a chance to say something for himself before he leaves. It's not his fault that he wasn't here earlier."

Stuart was saying nothing though. Nor was he doing anything but merely looking on, which of course infuriated Eliza all the more. In truth, Stuart was too dumbstruck to speak. Not only had he become dumbstruck at the wrath that he saw in Eliza's eyes—he was positive that he saw fire leaping in them—but he was astounded to find that he no longer feared Eliza Heyward! To his amazement, the fright and doubt that had ever seized him in her presence, had vanished like a gust of wind. He had no idea why he felt as he did but thought that perhaps his bursting into tears had had something to do with it, that and the fact that Jane Anne, only a moment earlier, had declared her love for him. Jane Anne not only needed him, she loved him and that had changed the whole run of things as far as Stuart was concerned, imbuing him with a composure that he found hard to believe.

At any rate, after a long moment of merely observing Eliza Heyward's obvious aversion to him, Stuart, feeling cool as a cucumber, finally said, "Mrs. Heyward, since the delicacy of this situation puts me at a disadvantage to start with, I see no point in trying to say anything for myself so I won't make any attempt to. However, I do want to state here and now before you and Mr. Heyward both that I'll ever regret that the circumstance of Jane Anne's pregnancy could not have occupied inside of God's law rather than outside of it. For that I'm truly regretful; and also deeply deplore the burden and anxiety that it's brought to both you and Mr. Heyward, and, no doubt the sorrow and pain that both of you still carry.

"Still, what concerns me the most, Mrs. Heyward, is Jane Anne's health and her well-being. So for her, not me, I'm not asking, I'm begging for yours and Mr. Heyward's forgiveness and, that whatever differences that you and I share now, Mrs. Heyward, will be laid aside and forgotten so we can be a family together rather than a family that's divided. I ..."

"Did you hear that, Luke?" Eliza rapped out, cutting in on Stuart's say with a voice that split the air like a peal of thunder. "Him having the boldness to stand there and talk about forgiveness and being family after all the shame and trouble he's brought down on us and our family! The nerve of him! All this time, sneaking our daughter off in the bushes behind our backs when we thought she was in school studying! He never had no intention of marrying Jane Anne, Luke, and won't now unless you force him to! He..."

"No, Mother! Stuart doesn't deserve that!" Jane Anne suddenly shrieked. "You're accusing him of things he's never done or would ever think of doing. "She dropped her face in the palm of her hands and started sobbing.

"Well, I don't hear him giving the lie to it." Eliza snorted back, seeming oblivious to the sound of Jane Anne's weeping or the obvious distress that she was burdened with. "He can't and tell the truth!"

Dear Father, the woman's impossible, thought Stuart. Feeling his composure beginning to slip from him like ice cream melting in ninety-five degree temperature.

"Oh, but I can deny it, Mrs. Heyward, because I've never sneaked off with your daughter anywhere, not once," he said, his indignation plainly coming through in his voice.

The fire in Eliza's eyes leaped higher. "You mean to stand here in our house, Stuart Drakston, and have the defiance to deny that you got our daughter with child? I should think that even a Drakston wouldn't be as foolhardy as that!" Her anger was so intense she came darn near spitting in his face.

With the vague memory of his father's death suddenly flashing through his mind—something that further rattled Stuart because he was left wondering why his mind had seized on it—he said, "No, certainly not, Mrs. Heyward, you can rest assured of that. But you twisted the meaning of my remark. What I meant was is that I'll forever deny what apparently you have conjured up in your mind and that is, that I was waiting my every chance to copulate with your daughter, which, of course, is plain absurd and couldn't be any wider from the actual facts involved." He, instantly, drew Jane Anne closer.

"Oh, I see," Eliza flared back. "Then, you too, would have Luke and me to believe some outrageous account like Jane Anne told us about you two meeting by accident on the old timber trail, though we never asked her for any details. Well, spare us the trial of listening to any more of that nonsense!"

"And, what nonsense was that, Mrs. Heyward, if I may ask? I'd certainly like to know." Stuart set his jaw in a hard line, waiting,

"Wanted her father and me to believe that—that you two were together only once. The most ridiculous thing I've ever heard tell of?" Eliza violently obliged. Then, looking as though it was all she could do to keep her hand from landing in Stuart's face, she went on to add, screaming each word, "I was married seven years, Stuart Drakston, seven years mind you, before I had a baby!"

Nonetheless, although his newfound cool was about battered to pieces by now, Stuart stayed to the battle, holding on by sheer will power.

Planting a stern and unrelenting gaze squarely on Eliza's face, he said, "And, thanks to that seven-year barrenness, Mrs. Heyward, I can see that your daughter has had to endure a lot of undue hurt that, no doubt, she would have been spared had it been otherwise with you. I should think, Mrs. Heyward, that fertility is a unique and single function in each and every individual and should not be viewed like some genetic feature or characteristic trait. Certainly, to compare its rate of success or failure between individuals, even mother and daughter, is not only in error but also unjust I should think."

Looking as though she was now near ready to fall with a stroke, Eliza blazed back, "And so you shall, the virile and mighty potently powered Stuart Drakston! I said get out of my sight and don't you ever set foot in this house again unless you have my consent also! Is that understood?" She had slowly overstepped this last remark.

Before Stuart could reply, Luke, who up until now had been giving impressions of having a gag in his mouth, said, "I think it's best that you leave, Stuart. Nothing's ever been settled yet by embittered retaliation. It only makes matters worse."

However, before Stuart could, once again, respond or make one move toward carrying through with Luke's suggestion, Jane Anne was intervening. She had already ceased her sobbing, having ceased it during Stuart's counter blow on fertility and now seemed to be seeing him in a light that she had just discovered—a praising and approving light.

Likewise, to her mother in giving point to her words, she said, "If Stuart leaves here, Papa, under the orders that Mother has just decreed to him, I leave, too, and won't come back to Green Sea until he's made welcome to come with me."

"Oh, but I haven't heard him ask you to leave with him yet." Eliza heatedly cried. "And furthermore, if that's your choosing to throw yourself at Stuart Drakston's feet and stay away from Green Sea because I won't welcome him here, so be it!" Jane Anne wasted all of two seconds of thinking better of her threat.

Promptly breaking her hold on Stuart's arm, she told him as she started to move from his side, "I'll be ready shortly, Stuart. I'll have Bessie to help me," surprising everybody by the grit that flowed underneath that gentle mien.

Feeling as though he had been rescued from some untimely end, Stuart sprang forth to stop Jane Anne and tell her, as he let his arm circle her middle once more, "I have to go back to Drakston Hall first, sweetheart, to get the carriage. I'm riding horseback. Encountering no difficulty, I'll be back no later than a couple hours from now." Turning back to Eliza he went on to add, "You will allow me to return here for Jane Anne, will you not, Mrs. Heyward?"

In tense silence, the question began to hang and it continued to hang while everybody waited. Finally, with no less impact than the sound of glass shattering on cement, Eliza retorted, "I've heard nothing said about marriage yet."

"Of course we'll be married by Revered Reed no later than this very day, Mrs. Heyward. Just as quickly as I can make the arrangements, I promise you that. Still, I feel I must say this too. As much as I'm grateful to make Jane Anne my wife before our baby's born, that is not the foremost reason why I want to marry her. I yearn to marry Jane Anne, Mrs. Heyward, because for most of my adult life I've been in love with her. And I vow to you and Mr. Heyward both that I'll do my every best to be a deserving husband to her and try to make our marriage a good marriage, too."

Eliza's hand had suddenly shot up, cutting off Stuart's declaration, and, at the same time, brusquely indicating to him that she had already endured more of his say than she had intention of continuing to bear with even before she went on to retort, "You've made your point; and also made good your long ago threat to me, Stuart Drakston! Yes, you may come back after her, so now get out!"

Stuart was positive that he now knew what a beaten dog felt like. Never had he felt so humiliated and put out. In his effort to try to ease Eliza Heyward's mind and convince her of his love for her daughter, he saw that he had done nothing but make himself more vulnerable to her insults and rebuffs.

Silently, and wondering which was worse to endure humiliation or fear, Stuart let his arm drop from Jane Anne's waist. Then, giving her hand a hard squeeze, he let it drop and turning to where his hat lay, he picked it up and made straight for the doorway. Not another word had he uttered.

As Luke Heyward turned and followed through the doorway on Stuart's heels, Jane Anne, turning a grim expression upon Eliza said, "Mother, you could've been more kind and tolerant of Stuart's feelings."

With her head dropped and her eyes staring at nothing, Eliza muttered back, "And you, Jane Anne, might've thought of your poor father's and mine before giving yourself to Stuart Drakston."

Saying nothing else, Jane Anne also made for the doorway.

Finally left to herself, Eliza lifted her head and fixed her blurry eyes on the only source of comfort that she felt was available to her right then. The portrait of the late Anne Carson hanging over the green sofa. She stared long and hard at it through her tears.

Once again, Elizabeth Drakston came outside to the veranda at Drakston Hall and peered intently down the long avenue. Had Elizabeth not known better, she would have sworn that some unknown force had actually picked her up and set her back down in the fright and calamity of that long ago night when Blossom had brought Frank to the front steps, bloody and sagging in the saddle. Of course, seeing her son set out for Green Sea when she knew he was not welcome there would have been disturbing for Elizabeth in any case, but knowing the circumstances that had persuaded Stuart that he must make an appearance there on this day, had made a nervous wreck out of her. If Elizabeth had traipsed to the front veranda one time after Stuart had left for Green Sea, she had traipsed there one dozen to see if he were returning, peering long and hard down the avenue with a taut expression.

But now, Elizabeth's taut features were suddenly relaxing. Far like a thunderclap and obviously in control of his mount at that, Stuart was back, reining General in from the river road onto the avenue and thundering on toward her. But as Stuart's mount thundered on, bringing him nearer, Elizabeth's face began to tighten all over again, because she could see that his trip to Green Sea had certainly given him no lightness or anything that paralleled it.

"Stuarts what is it, what's wrong?" she cried, as Stuart hastily reined General in at the end of the walk and, literally, sailing from the saddle, sped toward her.

"Everything, Mother!" He shot back, taking every one of the steps in one leap and hitting the porch. "Save death, things couldn't be much worse. It's Jane Anne!" He jerked his hat off and sailing it in the nearest chair he reached for his handkerchief that was already sopping wet and began wiping his face.

"Y-es, w-hat, what about Jane Anne?" Elizabeth croaked, her heart suddenly moving up in her throat.

"She's—well. . ." He stopped. Then he suddenly blurted, "Oh, hell, Mother! I couldn't feel more like a heel, more ashamed, or humiliated! Jane Anne's almost six months pregnant with my baby, so you can imagine what her mother's put me through! Still, that's not the worst of it or the part that's got me so upset that I hardly know what I'm doing, or saying for that matter"—using strong language was a vice that Stuart rarely fell to—"It's Jane Anne's appearance.

She doesn't look well at all, Mother, nothing like your typical pregnancy. Her color's bad and she's—well, she's so bloated looking. I know Mr. and Mrs. Heyward are awfully upset and worried about her, too, and they have good cause to be. In fact, the more I think about it, I guess I deserve everything Mrs. Heyward said to me." He stuffed his handkerchief back inside his pocket. "I've got a lot to do and I don't have much time to do it in, so I'd better be moving. I told Jane Anne I'd be back after her with the carriage in no less than two hours."

"You're going back to Green Sea—back after Jane Anne? But isn't that chancing an awful lot, Stuart?" Elizabeth's face grew tighter still.

Stuart laid his hand on Elizabeth's arm. "Don't worry about it, Mother. I asked and finally got Mrs. Heyward's permission to go. Mrs. Heyward made it plain to me though that that would be the limit of her consideration or her tolerance as far as I'm concerned. I did my best to reach Mrs. Heyward, but I got nowhere. All the same, Jane Anne and I will be married at the parsonage by Reverend Reed sometime this afternoon. Then, we'll be coming back here to Drakston Hall." He started to walk on but suddenly turned back, asking, "By the way, you wouldn't happen to know where Grandfather Matthew is, would you?"

"I think he's in the library reading. Is it something, Stuart, that I can take care of for you?"

"No, but thanks anyway, Mother. It's something I feel I should do myself. You see, through Mr. Heyward, he followed me out a while ago, I learned that aside from Aunt Martha, and she just found out about it recently, and Mr. Phil Carson and Doctor Seth, nobody else even knows that Jane Anne is home, let alone knowing that she's pregnant. I take it that Mrs. Heyward forbid any of them letting the word leak out, and especially to Grandfather Matthew."

"But that's acting senseless on her part." Elizabeth said. "Doesn't she realize that it's impossible to hide things of that nature?"

"Obviously not. And Mr. Heyward told me that she's quit attending church too. Said she hadn't gone to church in three months."

"Pray tell me, what excuse did she send, or did she say?"

"She sent word she had the flu."

Elizabeth shook her head. "Some flu to last over three months.

God forbid it drifting to Drakston Hall."

"Well, anyway, I'm going to prepare Grandfather Matthew and Grandmother too, if she's around for the shock of Jane Anne's pregnancy. I think they should've already been told about it, especially Grandfather Matthew. Certainly, I'd never consider springing the news of my marriage to Jane Anne on either Grandfather Matthew or Grandmother Amy without them having some knowledge of my intentions first, let alone expose them to the shock of Jane Anne's pregnancy without preparing them for it beforehand."

"I should think not," said Elizabeth, "If I know Father Matthew though as well as I think I do, I'm sure he'll take it all in stride and won't come down on you too hard. The fact is, although I'm certain he doesn't or won't even condone your and Jane Anne's behavior, I still wouldn't put it past him to want to mark the occasion with some kind of celebration."

"Well, he could at that, knowing him. But I'm afraid it'll be a long time before Jane Anne and I will be celebrating it, if ever," said Stuart, feeling that the price that he and Jane Anne were paying, and would continue to pay for that one idyllic hour that they had shared, and particularly in Jane Anne's case, was indeed too steep. Not only had it robbed Jane Anne of the home wedding that she had wanted and had looked forward to having for so many years, but it had also cheated them out of ever delighting in the thrill of a honeymoon, or certainly the kind of honeymoon that two people in love deserved to have.

"It'll work out, Stuart, you're not the first, and I feel that Jane Anne's going to be all right too," said Elizabeth, trying to lighten her son's obvious despondency.

"I pray you're right, Mother, but it seems nothing's as it should be. I don't even have a ring to put on Jane Anne's finger and there's no time to go to Charleston and buy one. In fact, my time's running short, I've got to run." He whirled to go on inside.

"Wait, Stuart!" Elizabeth cried, dashing after him and tugging at the diamond-circled wedding band that Frank Drakston had slipped on her finger so many years ago. "Here, take this." She held the ring out to him.

"But, Mother, are you sure you want to part with it?"

"I'm sure, go on and take it," insisted Elizabeth. "With your father gone so many years, I've worn it too long as it is. Besides, I'm still wearing the solitaire that he gave me to mark our engagement, so I know he'd be pleased to know that your wife's wearing this." She reached for Stuart's hand and dropped the ring inside his palm.

Stuart stared down at the blue-white, sparkling wedding band. Then, he raised his head and said, "Charleston can't have a wedding band in it, Mother, that tops this. My father sure had exquisite taste when it came to gems, or picking his wife for that matter. I'm sure Jane Anne will treasure it and be proud to wear it, too. As for myself, have I ever told you that you're the best mother a son could ever have?"

Ignoring his question, Elizabeth smiled, "I hope I'm the best that you could've ever come by!

Now, before you're late for your own wedding, you'd best not tarry any longer." She bent forward and kissed him on the cheek.

When Stuart turned to go on inside, Elizabeth turned and walked to the end of the long columned porch to where she could get a view of the Drakston burial plot. She did not know why she was impelled to seek a view of her late husband's resting place when so many other things were crowding her mind, but reasoned as she stood there gazing across the flower-scented terrace landscape at his tomb that undoubtedly it was due to her having parted with her wedding band.

Elizabeth held no regrets about parting with the ring and, suddenly, felt assured that there would be none in the future. For that same spiritual affinity with Frank that had ever been hers to experience at these moments, was still with her and keen as ever besides. Still, as she broke her gaze from Frank's tomb and cast it back down to the polish line on her finger where her wedding band had rested for so many ears, Elizabeth was starting to realize that the wedding band was not the only thing that she had let go of in the last little while. To her amazement she found that she no longer wanted to wring Eliza Heyward's neck! Indeed, Elizabeth was finding that she was very much in sympathy with Eliza Heyward, and, in addition, felt that Eliza Heyward and herself were even sharing a kindred like-mindedness at the moment!

Jane Anne Drakston, she had become. And now she softly closed the bedroom door and turned to face her new surroundings. Stuart Drakston, whom Jane Anne had finally married no more than three hours ago, had just made his excuses to her and headed back downstairs. However, even though circumstances had plummeted her into this unfamiliar setting—never before had Jane Anne set foot on Drakston Hall's upper floor—she did not feel abandoned nor out in the cold, so to speak. For not only had Stuart Drakston insisted on escorting Jane Anne upstairs to their appointed suite himself, but he had also not hesitated in the least about swooping her bulky body up in his arms and crying her over the threshold as well.

But now with Stuart no longer by her side, Jane Anne found herself alone, alone in an overlarge bedroom that was strange and unfamiliar to her. Still, as Jane Anne stood there and observed that there was nothing about the room, or its handsome Chippendale furnishings, that put her in mind of her pink and white bedroom at Green Sea, she nevertheless had to admit to herself that everything was strikingly pretty.

The motif was neither masculine nor feminine but a striking balance somewhere between the two that made for an instant eye opener. From the mint green and white damask pattern wallpaper to the green-hued Oriental rug, the look was nothing but cheerful and inviting, a blend of total charm, Jane Anne observed and also noted, at the same time, a number of things that helped make it appear as such. For instance, the ornately carved mahogany canopy that sheltered the huge Chippendale bed was draped with fabric of the same design and color as that in the wallpaper; and Jane Anne fancied that idea and wondered which of whom, her step-grandmother Amy Drakston Carson or Elizabeth Drakston, might take credit for it. She also took a fancy to the solid white damask lounge chairs that set on either side of the marble-mantled fireplace. Still, what attracted Jane Anne's eye the most and, in the same breath, made her feel as if she were any ordinary chastening and virtuous bride, was the added number of personal effects that had been made in her behalf. Looking as though they were actually growing in the tall crystal vases that they had been arranged in, fresh cut May roses glowed from chests and tables alike throughout the room. A box of French imported bonbons and chocolates set on the nightstand. A pitcher of ice water and two tumblers set beside it. The coverlets on the bed already been turned back and, Jane Anne was not sure whether it came from the exposed lacy, monogrammed bed linens that she had stepped nearer to or all the fragrant roses setting about, but a sudden whiff of something like French cologne hit her nose!

Venturing on across the room and on into the water closet in anticipation of starting her toilet and being all through with it before Stuart returned, Jane Anne took note that not one thing toward one achieving that purpose had been overlooked there either, it seemed. Even the washbowl on the washstand and the bathtub, too, had already been filled with water. Wondering about that also, Jane Anne stuck her finger in the washbowl and finding that the water was delightfully warm to the touch, stood in awe, for at least a full minute, and marveled at the amazement of someone's timing!

For the first time in long, nerve-wrecking hours, Jane Anne had begun to feel completely at ease, hugging all this welcome as tightly to her bosom as she had ever embraced any person, or any one thing, in her whole life. She turned and going back into the bedroom, she made for the one and only piece of luggage that she had arrived with. Though they had stopped at opening the small valise, Jane Anne noticed that someone had still taken the liberty of setting it upon the blanket chest at the foot of the bed. No doubt reasoning that I'm too cumbersome to step any further down than this convenient level, she thought to herself, and went on to reflect over the day's events as she opened the valise and pulled forth a pretty white gown that was embroidered in pink rosettes.

When Stuart had left Green Sea to come back to Drakston Hall to get the carriage earlier today, her father had come upstairs to her bedroom where she was busy packing her clothes and had suggested that she stop and not worry herself with trying to see to everything on such short notice, and especially since it was her wedding day, he had pointed out. He promised that he would have Bessie to see to all her belongings, and, he himself, would deliver everything to her to Drakston Hall on the morrow. Poor Papa, she was positive that never in her memory would she be able to erase how his face had looked when she had hugged him goodbye and then turned to Stuart for him to assist her in getting from the ground into the carriage! That had been the one trial that she had meant her father would be spared! But, even so, his pain had still been obvious, so obvious that she had stopped at uttering one word to him. Nor had he said one word to her. She and Papa had waved to one another though—waved until the carriage had gone through the archway out of sight. She liked to think that they both had let their waves express all they might have said but had found too difficult to voice to one another.

Her mother was not there to see her off as her father was. Mother had informed Bessie to tell her that she was indisposed with a migraine. Well, although she was much in sympathy with her mother's migraine, maybe it was just as well that Mother and Stuart had not encountered one another again today.

She wished her mother could see fit to be as warm toward Stuart as Miss Elizabeth was toward her. When Stuart had brought her to Drakston Hall today after their marriage at the parsonage by Revered Reed, Miss Elizabeth had been waiting on the porch to welcome her to Drakston Hall—a welcome that was as natural and commonplace with Miss Elizabeth had Stuart been bringing her home from a long honeymoon still slender as a reed! The truth was, everyone here at Drakston Hall seemed to view her pregnancy as a matter-of-fact and nothing more. And this seemed to be the case all the more with her Grandfather Matthew and Grandmother Amy. Still, she much would have preferred that Grandmother Amy stayed silent on the subject instead of telling her at supper, when she had picked at the food on her plate, that she must eat more for the baby's sake! Grandmother Amy had acted as though she and Stuart had been married three years ago instead of three hours ago! Grandfather Matthew had saved the moment, though, by cracking, in his ever-ageless manner, "She's merely doing what every bride does, Amy. I remember that you did the very same thing. You picked at your plate for an entire week after we were married, The fact is just as I was beginning to think that you'd come to regret your decision to marry me, you up and cleaned your plate of every morsel on it and asked for a second helping!"

Looking abashed, Grandmother Amy had cried, "Matthew! I don't recall that I've ever asked for a second serving of food in my whole life!"

"Of course, you don't recall the incident, dear, You were too nervous at the time," Grandfather Matthew said, and as Grandmother Amy had calmly come back and informed grandfather that no doubt his political activities had caused her nervousness and then had gone on into a long spill about Washington D.C. and its politics, Grandfather Matthew had caught her eye across the table and winked at her. She was certain that had been grandfather's way of telling her that she need have no fear that the baby subject would arise again for some while, because Grandmother Amy was still on the subject of Washington D.C. and its politics even after supper was already over and everybody was leaving the dining room and heading their separate ways.

Thinking about how shrewdly Matthew Carson had veered the

course of conversation at the supper table, Jane Anne smiled to herself and taking her gown, she turned back once more toward the water closet. However, she had only taken a step or two when, suddenly, a full-length reflection of herself in the mirrored door of the huge armoire across the room brought her feet to a standstill and, in addition, turned her smile to an appalled grimace as well. Though she had noted the full-length mirror on the door of the armoire as she had observed the room earlier, in some way up until now, her steps had prevented her from catching a full view of herself in it. But that was not the case no longer. For now, Jane Anne was looking and looking hard at herself; and the longer she looked, the more appalled and unhappy she became over what the mirror reflected back to her, which was the all-out change that had occurred in her appearance and which, up until now, she had been spared the shriek of seeing since the mirror in her bedroom at Green Sea was not full-length.

Even though she had chosen to wear her most attractive and best dress to be married in, which lucky for her was cut with a wide flowing skirt and was a pretty blue color besides that did enhance her coloring she thought, Jane Anne saw now that even her best with all its advantage might as well have been a drab shapeless gunny sack for all the good it was doing toward improving her appearance. The dress not only was much too short in front—hanging way above the tops of her shoes—but it was also doing nothing for her sallowness, or the swell in her stomach and breasts.

Indeed, she saw that instead of obscuring her pregnancy, to any degree, that the style and cut of the dress seemed to bare its existence all the more and, with this discovery hitting at her insides like the shock of a cold knife blade, she felt her throat constrict and suddenly all the quietude that she had come by was all but swept away by sobs gushing rampant upon the stillness,

Now feeling that she had to be the most awful-looking bride who had ever awaited her bridegroom, Jane Anne turned and falling into a straight chair along the wall, she continued to weep so hard and let all the unsightly things that the mirror had exposed to her engulf her, that she was not even aware of Stuart's presence until he was falling on his knee at her feet, anxiously crying her name.

Her wretchedness had gained such a grip on her that never once had Stuart's frantic knocks upon the door reached her, nor had any other move or utterance that he had made in gaining her side; that is, until now when he cried once more, "Darling, what is it? What's happened? Have you taken ill? Shall I go for Doctor Seth?" This last question made Jane Anne's sobs break all the harder as she thought to herself, her belly was so big that here was Stuart thinking she needed a doctor! Still holding onto the decanter of spirits that Matthew Carson had just slipped to him as he started to mount the staircase, Stuart, his nerves building to the point of exasperation, set the decanter on the floor and grabbing hold of Jane Anne's arms and punctuating his remarks with iron weight, he attempted to reach for her a third time, crying, "Darling, you must tell me! I have to know what's happened to you! If you don't tell me, and I mean this instant, I'm sending for Doctor Seth!"

The force in Stuart's voice, which Jane Anne was unacquainted with, turned the trick. Besides, requiring the attendance of a doctor on her wedding night was the ultimate in her opinion.

So, gathering all her will and managing a long, deep sniff that all but buried her erupting sobs, Jane Anne, still clutching her gown that was lying across her lap, croaked, "It's—I'm ugly, ugly as homemade soap, Stuart, and look like a scarecrow besides!"

Relieved, but not without reservations, Stuart repeated, "Ugly? Whatever gave you such a notion as that?"

"That full-length mirror over there, that's what." Jane Anne replied, "When I saw myself in it, I wondered why it didn't crack and shatter to the floor!"

Now it was Stuart who was experiencing the unexpected—appreciating Jane Anne's dry humor that was new to him.

Instinctively turning his head toward the armoire and then back to her, he smiled, "Well, you see it's still holding and with you looking in it, it's bound to hold for many a year, no matter how many babies we have." Reaching for the decanter and rising from his kneeling position, he went on as he gave the decanter a close scrutiny, "I'd say what you and me both need to do right now is forget about mirrors and have a sip or two of this."

"Spirits?" Questioned Jane Anne, lifting her head and appearing to notice the decanter for the first time. "No, I don't think I care to sip it, Stuart, I don't like the taste of hard liquor."

"Well, neither do I to tell the truth," said Stuart, "but apparently Grandfather Matthew thinks we both stand in need of something to settle our nerves, because he just slipped this to me and said for us to at least give it a try."

"What is it? Did he say?" Jane Anne asked, her interest

obviously perking up now that she knew the idea of their indulging in strong drink was actually her grandfather's doing.

"No, not really," Stuart replied "You know how Grandfather Matthew is, anything to make the best of all occasions. Sending me a wink, he told me that it's a concoction of his own that he makes for newlyweds only. He also said to not let grandmother know about it, said she'd give him hell"

"Well, maybe one little sip, Stuart." Jane Anne said, the hush-hush connected with the idea winning her change of mind more than anything else. "I know grandfather wouldn't put anything in it that would harm us."

Harm us, no. But make us three sheets in the wind, yes, Stuart thought to himself as he turned and made for the two tumblers sitting on the nightstand.

Thinking likewise to Matthew Carson that if Jane Anne and he both had ever had good cause to dull their sense to a situation it was now, Stuart poured from the decanter what he determined was a good man-sized drink into both tumblers. Then walking back to Jane Anne and handing one tumbler to her and raising the other one high in the air before him, he said, "Here's to our day and our baby, darling, and all conjectures about us and all tongue-waggers be damned."

He downed the whole portion in one gulp and had to strive with all his might to keep his breath in the process.

After raising her own tumbler to Stuart's toast and then taking a sip from it, Jane Anne said,

"Stuart, this stuff tastes awful."

"I know, sweetheart, but sip again. Actually, Grandfather Matthew said not to judge its taste by the first sip, anyway. He said to let it sort of roll around on your tongue a bit before swallowing it."

Raising the tumbler to her mouth again and taking another sip, Jane Anne did as Stuart had suggested. Then letting the liquor slide slowly down her throat, she said, surprise spreading across her face, "Grandfather's right. It's not bad at all that way!" She followed that sip with another.

"Well, since I gulped mine down like taking the worst kind of medicine, I think it only for the sake of being able to say a good word for it, I'll pour me another drink." Stuart said as he headed for the nightstand again.

Pouring another generous amount of Matthew Carson's special

concoction for himself, Stuart came back and pulling another straight chair up alongside Jane Anne's he fell into it and laughed, "I wonder what our neighborhood tongue-waggers would say if they could see us now, sitting here sipping this grog like two high society matrons sipping on a mint julep."

"It's my opinion that they'd say plenty and it wouldn't be very praiseworthy, though you deserve better," said Jane Anne. "Certainly, you don't deserve having a bride who looks like she might take to childbirth on your wedding night."

"No," said Stuart, growing serious all of a sudden and quickly reaching for Jane Anne's hand. "I won't listen to that kind of talk. You're the one who deserves better, having to bear the whole physical crux of this matter while I'm set free from it. That in my book is not fair play. No two ways about it, the woman is dished a raw deal in this love-making business. From the first second that I set eyes on you today, it seems I've thought of nothing else, Though I want you to know that you're still beautiful to me as you are, I must confess that it tears me apart every time I look at you. One mere sexual encounter and look where it got you." His seriousness was plenty evident, too much so for Jane Anne to take lightly.

"Don't, Stuart," she said. "Though, physically, I am bearing the consequences of our wrongdoing, that's the way it is with things of this nature, the way God saw fit to have it; and I should think that we wouldn't want to scorn His way. I'm going to be fine I promise you that. So please, darling, don't fret about it. After all, today did see us finally married to one another so that fact in itself should be reason enough for us to be happy and also optimistic about the future." Suddenly letting go with a loud burp and instantaneously jerking her hand from Stuart's and covering her mouth in order to suppress the inelegant act, she went on saying, "Oh my! Excuse me! I'm afraid me and the baby both are having trouble with our digestive systems. Do you suppose Grandfather Matthew put baking soda in this drink?" She gave a trivial little laugh that whispered of not caring one way or the other if he had.

"The baby—baking soda?" Stuart gasped, whirling his head to look at her. "You don't think it's—it's. . ." Stark fear that she might be going into labor had frozen his tongue all of a sudden.

"Time?" she finished for him and laughed again, beginning to feel free as air, and as unbound and uninhibited about her pregnancy had her stomach shown no bulge whatever. "Of course not, silly. It's just become awfully active, all of a sudden. Want to feel?" Without giving Stuart a chance to say whether he did or did not, she reached for his hand again and laid it on her stomach.

On the instant, awe and wonder gripped Stuart's face.

From his first suspicion that Jane Anne was carrying his baby as well as from the instant that his eyes had convinced him of it, Jane Anne's pregnancy, to Stuart, had more or less been just that, a pregnancy—a circumstance of their making that they not only were going to have to deal with and see through regardless, and especially in Jane Anne's case, but saddled with besides.

But now, in no more time than the length of a breath, Stuart's whole attitude had changed. No longer was this moving, quivering sensation that he felt rippling beneath his hand, just a pregnancy. It was life! A living being! A life of his and Jane Anne's flesh. A life of his and Jane Anne's blood.

Though he felt that he might burst into tears, Stuart, holding his emotion in check, said, "Darling, I think maybe he's trying to tell you that you've had enough of Grandfather Matthew's spirits for this once. Besides, it's time you were in bed. It's been a long, trying day for you, too long, in fact." He reached for the empty tumbler in her hand, which she had just drained, and took it and his own that still had some spirits in it back to the nightstand.

"What if it's a girl?" Jane Anne quipped to his back.

"Huh—what did you say?" Asked Stuart, turning around to face her.

"I said, what if it's a girl?" Jane Anne re-echoed, still sticking fast to her chair.

Stuart smiled. "I'll be more than happy to welcome her too," he said, retracting his steps back to where Jane Anne sat. "Now, what about your taking that gown there and get on with making ready for bed?" Suddenly, not only was Jane Anne's frivolous mood plainly disappearing before Stuart's eyes, but it was also obvious to him that she was hanging back from his suggestion.

Seeing now that Jane Anne had not become so giddy that she had forgotten what bedtime was going to involve on this occasion, Stuart, swiftly weighing the situation and taking a chance on an idea that had just come to him, said, "Listen, sweetheart, if it'll make you feel more comfortable, I'll sleep somewhere else."

"Where else will that be?" She asked, looking up at him with a most attentive gaze.

"Only a little way from you," he lied, "actually just beyond that other door inside the water closet there. You did notice there's another room adjoining the water closet, did you not?" He regarded her closely, trying to keep a straight face, because the door that he was referring to gave access to no bedroom. There was nothing behind it but a large linen closet. Still, he was pretending otherwise and hoping that she knew no better; in that, he was merely feeling out her attitude about them sharing the same bed, hoping that it would all eventuate to her inviting him to share it, He had not considered what he was going to do if he got no invitation.

Appearing now to be more let down than relieved at his suggestion, which, of course, raised Stuart's hope of getting the invitation he wanted, Jane Anne said, "No, I never noticed. I haven't had time to count the doors yet!"

There's that dry wit again, Stuart thought to himself as he smiled and said, "Well, that's where I'll be." Bending over and brushing her cheek with a kiss, he went on, "Before I do turn in though, I'll be back, darling, to tell you goodnight and check on you, So please, won't you get out of your clothes and into your gown, and be all snuggled down in that bed over there when I do get back." And, with that plea finally sounded, he turned and proceeded to leave the bedroom through the same door that he had entered it through.

Jane Anne never noticed though. Neither did she pay any attention to the door inside the water closet that Stuart had referred to when she reentered it to make ready for bed. For no sooner than he had turned his back and she rose to her feet to comply with his wishes, all her awareness, more or less, became claimed by the strange, but powerful exhilarating, feeling that stormed her whole body, a feeling of feather lightness that made her feel as though her feet were no longer on the floor, but floating inches above it instead. She looked down to check, and was not only surprised to note that she was indeed still standing on them, but was also astonished to find that she no longer looked on herself as being heavy and unattractive, despite the fact that she could barely see her feet—only the tips of her shoe toes—over the hump of her protruding stomach.

The fact was, to Jane Anne's amazement, she felt as graceful and light as a bird sailing on air and, literally, skipping inside the water closet she began to sound something like the feathered species, bursting forth with a marry little tune that she attempted to hum through frequent giggles! The shyness and self-doubt that had surfaced in her and threatened to undo her once more a few moments before, were no more, having completely dissolved to nothing.

Hurrying through her toilette and pulling the white gown with the pink rosettes down over her body, Jane Anne near about ran to the large fourposter, blithely falling between its covers and waiting for Stuart as eager as any bride had ever waited for her bridegroom.

And presently Stuart was back and approaching the bedroom door. However, as he lifted his hand and gave the door a light tap to signal his presence, he was thrown somewhat, wondering if that cheerful call of "Come in, darling" that had instantly met his ears was only his imagination since he had yearned for this same sort of happening for so many years, or the real thing voiced by Jane Anne. All the same, the matter was cleared up for him in nothing flat. For as he proceeded to go on and turn the doorknob and softly push the door wide enough for him to step through, there was Jane Anne lying abed with both arms outstretched toward him, crying, in that same gleeful voice, "Come here, darling!"

Though Stuart was gladdened by Jane Anne's most affectionate welcome and a little amused too, he was also somewhat wary, telling himself that with circumstances being as they were that he could not afford to go diving headlong into his bride's bed. In brief, he must make his moves with caution and discipline himself to be in no hurry.

So turning and seeing that the door was closed firmly behind him, Stuart, turning back and making his way toward the bed, said, a smile playing around his mouth, "You aren't, by any chance, luring me over here only to push me in that other room later, are you, sweetheart?"

Letting an arm fall flat upon the covers and using the other to prop her head on her elbow, Jane Anne, taking on a look that was anything but saintly, said, "The other room was your idea, not mine!" Startling Stuart again.

"Well—I—thought... " He stopped, realizing now that in addition to not being able to come up with something that made sense and prudently express it on the spot, that the lie that he had made up about the linen closet was going to be all the more difficult to explain when she found out.

Sober enough to see that she had stumped Stuart and also not too drunk to press the advantage that she saw in it Jane Anne giggled, finishing for him, "That the bed wouldn't be big enough for all three of us! Well, I should think, darling, with it being our wedding night, that you wouldn't be all that concerned about us not having enough room!"

Then, with her expression growing more wayward by the second, she let another giggle roll and went on, "Besides, whether it'll be or not, I know one thing and that is, it's a lot more comfortable than what that bed of dogwood leaves was on the old timber trail last November!"

Suddenly, as Stuart scrutinized his tipsy and forward bride, it happily came to him that the state of Jane Anne's health, as a whole, was not near as serious and alarming as he had thought. He was able to see now, as he studied the lively dance taking place in Jane Anne's deep-grey eyes, that what had mostly overwhelmed him and misled him into thinking her health was rapidly deteriorating was being forced to come face to face with the state of her glaring pregnancy all at once, instead of having the chance to witness its development on a gradual scale.

So, continuing to eye her, Stuart, letting an easy laugh roll too, said, "Well, that being the case, I can't imagine us not making a good thing of it, can you? And, instantly, he was untying the belt to his bath robe. Then, all in one quick move it seemed, he was out of it and falling down beside her, finding ever so quickly again as he gently—and with forethought too—reached for her, that everything was, indeed, going to be all right. No, not as simmering and volcanic as It had been with them upon the bed of dogwood leaves, on no account, she was thinking. But still blissfully satisfying, nevertheless. Yes, the invitation that he had wanted, he had gotten and more. His step grandfather Matthew Carson had seen to that! Christ! The wisdom of the man!

Stuart reached back over his shoulder and feeling for the lamp turned down its wick. And, back at Green Sea, Eliza looked back on her wedding night with Luke and wept for them.

August it was. And it also happened to be exactly nine months to the day that Jane Anne Heyward had headed her mare up the old overgrown timber trail, And moreover, it was also a day that saw the calendar counting Jane Anne's marriage to Stuart Drakston as having occurred no more than a little over three months past a fact that Eliza was still unable to lay aside, churning her blood to a boiling point when Luke said, in answer to her question about the message which had just been delivered to Green Sea and which he still stared at, "It's from Stuart. Kitten's in labor, taken to childbed about dawn this morning."

Pressing on with an anger so heatedly riled that she could

actually see little pinpoints of red before her eyes, Eliza cried, "Is that all the word he sent, only that she's in labor? No word about how she's doing or anything?"

"Yes, there's more, quite a bit more," murmured Luke. Then, lifting eyes that were obviously not paying any attention to his surroundings, he added, "Here, you can read it for yourself." He held the message out for Eliza to take.

Though it grated on Eliza something awful to even touch Stuart Drakston's message that was scribbled on stationery that had his family's armorial insignia blaring on it, something that set her anger aflame all that much more when she spied the Drakston logo, she nevertheless reached for the message and rapidly scanning it began to read in part:

...both Doctor Seth Sr. and Maggie are here with Jane Anne. The doctor says everything in progressing along at a normal pace and that if no drawback arises, which he does not foresee, the baby will come within a few hours from now. No doubt, as they are likewise with me, these hours of waiting are anxious ones for you both. Therefore, instead of waiting them out at Green Sea and wondering how things are going here, why not the both of you come on to Drakston Hall where you'll not only be closer to all firsthand information regarding Jane Anne, but will also be here with the rest of us to hail the baby's arrival and toast its birth, which, in all consciousness, is what I feel should be and what I also feel you both desire in your hearts and what to do. In any event, I will do my best to keep you informed.
Stuart Drakston

Letting Stuart's message fall from her hands and then pushing it as far away from her as she could reach from where she sat at the kitchen table, Eliza said, her voice as deadpan with emotion as her expression, "That man's got crust as thick as an alligator's hide, suggesting that we go to Drakston Hall and hail this baby's birth like no wrongdoing or shame is connected with it at all. Besides, can you, Luke, even imagine seeing anything as preposterous as me and Stuart Drakston drinking a toast together after all the trouble he's put us through?"

"I can certainly imagine seeing worse things and more absurd too, for that matter." Luke hastily shot back.

"What!" Eliza shrieked, losing her deadpan expression on the instant, "You're not suggesting that I—that we..." Her voice trailed in disbelief.

"Take Stuart Drakston up on his proposal?" Luke asked, posing the question for her. "No, not to the letter I'm not, because deep wounds don't heal at the snap of a finger, let alone painful disappointments. It takes time. Still, regarding this troublesome matter, the time factor is over with, finished with; that is, if we are to show that we hold any concern or interest in our daughter's plight as well as let her know that she has our love and understanding. Present circumstances has seen to that, whether we like it or not.

"So, yes, I suppose what I am saying dear, is, that I think we both should head for Drakston Hall just as quickly as we can make ready to head there. However, the question of your drinking a toast with Stuart Drakston, if the occasion should call for it once we do arrive there, is something else again and something that'll be your own affair. In brief, you'll have to decide that for yourself."

Luke stopped and waited, contemplating Eliza and her stunned silence with a wary eye. Finally, as the silence began to stretch on and on, he said, "Well, will you be accompanying me to Drakston Hall, dear?"

"Then, you have made up your mind to go?" She finally asked, side-stepping his question by raising one of her own.

"Of course, I'm going, and as I've just stated, I think you should go, too. The fact is, I should think you'd prefer to be there rather than stay here alone."

"I can't go, Luke. Abiding Stuart Drakston's company in the best of circumstances would drive me bereft of reason, or close to it, much less today of all days when our daughter is laboring to bring forth his child. I simply don't have that kind of tolerance and understanding. You do, but I don't. Besides, I won't be alone. Bessie's always within earshot, Pete too, and Sam's always around some place."

Knitting his brows together in a knot of worry and something close to agitation too, Luke protested, "But, what will you do to fill the hours? You do realize that it's going to be a long and dragging day, do you not? All things considered, it'll probably be dark before I get back, if then. "

"I've thought of that, but I'll be all right. I'll find something to keep me busy."

"Physical labor isn't, exactly, what I'm driving at, dear. I'm well aware of the fact that reposing on your laurels is something you don't do very often. I was thinking how terribly exhausting this waiting is going to be for you. I'd feel much easier about this whole matter if you'd go ahead and make ready to come with me."

"I can't, but come home as quickly as you can, and give Father my love."

What about sending your daughter your love, Luke thought, eyeing his wife none too pleasantly. Still, he never aired his pique. Nor did he let his disappointment in her spill out. Indeed, he did not utter another word because he knew, from past experience, that he might as well save himself the effort. That is, when it came to changing his wife's attitude about Stuart Drakston, or the circumstance of Jane Anne's pregnancy and subsequent marriage to Stuart. So continuing to hold his silence, Luke pulled his gaze away from Eliza and made for the outside kitchen door.

However, Eliza was not surprised at Luke's behavior. Nor was Luke surprised himself. For this was not the first time, in recent months, that her unbounding attitude had induced him to act in this very same manner. In fact, Luke had tried so many times, since Jane Anne's marriage, to change his wife's attitude and gotten nowhere, that stalking away from her and heading for Drakston Hall alone to visit their daughter was getting to be a habitual thing with him. Still,

Luke's disappointment with Eliza had cut a lot deeper today, because he had held hope that Jane Anne's confinement would persuade her to finally set her grievances at rest, but nothing of the kind had happened.

And now as Luke traveled on toward Drakston Hall with his disappointment and dashed hopes, mulling over the situation, he made up his mind that he would offer no more suggestions to Eliza on the subject. In short, Luke had tried and he had failed and he was through! Eliza was going to have to find her own way, he told himself. Her father said she would, said just give her time. Well, he wondered if Matthew Carson's faith in his daughter having a change of heart was going to be all that positive after today, Still, Phil had spent the same opinion about the matter before he had taken off for Lexington last week to visit Beth Anne and Carr, and also, Gilford Sloan and Lucy. Although Phil had been much against Eliza's stand from the first, he was still optimistic that, given time, she would come to view the situation in a different light. Well, how much time was it going to take? A year? Five years? A lifetime? Never? Come to think of it, with Eliza refusing to give in and come to Drakston Hall today, he himself would not be too surprised if the never question were to come to be the draw.

Pushing the horse on toward Drakston Hall, Luke shook his head and, hopelessly, shrugged his shoulders in distaste.

Be that as it may, the broken relationship between herself and her daughter was no merry whirl for Eliza, either. The fact was, had Eliza been called upon to define the turmoil that dwelled within her, she would have found herself as helpless and lost for words had she been born deaf as stone. Certainly, the pain, and hurt were both there, grating on every nerve it seemed. But, even so, by this date, her suffering had become so wretchedly twisted that explaining its ache, or the timing of its beginning, for that matter, would have been impossible for her. Granted, her suffering was far more violent in its wake and far more complex than any measure of thwarted hope or disappointment, no matter how great, that Luke had known, or was experiencing now, for that matter.

For it was Eliza who was marked by the late Frank Drakston's lust—a violation of her body that she had overcome and learned to live with and forgotten, she had thought, until the day her daughter had unexpectedly come home and made the shattering announcement that she was carrying Stuart Drakston's baby and carrying it out of wedlock to boot. Moreover, it happened to be Eliza who was born to the Carson dynasty, a dynasty that she had struggled to keep and hold together with all her might; and one that was also innately ingrained in her and as inseparable from her as the very skin that covered her body. And yet, though Early Cole and Early Cole's sons, the late Frank Drakston had left his mark on this dynasty too, because he could not have what was not his to have in the first place—a mark of grey, smoldering ashes sifting in a March wind— a mark that Eliza had still to overcome when she let her mind stray back to the grand and unique mansion that had made those ashes. And now, from all appearances it seemed Stuart Drakston was about to accomplish what his late father's deeds had failed to do and that was, flag Eliza's spirit and will to a finish. For struggling against an adversary with an objective in mind was one thing, dealing with disgrace and shame; however, to Eliza's way of thinking, was quite another.

Finally pulling herself up from where she sat at the kitchen table,

Eliza also turned and made for the outside kitchen door, Even though the August morning was hot and humid, she walked right on out into the blaring sun without placing a thing on her head to protect her somewhat from the sun's rays—almost a must in the low country's summer heat. At that time; however, even had the blazing heat of a tropic jungle been pouring through the pores of Eliza's body, it is doubtful that she would have taken note of her discomfort. For Eliza was paying no attention to anything. Involuntarily bending her head against the sun, she was merely on the move with no motivation or idea in mind—no thought of where she was headed to, where she wanted to head to, or what she wanted to do. That is, until a short while later when she suddenly found herself on the garden path coming face to face with Pete, who was carrying a large basket on either arm filled with fresh garden vegetables and a number of large ripened apples lying on top of the vegetables, she observed. That's it, she thought to herself as she slowed her steps to a stop. I need to work the time away, stay busy, because idle hands make for nothing but a heavy mind and if mine becomes any heavier, it just might collapse!

Noting that Eliza was pausing her steps, Pete took a step off the pathway and stopped too, thinking as he eased the baskets off his arms and let them rest at his feet that Eliza wanted to have a word with him pertaining to the preparation of the noonday meal.

However, seeing that his mistress appeared to be rather slow about coming out with her suggestions on this occasion—actually preoccupied—Pete took the initiative and spoke first saying, as he wondered why Eliza was not wearing a sunbonnet, "Some powerful hot day we're going to have, Miss Eliza."

"W-hat? Oh! Yes, it's hot already, Pete," she agreed, automatically sweeping a hand to her head and seeming to be surprised that she found no sunbonnet to push back. Letting her hand fall, she added, "August is always like this though. Never remember when it wasn't."

"Yes'um, that's sure fact, Miss Eliza," agreed Pete, pulling his handkerchief forth and wiping the sweat off his face.

"Pete, how long has it been since you've gone into Charleston?" Eliza suddenly blurted.

"Charleston?" Questioned Pete, now taking on a look of surprise himself as he stuffed his handkerchief back in his pocket. "I was there a couple weeks ago, Miss Eliza, with Mister Phil."

"I mean all by yourself to do what you want to do with you time." Eliza said.

"Can't rightly remember that, Miss Eliza," smiled Pete.

"Well, you want to go there today, or if there's some place else you'd like to go to, the rest of the day is yours to do so. I'm going to cook today!"

"But you do that, most every day, Miss Eliza, cook someth'em, I mean," reminded Pete, his smile waving in puzzlement.

"I know, but I'm going to do all the cooking today, dinner and enough for supper, too, while I'm at it. It's been ages since I've cooked a whole meal by myself. So, if you'll just bring the vegetables and apples on to the kitchen, I'll take care of the rest. I think those apples will make real nice apple dumplings, don't you," said Eliza, and whirling around she started back toward the house.

"Yes'um, that's the very thing I gather'em for," replied Pete, more for his own ears than Eliza's, though, because her fast steps had already put a lot of ground between them; and momentarily she was lost from sight, bringing Pete to wonder for a fleeting second if he had encountered his mistress at all, much less heard her right.

Bending down; however, and letting the basket handles slip back over his arms, Pete took on his full smile again, telling himself as he straightened back up and resumed his own steps, "Yes, she was here all right and I didn't misunderstand her, because that's Miss Eliza for you, always full of surprises." Still, he had to admit that when Miss Eliza's surprises concerned him, they were always in his favor rather than against him. However, he thought Miss Eliza's lasting devotion for the slave girl Julia, who had lived at Green Sea long ago and whom Miss Eliza had told him so much about, had had a lot to do with these favors, not to mention all the other good turns that he had come by over the years. Although she had never come right out and said so, it was his belief that Miss Eliza looked on him as being Julia's son. Was he Julia and Jake's son? Oh, yes, he had also heard plenty about Jake too, Julia's husband and Drakston Hall's one-time butler. Lord, how Miss Eliza despised him! She had never forgiven Jake for persuading Julia to leave the security of Green Sea and go away with him when he had had not one thing, by way of advantage, to offer her but plain hearsay.

Well, whatever the case was concerning his parentage as well as the circumstance of his abandonment, if it had to be that he was to be left on someone's doorstep, which he was, he was grateful that they had picked Mister Luke and Miss Eliza's doorstep. For to his way of thinking, he was very much doubtful that he could have come by a better life anywhere. When it came to the ups and downs of life, he could say in all honesty that he had yet to suffer one hardship. He did no field work, nor had he ever done any. He gathered a few vegetables and picked a little fruit from time to time, as he had done today, but nothing more in point of outside work and it had ever been thus for as long as he could remember. In short, when it came to the question of his duties at Green Sea, he was head cook and that was pretty much the scope of it.

The house that he lived in—the small grey house that the Heyward's had lived in for several years—was furnished to him rent free, The Heyward's also provided all his medical needs and all the food he ate. As a matter of fact, he filled his own plate from the same dishes that the

Heyward's filled theirs from. In addition, the Heyward's provided some of his clothing—mainly the lightweight cottons that made up his chef's outfit—and paid him a monthly minimum wage besides, which had enabled him to purchase and own several things for himself. For example, he owned his own horse, a final blooded riding mare that he also had the privilege of housing in Green Sea's stable free of charge. He owned a brand-spanking new buggy, too. Bought it two weeks ago, the same day that he had rode into Charleston with Mister Phil.

Yes, he was grateful for what he deemed his good fortune and, more than satisfied with his role as chef because he truly enjoyed cooking. Still, he could not say that he was not delighted about not having to sweat over the cookpots today. Indeed, it was a most astonishing thing to have happen, considering that it was only no later than yesterday that he heard Miss Eliza say that she was still sick with the flu!

Pete suddenly let his reflecting go and hastened his steps. He was bound for Charleston as soon as he could make ready to leave. His sweetheart lived in Charleston!

Eliza did make the apple dumplings. The golden, crispy mounds now anchored in a rivulet of sweet, spicy apple juice was setting on a back eye of the oversized wood-burning range. In addition, there were a numerous number of other tempting dishes setting around. Some on the stove and some on the kitchen table and some on the sideboard in the dining room, dishes that would have lured the weakest of appetites! There was a big platter of golden fried chicken, corn on the cob, stewed tomatoes, fried okra, potato salad, deviled-eggs, a pot of green beans and small white potatoes seasoned with pork, summer squash, creamed onions, a large platter of fried ham, steamed rice, red gravy and buttermilk biscuits, and cucumber and water cress salad. And, to top all those delectable dishes off, there were two kinds of pie for dessert—chess and chocolate—setting on the sideboard in the dining room! Each and every dish typical low country cuisine.

Eliza had cooked all day and to observe this handiwork of hers from a standpoint of quantity and culinary skill, not only would one have sworn that she had prepared for a barn raising but had been born to the task as well.

But now with the waning sun casting its last glint of sunlight upon the fertile and fruitful land—a time that told one the supper hour was drawing near, Eliza took a long look at her overladen kitchen and realized, for the first time, that there was not one soul there to set the table for but her lone self! So resolved she had been to keep going and not sit and dwell on the momentous event taking place at Drakston Hall, that never once had she stopped to consider that she was cooking all these dishes for a total empty table, so to speak! But, all the same, even as she became mindful of the matter and felt the stillness of the house raining down on her, Eliza knew what she was going to do and promptly lifting her voice she called out to Bessie.

Bessie was on the back porch and there was where she had been for the greater part of the day. She was occupied with the weekly ironing, having taken the advantage of heating the flatirons that she was using on the cook stove while Eliza was cooking. Bessie had wondered, all day, if there were going to be a barn raising at Green Sea that she had not heard about, as she had gone back and forth in the process of exchanging her irons. So now looking forward to having the question finally put to an end, Bessie stood her flatiron up and went spurting into the kitchen.

"Yes'um, Miss Eliza," she said, taking in once again all the filled platters, bowls and steaming pots.

Turning around from where she was staring through the kitchen window, Eliza said, "Bessie, as you see, there's a lot of food here that's going to spoil if it isn't eaten today, So..."

"Yes' um, fo' the last little while, I've been thinkin' that very thing myself, Miss Eliza, since I know no barn raising's goin' get started today. The sun's too low to start now," interrupted Bessie.

"A barn raising?" Questioned Eliza. "You've been thinking I was cooking for a barn raising? I should think, Bessie, that you'd know that we don't have barn raisings in the hot summertime unless we lose one and see we can't save the tobacco crop without replacing it." A sudden undertone of pique had entered Eliza's voice.

"Yes'um, I do know that, but..." Bessie stopped suddenly mindful that she had already jumped at one conclusion too many.

"I know." Eliza suddenly smiled, easing Bessie's obvious chagrin. "You couldn't see me or anyone else cooking this much food unless there were going to be a dozen hungrier men around to eat it up. Well, to tell you the truth, Bessie, neither can I. But I had to keep busy and I felt that cooking was what I wanted to do. Anyway, that's why I called you. Before it gets any later and they leave work to fix their supper, I want you to run to the tobacco barn and tell Ruth, Daisy, and Prudence not to cook one bit tonight. There's enough food here for them and their families and yours too. You're welcome to eat here or take it to your own house, whatever suits you best. See that there's a plate left for Pete, though, in case he hasn't eaten when he gets home," Slipping out of her apron, which protected her pretty blue and white checked gingham dress from grease and spills, and hanging it on the wall rack, she added, "I'm going to get a breath of fresh air. The sun's down now, it'll be refreshing to be outside." She headed for the outside door.

"What about you and Mister Luke, Miss Eliza, your supper, I mean?" Bessie called to her back.

Eliza stopped and after a long minute, in which she had appeared to be weighing the question, she finally said, "I have a feeling, Bessie, that Luke's fasting today. He's at Drakston Hall, Jane Anne was taken to childbed this morning. You might take out a couple chicken legs though and leave a piece of chess pie for him, in the event I'm wrong. As for myself, I don't want one bite." She went on through the door,

"Yes' um." Bessie murmured, fully aware now why there were so many eatables waiting to be devoured. And then, making sure that her voice spanned the mounting distance between herself and Eliza's departing back, she hollered, "I'll take care of it, Miss Eliza." And, as Bessie took another fast look around the kitchen and made for the outside door herself, she was thinking, "I sure enough will, not only

---

take out enough for Mister Luke's supper, Miss Eliza, but fix you a plate, too, because who else would stand and cook over a hot cook stove all day just for the sake of keeping busy!" Still she was not surprised even if Miss Eliza had overleaped the bounds of her good brains today because Miss Jane Anne was in labor. For nobody worked any harder than Miss Eliza. Mister Luke shouldered his share too. They were good people, Mister Luke and Miss Eliza, the very best. No wonder their sharecroppers and tenants stayed on at Green Sea year after year after year. As for Sam and herself, they would not live no place else. Sam was born at Green Sea. Green Sea was his home and, from the day Sam had brought her there, she had felt that it was her home too. In fact, she intended to be buried at Green Sea. No sirree, she had no intentions of ever leaving Green Sea!"

Bessie quickened her pace into a run. She had a number of errands to carry through with.

Pulling on the horse's reins and stopping the buggy, Luke peered through the gathering darkness and called, his voice high-pitched with anxiousness, "Sweetheart, is that you?" Though he had mouthed the question, he could hardly believe that he had guessed the true identity of the lone figure walking on the shoulder of the road toward Drakston Hall.

"Oh! Yes—Yes, Luke, it's me!" Eliza called back, running fervently toward the stalled buggy.

Throwing the reins down and leaping to the ground, Luke, hurrying forth to shorten the distance between them, cried aloud, "Everything's fine, dear! But, pray tell me, what are you doing way out here? Where are you walking to, anyhow? Do you realize you're over halfway to Drakston Hall?"

"Never mind how far I've walked, Luke, it doesn't matter!" Eliza gasped, as the distance between them was finally closed. "You say she's all right? What—What about the baby? Is it all right, too? You've been gone so long and I was so worried." Her voice sounded tired but suddenly more relaxed.

"The baby?" Laughed Luke, his laughter sounding happy. "You want to know about the baby? What about both babies, sweetheart?"

"Both—Both babies, Luke? Are you saying there's two babies, that Jane Anne's given birth to two babies today—twins?" The enormity and girth of Jane Anne's belly was suddenly arresting Eliza's mind and not without some conscience to boot.

"You bet, I am!" Luke guffawed again. "And I could simply

shout from the pure joy of it!"

Twins! Two perfect, darling babies, a boy and a girl! None of us could believe it, Seth least of all. It staggered him, too, and your father teased the poor man something awful. He told Seth that he would've liked to have some warning that the shock of being great grandfather to twins was no small matter to take in, and especially for someone who had climbed to the age he had.

"And guess what, sweetheart! They already have names. They've been named for both sets of grandparents. The boy's name is Luke Franklin, and they've named the girl Mary Elizabeth. Twins! I still can hardly believe it. Just think, Eliza dear, we've become grandparents and grandparents of twins at that!"

In a voice that sounded as utterly drained of emotion as one might come out with, Eliza said, "And to think they had to be born in shame," abruptly silencing Luke's happiness as still as the quiet of the night falling around them.

Finally, as the crowding hush between them continued to lengthen and build, Luke said, his voice void of all gladness, "Come on, dear, let's get on to the house. It's been a long day for the both of us."

He reached for Eliza's hand and graciously assisted her in gaining the buggy seat.

The latter part of September, Eliza and Luke journeyed to Lexington, Virginia. The news that Beth Anne Carson Heyward had been safely delivered of a strapping seven-pound baby boy was the main, if not the sole, reason for their making the trip. Yes, after a long seven months seclusion, Eliza Heyward had finally emerged from behind Green Sea's closed doors—closed so to speak because not since the previous February had one social event come off at Green Sea. No dinner parties, no visiting or social doings of any kind, had Eliza Heyward been involved in. That is, not counting those occasions when Martha Randolph and Mollie Cooper had dropped in at Green Sea to check on her lingering "flu" and she had been forced to receive them and visit!

The truth was, up until now, it was almost as if a plague epidemic had been raging at Green Sea. At any rate, the birth of Philippe Matthew Carson—this was the baby's full Christian name—had brought Eliza Heyward out of hiding at last; and as much as Luke was grateful and was taking joy from the gift of this additional grandchild in whom the Heyward family lineage continued, he did not go to Lexington without some misgivings and guilt too, due to the fact that Eliza had yet to go to Drakston Hall to see Stuart and Jane Anne's month-old twins. And in addition, what seemed, to Luke, to make the situation worse, certainly widening the gap between Jane Anne and her mother even further, was Jane Anne's steadfast refusal to accept Eliza's invitation to visit at Green Sea with the twins without Stuart being made welcome too. In brief, Luke had found that his quiet and gentle daughter, if she was so minded to be, was just as strong-willed and rigid in her convictions and beliefs as her fiery and highly emotional mother was or ever could be. Still, the essence of his daughter's stand Luke did see and sympathized with, and in so doing, it was impossible for him to journey to Lexington in the spirit that he would have liked to gone there with.

The journey turned out to be rewarding enough though, Indeed, for all the good and many blessings that were to come of it, it also set afloat the making of another reward that not only came at a later date but proved to be something that neither Luke or Eliza banked on happening or was aware of at the time.

For then; however, besides having plans to visit with Tom and Betsy Green on their return trip home, which naturally gave Luke and Eliza both an additional something to look forward to, there was the thrill of hearing Carr's hearty yell upon their arrival at the train depot in Lexington; and, at the same time, knowing the joy of a divine grace and reveling in it, as Carr came racing toward them with his beaming face and open arms. Then presently, there was the warm and tender meeting with Beth Anne, and the moving experience of looking upon the new baby for the first time. Matthew, they were already calling him; and both Luke and Eliza were quick to note, that if looks meant anything, that a more deserving name he could not have come by. For a miniature Matthew Carson, he was! Little wonder of that fact though, considering that both his parents before him had inherited the same dominant Carson features—dark brown curly hair and deep-set violet-blue eyes.

Philippe Carson, who was still visiting in Lexington, simply adored the baby. In fact, Matthew was so cuddling and such a lamb besides that everybody adored him, family and friends alike and that included Gilford and Lucy Randolph Sloan as well as the Simpson family next door who, by this date, had finally reconciled themselves to Beth Anne and Carr's marriage because the young couple ever appeared to be so delighted with one another, to say nothing of the apparent joy that they seemed to draw from the marriage institution itself.

At any rate, the newborn Heyward baby did have plenty admirers and was passed from one pair of loving arms to another rather frequently. That is, this was the way of things until Eliza's arrival. For once the baby was passed to Eliza's arms, that was where he stayed no matter how many more arms were waiting to hold him. For hours on end, she sit and rocked Matthew, not only wrapped up in her adoration of him as she kept the rocker going at an easy pace, but also overwhelmed over the fact that she was truly rocking the future heir to Green Sea. Though she did think when she allowed herself to give thought to it, and especially since the Carson features were so prominently present in the baby, that it was somewhat ironic that his surname was Heyward rather than Carson. Still. Eliza did not let this aspect regarding the heirship bother her. The important thing was, Matthew was the heir and hearing his feet pattering through the house at Green Sea was something that she was awaiting most expectantly. For, although it would not happen until his father completed another full year of law school, Matthew and his parents would be coming to Green Sea to dwell where they belonged.

Granted, to Eliza, the visit to Lexington was like taking a soothing sedative every day—the kind of prescription that both her mental and physical makeup had required so desperately and one that Doctor Seth Roalf would not have found for her had he experimented and given her every kind of medicine that was known to his profession. For the mitigator that was calming Eliza's wounded spirit and bringing a degree of balance to her conflicting emotions was not to be found in a medicine bottle.

Indeed, the soother that Eliza had come by was made of original and firsthand things, ingredients that only Lexington could provide and make available to her. For example, the unique delight that was hers to relish in her self-appointed role as baby sitter to Matthew, the easy, harmonious friendship that was taking root and growing more solid each day between herself and her daughter-in-law who was also her blood niece, the long affable chitchats with her beloved son and all those other animated visits that she took part in when Carr and all the rest of the Lexington family members as well and often as not Gilford and Lucy Sloan too, gathered in the warmth of the fireplace in the evenings to exchange notes and happenings of the day—all this, was that special prescription which Eliza's soul was feeding on and which, in due course, would help her make the move that would make her whole again and set her free.

The close relationship between Gilford Sloan and vibrant Beth Anne was still intact and solid as ever. Although they were not related by blood one fraction, to Beth Anne, Gilford Sloan was no less an uncle than had he been related to her not once but twice over by blood. He was "Uncle Gilford" and she adored him and that was that. Therefore, Lucy Randolph upon her marriage to Gilford Sloan, had, automatically, become "Aunt Lucy" to Beth Anne. So, since it was only natural that Carr follow suit and do the same, the Sloan's had become uncle and aunt to Carr, too.

The Sloans and the young Heywards saw a lot of one another. In fact, hardly a day passed that Gilford Sloan did not drop in to check on the Heyward's. He had taken up the habit when Philippe Carson had gone back to live at Green Sea. And although he was understanding over the fact that Carr, Beth Anne, and the baby would be making their home at Green Sea, once Carr finished law school, and reasoned that this was the way things should be, Gilford Sloan deeply regretted to see the day come. Still, knowing that there would be intermittent visiting back and forth, and in the case of Lucy and himself not only paying visits to Green Sea but Oak Grove too, Gilford Sloan took solace from this promising prospect and bore up to his disappointment, determined that when time did bring the young family's absence about, that he would make something good out of the situation rather than being low and sorrowful over it. Of course, the regret that Gilford Sloan carried over the young Heyward's leaving Lexington was not as poignant and sharp with him as it would have been had there been no Lucy Randolph to share his life with. For what, actually, gave substance to Gilford Sloan's wills, his hopes and desires and made them meaningful to him nowadays, was Lucy, his wife. She was the nutriment that sustained his self-discipline and upheld and braced his determinations.

Yes, because of his marriage to Lucy Randolph, Gilford Sloan had finally become an untroubled and well-contented man. And, if the light that seemed to ever shine on Lucy's face was any sign, one would have said the same for her.

Eliza, observing this radiance now on Lucy's face, spoke of it to her as the two of them were conversing for still another time since Eliza had arrived in Lexington. Eliza and Luke had called on the

Sloan's and as the faint hum of Gilford Sloan's printing press came from downstairs where he was busy showing Luke around, Eliza said, "Lucy, it makes me truly feel good to look at you. You seem so happy and contented."

Handing Eliza a cup of freshly-brewed tea, Lucy smiled and said, "Does it stand out all that much?"

"On my word of honor," laughed Eliza as Lucy poured herself a cup of tea and took a seat opposite Eliza.

"Well, I'm glad it shows because I am happy, Eliza," declared Lucy, as she settled back in her chair, "more than I ever dreamed possible. You must know, I can't ever remember when I didn't love your brother, Nat. In fact, my love for Nat was so deep and compelling, that never did I give one thought to marrying anyone else. Then, Nat was killed at Yellow Tavern, and after the horror of that experience, knowing that I'd never see him again, let alone being prevented the opportunity to marry him, I was certain I'd live out the rest of my days in spinsterhood. I think Gilford felt likewise after experiencing the tragic death of his wife there at the end of the war. Anyway, maybe this common bond of loss and grief made us vulnerable to one another, I don't know. What I do know is, from the first moment I met Gilford, I was to see everything in a different light. As near as I can explain my feelings at the same time, I felt as though I'd suddenly untied a blindfold from around my head."

"But Nat's been gone such a long time, Lucy. Maybe that's why you felt as you did and was, eventually, able to love again."

"No doubt about that," agreed Lucy. "Still, I should think that since Gilford and I were attracted to one another when we did finally meet, that no matter what period in our lives we have may met that our feelings would've been no different. I deeply regret that we didn't meet in earlier years, those years following the war I mean, because there's no question in my mind that had that been our fortune, both our lives as a whole, would've been so much lighter and rewarding in many ways."

"Such as, if I may venture to ask, Lucy?" Eliza said, her gaze on Lucy's face becoming more attentive—searching.

"Well, for one thing, being able to give Gilford a child. He simply adores children, but our having a child together at the age I've become now, is unthinkable. I'm too old." Lucy's face, as well as her voice, suddenly lost its lightness.

"Oh, Lucy, I'm so sorry," murmured Eliza, a poignant sadness piercing her heart. "Time does have a way of altering so many things about our lives that, as a rule, we never give a thought or apply it to ourselves until we're suddenly forced to face the fact that we're no exception in the case. That doesn't mean though that I'm agreeing with that remark that you've just made about you being old. You're still a very vital and attractive woman and I don't want you to forget it!" All at once, Eliza's words were coming through with a driving force. "So the springtime of your life has disappeared, and mine, too, for that matter, I should think that that's no reason for either of us to start thinking in terms of winter yet! Maybe midsummer or early autumn, but certainly not winter, by no means!"

Dropping her gloom as quickly as she had taken it on, Lucy laughed, "That's what Gilford tells me, though I must admit never as quaintly as that in spite of all the experience he's had in dealing with words, either! Gracious no, I should say not!" She shrugged at the thought and laughed again. Then just as quickly her face was straight once more and she was adding, changing the subject altogether, "Tell me, Eliza, what's new back home? We really haven't had the chance to talk like this, to ourselves I mean, since your arrival here in Lexington. How's Martha doing? Is she still up in arms over Laura marrying that stage performer? And what about Grace Cooper's marriage? Is it working out? Most of all though, I want to hear about Jane Anne and those darling babies that she's given birth to." Lucy leaned forward somewhat, her face most expectant—waiting.

Appearing to be rather hesitant about granting Lucy's request, Eliza, draining the last sip from her teacup and setting it aside, finally said, "I truly don't know very much to tell, Lucy, firsthand I mean, because this is the first time I've ventured from the premises of Green Sea for months. First things first though, I'll venture to say that I believe Martha has come to accept the fact that she's going to see mighty little of Laura unless this Cornwallis Silverspoon, who Laura married, decides to abandon the stage for some other type of work. I understand the troupe that he performs with is in Chicago at the present time, and Laura writes that, eventually, it will come to Charleston. I truly hope so, not only for Martha's sake but for Laura's too."

"Oh, I hope so too!" Lucy cried. "That's wonderful news. I'd so much love seeing her."

"Yes, and so would I, and if all goes well and Cornwallis Silverspoon doesn't fall down on the job like breaking a leg or something, while he's up there on that stage flouncing around as

Martha says, maybe we will." Eliza said, her voice no less sober than had she been a judge handing down a sentence. Then after giving a rather long and wearisome sigh, she went on to oblige, "I gather Grace Cooper's married life, or Grace Blake's I should say, is just as orderly and serene as her single days ever were. Mollie tells me that Cyrus Blake's medical practice is flourishing and that he and Grace are expecting their first child in early spring.

"I guess you already know that Bill Cooper also married into the Blake family, Harriett Blake the doctor's sister. I understand that he and Harriett spend about as much time at Foxwood, that's Harriett's home in Mississippi, as they do at the Cooper residence in Charleston. The word is going around that Foxwood is one of the show places in Mississippi."

"So I've heard." Lucy averred.

"Well," Eliza went on, the tone of her voice bland as water still, "Mollie says that everything about it is nothing but pure grandeur, so I reckon you've heard right. Yes, the Cooper children have done their parents proud. It's a pity and a shame, a shame that I might add that's about done me in, that I can't say the same; that is, in my daughter's case, I mean."

"But you can be proud of your daughter, Eliza!" Lucy promptly cried, astonished that Eliza would speak of Jane Anne in this manner.

Countering right back with a reproving look, Eliza said, "Proud that she and Stuart Drakston have blackened my family's good name for all time. No, I should think not, Lucy. Besides, I should also hope that you realize that's not only asking the ultimate of one's tolerance but going far beyond all I'm ever possessed with or have to give in the first place."

"I'm sorry, Eliza, I didn't mean to give offense. Nor do I mean to probe where I have no business. But I still maintain that regardless of any premature timing connected with those twins' birth that Jane Anne is a daughter whom you can take pride in." Challenging Eliza's reproving gaze, she added, "I, too, should think that you, Eliza, least of all, would denounce this one wrong on your daughter's part, so severely."

Obviously piqued, Eliza snapped, her voice sounding calm no longer, "What would you have me do then, uphold it, when I feel humiliated and ashamed that even thinking about attending church again, let alone having to face my neighbors and friends, near makes me ill?"

"No, not uphold it, Eliza, but accept it." Lucy replied. Then rising to her feet she moved to where Eliza sit and squatting down she reached for Eliza's hand and went on, "It's not the end of the world, Eliza. You know, it's like Gilford says. He has so much wisdom when it comes to things of this nature, or at least I've come to think so and I believe you will, too, when you've had time to give some thought to his way of thinking.

Gilford says we all prize and place too much emphasis on public opinion when in the long run, it has very little if anything at all, to do with having happiness and peace of mind. He says the things that truly sustains us, the things that inspires our hopes and our dreams and makes for our happiness as a whole are love of God, good health, and devotion of family and friends. Gilford says without these things our existence here comes to be nothing. Further, you aren't responsible, Eliza, for someone else's mistakes. Please, won't you give thought to that too? Promise?"

Unable to dismiss the earnestness that she saw on Lucy's face as well as the validity of her request, Eliza, forcing herself to bury her pique then and there, said, "I promise, Lucy."

No sooner than they had taken their departure of the Sloan residence, Luke noted there was something different about Eliza. Though he had no name or answer for it, he knew her too well not to know that it was there. Even though she was and continued to be obliging and receptive, responding to family members and friends and the bustle and flatter of each day's activity as normally as one would expect of a guest for the remainder of their stay in Lexington, he nevertheless knew that something was amiss with Eliza regardless of how much she tried to hide it from him—something in the wind so to speak that not only was testing her will and her courage but all her patience as well.

Still, Luke let the matter rest, asking no questions due to the fact that, aside from himself, it seemed nobody else was aware that something was going on with Eliza. In addition, and most important too, Eliza did not appear to be depressed in the least, which, of course, Luke silently thanked his maker for many times oven For, to Luke, seeing Eliza merely harboring a doubt or some impression was one thing, Seeing her submerged in a pool of gloom though was quite another.

Nonetheless, to Luke's bewilderment, he saw no change in Eliza's manner. That is, no change that unfamiliar that he was seeing in her. Nothing seemed to dissolve it, not even on the day of their departure from Lexington when Carr had announced that he, Beth Anne, and baby Matthew would be coming to Green Sea at Christmastime, and this joyous news was hers to hold, to say nothing of the pleasant visit that was to come a day or two later with Tom and Betsy Green. Of course, Luke would have been the first to admit that Eliza had appeared and was; indeed, overjoyed at Carr's news. And further, he also would have acknowledged that Eliza had been most agreeable and affable during their stay with Tom and Betsy. But, even so, by the time that he and Eliza returned back to Green Sea, Luke was beginning to feel as if he and Eliza were talking to one another through a wire fence,

Be that as it may; however, more surprises were yet to come from Eliza. For in less than no time after her arrival home, she was back in the kitchen embarking on another cooking spree! Phil, who had accompanied the Heyward's back to Green Sea, brought the matter to Luke's attention as the latter sat in his study going over his account books.

The three had arrived home early that Saturday morning. Now approaching Luke's desk, Phil said, "Luke, is there some kind of celebration taking place around here tomorrow that I haven't heard about?"

"Celebration?" Luke repeated, wondering what had prompted Phil to raise such a question.

Not that I'm aware of, why?"

"Well, considering all the eats that Eliza and Pete are busy preparing, one would think so. The sideboard in the dining room is already loaded from end to end with different pastries, besides all the other dishes they're busy with. It looks like Christmas back there, I asked Eliza if we were celebrating something tomorrow, like someone's birthday or anniversary because I'd prefer to be set for it rather than caught empty-handed, and you know what her reply to me was?"

"What?" Luke asked, his curiosity beginning to run like wildfire.

"We'll see," said Phil, plainly showing his fret over the matter by punctuating the remark with emphasis. "Now what kind of an answer is that, pray tell me! Makes me think something's going on that I'm not supposed to know about."

"No, I don't think it's anything like that, I mean anything that concerns you." Luke quickly assured. "I think it's safe to bet though that your sister and my wife is up to something in spite of all the cooking that's going on."

"What are you getting at?" Queried Phil, pricking up his ears for the ready.

"You mean to say that you haven't noticed that Eliza seems different these past few days, sort of—well—sort of preoccupied and elsewhere at times—distracted with some matter that not only appears to be weighing on her, but one that she's counting time against besides? For if you haven't, you take me by surprise, because when it comes to make-up and inner nature, I see yours and your sister's as being pretty much the same. That also applies to Mr. Carson, your daughter, and my son as well. In substance, I see the whole lot of you as having the same infixed spirit of manner and disposition. Anyhow, getting back to Eliza, I've detected a vast change in her. Yes, I'm positive, despite all the cooking that you say she and Pete are doing this morning, that something's going on with her and has been for several days now."

"For several days," echoed Phil, his voice betraying his agitation with Luke because the latter had come no closer in answering what he was trying to find out than Eliza had. All he had gotten, he felt, had been a brief in personality make-up. He went on, "It's my opinion, Luke, that something's been going on with my sister far longer than a few days! In fact, I'd say since last February when she let this matter concerning Stuart Drakston and Jane Anne get out of hand. No, I did not approve of their conduct and still don't. But, the thing is, it's time that Eliza laid it aside and quit passing judgment on them. Christ! We all make mistakes! Can't she accept that fact and live with it?"

"She's suffered a terrible blow," Luke defended. "Besides, Mr. Carson says she'll come around, says just give her time."

"Time," echoed Phil again as he let an incredulous gaze hang on Luke's face. "Heavens! That's the very thing, Luke, I'm trying to call your attention to. For this matter in question didn't happen just last week or a few days back. It happened over eight months ago, and appears to be as fresh as ever with Eliza. Can't you and Pa see this?" Thinking it was wiser to let his question hang and make his exit, then and there, he shrugged his shoulders and made for the door.

Although both of them staunchly refused to acknowledge its presence by being as amicable toward one another as always, something remarkably close to a chill—the first—hang between

Luke and Phil at the breakfast table next morning. In fact, both men were so preoccupied with trying to be overly pleasant to the other, doing their best to pretend that no difference of opinion had come up and stood between them concerning the matter of Eliza's behavior, that neither seemed to be aware that she was also at the breakfast table too.

However, the situation was to change, and change so startlingly fast that not only were Luke and Phil left silently wide-eyed and open-mouthed, but Pete too. For as Luke interrupted his pleasantries with Phil to ask Pete, who had stepped into the dining room to refill everybody's coffee cup, to tell Sam that it was time to ready his horse and buggy to drive to church, Eliza cheerfully piped, "No, Pete, tell Sam to prepare the surrey instead, for I'll be attending church today also! "

Now it was fact that Pete's sense of hearing was sound and had ever been true in maximum strength. It was also fact that Pete was not in the habit of commenting upon his mistress' statements. Nor did he ever appraise them or question them.

However, considering that Pete had heard Eliza state numerous times, in past months, that she did not know when she would dart the door of the Baptist Church again, if she ever did, not to mention that he was also well aware that Eliza continued to maintain to whomever happened to inquire that she still suffered from the flu, it came only as a natural reflex that Pete felt compelled to blurt now, as he gathered his wits about him and clutched the coffeepot tighter to keep from dropping it, "Did you say, for sure, to have the surrey readied, Miss Eliza?"

Taking a sip of coffee and then endeavoring to peer at Luke and Phil over the rim of her coffee cup as she responded, Eliza said, "Yes, I said for sure, Pete, because I have no intention of riding all the way to church and back squeezed in between two grown men on a small buggy seat! I should imagine what my dress would look like, no doubt give every appearance that I'd been using it to sleep in all these past months! Besides, I want to look as personable when I arrive as I possibly can so everybody can see that, despite fighting the flu for well into a year now, I'm still fairly steady and enduring, too, I hope!"

"Yes'um, you bets Miss Eliza, and the surrey it is," assured Pete. And turning back to the kitchen he smiled and told himself that Miss Eliza's reappearance at the Baptist Church was going to be one event

The Gathering

that he would sure like to see. Still, on second thought, he was thinking he was not so certain that he wanted to witness the event after all; that is, unless he wanted to see the Reverend Marsh Reed rendered out cold. For taking into account the many times that he had overheard the reverend trying to get Miss Eliza to go back to church and getting nowhere, he was sure that that was going to happen to the reverend when he saw Miss Eliza today!

Though Luke Heyward might have turned to Phil Carson and said "I told you so", he was never moved to do so simply because crowing, or handing bouquets to himself, was not his style. Instead, he reached across the table and laying his hand on his wife's arm, he said, "That's the best news I've heard for many a day, darling. Of course, we'll drive the surrey. The weather out there today couldn't be better for traveling in it."

Phil Carson, still gaping at his sister with arched brows, said nothing.

As for Eliza herself, she merely gave Luke a slight nod and then asking to be excused, she fled the table in a hurry.

In truth, Eliza's sudden decision to attend church had been spontaneous and not planned, actually having surprised herself when she had popped out with it almost as much as she had surprised anyone else. Although, ever since her talk with Lucy Sloan, she had known that she was going to do something about the estrangement that existed between her daughter and herself, she had not known what she was going to do, or when, until now.

The cooking spree that Eliza had embarked on the day before had, more or less, been a way of dispelling her nervous energy once more; and also, making certain at the same time that there would be plenty of food on hand to feed the usual flock of Sunday guests, as well as those of whom who happened to drop in at Green Sea by chance.

Still, if that were the case, Eliza was now thinking as she pulled the new gold-colored dress that she had purchased in Lexington over her head and smoothed it down over her hips, why had she gone to all the trouble yesterday to make certain that her daughter's two favorite dishes _lemon meringue pie and Southern-fried chicken— would be among the array of edibles served at Green Sea today?

And further, since she was aware that Jane Anne was attending church again and also taking the twins along with her instead of leaving them behind at Drakston Hall with a wet nurse—she had

337

heard Luke praising their daughter for this—had she known all along that she, too, would be resuming her churchgoing today as well; and, no doubt, resuming for the sole purpose of seeing Jane Anne and those two babies whom she yet had to cast her eyes upon?

Well then, since she was finally getting the whole picture of her recent moves together and also admitting to herself why she had and was making them, what did she have in mind to do, or say, when she saw Jane Anne? Moreover, what about Stuart Drakston? How was she going to deal with him? Certainly, her hostility toward Stuart Drakston had grown no less. So, taking that fact into account, was she planning on addressing him and let it go at that, or just ignore him completely, because it was inconceivable to see herself hiding her feelings and trying to be pleasant toward him to any degree. However, she must not forget that if she were to choose to do the latter, act as if Stuart Drakston were totally out of the picture, Jane Anne just might retaliate by brushing any gesture that she might make toward her aside; and that possibility was too upsetting to even take into consideration, let alone trouble her mind with!

Oh dear, the whole troublesome matter was enough to addle her wits for all time, not to mention putting grey hairs in her head. Grey hairs? She must check! Oh fiddle-faddle, she couldn't even see her hair because of this stupid-looking hat that she had on her head! As a matter of fact, with its oversized brim and all those gold plumes dangling over and around it, she could barely see her face, let alone her hair!

Why she had bought such an outlandish hat was a riddle to her to start with! She supposed it was on account of Lucy Sloan saying that she looked like a million in it and going on to point out that its color, which did match her dress to a T, was not only great for her but would also get her away from the habit of wearing blue so much because blue was Luke's favorite color!

Well, she guessed she had needed Lucy's advice and compliment. Certainly, she could see now that she had needed the flattery far more than she had needed the hat though! What on earth would Luke think when he saw her? Would he go for the hat and its gold plumes? Come to think of it, Rebecca had caught Luke's eye when she had worn her plumes!

Poor Rebecca, the news of her death that day years ago had been so sudden and unexpected. It had truly shocked Luke and her both. The fact was, Luke had deeply mourned Rebecca's death. To tell the truth, although Luke had ever denied it, she was positive that he had been attracted to the late Rebecca Wainwright Drexwell, and she to him, but the circumstance of Rebecca having married Luke's guardian and friend, Hugh Wainwright and Luke's high morals—she was certain Rebecca would not have given a hoot about morals—had kept their relationship in check and, in every respect, strictly platonic.

At any rate, it had been a long time since Rebecca's plumes had forced Luke's morals to make a run for it, and she surely hoped hers would do no less even if she yet had to see the day when she found herself in want for his attention! Most assuredly, she was going to trust that when Luke saw her and those dangling plumes, that he was going to be inclined to like and appreciate what he saw, instead of letting himself be persuaded to think that she looked like the late plume—crowned Jeb Stuart riding forth to battle! In any event, she must stop fretting over the matter and move on or by the time she got to church, the Reverend Marsh Reed could very well be already drained and petered out of all and any spiritual guidance that was his to offer a sinner; and, in her view, she was one who needed all the help, in that respect, that she could come by!

Immediately quelling her rambling thoughts, Eliza hesitated a moment longer and, once again, peered intently into the mirror, Then suddenly shrugging off the plume-decked hat, which she gazed at and which she saw was all but threatening to engulf the image that she saw staring back at her, she went rushing toward the door.

If Luke or Phil for that matter, was reminded of the Civil War cavalry leader, the late flamboyant J.E.B. Stuart when Eliza came rushing down the front steps toward the waiting surrey In all her gold-colored, plume-decked finery, he did not speak of it. Phil merely let forth with a loud whistle and Luke—though he was rather surprised that Eliza had decided to swathe herself in bright gold from head to foot—only expressed his delight in seeing her in the new outfit, which, to him, did seem to make Eliza shimmer as radiant and bright as the October gold's that decked the countryside even if the color blue did take precedence with him.

However, as the surrey began to roll along toward the Baptist Church and Eliza began over again to acquaint herself with the good of the land and revel in it—creative goodness like the beaming, bright sky that shone above her and the throng of wildlife that sang and flounced in its halcyon warmth—spiritual food an essential that

Louise Gore Sayre-David

her very soul had ever needed and cried for and one that she had deprived it of for so many months, she began to experience such a thankfulness for the world and life itself, that fretting over something as insignificant as the plumes on her hat counted no more with her. The fact was, her concern over her appearance vanished. No more did she care if she did remind Luke of the late J.E.B. Stuart!

Eliza felt good, better than she had felt for a long, long time and the feeling continued to hold. Even when she finally swept inside the church on Luke's arm—procrastinating at her mirror had made them a little late—and spied Stuart Drakston sitting only a few pews away, she did not feel any less exhilarated or unhappy. Nor was she vexed when the Reverend Marsh Reed chose to stretch his damning sermon way beyond his usual time limit. As a matter of fact, she became so busy and preoccupied with receiving and returning numerous smiles and nods of welcome that had come her way throughout the service, that concentrating on other matters had simply been out, the presence of Stuart Drakston and the reverend's damnatory raps included— raps that she was positive Marsh Reed had made for her benefit alone; that is, when one did happen to make its dent upon her!

At any rate, her presence in church had stirred an awful lot of attention and when Marsh Reed had finally ceased his flailings and dismissed the congregation, Eliza found the attention all the more overwhelming. In brief, she became center of attraction and could not help thinking that her crazy hay was, no doubt, luring part of it! Swamped by the curious as well as those of whom who were truly devoted to her, she became besieged by hugs and kisses alike and not only was forced to inch her way down the church aisle toward the door, but became separated from Luke in the process.

Marsh Reed—no, he had not fallen dead as Pete had feared, but looked like he was pretty close to it—managed to reach her and pumped her hand for at least five minutes, or at least long enough that it dawned on Eliza, that he was probably waiting to be invited to Green Sea for dinner! She issued the invitation. Martha Randolph was another who finally made it to Eliza, and linking her arm in Eliza's arm, she never let go until she had shepherded Eliza through the throng of greeters and on to the outside grounds where the latter suddenly found herself within an arm's reach of Jane Anne and Stuart as well as seeing the twins for the first time.

In any event, aside from Martha who was still very much present beside her, the crowd that had flocked around Eliza had finally

340

disappeared. And now, not only was she face to face with her daughter whom she had not seen for months but also face to face with Stuart Drakston whom she thought she loathed. Both Jane Anne and Stuart, Eliza observed, were both holding an infant baby in their arms. She also observed that both babies were swaddled in light woolen shawls of the same make but of a different color. The baby in Jane Anne's arms was swaddled in pink. The other baby's shawl was blue, Eliza noted.

Though Eliza's devotion for her daughter had truly never wavered and was as deep and abiding as ever, and she was deeply moved to see Jane Anne, it nevertheless was the bundle in Jane Anne's arms that stirred her emotions the most—the key that finally turned the lock in Eliza's heart and reconciled it to the inevitable.

So powerfully drawn Eliza had become toward the pink-swaddled infant, hungering to touch this small bundle of humanity who not only was flesh of her daughter's flesh but flesh of hers and Luke's own bloodline as well, that it might have been some magnetic device pulling her hand forward.

In a voice as calm and loving as she had ever spoken with, she heard herself say, as her hand automatically went forward to make contact with the baby's shawl, "It's so good to see you, dear, may I take a peep at her?"

"Of course, Mother, and it's wonderful to see you too," smiled Jane Anne.

Easing the shawl back from the sleeping baby's face, instead of taking a peep, Eliza looked, examining and studying every feature that the blonde-haired baby possessed; that is, aside from its eyes which were shut fast in sleep. Then suddenly, she was exclaiming, "Well, did you ever!

Why this baby's going to be a carbon copy of Elizabeth!" The idea of the baby favoring Elizabeth seemed to startle her.

Jane Anne laughed, "That's what everybody says,"

"All except me, sweetheart." Stuart quickly put in. "And if she had her eyes open, Mrs. Heyward, I have a feeling you'd be inclined to go along with me. Their as grey as grey ashes, the very same color as Jane Anne's.

"You don't say!" Eliza sang right back, obviously elated to hear this news. Though it was also obvious that the person who had furnished her with the information had yet to receive one fraction of recognition from her. In short, when it came to acknowledging

Stuart's presence, Eliza, so far, had cut him dead.

But then, as Martha and Jane Anne, and Stuart too for that matter, began to hold their breath in anticipation of what Eliza might do or say next, she suddenly turned to Stuart—the first glance that she had spared him—and said, as she set her eyes on a square level with his, "And what about this one, did his eyes take after his mother's too?"

"No, I'm afraid not, Mrs. Heyward. They're ...."

"Brown, Eliza! The very same color as Stuart's". Martha forcefully interrupted, the tone of her voice making it plain to Eliza whose side she was going to be on if Eliza started any nonsense, to say nothing of making clear, that she had better not!

However, to Martha's amazement, Eliza appeared to be thrown off guard for change, deliberating over her next move. Then, just as Martha had begun to think that it was going to be left up to her and her alone to get the conversation started again, Eliza finally muttered, "I see. May I hold him?" taking Martha and all the rest by complete surprise.

"Yes—certainly ..." Stuart managed to croak. Then giving a little nervous laugh, he added, "But he's sleeping too. What one baby does, the other follows with, we've noted."

He promptly, but gently, laid the baby in Eliza's waiting arms.

Easing the shawl back from the baby's face and seeing that he was opening his alert, brown eyes, Eliza said, "Oh, we've awakened him."

"Don't fret about it, Mrs. Heyward." Stuart quickly assured. "With all the sleep they both get, I'm certain missing out on a few winks isn't going to hurt either of them."

Looking up and seeing that Stuart had relieved Jane Anne of the girl twin, no sooner than his arms had become vacant, and was now holding her, Eliza asked, her face flooding over with curiosity, and wonder too, "Did she awaken with him?"

"Sure thing. They're right on target with one another as usual," laughed Stuart in a more relaxed manner. Taking a step forward and pushing the baby's wrappings back, he went on, "Here's those ash-grey eyes I was telling you about."

"Well, fancy that! Eliza cried as she leaned over the boy baby in her arms and took in the other twin's eyes for the first time. "They are grey, aren't they!"

"Like I said, grey as ashes." Stuart replied, and wondered as he did if he had taken leave of reality or not. For those few remarks that he and Eliza Heyward had and were exchanging were the first, as far back as he could recall, that had not been exchanged in animosity.

But even as this startling fact was making its dent upon Stuart and he was trying to absorb it as well as concern himself with his and Eliza Hayward's last and most rancorous encounter, it suddenly hit upon him that Eliza Hayward had become silent and distant again. What's more, if her appearance told him anything, she was going to be holding to this mien indefinite. Indeed, although she had shifted her gaze back to the twin in her own arms and was staring down at him, she appeared to be seeing and thanking about something else. And, not only did she appear to be lost to the present, but she also looked like she was greatly burdened and sorrow-stricken. In fact, Stuart was positive that Eliza Hayward was about to break down and weep, and seeing her dissolve in tears was the last thing that he would ever have expected to see out of her. It bothered him.

Although Stuart would have had another surprise to learn of it, Eliza's sudden withdrawal was spontaneous and not by choice. Indeed, she was not even aware of the sudden distance that she had put between herself and those of whom she was in company with because, as Stuart had reasoned and decided, she was lost, lost in the eyes of the baby she held and the volumes of facts that it's fixed gaze was finally exposing to her—facts that were hammering Eliza's heart and conscience so hard that she felt as though she was being killed by inches.

Yes, the baby was staring up at Eliza as hard as she was staring at him, a sweet and innocent gaze. And yet, despite all its newborn purity, Eliza had readily seen that it was also a gaze that was identical to the way the late Frank Drakston could eye one, bold and challenging, daring her—she felt like - to scorn him another time!

No! Eliza thought to herself and shuttered, I must not, will not, regard this precious baby in such a vicious light, let alone be so small-minded as to identify its gaze with Frank's. Still, she had to admit the look was real enough. She could not deny that, she reflected. But even so, why was she standing here thinking about Frank and seeing him so vividly in this baby's gaze when he was the last person she wanted to think about?

No! Eliza told herself again and shouldered for a second time as another distressing thought entered her mind. She had forgiven Frank that day, or thought she had! Who would not forgive, if one asked

from one's deathbed as Frank had? Still, why did she feel as though
Frank had actually emerged from his grave and was here now,
accusing her of never forgiving him when he had asked it of her?
And worse still why had she felt from the instant that she had looked
into this baby's eyes that it was Frank staring at her instead of it—
staring at her with that gaze of his that was like no other; and not
only accusing her of transferring the bitterness that she had ever felt
toward him to his innocent son and despising Stuart, too, for no other
reason than the fact that he was born a Drakston, but also blaming
her for the disgrace that Stuart and Jane Anne had brought to both
the Drakston and Heyward family as well, causing her to feel no less
at fault for the whole unhappy matter than had she taken Stuart and
Jane Anne by the hand and led them to the old timber trail and left
them there alone together?[1]

Well, regardless of how she was feeling at the moment, it
happened to be a matter of mind over body with her and push these
crazy thoughts out of her head, she must! Stuart and Jane Anne both
were mature adults. She was not responsible for their conduct, they
were. She had had nothing to do with these two babies having been
conceived out in the bush, like they had been! In fact, why her mind
had latched onto all this crazy mess was a mystery to her to begin
with. No, that was not true because it happened to be this baby's gaze
that had prompted all of it. Well then, was there more truth here then
what she wanted to admit there was? Had this baby, whose features
were so much like Frank's and especially his eyes, been put in her
arms today to show her that? Had she truly let her bitterness toward
Frank for raping her become so deep-seeded that it had served as a
route for all the trials and tribulations that had befallen her over the
years to grow from, not to mention all the heartbreak her beloved
daughter had suffered as well? And what about Stuart Drakston? Had
she actually been judging him, all along, buy his father's
shortcomings rather than by the good in his own character? If that
were the case, she did not need Marsh Reed or anyone else to point
out to her that she had and was doing Stuart Drakston a gross
injustice. Thus she must set a different course for herself and see.
After all, Frank had been gone a long time. It was only fitting that
she lay it all aside and let his soul rest in peace, let bygones be
bygones and live in the present.

Yes, bless this beautiful baby, she could see it also clearly, see
what she must do as clearly as if she were actually holding Frank's

spirit in her arms; and, in a way, she felt that was what she was doing. Besides, fighting one in physical body was one thing, continuing to fight one soul was quite another!

All at once, Eliza felt such a softening of heart and quietening of mind that, for a fleeting second, she wondered if she had swallowed a sedative!

In fact, knowing that she had truly forgiven frank, at last, coupled with her deliverance from the turmoil that had raked her and obscured her ability, up until this moment, to see the late Frank Drakston and Stuart Drakston as being too diverse and separate individuals instead of molding them in the same cast, was so intense that there was no way that she could stop the tears coursing along her insides. And as they abruptly broke upon the surface of her eyes, with her peering harder through them still at the baby who had finally delivered her—feeling no less cleansed in heart and mind than newly plowed earth after a spring rain, she felt an anxious hand grip her arm and knew the touch even before she heard her daughter say in a much disquieted voice, "Mother—perhaps we should go on to the carriage where we can sit down. Here let me take the baby. I'm afraid he's going to tire you too much."

Thinking that her crazy hat was coming in handy after all because it was providing a shelter for some of her tears, not to mention hiding a great deal of her distress besides, Eliza, clasping the baby tighter to her bosom, murmured, "N-o-o, just give me a minute dear, and I'll be fine. Besides, he's not all that heavy." Then, after a rather long pause, one in which Jane Anne and Stuart, and Martha too, had all exchanged disconcerting looks, she abruptly asked, "What name does he go by, Luke or Franklin, or do you call him by his full name?"

Jane Anne laughed, her voice somewhat trembled, "Well, so far, he's mostly been tagged 'Him' or 'He', but in the long run I think Frankie might win out."

Appropriate enough, if looks mean anything, Eliza thought to herself again; and much to her surprise not only found that she was pleased with the nickname, but she was also certain that she was going to be contented with addressing the boy twin as such.

However, her thoughts and her sentiments regarding the nickname, Frankie, Eliza kept to herself and made no further comment about it. Instead, she unexpectedly raised her head and looking at Jane Anne she smiled and said, "It's such a beautiful day, dear, one will never be prettier, I'm sure, for Frankie and his sister to make their first visit to Green Sea in! Won't you agree?" her bold approach igniting a fire in Martha's eyes and causing what little encouragement that Jane Anne and Stuart both had taken from the encounter, so far to perish on the spot, to say nothing of the uncomfortable silence it began to raise.

All the same, if Eliza were aware of having thwarted anyone's feelings or impaired the meeting to any degree, her next remark lacked one suggestion of it.

Still smiling and giving every impression of having her heart and soul set on making amends to her daughter, she broke the growing and uneasy hush by adding, "I have your two favorite dishes, lemon meringue pie and Southern-fried chicken prepared for dinner."

Seeing that his wife was procrastinating, obviously still bowled over and also at a nonplus as well over her mother's pressing suggestion—it put Stuart in mind of one baiting a fish—Stuart, endeavoring to make the best of the fact that the invitation had not included him, laughed, "Sounds mouth-watering to me, sweetheart. Surely you aren't thinking of turning those palatable dishes down."

But Jane Anne was thinking just that, and finally finding her voice, she made no attempt to mince the matter as she turned to Stuart and said, "But how would I handle two babies, Stuart, without your helping me? And besides, by rights, Mother should've invited you too, you know."

"Oh, my! No, dear!" Eliza exclaimed on the dart, even before Stuart could open his mouth, "I meant—I mean—I'd like for Stuart to come with you, dear! Of course, you need him to help you with these darling babies. I intend to hold this one though, all the way to Green Sea, so don't you or Stuart try to take him from me!" Like a snap, she brought her head around to face Martha, who was sending her an incredulous look, and added, "Martha, I want you and Bruce to come too. Marsh Reed's already said he'd be there. In fact an idea's just come to me! Why not all the family and our close friends come, and we'll call it a celebration in honor of the twins? Yes, that's what we'll do! There's enough food already cooked and baked at Green Sea to feed an army anyway!" She quickly turned her head and let her gaze move anxiously over the churchyard. "We must tell the rest before they leave for home. Oh, where in the world are they? There's Father and Aunt Amy and Elizabeth, and Seth and his family must be told. "

"Yonder's Uncle Matthew and Mother standing over there under that oak talking with Luke," interrupted Martha, still daring to believe Eliza's sudden sweet temper toward Stuart—not to mention good manners—at the same time that her cousin was not headed in the direction of being a borderline case." And, yes, I think I see all the others bunched together over there too, including Bruce."

"Where—oh—yes, I believe they are! Well, as long as they're visiting and not leaving before they know," Eliza sang again. Then, she turned back to Martha, asking, "You will come won't you, Martha, and help make it a celebration?"

"I wouldn't advise anyone to try and keep me away," smiled Martha, her pique toward Eliza vanished. "Of course, Bruce and I will come."

"And what about you two?" Eliza sang on, searching Stuart's and Jane Anne's face in earnest. "Neither of you have said a word yet. You will come won't you, or don't you go for the idea of my calling it a celebration in honor of the twins, after all this time?" All of a sudden her expression fell, at least, a foot!

Observing that Jane Anne was obviously lost in amazement—looking at her mother like she had never seen her before—Stuart, taking it upon himself to speak for both of them, quickly said, "No, Mrs. Heyward, don't think that even for a second. We think it's a great idea, and we'll be happy to go to Green Sea and help you celebrate. In fact, I'll ever feel that I'm indebted to you for suggesting it."

Continuing to hold her fallen expression she regarded Stuart with a rather thoughtful and penetrating gaze, Eliza muttered, somewhat unevenly, "No—I—I'd much prefer that you don't feel beholden to me ever, or feel that you're under obligation to come to Green Sea today or at any other time in the future." She drew a deep breath and appearing to be suddenly braced up went on, "You see, from this day forward, I want our relationship to have every chance to grow to one of harmony and understanding, with no barriers to hold back that growth. I want you to feel good about visiting at Green Sea, feel that you're welcome to come there for yourself alone, instead of feeling that you're invited only because of family connections.

"I suppose what I'm trying to say to you, and doing a rather poor job of it in my opinion, is, regardless of the blood relation between us or the family tie through your marriage to my daughter, I want us to become friends and, as of now, begin working toward that objective by holding no reservations over anything that's hurt or troubled either of us, in the past.

"In some instances, I feel I've made mistakes judging you too harshly and, sometimes, even unjustly. Therefore, for those wrongs, I'm asking your forgiveness so our relationship can truly start anew." Though her say was finally ended, Eliza continued to peer at Stuart more earnest than ever.

Astounded, Stuart merely peered back, saying nothing. Intrusive, he was actually indisposed to believe what his ears had just heard.

All the same, suddenly realizing that he was doing nothing but silently gaping back at Eliza and knowing, too, that giving her the impression he was not willing to compromise was the last thing he wanted to do, Stuart, abruptly finding his tongue, said, "Your capacity for understanding and being bighearted, Mrs. Heyward, if you think circumstances warrant it, overwhelms me. Of course, I forgive you of all or any wrong that you feel you may have inflicted upon me.

"However, you and I both must not forget that I've committed wrongs, too; and some that were inexcusable besides. So for those flaws of character on my part and because I've also come to know and am experiencing every waking moment of every day the love and sense of protection that one feels for one's child, I'm also asking and beseeching of you no less indulgence and forgiveness for my shortsightedness and my mistakes than you've asked of me." Letting the last of his astonishment vanish like a breath, he sent her a warm smile.

Promptly accepting his smile by sending him a friendly one in return, Eliza said, "So shall it be then. It is done." Turning her head and looking toward the oak tree once again, she went on, "Now let's all go and join the others so we can head on to Green Sea for dinner." And so everybody started to move on, feeling easy and joyful for a change, Eliza let one of her hands fall to lock with one of Jane Anne's and thought to herself, one of the most difficult things that I ever imagined doing and it turned out to be so easy, made easy because of this blessed baby in my arms and yes, because of you, too, Frank. I wish you could be here with us.

She gripped her daughter's hand tighter than ever.

www.ingramcontent.com/pod-product-compliance
Lightning Source LLC
Chambersburg PA
CBHW070623260626
47161CB00007B/2563